ONESS

Henning Mankell was born in Stockholm in 1948.
He is the author of many works of fiction, among
them the nine books in the Kurt Wallander series. His
books have been translated into 19 languages. He has
worked as an actor, theatre director and manager in
Sweden and more recently in Mozambique, where he
now lives and is the head of the Teatro Avenida in
Maputo. He won the Swedish Academy of Crime
Literature award for *Faceless Killers*, and the CWA
Gold Dagger 2001 for *Sidetracked*.

Laurie Thompson has been editor of *Swedish Book
Review* since 1983 and has translated over a dozen
books from Swedish, including three Inspector
Wallander novels by Henning Mankell.

BY HENNING MANKELL
(in chronological order)

Faceless Killers
The Dogs of Riga
The White Lioness

*

Sidetracked
The Fifth Woman
One Step Behind

Henning Mankell

THE WHITE LIONESS

TRANSLATED FROM THE SWEDISH BY
Laurie Thompson

V

HARVILL CRIME IN VINTAGE

Published by Vintage 2003

2 4 6 8 10 9 7 5 3 1

Copyright © Henning Mankell, 1993 and 2003
English translation © Laurie Thompson, 1998 and 2003

Henning Mankell has asserted his right under the Copyright, Designs and Patents Act, 1988 to be identified as the author of this work

First published with the title *Den vita lejoninnan* by Ordfront Förlag, Stockholm, 1993

English translation first published by The New Press, New York, 1998

First published in Great Britain in 2003 by The Harvill Press

Vintage
Random House, 20 Vauxhall Bridge Road,
London SW1V 2SA

Random House Australia (Pty) Limited
20 Alfred Street, Milsons Point, Sydney
New South Wales 2061, Australia

Random House New Zealand Limited
18 Poland Road, Glenfield,
Auckland 10, New Zealand

Random House (Pty) Limited
Endulini, 5A Jubilee Road, Parktown 2193,
South Africa

The Random House Group Limited Reg. No. 954009
www.randomhouse.co.uk

A CIP catalogue record for this book
is available from the British Library

ISBN 0 09 946469 1

Maps drawn by Reg Piggott

Papers used by Random House are natural, recyclable products made from wood grown in sustainable forests. The manufacturing processes conform to the environmental regulations of the country of origin

Printed and bound in Great Britain by
Cox & Wyman Limited, Reading, Berkshire

As long as we assign value to the people of our country on the basis of their skin colour, we will force them to endure what Socrates termed the lie at the depths of our souls.

JAN HOFMEYR, 1946

Who dares to play while the lion roars?

AFRICAN PROVERB

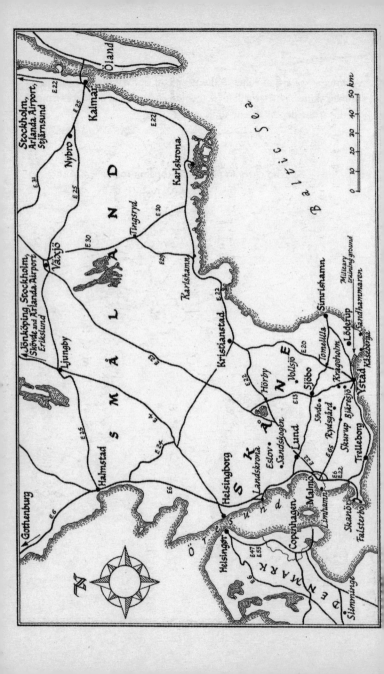

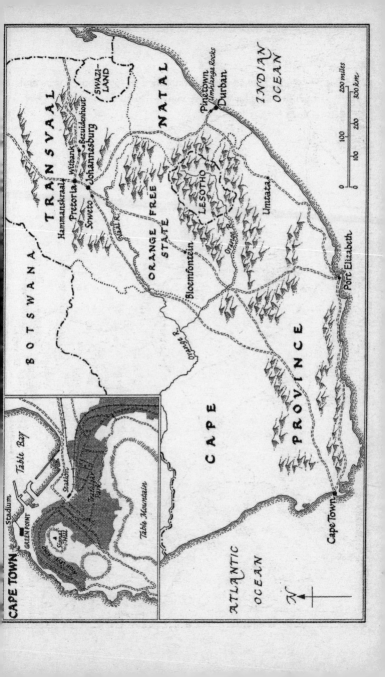

Since *The White Lioness* was first published in 1993, some towns and areas in South Africa have been renamed. The names in use then have been retained here.

PROLOGUE

In 1990 Nelson Mandela was released from Robben Island, where he had been a political prisoner for almost 30 years.

While the world rejoiced, many Afrikaners regarded the release of Nelson Mandela as an unspoken declaration of war. President de Klerk became a hated traitor.

At the time of Mandela's release, a group of men met in secret to take upon themselves responsibility for the future of the Afrikaners. They were ruthless men, and they would never submit.

They met in secret and reached a decision. They decided to create the conditions that would spark off a civil war which could end only one way: in a bloodbath.

The Woman from Ystad

CHAPTER ONE

Louise Åkerblom, an estate agent, left the Savings Bank in Skurup shortly after 3.00 in the afternoon on Friday, April 24. She paused for a moment on the pavement and sucked the fresh air into her lungs, deciding what to do next. What she wanted to do most of all was to leave work straightaway and drive home to Ystad. She had promised a widow who had called her that morning to visit a house the woman wanted to sell.

She worked out how long it would take. An hour, maybe; hardly more. And she had to buy bread. Her husband Robert usually baked all the bread they needed, but that week he hadn't had time. She crossed the square and turned to the left where the bakery was. An old-fashioned bell tinkled as she opened the door. She was the only customer. Later, the lady behind the counter would remember that Louise Åkerblom seemed to be in a cheerful mood, and remarked how good it was that spring had arrived at last.

She bought some rye bread, and decided to surprise the family with napoleons for dessert. Then she returned to the bank, where her car was parked at the back. On the way she met a young couple from Malmö to whom she had just sold a house. They had been at the bank tying up the loose ends, paying the seller his money, signing the contract and the loan agreement. She was delighted for them, for their joy at owning their own home. She felt, all the same, uneasy. Could they manage the mortgage and interest payments? Times were hard, and hardly anybody was able to feel secure in their work any more. What would happen if he lost his job? She had made a careful check on their finances. Unlike many other young people, they had not run up credit card debts, and the wife seemed to be the thrifty type. They would no doubt cope with buying their house. If not, she would see it advertised again soon enough. Maybe she or Robert would be the one to sell it. It wasn't unusual nowadays for her to sell the same house two or three times in the course of a few years.

She unlocked the car and called the Ystad office on the car phone. She heard Robert's voice on the answering machine informing callers that Åkerblom's Estate Agency was closed for the weekend, but would reopen Monday morning at 8.00.

At first she was surprised to hear Robert had left so early. Then she remembered he was due to meet their accountant. She left a message: "Hi! I'm just going to take a look at a house at Krageholm. Then I'll be on my way home. It's 3.15. I'll be back by 5.00." Robert might go back to the office after his meeting with the accountant.

She pulled over a plastic folder lying on the seat, and took out the map she had drawn from the widow's description. The house was on a side road between Krageholm and Vollsjö. It would take a little over an hour to get there, look at the house and grounds, then drive back to Ystad.

Then she hesitated. It can wait, she thought. I'll take the coast road home and stop for a while and look at the sea instead. I've already sold one house today: that'll have to be enough.

She began humming a hymn, started the engine, and drove out of Skurup. But when she came to the Trelleborg turning she changed her mind once more. She wouldn't have time to look at the house on Monday or Tuesday. The lady might be disappointed and turn to some other agency. They couldn't afford to let that happen. Times were hard enough, and the competition was getting tougher. Nobody could afford to pass up anything that came their way, unless it was quite out of the question.

She sighed and turned off in the other direction. The coast road and the sea would have to wait. She kept glancing at the map. Next week she would buy a map holder so she wouldn't have to keep turning her head to check that she was on the right road. The widow's house shouldn't be all that hard to find even though she had never been on the road itself. She knew the district inside out. She and Robert would have been running the agency for ten years next year.

That thought surprised her. Ten years already. Time had passed so quickly, all too quickly. During those ten years she had given birth to two children and worked diligently with Robert to establish the firm. When they started up, times were good; she could see that. Now, they would never have managed to break into the market. She ought to feel pleased. God had been good to her and her family. She would talk to Robert again and suggest they could afford to increase their contributions to Save the Children. He would be hesitant, of course; he worried about money more than she did. No doubt she could talk him into it, though. She usually did.

Then she realised she was on the wrong road, and braked. Thinking about the family and the past ten years had made her miss the first exit. She laughed to herself, shook her head, and looked around carefully before making a three-point turn and retracing her route.

Skåne is a lovely place, she thought to herself. Pretty and open. Yet secretive as well. What seemed at first sight to be so flat could unexpectedly change and reveal deep hollows like isolated islands with houses and farms. She never ceased to be amazed by the changing nature of the landscape when she drove around to look at houses or show them to prospective buyers.

She pulled onto the shoulder after Erikslund to check her directions. She was right. She turned left and could see the road to Krageholm ahead of her; it was beautiful. The countryside was hilly, and the road wriggled its way through the Krageholm forest where the lake lay glittering through the deciduous woods to the left. She had often driven along that road, and never tired of it.

After some seven kilometres she started looking for the final turn. The widow had described it as a dirt road, ungravelled but easily negotiable. She slowed down when she saw it and turned right; according to the map, the house would be on the left-hand side in about one kilometre.

After three kilometres the road petered out, and she knew she must be wrong after all.

For just a moment she was tempted to forget about the house altogether and drive straight home, but she resisted the thought and went back to the Krageholm road. About 500 metres further north she found another right turn. There were no houses answering to the description here either. She sighed, turned around, and decided to ask someone the way. She had just passed a house half hidden behind a clump of trees.

She stopped, switched off the engine and got out of the car. There was a fresh smell from the trees. She started walking towards the house, a white-painted, half-timbered, U-shaped building, the kind Skåne is full of. Only one of the wings was still standing, however. In the middle of the front yard was a well with a black-painted pump.

She hesitated, and stopped. The house seemed deserted. Maybe it would be best to go home after all, and hope the widow wouldn't be upset.

I can always knock, she thought. That doesn't cost anything.

Before she came to the house, she passed a large, red-painted barn. She couldn't resist the temptation to peer in through the high, half-open doors.

She was surprised by what she saw. There were two cars. She was not knowledgeable about cars, but she couldn't help seeing that one was a top of the range Mercedes, and the other one a BMW.

There must be somebody in, then, she thought, and continued towards the whitewashed house. Somebody not short of cash.

She knocked at the door and waited. She knocked again, harder this time; still no answer. She tried to look in through a window next to the door, but the curtains were drawn. She knocked a third time, before walking round to see if there was a back door.

Behind the house was an overgrown orchard. The apple trees had certainly not been pruned for 20 or 30 years. Some rotting garden furniture was standing under a pear tree. A magpie flapped its wings loudly and flew away. She couldn't see a door, and returned to the front of the house.

I'll knock just one more time, she thought. If nobody answers, I'll go home. There'll be time to stop by the sea for a while before I need to start making dinner. She hammered on the door. Still no answer.

She felt rather than heard that someone had come up behind her from the courtyard. She turned abruptly. A man was about a metre away from her, looking straight at her. She saw he had a scar on his forehead. She was instantly uneasy.

Where had he come from? Why hadn't she heard him? The courtyard was gravelled. Had he crept up on her?

"I hope I'm not intruding," she said, trying to sound normal. "I'm an estate agent, and I'm lost. I just wanted to ask my way."

The man did not answer.

8

Maybe he's not Swedish, she thought. Maybe he couldn't understand what she was saying. There was something strange about his appearance that made her think he could be a foreigner.

She knew she had to get away. The man's cold eyes were frightening her.

"I won't disturb you any longer," she said. "Sorry to intrude."

She started to walk away but stopped in mid-stride. The man had come to life. He took something out of his jacket pocket. At first she didn't see what it was. Then she realised it was a pistol.

He raised the gun slowly and pointed it at her head.

Good God, she managed to think.

Good God, please help me. He's going to kill me.

Good God, help me.

It was 3.45 on the afternoon of April 24, 1992.

CHAPTER TWO

When Detective Chief Inspector Kurt Wallander arrived at the police station in Ystad on Monday morning, April 27, he was furious. He couldn't remember the last time he'd been in such a bad mood. His anger had even left its mark, a plaster where he had cut his cheek shaving.

He muttered a reply to colleagues who said good morning. When he got to his office, he slammed the door behind him, took the phone off its hook, and sat staring out the window.

Kurt Wallander was 44 years old. He was considered a proficient policeman, persistent and occasionally astute. That morning, though, he felt only irritation and an increasingly bad temper. Sunday had been one of those days he would have preferred to forget all about.

One of the reasons was his father, who lived alone in a house on the flat land outside Löderup. His relationship with his father had always been complicated. Things had not improved over the years. Wallander realised, with an increasing annoyance, that he was becoming more and more like him. He tried to imagine himself at the same age as his father, but this induced in him only despair. Was he to end up a sullen and unpredictable old man, capable, out of the blue, of doing something absolutely crazy?

On Sunday afternoon Wallander had visited his father as usual. They played cards and drank coffee on the veranda in the warm spring sunshine. And then without warning, his father announced that he was getting married. Wallander thought at first he had misheard.

"No," he said, "I have no intention of getting married."

"I'm not talking about you," his father said, "I'm talking about me."

Kurt Wallander stared at him in disbelief. "You're almost 80," he said. "You aren't getting married."

"I'm not dead yet," his father said. "I'll do whatever I like. You'd be better off asking me who I'm marrying."

Wallander did as he was told.

"You ought to be able to work it out for yourself," his father said. "I thought policemen were paid to draw conclusions?"

"But you don't know anybody your age, do you? You keep pretty much to yourself."

"I know one," his father said. "And anyway, who says you have to marry somebody your own age?"

Wallander realised that there was one possibility: Gertrud Anderson, the 50-year-old woman who came to do the cleaning and wash his father's feet three times a week.

"Are you going to marry Gertrud?" he asked. "Have you thought of asking her if she wants to? There's 30 years between you. How do you think you're going to be able to live with another person? You've never been able to. Not even with my mother."

"I've grown better tempered in my old age," said his father mildly.

Wallander couldn't believe his ears. His father was going to get married? Better tempered in his old age? Now, when he was more impossible than he'd ever been?

Then they had quarrelled. It ended up with his father throwing his coffee cup into the tulip bed and locking himself in the shed where he painted his pictures, all with the same subject, repeated over and over again: sunset in an autumnal landscape with or without a wood grouse in the foreground, depending on the preference of whoever had commissioned it.

Wallander drove home much too fast. He had to put a stop to this absurd business. How on earth could Gertrud Anderson work for his father for a year and not see that it was impossible to live with him?

He parked the car on Mariagatan in central Ystad where he lived, and decided to call his sister Kristina in Stockholm. He would ask her to come to Skåne. Nobody could change his father's mind. But perhaps Gertrud Anderson could be made to see sense.

He never called his sister. When he got to his apartment on the top floor, the door had been broken open. Moments later it was clear the thieves had marched off with his brand-new stereo equipment, CD player, all his discs and records, the television, radio, clocks and a camera. He slumped into a chair and just sat there for a long while, wondering what to do. In the end, he rang the police station and asked to speak with one of the CID inspectors, Martinsson, who he knew was on duty that Sunday.

He was kept waiting for an age before Martinsson came to the phone. Wallander guessed he'd been having coffee and chatting to some of the officers who were taking a rest from the big traffic operation they were mounting that weekend.

"Martinsson here. How can I help?"

"It's Wallander. You'd better come over here."

"Where? To your office? I thought you were off today."

"I'm at home. Get over here."

Martinsson asked no more questions.

"Right," he said. "I'm on my way."

The rest of Sunday was spent doing a forensic investigation of the apartment and writing a case report. Martinsson, one of the younger policemen Wallander worked with, was sometimes careless and impulsive. All the same, Wallander liked working with him, not least because he often proved surprisingly perceptive. When Martinsson and the forensic technician had left, Wallander did a provisional repair job on the door.

He spent most of the night lying awake, thinking about how he'd beat the shit out of the thieves if he ever laid hands on them. When he could no longer bear to torture himself thinking about the loss of all his music, he lay there worrying about what to do with his father, feeling more and more resigned to it all.

At dawn he got up, brewed some coffee and looked for his home insurance documents. He sat at his kitchen table going through the papers, getting crosser by the minute at the insurance company's incomprehensible jargon. In the end he flung the papers to one side and went to shave. When he cut himself, he considered calling the station and telling them he was sick, then going back to bed with the duvet over his head. But the thought of being in his apartment without being able to listen to a CD was too much for him.

It was 7.30 a.m. and he was sitting in his office with the door closed. With a groan, he forced himself to become a policeman again, and replaced the phone.

It rang immediately. It was Ebba on reception.

"Sorry to hear about the burglary," she said. "Did they really take all your records?"

"They left me a few 78s. I thought I might listen to them tonight. If I can get hold of a wind-up gramophone."

"It's awful."

"That's the way it goes. What do you want?"

"There's a man out here who insists on talking to you."

"What about?"

"About a missing person."

Wallander looked at the heap of case notes on his desk. "Can't Svedberg look after him?"

"Svedberg's out hunting."

"He's what?"

"I don't quite know what to call it. He's out looking for a young bull that broke out of a field at Marsvinsholm. It's cantering around on the E14, playing havoc with the traffic."

"Surely the traffic people can deal with that? Why should one of our men have to get involved?"

"It was Björk who sent Svedberg."

"Oh, my God!"

"Shall I send him in, then? The man who wants to report a missing person?"

"All right," Wallander said.

The knock on his door a few minutes later was so discreet, Wallander wasn't sure at first whether he'd heard anything at all. When he shouted "Come in", however, the door opened right away.

Wallander had always been convinced the first impression a person makes is crucial. The man who entered Wallander's office was in no way remarkable. Wallander guessed he was about 35, he was wearing a dark brown suit, he had close-cropped blond hair, and glasses.

Wallander noticed something else as well. The man was obviously worried. Wallander was not the only one with a sleepless night behind him. He got to his feet and offered his hand. "Kurt Wallander. Inspector Wallander."

"My name is Robert Åkerblom," the man said. "My wife has disappeared."

Wallander was surprised by the man's forthright statement. "Please

13

sit down. I'm afraid the chair's a bit old. The left armrest keeps dropping off. Don't worry about it," he said. "Let's start from the beginning."

The man sat down on the chair. Then he started sobbing, heartbroken, desperate.

Wallander remained standing behind his desk, at a loss.

The man in the visitor's chair calmed down after a couple of minutes. He dried his eyes and blew his nose. "I'm sorry," he said. "Something must have happened to Louise, though. She would never go away of her own accord."

"Can I get you a cup of tea?" Wallander said. "Maybe we can get a pastry or something as well."

"No, thank you," Åkerblom said.

Wallander nodded and took a notebook out of one of the desk drawers. He used regular note pads he bought himself at the local book shop. He'd never managed to cope with the flood of printed report forms the Central Police Authority used to overwhelm the force with. He'd sometimes thought of writing to *Swedish Policeman* proposing that whoever invented the forms should be presented with pre-printed responses.

"You'd better start by giving me your personal details," Wallander said.

"My name is Robert Åkerblom," the man said. "I run Åkerblom's Estate Agency with my wife."

Wallander nodded as he wrote. He knew the offices, close to the Saga cinema.

"We have two children, four and seven. Two girls. We live in a terrace house, 19 Åkarvägen. I was born in this town. My wife comes from Ronneby."

He broke off, took a photograph out of his inside pocket, and put it on the desk in front of Wallander. It was of a woman; she looked like any other woman. She was smiling at the photographer, and Wallander could see it was taken in a studio. He contemplated her face and decided it was somehow or other just right for Robert Åkerblom's wife.

"That photograph was taken only three months ago," Åkerblom said. "That's exactly what she looks like."

"And she's disappeared, has she?"

"Last Friday she was at the Savings Bank in Skurup, clinching a house sale. Then she was going to look at a house somebody was putting on the market. I spent the afternoon with our accountant, at his office. I stopped in at the office in Ystad on my way home. She'd left a message on the answering machine saying she'd be home by 5.00. She said it was 3.15 when she called. That's the last we know."

Wallander frowned. Mrs Åkerblom had been gone two-and-a-half days, with two small children waiting for her at home. He felt instinctively that this was no routine disappearance. Most people who went missing came back sooner or later, and a natural explanation would emerge. It was common enough for people to go away for a few days, even a week, and forget to tell anybody. On the other hand, he knew that women rarely abandoned their children. That worried him.

He made a few notes on his pad.

"Do you still have the message she left on the answering machine?" he said.

"Yes," Åkerblom said. "I didn't think of bringing the cassette with me, though."

"That's OK, we'll sort that out later," Wallander said. "Was it clear where she was calling from?"

"She was using the car phone."

Wallander put down his pen and contemplated the man on the visitor's chair. His anxiety seemed absolutely genuine.

"You can't think of any reason she might have had to go away?"

"No."

"She can't be visiting friends?"

"No."

"Relatives?"

"No."

"There's no other possibility you can think of?"

"No."

"I hope you won't mind if I ask you some personal questions."

"We've never quarrelled, if that's what you were wanting to know."

Wallander nodded. "That was what I was going to ask," he said. Then he started all over again. "You say she disappeared on Friday afternoon. But you waited until Monday before coming to us?"

15

"I was afraid," Åkerblom said.

Wallander stared at him in surprise.

"Going to the police would be like accepting that something awful had happened," Åkerblom said. "That's why I didn't dare."

Wallander knew exactly what Åkerblom meant. "You've been out looking for her, of course," he said.

Åkerblom nodded.

"What other steps have you taken?" Wallander said, starting to make notes again.

"I have prayed to God."

Wallander stopped writing. "Prayed to God?"

"My family are Methodists. Yesterday, we joined the whole congregation and Pastor Tureson in praying that nothing unthinkable has happened to Louise."

Wallander could feel something gnawing away in his stomach. He tried to conceal his disquiet from the man in the chair before him.

A mother with two children, member of a church, he thought to himself. She wouldn't disappear of her own accord. Not unless she'd gone out of her mind. Or been possessed by religion. A mother of two children would hardly stroll into the forest and take her own life. Such things do happen, but only once in a blue moon.

Wallander knew that either there had been an accident or Louise Åkerblom was the victim of a crime.

"You realise, of course, there might have been an accident," he said.

"I've called every hospital in Skåne," Åkerblom said. "She hasn't been admitted anywhere. Besides, a hospital would have been in touch with me if anything had happened. Louise always had her ID card on her."

"What make of car did she drive?"

"A Toyota Corolla. 1990 model. Dark blue. Registration number MHL 449."

Wallander wrote it all down. Then he went back to the beginning again, methodically going through the details Åkerblom knew about what his wife was doing that afternoon. They looked at maps, and Wallander could feel unease growing within him.

For God's sake, let's not have the murder of a woman on our hands, he thought. Anything but that.

Wallander put down his pen at 10.45.

16

"There is no reason to suppose that your wife won't be found safe and sound," he said, hoping his scepticism was not apparent. "But we'll treat your report with the utmost seriousness."

Åkerblom was slumped down in the chair. Wallander was afraid he might start weeping again. He felt incredibly sorry for him. He would have loved to console him. But how could he do that without showing how worried he himself felt?

He got up from his chair. "I'd like to listen to her telephone message," he said. "Then I'll drive over to Skurup and call in at the bank. Have you got somebody to help out with the children?"

"I don't need any help," Åkerblom said. "I can manage on my own. What do you think has happened to Louise, Inspector?"

"I don't think anything at all as yet," Wallander said. "Except that she'll soon be back home again."

I'm lying, he thought. I don't think that. I'm just hoping.

Wallander followed Åkerblom back into town. As soon as he had listened to the message on the answering machine and gone through her desk drawers, he'd go back to the office and talk to Björk. Even if there were specific procedures for how to go about looking for a missing person, Wallander wanted all available resources placed at his disposal right away. The disappearance of Louise Åkerblom, his instincts told him, involved a crime having been committed.

Åkerblom's Estate Agency was located in a former grocery shop. Wallander recalled it from his first year in Ystad, when he'd arrived as a young policeman from Malmö. There were a couple of desks, and some stands with photographs and descriptions of properties. There was a table with visitors' chairs where clients could delve into the details of the houses they were interested in. On the wall were a couple of Land Survey maps, with pins on in various colours. Behind the office there was a small kitchen.

They went in the back way, but even so Wallander noticed the handwritten card taped to the front door: CLOSED TODAY.

"Which is your desk?" Wallander said.

Åkerblom pointed. Wallander sat down at the other one. Apart from a diary, a photograph of the daughters, a few files, a green blotter and a pen stand, the desk top was empty, and Wallander had the impression it had only recently been tidied.

17

"Who does the cleaning?"

"We have a cleaner who comes in three times a week," Åkerblom said. "Mind you, we generally do the dusting and empty the waste baskets every day ourselves."

Wallander made a note, then he took a look around the office. The only thing that struck him as odd was a little crucifix on the wall by the kitchen door.

Then he nodded at the answering machine.

"It'll come right away," Åkerblom said. "It was the only message we had after 3.00 p.m. on Friday."

First impressions, was what Wallander was thinking. Listen carefully now.

Hi! I'm just going to take a look at a house at Krageholm. Then I'll be on my way home. It's 3.15. I'll be back by 5.00.

Cheerful, Wallander thought. She sounds happy and keen. Not threatened, not scared.

"One more time," Wallander said. "But first I want to hear what you yourself say on the tape. If you still have that?"

Åkerblom rewound the cassette, and pressed a button.

Welcome to Åkerblom's Estate Agency. We're out on business at the moment, but we'll be open again as usual on Monday, 8.00 a.m. If you would like to leave a message or send a fax, please do so after the beep. Thank you for calling, and we look forward to hearing from you again.

Wallander could hear that Åkerblom had not been comfortable speaking the message into the answering machine's microphone. He sounded rather strained.

Then he turned his attention again to Louise Åkerblom and asked her husband to wind the tape back time after time.

Wallander tried to listen for some message that might have been concealed behind the words. He had no idea what it might be. But he tried even so.

When he had heard the tape ten times, he nodded to Åkerblom.

"I'll have to take the cassette with me," he said. "We can amplify the sound at the station."

Åkerblom took out the little cassette and handed it to Wallander.

"I'd like you to do something for me while I'm going through the drawers in her desk," Wallander said. "Write down everything she did

18

or was going to do last Friday. Who she was due to meet, and where. Write down what route you think she would have taken as well. Make a note of the times. And I want an exact description of where that house is, the one she was going to look at near Krageholm."

"That I can't tell you," Åkerblom said. "It was Louise who took the call from the lady who wanted to sell the house. She drew herself a map and took it with her. She wouldn't be putting all the details into a file until today. If we'd taken on the house either she or I would have gone back there to take photographs."

Wallander thought for a moment. "In other words, at the moment Louise is the only one who knows where the house is," he said.

Åkerblom nodded.

"When would the house owner get in touch again?" Wallander said.

"Some time today," Åkerblom said. "That's why Louise wanted to try and see the house on Friday."

"It's important that you're here when she calls," Wallander said. "Say that your wife has taken a look at the house, but unfortunately she's sick today. Ask for a description of how to get there again, and get her telephone number. As soon as she's been in touch, give me a call."

Åkerblom sat down to write out the details Wallander needed.

Wallander went through the desk drawers. He found nothing that seemed significant. None of them appeared to have been tidied recently. He lifted the green blotting pad, and found a recipe for hamburgers, torn from a magazine. Then he studied the photograph of the two daughters.

He went out into the kitchen. Hanging on one of the walls was a calendar and a sampler with a quotation from the Bible. A small jar of coffee was on one of the shelves, unopened. On another were several kinds of tea. He opened the refrigerator. A litre of milk and some margarine.

He thought of her voice, and what she had said in the message. He was sure the car had been stationary when she made the call. Her voice was steady. It would not have been if she had been concentrating on driving at the same time. Later, when they amplified the tape at the station, he was proved to have been right. Besides, Louise Åkerblom was bound to be a careful, law-abiding citizen who would not risk her life or anybody else's by using the phone while driving.

If the times she mentioned are accurate, she'll have been in Skurup,

Wallander thought. She'll have done her business at the bank and be about to set off for Krageholm. But she wants to call her husband first. She's pleased that everything went well at the bank. Moreover it's Friday afternoon, and she's finished work for the day. It's nice weather. She has every reason to feel happy.

Wallander went back and sat at her desk once more, leafing through the desk diary. Åkerblom handed him his list.

"I have one question more for the moment," Wallander said. "It isn't really a question. But it is important. What kind of a person is Louise?" He was very careful to use the present tense, as if nothing had happened. In his own mind, however, Louise Åkerblom was already someone who no longer existed.

"Everybody likes her," Åkerblom said, straightforwardly. "She's even-tempered, laughs a lot, finds it easy to talk to people. Actually, she finds it hard to do business. Anything to do with money or complicated negotiations, she hands over to me. She's easily moved. And upset. She's troubled by other people's suffering."

"Does she have any special idiosyncrasies?" Wallander said.

"Idiosyncrasies?"

"Well, we all have our peculiarities," said Wallander.

"I can't think of anything," Åkerblom said, eventually.

Wallander nodded and got to his feet. It was already 11.45. He wanted to have a word with Björk before his boss went home for lunch.

"I'll be in touch later this afternoon," he said. "Try not to worry too much. See if you can think of anything you've forgotten. Anything I ought to know."

"What happened, do you think?" Åkerblom said as they shook hands.

"Probably nothing at all," Wallander said. "There's bound to be a natural explanation."

Wallander got hold of Björk just as he was about to leave. He was looking harassed, as usual. Wallander didn't suppose that a chief constable's job was something to feel envious about.

"Sorry to hear about the burglary," Björk said, trying to look sympathetic. "Let's hope the newspapers don't get hold of this one. It wouldn't look good, a detective inspector's home being broken into. We have a high percentage of unsolved cases. The Swedish police force is pretty low on the international league table."

"That's the way it goes," Wallander said. "I need to talk to you about something else." They were in the corridor outside Björk's office. "It can't wait till after lunch."

Björk nodded, and they went back into the office.

Wallander reported in detail his meeting with Robert Åkerblom.

"A mother of two and religious," Björk said, when Wallander had finished. "Missing since Friday. Doesn't sound good."

"No," Wallander said. "It doesn't sound good at all."

Björk eyed him shrewdly. "You think there's been a crime?"

Wallander shrugged. "I don't really know what I think," he said. "But this isn't a straightforward missing person case. I'm sure of it. That's why we ought to mobilise the appropriate resources from the start. Not apply the usual wait-and-see tactics."

Björk nodded. "I agree," he said. "Who do you want? Don't forget we're understaffed as long as Hansson's away. He managed to pick just the wrong moment to break his leg."

"Martinsson and Svedberg," Wallander said. "By the way, did Svedberg pin down the young bull that was careering along the E14?"

"A farmer got it with a lasso in the end," Björk said, glumly. "Svedberg twisted his ankle when he tumbled into a ditch. But he's still at work."

Wallander stood up. "I'll drive to Skurup now," he said. "Let's get together at 4.30 and sort out what we know. We'd better start looking for her car right away."

He put a piece of paper on Björk's desk.

"Toyota Corolla, dark blue," Björk said. "I'll see to it."

Wallander drove from Ystad to Skurup. He needed time to think, and took the coast road. A wind was picking up. Jagged clouds were racing across the sky. He could see a ferry from Poland on its way into the harbour. When he got to Mossby Beach, he drove down to the deserted car park and stopped by the boarded-up hamburger stand. He stayed in the car, thinking about the previous year, when a rubber dinghy had drifted into land just here, with two dead bodies in it. He thought about Baiba Liepa, the woman he'd met in Riga. Interesting that he hadn't managed to forget her, despite his best efforts. A year ago, and he was still thinking about her all the time.

A murdered woman was the last thing he needed right now. What he needed was peace and quiet. He thought about his father getting married. About the burglary and all the music he'd lost. It felt as if someone had robbed him of a significant portion of his life.

He thought about his daughter Linda, at college in Stockholm. He had the feeling that he was losing touch with her. It was too much, all at once.

He got out of the car, zipped up his jacket and walked to the beach. The air was chilly, and he was cold.

He went over in his mind what Åkerblom had said, tried various theories yet again. Could there be a natural explanation, despite everything? Could she have committed suicide? He thought of her voice on the telephone. Her eagerness.

Shortly before 1 p.m. Wallander left the beach and continued his way towards Skurup.

He could not shake off the conviction that Louise Åkerblom was dead.

CHAPTER THREE

Kurt Wallander had a recurring daydream, which he suspected he shared with a lot of other people: that he'd pulled off the ultimate bank robbery and astounded the world. He wondered how much money was generally kept at a medium-sized bank. Less than one might think? But more than enough? He didn't have any idea how he'd go about it, yet the fantasy kept recurring. He grinned at the thought. But the grin quickly gave way to the stirrings of a guilty conscience.

They would never find Louise Åkerblom alive. He had no evidence; there was no crime scene, no body. And yet he knew.

He couldn't get the photograph of the two girls out of his mind. How do you explain what it's not possible to explain? How will Robert Åkerblom be able to go on praying to his God in the future, the God who's left him and two children so cruelly in the lurch?

Wallander wandered around the Savings Bank at Skurup, waiting for the assistant manager who had helped Louise Åkerblom with the property deal the previous Friday to come back from the dentist. When Wallander had arrived at the bank a quarter of an hour earlier, he had talked with the manager, Gustav Halldén, whom he had met once before. He also asked Halldén to keep his visit confidential.

"After all, we're not sure if anything serious has happened," Wallander said.

"I get it," Halldén said. "You just think something *may* have happened."

Wallander nodded. That's exactly how it was. How could you possibly be sure just where the boundary was between thinking and knowing?

His train of thought was interrupted by somebody addressing him. A fuzzy voice saying: "I believe you wanted to talk to me."

Wallander turned round. "Are you Moberg, the assistant manager?"

The man said that he was. He was young, surprisingly young according to Wallander's idea of how old an assistant manager should be. But there was something else that immediately attracted his attention.

One of the man's cheeks was noticeably swollen.

"I still have some trouble speaking."

Wallander couldn't understand what the man was saying.

"We'd better wait," Moberg said. "Shouldn't we wait until the injection has worn off?"

"Let's try anyway," Wallander said. "I'm short of time, I'm afraid. If it doesn't hurt too much when you talk."

Moberg shook his head and led the way into a small meeting room at the back.

"This is exactly where we were," the assistant manager said. "You're sitting in Mrs Åkerblom's chair. Halldén said you wanted to talk about her. Has she disappeared?"

"She's been reported missing," Wallander said. "I expect she's just visiting relatives and forgot to tell them at home."

He could see even from Moberg's swollen expression that he regarded Wallander's reservations with scepticism. Fair enough, thought Wallander. If you're missing, you're missing. You can't be partially missing.

"What was it you want to know?" asked the assistant manager, pouring a glass of water from the carafe on the table and gulping it down.

"All that happened last Friday afternoon," Wallander said. "In detail. Exact time, what she said, what she did. I also want the name of the parties buying and selling the house that was being exchanged, in case I need to contact them later. Had you met Louise Åkerblom before?"

"I met her several times," Moberg said. "We were involved in four of her company's property deals."

"Tell me about last Friday."

Moberg took his diary from the inside pocket of his jacket. "The meeting had been set for 2.15," he said. "Louise Åkerblom turned up a couple of minutes early. We exchanged a few words about the weather."

"Did she seem tense or worried?"

Moberg thought for a moment before answering. "No," he said. "On the contrary, she seemed happy. Before, I always thought she was uptight, but not on Friday."

Wallander nodded, encouraging him to go on.

"The clients arrived, a young couple called Nilson. And the seller, representing the estate of somebody who had died in Sövde. We sat down here and went through the whole procedure. There was nothing out of the ordinary. All the documents were just so. The deeds, the mortgage, the loan forms, the bank draft. It didn't take long. Then we broke up. I rather think we all wished one another a pleasant weekend, but I can't remember exactly."

"Was Louise Åkerblom in a hurry?"

The assistant manager thought it over again. "Could be," he said. "Maybe she was. I'm not sure. But there is something I'm quite certain about."

"What?"

"She didn't go straight to her car." Moberg pointed at the window, which looked over a small car park. "Those lots are for the bank's customers. I saw her park there when she arrived. It was a quarter of an hour after she'd left the bank before she drove off. I was still in here, on the telephone. That's how I could see everything. I think she had a bag in her hand when she got to the car. As well as her brief-case."

"A bag?" Wallander said. "What did it look like?"

Moberg shrugged. Wallander could see the injection was wearing off.

"What does a bag look like?" said the assistant manager. "I think it was a paper bag. Not plastic."

"And then she drove off?"

"Before that she made a call from her car phone."

To her husband, Wallander thought. Everything fits so far.

"It was just after 3.00," Moberg said. "I had another meeting at 3.30, and needed to prepare myself. My own call dragged on a bit."

"Could you see when she drove off?"

"I had gone back to my office by then."

"So the last you saw of her was when she was using the car phone."

Moberg nodded.

"What make of car was it?"

"I'm not so up on cars," said the assistant manager. "But it was black. Possibly dark blue."

Wallander shut his notebook. "If you think of anything else, let me know right away," he said. "Any little thing could be important."

Wallander left the bank after making a note of the names and telephone numbers of the seller and the buyers. He went out the front entrance, and paused in the square.

A paper bag, he thought to himself. That sounds like a bakery. He remembered a bakery on the street running parallel to the railway. He crossed over the square then turned off to the left.

The girl behind the counter had been working all day Friday, but she didn't recognise Louise Åkerblom from the photo Wallander showed her.

"There is another bakery," said the girl.

"Whereabouts?"

The girl explained, and Wallander could see it was just as close to the bank as the one he was in now. He thanked her, and left. He made his way to the bakery on the other side of the square. An elderly lady asked him what would he like as he entered the shop. Wallander showed her the photograph and explained who he was.

"I wonder if you recognise her?" he asked. "She might have been here shopping shortly after 3.00 last Friday afternoon."

The woman went to fetch her glasses to study the photograph more carefully.

"Has something happened?" she asked, curious to know. "Who is she?"

"Just tell me if you recognise her," Wallander said, gently.

The woman nodded.

"I remember her," she said. "I think she bought some pastries. Yes, I remember quite clearly. Napoleons. And a loaf of bread."

Wallander thought for a moment.

"How many pastries?" he asked.

"Four. I remember I was going to put them in a carton, but she said a bag would be OK. She seemed to be in a hurry."

Wallander nodded.

"Did you see where she went after she left?"

"No. There were other customers waiting."

"Thank you," Wallander said. "You've been a great help."

"What happened?" the woman said.

"Nothing," Wallander said. "Just routine."

He left the shop and walked back to the rear of the bank where Louise Åkerblom had parked her car.

Thus far but no further, he thought. This is where we lose track. She sets out from here to see a house, but we still don't know where it is. After leaving a message on the answering machine. She's in a good mood, she has pastries in a paper bag, and she's due home at 5.00.

He looked at his watch. 2.57 p.m. Three days exactly since Louise Åkerblom was standing on this very spot.

Wallander walked to his car, which was parked in front of the bank, put in a music cassette, one of the few he had left after the break-in, and tried to summarise where he'd got to so far. Placido Domingo's voice filled the car as he thought about the four pastries, one for each of the Åkerbloms. Then he wondered if they said grace before eating pastries. He wondered what it felt like to believe in a god.

An idea occurred to him at the same time. He had time for one more interview before the meeting at the station to talk things through.

What had Åkerblom said? Pastor Tureson?

Wallander started the engine and drove towards Ystad. When he joined the E14, he was only just within the speed limit. He called Ebba at the station reception, asked her to get hold of Pastor Tureson and tell him Wallander wanted to speak to him right away. Just before he got to Ystad, Ebba called him back. Pastor Tureson was in the Methodist chapel and would be pleased to see him.

"It'll do you no harm to go to church now and again," Ebba said.

Wallander thought about the nights he'd spent with Baiba Liepa in a church in Riga the previous year. But he said nothing. Even if he wanted to, he had no time to think about her just now.

Pastor Tureson was an old man, tall and well built, with a mop of white hair. Wallander could feel the strength in his grip when they shook hands.

The inside of the chapel was simple. Wallander did not feel the oppression that often affected him when he went into a church. They sat on wooden chairs by the altar.

"I called Robert a couple of hours ago," Pastor Tureson said. "Poor man, he was beside himself. Have you found her yet?"

"No," Wallander said.

"I don't understand what can have happened. Louise wasn't the type to get herself into dangerous situations."

"Sometimes you can't avoid them," Wallander said.

"What do you mean by that?"

"There are two kinds of dangerous situation. One is the kind you get yourself into. The other just sucks you in."

Pastor Tureson threw up his hands in acknowledgment. He seemed genuinely worried, and his sympathy for the husband and their children appeared to be real.

"Tell me about her," Wallander said. "What was she like? Had you known her long? What sort of a family were the Åkerbloms?"

Pastor Tureson stared at Wallander, a serious expression on his face. "You ask questions as though it were all over," he said.

"It's a bad habit of mine," Wallander said, apologetically. "Of course I mean you should tell me what she *is* like."

"I've been pastor in this parish for five years," he began. "As you can probably hear, I'm originally from Göteborg. The Åkerbloms have been members of my congregation the whole time I've been here. They both come from Methodist families, and they met through the chapel. Now they're bringing up their daughters in the true religion. Robert and Louise are good people. Hard-working, thrifty, generous. It's hard to describe them any other way. In fact, it's hard not to talk about them as a couple. Members of the congregation are shattered by her disappearance. I could feel that at our prayer meeting yesterday."

The perfect family. Not a single crack in the façade, Wallander thought. I could talk to a thousand different people, and they would all say the same thing. Louise Åkerblom doesn't have a single flaw. Not one. The only odd thing about her is that she has disappeared.

Something doesn't add up. Nothing adds up.

"Something's on your mind, Inspector?" Pastor Tureson said.

"I was thinking about flaws," Wallander said. "Isn't that one of the basic features of all religions? That God will help us to overcome our flaws?"

"Absolutely."

"But it seems to me that Louise Åkerblom didn't have any flaws.

The picture I'm getting of her is so perfect, I start getting suspicious. Do such utterly good people exist?"

"That's the kind of person Louise is," Pastor Tureson said.

"You mean she's almost angelic?"

"Not quite," Pastor Tureson said. "I remember one time when she was making coffee for a chapel social evening. She burnt herself. I happened to hear that she actually swore."

Wallander tried going back to the beginning and starting again. "There's no chance she and her husband were fighting?"

"None at all," Pastor Tureson said.

"No other man?"

"Of course not. I hope that isn't a question you'll put to Robert."

"Could she have felt some kind of religious doubt?"

"I believe that to be out of the question. I'd have known about it."

"Was there any reason why she might have committed suicide?"

"No."

"Could she have gone out of her mind?"

"Whyever should she? She's a perfectly stable character."

"Most people have their secrets," Wallander said after a moment's silence. "Can you imagine that Mrs Åkerblom might have had some secret she couldn't share with anybody, not even her husband?"

Pastor Tureson shook his head. "Of course everybody has secrets," he said. "Often very murky secrets. All the same, I'm convinced Louise didn't have any that could lead her to abandon her family and cause all this worry."

It doesn't add up, Wallander thought again. There's something in this picture of perfection that simply doesn't add up.

He got to his feet and thanked Pastor Tureson. "I'll be talking with other members of your congregation," he said. "If she doesn't turn up, that is."

"She'll have to turn up," Pastor Tureson said. "There's no other possibility."

It was 4.05 p.m. as when Wallander left the Methodist chapel. It had started raining, and he shivered in the wind. He sat in the car for a while, feeling how tired he was. It was as if he couldn't cope with the thought that two little girls had lost their mother.

*

At 4.30 they were all gathered in Björk's office at the station. Martinsson was slumped back on the sofa; Svedberg leaned against a wall. He was scratching his bald head as usual, as if searching absentmindedly for the hair he had lost. Wallander sat on a wooden chair. Björk was leaning over his desk, engrossed in a telephone conversation. At last he put down the receiver and told Ebba they were not to be disturbed for the next half-hour. Unless it was Robert Åkerblom.

"Where are we?" Björk said. "Where shall we start?"

"We are nowhere," Wallander said.

"I've filled in Svedberg and Martinsson," Björk said. "We've put out a search for Mrs Åkerblom's car. All the usual routines for missing person cases we consider to be serious."

"Not *consider* to be serious," Wallander said. "*Are* serious. If there had been an accident, we'd have heard about it by now. But we haven't. That means we're dealing with a crime. I'm sure she's dead."

Martinsson began to ask a question, but Wallander interrupted him and summarised what he'd been doing that afternoon. He had to get his colleagues to see what he had realised. A person like Louise Åkerblom would not of her own free will abandon her family. Somebody or something must have forced her to fail to arrive home at 5 p.m., as she had promised on the telephone.

"It sounds nasty, no doubt about that," Björk said, when Wallander had finished.

"Estate agent, free church member, family," said Martinsson. "Maybe it all got too much for her? She buys the pastries, drives off home. Then all of a sudden she turns around and heads for Copenhagen instead."

"We have to find the car," Svedberg said. "Without it, we won't get anywhere."

"First of all we have to find the house she was going to see," Wallander said. "Hasn't Robert Åkerblom called yet?"

No-one had heard from him.

"If she really did go to see that house somewhere near Krageholm, we ought to be able to follow her tracks until we find her, or until the tracks come to an end."

"Peters and Norén have been combing the side roads around

Krageholm," Björk said. "No Toyota Corolla. They did find a stolen truck, though."

Wallander took the cassette from the answering machine out of his pocket. With some considerable difficulty they eventually managed to find a machine to play it. They all stood around the desk, listening to Louise Åkerblom's voice.

"We have to analyse the tape," Wallander said. "I can't imagine what the technical guys could possibly find. But still."

"One thing is clear," Martinsson said. "When she left her message she wasn't threatened or pressured, scared or worried, desperate or unhappy."

"Which means something must have happened," Wallander said. "Between 3 p.m. and 5 p.m. Somewhere in the area of Skurup, Krageholm, Ystad. A little over three days ago."

"How was she dressed?" Björk said.

Wallander realised he'd forgotten to ask her husband this most basic question. He admitted as much.

"I still think there could be a natural explanation," Martinsson said, thoughtfully. "It's as you say yourself, Kurt. She's not the type to disappear of her own free will. But assault and murder are still pretty rare. I think we should go about it in the usual way. Not get hysterical."

"I'm not hysterical," Wallander said, knowing that he was getting angry. "I know what I think, though, and I think certain conclusions speak for themselves."

Björk was just about to intervene when the telephone rang.

"I said we shouldn't be disturbed," Björk said.

Wallander quickly put his hand over the receiver.

"It could be Åkerblom," he said. "Maybe it's best if I talk to him."

He picked up the phone and gave his name.

"Robert Åkerblom here. Have you found Louise?"

"No," Wallander said. "Not yet."

"The widow just called," Åkerblom said. "I have a map. I'm going there myself to take a look."

"I'll take you there," Wallander said. "That'll be best. I'll come right away. Can you make a few copies of the map? Five will do."

"OK," Åkerblom said.

Wallander thought how truly religious people were usually

law-abiding and compliant with authority. Yet nobody could have stopped Åkerblom from going out on his own to look for his wife.

Wallander slammed down the receiver. "We have a map now," he said. "We'll take two cars to start with. Åkerblom wants to come. He can come with me."

"Shouldn't we take a few patrol cars?" Martinsson said.

"We'd have to drive in a convoy if we did that," Wallander said. "Let's take a look at the map first, and draw up a plan. Then we can send out everything we've got."

"Call me if anything comes up," Björk said. "Here or at home."

Wallander almost ran down the corridor. He had to know if the track just petered out, or if Louise Åkerblom was still out there somewhere.

They took the map Åkerblom had sketched to the widow's instructions, and spread it out over the bonnet of Wallander's car, which Svedberg had dried first with his handkerchief.

"E14," Svedberg said. "As far as the exit for Katslösa and Lake Kade. Take a left to Knickarp, then a right, then left again, and look for a dirt road."

"Wait a minute," Wallander said. "If you'd been in Skurup, which road would you have taken then?"

There were lots of possibilities. After some discussion Wallander turned to Åkerblom. "What do you think?" he said.

"Louise would have taken a minor road," he said without hesitation. "She didn't like the traffic on the E14. I think she'd have gone by way of Svaneholm and Brodda."

"Even if she was in a hurry? If she wanted to be home by 5.00?"

"Even so," Åkerblom said.

"You take that road," Wallander said to Martinsson and Svedberg. "We'll go straight to the house. We can use the car phone if we need to."

They drove out of Ystad. Wallander let Martinsson and Svedberg pass, since they had the longer distance to travel. Åkerblom sat staring straight ahead. Wallander kept glancing at him. He was rubbing his hands anxiously, as if he couldn't make up his mind whether or not to clasp them together. Wallander could feel Åkerblom's tension. What would they find?

He slowed down as they approached the exit for Lake Krageholm, let a truck pass, and recalled having driven along this same road one early morning two years before, when an old farmer and his wife had been beaten to death in a remote farmhouse. He shuddered at the memory, and thought – as he so often did – of his colleague Rydberg, who died last year. Every time Wallander was faced with an investigation out of the ordinary, he missed the experience and advice of the older man.

What's going on in this country of ours? he said to himself. Where have all the old-fashioned thieves and conmen gone? Where does all this senseless violence come from?

The map was lying by the gear lever.

"Are we going the right way?" he said, to break the silence in the car.

"Yes," Åkerblom said, without taking his eyes off the road. "We should take a left just over the brow of this next hill."

They drove into the Krageholm forest. The lake was on their left, shimmering through the trees. Wallander slowed down, and they started looking out for the turning.

It was Åkerblom who saw it first. Wallander had already driven past. He reversed and came to a halt.

"You stay in the car," he said. "I'll go and look around."

The actual turning into the dirt road was almost overgrown. Wallander got down on one knee and could make out faint traces of car tyres. He could feel Åkerblom's eyes on his neck. He went back to the car and called Martinsson and Svedberg. They'd just got as far as Skurup.

"We're at the start of the dirt road," Wallander said. "Be careful when you turn in. Don't drive over the tyre marks."

"Roger," Svedberg said. "We're on our way now."

Wallander turned into the track, avoiding the tyre marks.

Two cars, he thought. Or the same one going in and coming back.

They shuddered along the muddy and badly maintained road. It was supposed to be a kilometre to the house that was up for sale. To his surprise, Wallander saw on the map that the house was called Solitude.

After three kilometres the track petered out. Åkerblom stared uncomprehendingly at the map and at Wallander.

33

"Wrong road," Wallander said. "We couldn't have missed the house. It's beside the road. Let's go back."

When they emerged onto the main road, they drove slowly and came to the next turning a few hundred metres further on. Wallander repeated his investigation. Unlike the previous road, this one had a great many tracks, one over the other. The road also gave the impression of being better maintained, but they could not find the house here, either. They caught a glimpse of a farmhouse through the trees, but it didn't look anything like the description they had. Wallander stopped after they had gone four kilometres.

"Do you have Mrs Wallin's number?" he said. "I get the feeling that she has a poor sense of direction."

Robert Åkerblom said that he had and took a small address book from his inside pocket. There was a bookmark shaped like an angel between the pages.

"Call her," Wallander said. "Explain that you're lost. Ask her to give you the directions again."

The phone rang for some time before the widow answered. It turned out that Mrs Wallin was by no means sure how many kilometres it was to the turn-off.

"Ask if there is some other landmark," Wallander said. "There must be something we can use to get our bearings. If not, we'll have to send a car and bring her here."

Wallander let Åkerblom talk to Mrs Wallin without switching the phone on to the loudspeaker.

"An oak tree struck by lightning," Åkerblom said. "We turn off just before we get to the tree."

They drove on, and after two more kilometres saw the oak. There was also a road going to the right. Wallander called Svedberg and explained how to find it. Then he searched for the third time, looking for tyre tracks. To his surprise he found nothing at all to suggest any vehicle had used this road for some time. That wasn't necessarily significant. The tracks could have been washed away by rain. Nevertheless, he felt something approaching disappointment.

The house was where it ought to have been, by the road, one kilometre in. They stopped and got out of the car. It had started raining, and the wind was blowing in gusts.

Åkerblom set off at once, running towards the house, yelling out his wife's name in a shrill voice. Wallander stayed by the car. It happened so quickly, he was taken by surprise. When Åkerblom disappeared behind the house, he ran after him.

No car, he thought. No car, and no Mrs Åkerblom.

He caught up with Åkerblom just as he was about to throw a brick through a window at the back of the house. Wallander grabbed his arm.

"It's no good," Wallander said.

"She may be in there," Åkerblom shouted.

"You said she didn't have any keys to the house," Wallander pointed out. "Put the brick down and we'll look for a door that's been forced. But I can tell you now, she's not there."

Without warning Åkerblom collapsed to the ground.

"Where is she?" he said. "What's happened?"

Wallander felt a lump in his throat. He had no idea what to say.

Then he took Åkerblom by the arm and helped him to his feet. "No point in sitting here and making yourself ill," he said. "Let's look around."

There was no door that had been forced. They peered in through uncurtained windows and saw only empty rooms. They had just concluded there was nothing else to see when Martinsson and Svedberg turned into the drive.

"Nothing," Wallander said. At the same time, he put his finger to his lips, discreetly, so that Åkerblom couldn't see. He didn't want Svedberg and Martinsson to start asking questions. He didn't want to have to say Louise Åkerblom probably never got as far as the house.

"We have nothing to report either," Martinsson said. "No car, nothing."

Wallander looked at his watch. It was 6.10 p.m. He turned to Åkerblom and tried to smile. "I think the most useful thing you can do now is to go back home to the girls," he said. "Svedberg here will drive you home. We'll make a systematic search. Try not to worry. We'll find her all right."

"She's dead," Åkerblom said, in a low voice. "She's dead, and she'll never come back."

The three policemen stood in silence.

"No," Wallander said, eventually. "There's no reason to think it's as bad as that. Svedberg will drive you home now. I'll get in touch later on."

Svedberg drove away.

"Now we can start searching in earnest," Wallander said, resolutely. He could feel the unease mounting in him all the time.

They sat in his car. Wallander called Björk and asked for all available personnel with cars to be sent to the split oak. At the same time Martinsson began planning how best to examine all the roads in a circle around the house as quickly and as efficiently as possible. Wallander asked Björk to make sure they got suitable maps.

"We'll keep looking until it gets dark," Wallander said. "We start again at dawn tomorrow if we don't find anything tonight. You can get in touch with the army as well. Then we'll have to consider a line search."

"Dogs," Martinsson said. "We need dogs tonight, right now."

Björk promised to come along in person and take charge of the operation.

Martinsson and Wallander looked at each other.

"Summarise," Wallander said. "What do you think?"

"She never came here," Martinsson said. "She could have been close to here, or a long way away. I don't know what can have happened, but we have to find the car. We're doing the right thing, starting the search here. Somebody will have seen it, surely. We'll have to start knocking on doors. And Björk will have to hold a press conference tomorrow. We have to let it be known we take the disappearance very seriously."

"What can have happened?" Wallander said.

"Something we'd rather not think about," Martinsson said.

The rain started drumming against the car windows and roof.

"Hell," Wallander said.

"Yes," Martinsson said. "Exactly so."

Shortly before midnight the policemen, tired and drenched, reassembled on the gravel in front of the house Mrs Åkerblom had possibly never seen. They had found no trace of the dark blue car, still less of Louise Åkerblom. The most noteworthy thing they found was a pair

36

of elk carcasses. And a police car almost crashed with a Mercedes travelling along one of the dirt roads at high speed.

Björk thanked all of them for their efforts. He had agreed with Wallander that they could be sent home. The search would begin again at 6 a.m.

Wallander was the last to leave. He had called Åkerblom on his car phone, and told him that he was sorry to have nothing new to report. Although it was late, Åkerblom expressed the wish that Wallander should come and see him at their house, where he was with the daughters.

Before Wallander started the engine he called his sister in Stockholm. He knew she stayed up late. He told her their father was planning to marry his home help. To Wallander's astonishment, she burst out laughing, but to his relief, she promised to come down to Skåne at the beginning of May.

Wallander replaced the telephone in its holder and set off for Ystad. Rain squalls hammered the windscreen.

He found his way to the Åkerblom home. It was a terrace house like hundreds of other houses. The light was still on downstairs. Before getting out of the car he leaned back in his seat and closed his eyes. She never got that far, he thought. What happened on the way?

CHAPTER FOUR

The alarm beside Wallander's bed rang at 4.45 a.m. He pulled his pillow over his face. I get far too little sleep, he thought dejectedly. Why can't I be one of those policemen who put everything to do with work aside as soon as they get home?

He stayed in bed, and turned his mind back to his brief visit to Åkerblom's house the night before. It had been pure torture to look into his distraught eyes and tell him they hadn't managed to find his wife. Wallander had escaped from the house as quickly as he could, and he felt unwell as he drove home. Then he had lain awake until 3 a.m. in spite of his exhaustion.

We've got to find her, he thought. Now. Soon. Dead or alive. We just have to find her.

He had arranged with Åkerblom that he would be in touch in the morning, once the search had begun again. Wallander realised he would have to go through Louise Åkerblom's belongings, to find out what she was really like. Somewhere in the back of Wallander's mind was the nagging thought that there was something very peculiar about her disappearance. There were peculiar circumstances every time a person went missing; but there was something in this case that was different from anything he had experienced before. He badly wanted to know what it was.

Wallander forced himself out of bed, switched on the coffee machine, and went to turn on the radio. He cursed when he remembered the burglary, and it occurred to him that nobody would now have time to deal with that investigation.

He took a shower, got dressed, and drank his coffee. The weather did not improve his temper. It was pouring, and the wind was up. It was the worst possible weather for a line search. All day long the fields and coppices around Krageholm would be full of tired, irritable policemen, dogs with their tails between their legs, and fed-up conscripts from the local regiment. Still, that was Björk's problem. His job was to go through Mrs Åkerblom's belongings.

He drove to the split oak tree. Björk was pacing irritably up and down the verge.

"What awful weather," he said. "Why does it always have to rain when we're out looking for somebody?"

"It's odd," Wallander said.

"I've talked to the lieutenant-colonel: his name's Hernberg," said Björk. "He's sending two bus-loads of conscripts, at 7 a.m. I think we might as well start straightaway. Martinsson's done all the spadework."

Wallander nodded appreciatively. Martinsson was good when it came to line searches.

"I thought we'd call a press conference for 10 a.m.," Björk said. "It would help if you could be there. We'll have to have a photograph of her by then."

Wallander gave him the one he still had in his inside pocket. Björk studied Louise Åkerblom's picture.

"Nice girl," he said. "I hope we find her alive. Is it a good likeness?"

"Her husband thinks it is."

Björk put the photograph into a plastic wallet which he carried in one of his raincoat pockets.

"I'm going to their house," Wallander said. "I can be of more use there."

As Wallander made to walk over to his car, Björk grabbed him by the shoulder.

"What do you think?" he said. "Is she dead? Is there some crime at the back of all this?"

"It can hardly be anything else," Wallander said. "Unless she's been hurt and is lying in agony somewhere or other. But I don't think so."

"I don't like the look of this," Björk said. "Not one little bit."

Wallander drove back to Ystad. The grey sea was very choppy.

When he entered the house in Åkarvägen, two little girls stood staring at him, wide-eyed.

"I've told them you're a policeman," Åkerblom said. "They know Mama's lost, and you're looking for her."

Wallander nodded and tried to smile, despite the lump that came into his throat. "My name's Kurt," he said. "What's yours?"

"Maria" and "Magdalena", the girls said, one after another.

"Those are lovely names," Wallander said. "I have a daughter named Linda."

"They're going to be at my sister's today," Åkerblom said. "She'll be here shortly to pick them up. Can I offer you a cup of tea?"

"Yes, please," Wallander said.

He hung up his overcoat, removed his shoes, and went into the kitchen. The girls were standing in the doorway, watching him.

Where shall I start? Wallander wondered. Will he understand that I have to open every drawer, and go through every one of her papers?

The girls were collected, and Wallander finished his tea.

"We have a press conference at 10.00," he said. "That means we shall have to make public your wife's name, and ask for anybody who might have seen her to come forward. As you will realise, that implies something else. We can no longer discount the possibility that a crime has been committed."

Wallander had foreseen the risk that Åkerblom might go to pieces and start weeping. But the pale, hollow-eyed man, immaculately dressed in suit and tie, seemed to be in control of himself this morning.

"We have to go on believing that there's a straightforward explanation for your wife's disappearance," Wallander said. "But we can no longer exclude anything at all."

"I understand," Åkerblom said. "I've been clear about that all the time."

Wallander pushed his teacup to one side, said thank you, and got to his feet. "Have you thought of anything else we ought to know about?"

"No," Åkerblom said. "It's a complete mystery."

"Let's go through the house together," Wallander said. "I hope you understand that I have to look through all her drawers, clothes, everything that could give us a clue."

"She keeps everything in good order," Åkerblom said.

They began upstairs, and worked their way down to the basement and the garage. Wallander noticed that Louise Åkerblom was fond of pastel shades. There was nowhere a dark curtain or tablecloth to be seen. The house exuded *joie de vivre*. The furniture was a mixture of old and new. When he was drinking his tea, he had noticed how well

40

equipped the kitchen was with machines and gadgets. Their everyday life was evidently not restricted by excessive puritanism.

"I'll have to drive down to the office for a while," Åkerblom said, when they had finished their tour of the house. "I take it I can leave you here on your own."

"No problem," Wallander said. "I'll save my questions till you get back. Or I'll give you a call. In any case, I have to leave for the station shortly before 10.00, for the press conference."

"I'll be back before then," Åkerblom said.

When Wallander was on his own, he began by searching every cupboard and drawer in the kitchen and examined the refrigerator and the freezer. One thing intrigued him. In a cupboard under the sink was a copious supply of alcohol. That didn't square with the impression he had of the Åkerblom family.

He continued with the living room, without finding anything of note. Then he went upstairs. He ignored the girls' room. He searched the bathroom first, reading the labels on bottles from the pharmacist and making a note of some of Louise Åkerblom's medicines in his note pad. He stood on the bathroom scales, and was dismayed to see how much he weighed. Then he moved on to the bedroom. He always felt uncomfortable going through a woman's clothes: it was as if somebody was watching him without his knowing it. He went through all the pouches and cardboard boxes in the wardrobes. Then he came to the chest of drawers where she kept her underwear. He found nothing that surprised him, nothing that told him anything he didn't already know. When he was finished, he sat on the edge of the bed and looked around the room.

Nothing, he thought. Absolutely nothing.

He sighed, and moved on to the next room, which was used as a study. He sat at the desk, opening drawer after drawer. He immersed himself in photograph albums and bundles of letters. He didn't come across a single photograph in which Louise Åkerblom was not smiling or laughing. He replaced everything carefully, closed the drawer, and tried the next one. Tax returns and insurance documents, school reports and conveyancing deeds, nothing out of the ordinary.

It was only when he opened the bottom drawer in the last of the chests that he was surprised. At first he thought it contained nothing

41

but plain white writing paper. When he felt the bottom of the drawer, however, his fingers came into contact with a metal object. He took it out and sat there, frowning.

A pair of handcuffs. Not toy handcuffs; real ones. Made in England. He put them on the desk in front of him. They don't have to be significant, he thought. But they were well hidden. And I suspect Åkerblom would have taken them away, if he had known they were there.

He put the handcuffs in his pocket and closed the drawer.

Then he went down to the basement rooms and the garage. On a shelf over a little workbench he found a few neatly made balsa wood model aeroplanes. He pictured Åkerblom in his mind's eye. Maybe once he'd dreamed of becoming a pilot?

The telephone started ringing in the background. He hurried to answer it.

By this time it was 9 a.m.

"Could I speak to Inspector Wallander?" It was Martinsson.

"Speaking," Wallander said.

"You'd better get out here," Martinsson said. "Right away."

Wallander could feel his heart beating faster. "Have you found her?" he said.

"No," Martinsson said. "Not her, and not the car either. But there's a house on fire not far away. Or, to be more accurate, the house exploded. I thought there might be a link."

"I'm on my way," Wallander said.

He scribbled a note for Åkerblom and left it on the kitchen table.

As he drove to Krageholm, he tried to work out the implications of what Martinsson had said. A house had exploded? What house?

He overtook three big trucks in succession. The rain was now so heavy that the wipers could only keep the windscreen partially clear.

Just before he reached the shattered oak tree, the rain eased a little and he could see a column of black smoke rising above the trees. A police car was waiting for him by the oak. One of the men inside indicated he should take the right-hand turning. As they swung in from the main road, Wallander noted the road was one of those he'd taken by mistake the previous day, the one with the most tyre marks. There was something else about that road, but he couldn't put his finger on what it was right now.

When he got to where the fire was, he recognised the house. It was to the left, and only just visible from the road. The firemen were already at work. Wallander got out of his car, and was immediately hit by the heat of the blaze. Martinsson was striding towards him.

"People?" Wallander said.

"None," Martinsson said. "Not as far as we know. In any case, it's impossible to go inside. The heat is terrific. The house has been empty for more than a year since the owner died. A farmer told me the background. Apparently, whoever was dealing with the estate couldn't make up his mind whether to rent it or sell it."

"So what happened?" Wallander said, eyeing the enormous clouds of smoke.

"I was out on the main road," Martinsson said. "One of the army search lines had got into a bit of a mess. Then there was this bang. It sounded like a bomb going off. At first I thought a plane had crashed. Then I saw the smoke. It took me five minutes at most to get here. Everything was in flames. Not just the house, but the barn as well."

Wallander tried to think. "A bomb," he said. "Could it have been a gas leak?"

Martinsson shook his head. "Even 20 canisters of calor gas could not have made an explosion of that force," he said. "Fruit trees in the back have snapped off. Or been blown up by the roots. It must have been deliberate."

"The whole area is crawling with police and soldiers," Wallander said. "An odd time to choose for arson."

"Exactly what I thought," Martinsson said. "That's why I thought right away there could be a connection."

"Any ideas?"

"No," Martinsson said. "None at all."

"Find out who owns the house," Wallander said. "Who's responsible for the estate. I agree with you, this seems to be more than just a co-incidence. Where's Björk?"

"He already left for the station, to get ready for the press conference," Martinsson said. "You know how nervous he gets when he has to face journalists who never write what he says. But he knows what's happened. Svedberg's been speaking to him. He knows you're here as well."

"I'll have a closer look at this when they've put the fire out," Wallander said. "But it would be a good idea for you to detail some men to run a fine-tooth comb over this area."

"Looking for Louise Åkerblom?" Martinsson said.

"For the car in the first place," Wallander said.

Martinsson went off to find the farmer. Wallander stayed put, staring at the raging fire.

If there is a connection, what is it? he wondered. A woman goes missing and a house explodes. Right under the noses of a huge search party. He looked at his watch: 9.50. He beckoned to one of the firemen.

"When will I be able to start rooting around in there?" he said.

"It's burning pretty fast," the fireman said. "By this afternoon you should be able to get close to the house."

"Good," Wallander said. "It seems to have been a hell of a bang."

"That wasn't started with a match," the fireman said. "I wouldn't be surprised if a 100 kilos of dynamite went off."

Wallander called Ebba in the station and asked her to tell Björk he was on his way, and drove back to Ystad. Then he remembered what it was he'd forgotten: one of the patrol car crews had reported they'd nearly been hit by a Mercedes going at a hell of a speed down one of the dirt roads. Wallander was pretty sure it was the very track where the house on fire was.

Too many coincidences, he thought. Soon we'll have to find something that starts to make it all add up.

Björk was pacing restlessly up and down in the reception area when Wallander got there.

"I'll never get used to press conferences," he said. "What's all this about a fire that Svedberg tells me? He expressed himself very oddly, I must say. He said a house and barn had exploded. What did he mean by that? What house was he talking about?"

"The description was probably accurate," Wallander said. "It can hardly have anything to do with the press conference on the disappearance of Louise Åkerblom, though, so I suggest we talk about it later. The team might have more information by then, anyway."

"OK, let's keep this simple," Björk said. "A straightforward reference to her being missing, hand out the photos, appeal to the general public. You can deal with questions about how the investigation is going."

"The investigation isn't really going at all," Wallander said. "If only we'd traced her car. But we've got nothing."

"You'd better make something up," Björk said. "Police who claim they have nothing to tell reporters are sitting ducks. Never forget that."

The press conference took just over half an hour. In addition to the local papers and local radio, the stringers for *Expressen* and *Idag* had shown up. Nobody from the Stockholm papers, though. They won't arrive until we've found her, Wallander thought. And if she's dead.

Björk opened the conference and announced that a woman was missing in circumstances that the police were taking very seriously. He described the woman and her car, and distributed photographs. Then he invited questions, nodded towards Wallander, and sat down. Wallander took his place on the little dais podium and waited.

"What do you think has happened?" the reporter from the local radio station said. Wallander had never seen him before. They seemed always to be changing staff.

"We don't think anything," Wallander said. "But the circumstances suggest we should be taking the disappearance of Louise Åkerblom seriously."

"Tell us about the circumstances, then," the reporter said.

Wallander waded in. "We must be clear that most people in this country who go missing in one way or another turn up again sooner or later. Two times out of three there is a perfectly simple explanation. One of the most common is forgetfulness. Just occasionally there are signs to suggest there could be another explanation. Then we treat the disappearance very seriously."

Björk raised his hand. "Which is not to say, of course, that the police don't take all cases of missing persons very seriously," he said.

Oh my God, Wallander thought.

The man from *Expressen*, a young man with a red beard, raised his hand and said, "Can't you be a bit more precise? You're not excluding the possibility that a crime may have been committed. Why aren't you? And one more thing: it's not clear where she disappeared, and who was the last to see her."

The journalist was right. Björk had been vague on several counts.

"She left the Savings Bank in Skurup just after 3 p.m. last Friday," Wallander said. "An employee at the bank saw her drive off around

45

3.15. Nobody saw her after that. We believe she took one of two routes. Either the E14 towards Ystad, or she might have driven past Slimminge and Rögla towards the Krageholm district. As you heard, Louise Åkerblom is an estate agent. She may have gone to see a house that was being put up for sale. Or she may have driven straight home. We are not sure what she decided to do."

"Which house?" one of the local press reporters said.

"I can't answer that question – for reasons connected with the investigation," Wallander said.

The press conference died out of its own accord. The local radio reporter interviewed Björk. Wallander talked to one of the local press reporters in the corridor. When he was alone, he made himself a cup of coffee, went into his office and called the scene of the fire. He got hold of Svedberg, who told him that Martinsson had already diverted a group of searchers to concentrate on the area around the burning house.

"I've never seen a fire like this one," Svedberg said. "There won't be a single roof beam left when it's over."

"I'll be out this afternoon," Wallander said. "I'm going to Åkerblom's place again. Call me there if anything comes up."

"We'll call you," Svedberg said. "What did the press have to say?"

"Nothing of note," Wallander said, and put the phone down.

At that moment Björk knocked and came in. "That went pretty well," he said. "No dirty tricks, just reasonable questions. Let's just hope they write what we want them to."

"We'll have to detail a few extra people to man the phones tomorrow," Wallander said, not bothering to comment on his assessment of the press conference. "When a church-going mother of two disappears, I'm afraid lots of people who've seen nothing at all will be calling in, giving the police the benefit of their blessing and prayers. Quite apart from those we hope might really have something useful to tell us."

"Assuming we don't find her in the course of today," Björk said.

"I don't believe that, and neither do you," Wallander said.

Then he told him all he knew about the fire. The explosion. The fireman's assessment. Björk listened, looking more and more worried. "What does all this mean?" he said.

46

Wallander stretched out his arms. "I don't know. I'm going back to see Åkerblom now, though, to find out what else he's got to say."

Björk stood in the door.

"We'll have a debriefing in my office at 5.00," he said.

Just as Wallander was about to leave his office, he remembered he'd forgotten to ask Svedberg to do something for him. He called the scene of the fire again.

"Do you remember that a police car nearly crashed into a Mercedes last night?" he said.

"It rings a bell," Svedberg said.

"Find out all you can about it," Wallander said. "I have a strong feeling that that Mercedes has something to do with the fire. I'm not so sure whether it has anything to do with Louise Åkerblom."

"OK," Svedberg said. "Anything else?"

"We have a meeting here at 5.00," Wallander said, and replaced the receiver.

A quarter of an hour later he was back in the Åkerbloms' kitchen. He sat on the same chair he'd occupied a few hours earlier, and had another cup of tea.

"Sometimes you get called out on some emergency," Wallander said. "There's been a major fire, but it's under control now."

"I understand," Åkerblom said, politely. "It can't be easy, being a policeman."

Wallander observed the man opposite him at the table. At the same time, he could feel the handcuffs in his trouser pocket. He wasn't looking forward to the interrogation he was about to embark upon.

"I have a few questions," he said. "We can talk just as easily here as anywhere else."

"Of course," Åkerblom said. "Ask as many questions as you like."

Wallander noticed he was irritated by the gentle and yet unmistakably admonishing tone in the man's voice.

"I'm not sure about the first question," Wallander said. "Does your wife have any medical problems?"

The man looked at him in surprise. "No," he said. "What are you suggesting?"

"It just occurred to me she might have heard she was suffering from some serious illness. Has she been to the doctor lately?"

"No. And if she'd been ill, she'd have told me."

"There are some serious illnesses that people are hesitant to talk about," Wallander said. "Or at least, they need a few days to gather their thoughts and emotions. It's often the case that the sick person is the one who has to console whoever it is he or she tells."

Åkerblom thought for a moment before answering. "I'm certain that's not the case here," he said.

Wallander nodded and went on. "Did she have a drinking problem?"

Åkerblom winced. "How can you ask such a question?" he said, after a moment's silence. "Neither of us so much as touches a drop of alcohol."

"Yet the cupboard under the sink is full of bottles," Wallander said.

"We have nothing against other people drinking," Åkerblom said. "Within reason, of course. We sometimes have guests. Even a little estate agency like ours needs to entertain its clients occasionally."

Wallander nodded. He had no reason to question the response. He took the handcuffs out of his pocket and put them on the table. He watched Åkerblom's reaction the whole time.

It was exactly what he had expected. Incomprehension.

"Are you arresting me?" he said.

"No," Wallander said. "But I found these handcuffs in the bottom drawer to the left of the desk, under a stack of writing paper, in your study upstairs."

"Handcuffs?" Åkerblom said. "I've never seen them before in my life."

"As it can hardly have been one of your daughters who put them there, we'll have to assume it was your wife," Wallander said.

"I just don't understand it," Åkerblom said.

Wallander knew at once that the man was lying. A barely noticeable shift in his voice, a sudden insecurity in his eyes. Enough for Wallander to register it.

"Could anybody else have put them there?" he said.

"I don't know," Åkerblom said. "The only visitors we have are from the chapel. Apart from clients. And they never go upstairs."

"Nobody else at all?"

"Our parents. A few relatives. The children's friends."

"That's quite a lot of people," Wallander said.

"I don't understand it," Åkerblom said, again.

Maybe you just don't understand how you could have forgotten to take them away, Wallander thought. For now, the question is: what do they mean?

For the first time Wallander asked himself whether Åkerblom could have killed his wife. But he dismissed it. The handcuffs and the lie were not enough to overturn everything Wallander had already established.

"Are you certain you can't explain these handcuffs?" Wallander said again. "Perhaps I should point out it's not against the law to keep a pair of handcuffs in your home. You don't need a licence. On the other hand, of course, you can't just keep people locked up however you like."

"Do you think I'm not telling you the truth?" Åkerblom said.

"I don't think anything," Wallander said. "I just want to know why these handcuffs were hidden in a desk drawer."

"I've already said I don't understand how they could have got into the house."

Wallander nodded. He didn't think it was necessary to press him any further. Not yet, at least. But Wallander was sure he was lying. Could it be that the marriage concealed a strange and possibly dramatic sex life? Could that in its turn explain why Mrs Åkerblom had disappeared?

Wallander pushed his teacup to one side, indicating that the conversation was over. He put the handcuffs back in his pocket, wrapped in a handkerchief. A forensic analysis might reveal more about what they'd been used for.

"That's all for the time being," Wallander said, getting to his feet. "I'll call the minute I have anything to report. You'd better be ready for a bit of a fuss tonight, when the evening papers come out and the local radio has broadcast its piece. We'll have to hope it all helps us, of course."

Åkerblom nodded, but said nothing.

Wallander shook hands and went out to his car. The weather was changing. It was drizzling and the wind had eased off. Wallander drove to Fridolf's Café near the bus station for a coffee and a couple of sandwiches. It was past noon before he was on his way to the scene of the fire. He parked, clambered over the barriers, and saw that both the house and the barn were now smoking ruins. It was still too soon for the forensic team to start their investigation. Wallander approached the edge of the fire and had a word with the man in charge, Peter Edler, whom he knew well.

"We're soaking it," he said. "Not much else we can do. Is it arson?"

"I've no idea," Wallander said. "Have you seen Svedberg or Martinsson?"

"I think they've gone for something to eat," Edler said. "In Rydsgård. And Colonel Hernberg has taken his wretchedly wet recruits back to their barracks. They'll be here again later."

Wallander nodded, and left the fire chief.

A policeman with a dog was standing a few metres away. He was eating a sandwich, and the dog was scratching away at the sooty, wet gravel with one paw. Suddenly the dog started howling. The policeman tugged impatiently at the leash a couple of times, then looked to see what the dog was digging for. Then Wallander saw him draw back with a start and drop his sandwich. Wallander couldn't help being curious, and walked over towards them.

"What's the dog found?" he said.

The policeman turned round to face Wallander. He was white as a sheet, and trembling. Wallander hurried over and bent down. In the mud was a finger. A black finger. Not a thumb, and not a little finger. But a human finger. Wallander felt ill. He told the dog handler to get in touch with Svedberg and Martinsson right away.

"Get them here immediately," he said. "Even if they're halfway through their meal. There's an empty plastic bag on the back seat of my car. Get it."

The policeman did as he was told.

What's going on? Wallander thought. A black finger. A black man's finger. Cut off. In the depths of Skåne.

When the policeman returned with the plastic bag, Wallander made a temporary cover to protect the finger from the rain. News of the discovery had spread, and several firemen gathered around the find.

"We have to start looking for the remains of bodies among the ashes," Wallander said to the fire chief. "God knows what's been going on here."

"A finger," Edler said, incredulously.

Twenty minutes later Svedberg and Martinsson arrived, and came running up to the spot. They stared, bewildered, at the black finger. In the end it was Wallander who broke the silence. "We can be sure of one thing," he said. "This isn't one of Mrs Åkerblom's fingers."

CHAPTER FIVE

They met at 5 p.m. in one of the conference rooms at the police station. Wallander could not remember a less talkative meeting. In the middle of the table, on a plastic cloth, was the black finger. He could see that Björk had angled his chair so he couldn't see it. Everyone else stared at the finger.

After a while, an ambulance arrived from the hospital and removed the finger. When it was gone, Svedberg went to get a tray of coffee, and Björk started the proceedings again.

"Just for once, I'm speechless," was his opening gambit. "Can any of you suggest a plausible explanation?"

Nobody spoke up.

"Wallander," Björk said, trying another angle, "could you perhaps give us a summary of where we are?"

"I'll give it a shot," Wallander said. "The rest of you can fill in the gaps."

He opened his notebook and leafed through. "Louise Åkerblom went missing four days ago," he began. "To be more precise, 98 hours ago. Nobody's seen her since, as far as we know. While we were looking for her, and for her car, a house exploded close to where we think she might be found. We know that the occupant of that house is deceased, and that the house was up for sale. The estate's lawyer lives in Värnamo. He's at a loss to explain what has happened. The house has been empty for more than a year. The new owners have not yet been able to decide whether to sell or to keep it in the family, or rent it. It's possible that some of the heirs might buy out the rest. The lawyer's name is Holmgren, and we've asked our colleagues in Värnamo to discuss the matter with him. At the very least, we want the names and addresses of all the beneficiaries."

He took a slurp of coffee before continuing.

"The fire broke out at 9 a.m.," he said. "There is evidence to suggest that some form of powerful explosive was used, with a timing device. There is absolutely no reason to suppose the fire was started by natural causes. Holmgren says that there were no gas canisters and the whole house was rewired last year. While the fire was being fought, one of our police dogs sniffed out a human finger some 25 metres from the blaze. It's an index finger or middle finger of a left hand. In all probability a man's. A black man's. The forensic team have run a fine-tooth comb over such parts of the heart of the fire and the immediate area as are accessible, but they have found nothing more. We've run a line search over the whole area, and found nothing. No sign of the car, no sign of Mrs Åkerblom. A house has blown up, and we've found a finger belonging to a black man. That's about it."

Björk made a face. "What do the medics have to say?" he asked.

"Maria Lestadius from the hospital was here," Svedberg said. "She says we should get onto the forensic lab. right away. She claims she's not competent to read fingers."

Björk squirmed on his chair. "Say that again," he said. "Read fingers?"

"That's the way she put it." Svedberg seemed resigned. It was a well-known peculiarity of Björk's, picking on inessentials.

Björk thumped the table almost absentmindedly. "This is awful," he said. "To put it bluntly, we don't know anything at all. Hasn't Åkerblom been able to give us any pointers?"

Wallander made up his mind there and then to say nothing about the handcuffs, not for now. He was afraid it might take them in directions that were of less than immediate significance. Besides, he was not persuaded that the handcuffs had any connection with her disappearance.

"Nothing at all," he said. "I think the Åkerbloms were the happiest family in the whole of Sweden."

"Might she have gone over the top, from a religious point of view? We're always reading about those crazy sects."

"You can hardly call the Methodists a crazy sect," Wallander said. "It's one of our oldest free churches. I have to admit I'm not 100 per cent clear just what they stand for."

"We'll have to look into that," Björk said. "What do you think we should do now?"

"Let's hope for what tomorrow might bring," Martinsson said. "We may get some calls."

"I've arranged extra personnel to man the telephones," Björk said. "Anything else we should be doing?"

"Let's face it," Wallander said, "we have nothing to go on. We have a finger. That means that somewhere there's a black man missing a finger on his left hand. That means in turn he needs help from a doctor or a hospital. If he hasn't shown up already, he will do sooner or later. He might contact the police. Nobody cuts his own finger off. Well, not often. In other words, somebody has subjected him to torture. It's possible he has fled the country already."

"Fingerprints," Svedberg said. "I don't know how many Africans there are in this country, legally or illegally, but there's a chance we might be able to trace a print in our files. We can send a request to Interpol as well. To my knowledge, many African states have been building up advanced criminal files in the last few years. There was an article about it in *Swedish Policeman* recently. I agree with Kurt. Even if we can't see any connection between Louise Åkerblom and this finger, we have to assume there might be one."

"Shall we give this to the newspapers?" Björk said. "The Ystad police are looking for the owner of a finger. That should get a headline or two, anyway."

"Why not?" Wallander said.

"I'll think about it," Björk said. "Let's wait a bit. I agree that every hospital in the country should be alerted, though. Surely the medics have a duty to inform the police if they suspect an injury may have been caused by a criminal action?"

"They're also bound by confidentiality," Svedberg said. "But of course the hospitals should be contacted. Health centres, too. Does anybody know how many doctors we have in this country?"

Nobody knew.

"Ask Ebba to find out," Wallander said.

"There are just over 25,000 doctors in Sweden," Wallander said, when she had reported to the conference room the result of her call to the secretary of the Swedish Medical Association.

They were astonished. Twenty-five thousand.

"Where are they all when we need them?" Martinsson said.

53

Björk was starting to get impatient. "Is this getting us anywhere?" he said. "If not, we've all got plenty to do. We'll have another meeting tomorrow morning at 8.00."

"I'll see to the hospital business," Martinsson said.

They had just collected their papers and got to their feet when the telephone rang. Martinsson and Wallander were already out in the corridor when Björk called them back.

"Breakthrough!" he said, his face flushed. "They think they've found the car. That was Norén. Some farmer showed up at the fire and asked the police if they were interested in something he'd found in a pond a few kilometres away. Out towards Sjöbo, I think he said. Norén drove to the spot and saw a radio aerial sticking out of the mud. The farmer, whose name is Antonson, was sure the car wasn't there a week ago."

"Right, let's get the hell out of here," Wallander said. "We've got to get that car up tonight. It can't wait until tomorrow. We'll have to find searchlights and a crane."

"I hope there's nobody in the car," Svedberg said.

"That's exactly what we're going to find out," Wallander said. "Come on."

The pond was difficult to get to, close to a thicket, to the north of Krageholm on the way to Sjöbo. It took the police three hours to get searchlights and a mobile crane on site, and it was 9.30 before they had managed to attach a cable to the car. Then Wallander contrived to slip and fall halfway into the water. He borrowed overalls from Norén, who had a spare set in his car. He hardly noticed how wet and cold he was. All his attention was concentrated on the car. He was also tense and uncomfortable. He hoped it was the right car, but he was afraid Louise Åkerblom might be found inside it.

"This was no accident," Svedberg said. "The car was driven into the mud so that it wouldn't be seen. Probably in the middle of the night. Whoever did it missed the aerial sticking up."

Wallander nodded. Svedberg was right.

The cable slowly tightened. The crane strained against its stanchions and started to pull. The rear end slowly rose into view. Wallander looked at Svedberg, who was an expert on cars.

"Is it the right one?" he said.

"Hang on a bit," Svedberg said. "I can't see yet."

Then the cable came loose. The car sank back into the mud. They had to start all over again. Half an hour later, the crane started pulling once more.

Wallander kept looking from the slowly emerging car to Svedberg, and back again.

And then Svedberg nodded. "It's a Toyota Corolla. No doubt about it."

Wallander aimed a searchlight. Now they could see the car was dark blue.

The car rose slowly from the pond. The crane stopped. Svedberg looked at Wallander. They walked over and looked in, one at each side. The car was empty. Wallander opened the boot. Nothing.

"The car's empty," he told Björk.

"She could still be in the water," Svedberg said.

Wallander nodded. The pond was about 100 metres in circumference, but the aerial had been visible, so it couldn't be very deep.

"We need divers," he said. "Now. Right away."

"A diver wouldn't be able to see anything, it's too dark," Björk said. "We'd better wait till the morning."

"They only need to wade along the bottom," Wallander said. "Dragging grappling irons between them. I don't want to wait till tomorrow."

Björk gave in. He went over to one of the police cars and made a call. Meanwhile Svedberg had opened the driver's door and poked around with a torch. He carefully detached the car telephone.

"The last number called is usually registered," he said. "She might have made some other call, as well as the one to the answering machine at the office."

"Good," Wallander said. "Good thinking, Svedberg."

While they were waiting for the divers, they made a preliminary search of the car. Wallander found a sodden paper bag on the back seat, with soggy pastries.

Everything fits so far, he thought. But then what happened? On the road? Who did you meet, Louise Åkerblom? Somebody you'd arranged to see? Or somebody else? Somebody who wanted to meet you, without your knowing about it?

"No handbag," Svedberg said. "No briefcase. Nothing in the glove compartment apart from the log book and insurance documents. And a New Testament."

"Look for a handwritten map," Wallander said.

Svedberg did not find one.

Wallander walked slowly round the car. It was undamaged. It had not been involved in an accident.

They sat in one of the patrol cars, drinking coffee from a thermos. It had stopped raining, and there was barely a cloud in the sky.

"Is she in the pond?" Svedberg wondered.

"I don't know," Wallander said. "Could be."

Two young men arrived in one of the fire brigade's emergency vehicles. Wallander and Svedberg greeted them – they had met before.

"What are we looking for?" one of the divers said.

"Maybe a body," Wallander said. "Maybe a briefcase, or a handbag. Perhaps something else we don't know about."

The divers made their preparations, then waded out into the black, stagnant water, holding a line with grappling irons between them.

The policemen watched in silence.

Martinsson showed up just as the divers had completed their first drag. "It's the right car, I see," Martinsson said.

"And she could be in the pond," Wallander said.

The divers were conscientious. One of them would stop occasionally and pull at the grappling iron. A collection of objects was starting to build up on the bank. A broken sleigh, parts of a threshing attachment, rotten tree branches, a rubber boot.

It was past midnight and still no sign of Louise Åkerblom.

"There's nothing more in there," one of the divers said. "We can try again tomorrow, if you think it would be worth it."

"No point," Wallander said. "She's not there."

They exchanged a few brief pleasantries, then drove home.

Wallander had a beer and a couple of crusty rolls when he got back. He was so exhausted, he couldn't think straight. He didn't bother to get undressed, just lay on the bed with a blanket over him.

*

By 7.30 on Wednesday morning, April 29, Wallander was back at the police station.

A thought had struck him while he was in the car. He looked up Pastor Tureson's telephone number. Tureson himself answered. Wallander apologised for calling so early, then asked if they could meet some time that day.

"Is it about anything in particular?" Tureson said.

"No," Wallander said. "I've just had a few thoughts that give rise to questions I'd like answering. You never know what might be important."

"I heard the radio reports," Tureson said. "And I've read the papers. Is there anything new?"

"She's still missing," Wallander said. "I can't say very much about how the investigation is proceeding, for technical reasons."

"I understand," Tureson said. "Forgive me for asking, it's just that I am worried about Louise's disappearance, naturally."

They agreed to meet at 11.00, at the Methodist chapel.

Wallander put the phone down, and went in to Björk's office. Svedberg was already sitting there, yawning, and Martinsson was on Björk's phone. Björk was drumming his fingers impatiently on the desk. Martinsson replaced the receiver, making a face.

"The tip-offs have started coming in," he said. "Nothing worthwhile yet. Somebody called to say he was absolutely certain he had seen Louise Åkerblom at Las Palmas airport last Thursday. The day before she vanished, that is."

"Let's get started," Björk said, interrupting him.

The chief constable had obviously slept badly. He was tired and bad tempered.

"Let's continue where we left off yesterday," Wallander said. "The car will have to be thoroughly gone over, and the telephone tip-offs dealt with as they come in. I intend to drive out to the scene of the fire again, to see what the technicians have found. The finger is on its way to forensics. The question is: should we let the media know about that or not?"

"Let's do it," Björk said, without hesitation. "Martinsson can help me write a press release. I expect there'll be an uproar once the reporters get hold of that."

"It would be better if Svedberg took care of it," Martinsson said. "I've got my hands full contacting 25,000 Swedish doctors. Plus an endless list of health centres and emergency clinics. That will take time."

"Fair enough," Björk said. "I'll get onto that lawyer in Värnamo. We'll meet again this afternoon, unless something crops up."

Wallander went out to his car. It was going to be a nice day in Skåne. He paused and filled his lungs with fresh air.

When he got to the burned-out house, there were two surprises in store for him.

The forensic team had done some fruitful work early that morning. He was met by Sven Nyberg, who had only joined the Ystad force a few months earlier. He had been working in Malmö, but did not hesitate to move to Ystad when the opportunity arose. Wallander had not had very much to do with him as yet, but the reputation that preceded him suggested he was a skilful investigator at the scene of a crime. Wallander had discovered for himself that he was also brusque and hard to make contact with.

"You ought to look at a couple of things," Nyberg said.

They walked over to a rain shelter that had been rigged up over four posts. Some twisted bits of metal were lying on a sheet of plastic.

"A bomb?" Wallander said.

"No," Nyberg said. "We've found no trace of a bomb so far. But this is at least as interesting. You're looking at some parts of a biggish radio installation."

Wallander stared at him aghast.

"A combined transmitter and receiver," Nyberg said. "I can't tell you what type or what make it is, but it's definitely an installation for radio buffs. You may well think it's a bit odd to find something like this in a deserted house. Especially one that's been blown up."

"You're right," Wallander said. "I want to know more about this."

Nyberg picked up another piece of metal from the plastic sheet.

"This is interesting too," he said. "Can you see what it is?"

Wallander thought it looked like a pistol butt. "Part of a gun," he said.

"A pistol," Nyberg said. "There was presumably a live magazine in place when the house blew up. The pistol was smashed to bits when the magazine exploded, due either to the fire or the pressure waves. I also have a suspicion this is a pretty unusual model. The butt is extended, as you can see. It's certainly not a Luger or a Beretta."

"What is it, then?"

"Too early to say," Nyberg said. "But I'll let you know as soon as we find out."

Nyberg filled his pipe and lit up. "What do you think about this little lot?" he said.

Wallander shook his head. "I don't think I've ever been so confused," he answered honestly. "I can't find any links. All I know is I'm looking for a missing woman, and all the time I keep coming across the damnedest things. A severed finger, parts of a radio transmitter, unusual weapons. Maybe it's precisely these unusual features I should take for a starting point. Something I haven't come across before in all my police experience."

"Patience," Nyberg said. "We'll establish the links sooner or later, no doubt about it."

Nyberg went back to his meticulous piecing together of the jigsaw. Wallander wandered around for a while, trying yet again to summarise everything to his own satisfaction. In the end he gave up. He called the station from his car.

"Have we had many leads?" he asked Ebba.

"The calls are coming in non-stop," she said. "Svedberg told me a couple of minutes ago that some of the people offering information seemed reliable and interesting. That's all I know."

Wallander gave her the number of the Methodist chapel, and made up his mind to do another thorough search of Louise Åkerblom's desk at the office, when he'd finished talking to the minister. He felt bad about not having followed up his first cursory search.

He drove back to Ystad. As he had plenty of time before he was due to meet Tureson, he parked at the square and went into the stereo shop. Without spending much time comparing one model against another, he bought a walkman. Then he drove home to Mariagatan. He'd bought a CD of Puccini's *Turandot*. He put on the earphones, lay back on the sofa, and tried to think of Baiba Liepa. But instead, Louise Åkerblom's face kept filling his mind.

He woke with a start and looked at his watch. He cursed when he realised he ought to have been at the chapel ten minutes ago.

Pastor Tureson was waiting for him in a back room, a sort of store-room and office combined. Tapestries with Bible quotations were hanging on the walls. A coffee machine stood on a window ledge.

"Sorry I'm late," Wallander said.

"I'm well aware you police have a lot to do," Tureson said.

Wallander sat down on a chair and took out his notebook. Tureson offered him a cup of coffee, but he declined.

"I'm trying to build up an image of what Mrs Åkerblom is really like," he said. "Everything I've found out so far seems to indicate just one thing: Louise Åkerblom was a woman at peace with herself, who would never voluntarily leave her husband or her children."

"That's the Louise Åkerblom we all know," Tureson said.

"At the same time, that makes me suspicious," Wallander said.

"Suspicious?" Tureson looked puzzled.

"I cannot believe that such perfect individuals exist," Wallander said. "Everybody has his or her secrets. The question is: what are Louise Åkerblom's? I take it she hasn't vanished because she hasn't been able to cope with her own good fortune."

"You'd get the same answers from every single member of our church, Inspector," Tureson said.

Afterwards, Wallander could never manage to put his finger on just what had happened; but there was something in Tureson's response that made him sit up and take notice. It was as if the minister were defending Louise Åkerblom's image, even though it was not being questioned. Or was there something else he was defending?

Wallander swiftly shifted his approach and put a question that had seemed less important before.

"Tell me about your congregation," he said. "Why does one choose to become a member of the Methodist church?"

"Our faith and our interpretation of the Bible stand out, quite simply, as right."

"Is that justified?" Wallander wondered.

"In my opinion and that of my congregation it is," Pastor Tureson said. "Needless to say, members of other denominations would disagree. That's only natural."

"Is there anybody in your congregation who doesn't like Mrs

Åkerblom?" Wallander said, and felt at once that Tureson hesitated a fraction too long before replying.

"I can't imagine there would be," he said.

There it is again, Wallander thought. Something evasive, something not quite straightforward about the answer. "Why don't I believe you?" he asked.

"But you should, Inspector," Tureson said. "I know my congregation."

Wallander could see he would have to put his questions rather differently if he was going to succeed in throwing the minister off balance. A full frontal attack it would have to be.

"I know that Louise Åkerblom has enemies in your congregation," he said. "Never mind how I know. But I'd like to hear your views."

Tureson stared hard at him for some time before replying.

"Not enemies," he said. "But it is true that one of our members had an unfortunate relationship with her." He got up and went over to a window. "I've been wavering. I almost called you last night, in fact. But I didn't. I mean, everybody hopes Louise will come back to us. That everything will turn out to have a natural explanation. All the same, I've been getting more and more worried. I have to admit that." He returned to his chair. "I also have responsibilities to all the other members of my church," he said. "I don't want to have to put anybody in a bad light, to make an accusation that later proves to be wrong."

"This conversation is not an official interrogation," Wallander said. "Whatever you say will go no further. I'm not taking notes."

"I don't know how to put it," Pastor Tureson said.

"Tell it as it is," Wallander said. "That's generally the simplest way."

"Two years ago, our church welcomed a new member," Tureson began. "He was an engineer on one of the Poland ferries, and he started coming to our services. He was divorced, he was 35, friendly and considerate. He soon became well liked and much appreciated by other church members. About a year ago, though, Louise Åkerblom asked to speak to me. She was very insistent that her husband Robert should not know anything about it. We sat here in this room, and she told me that the new member of our congregation had started pestering her with declarations of love. He was sending her letters, stalking her, calling her. She tried to put him off as nicely as she could, but he persisted and the situation was becoming intolerable. Louise asked me to have a word with him. I did so, and suddenly he seemed to change into an altogether different person. He fell into a terrible rage, claimed that Louise had let him down, and that he knew that I was the one having a bad influence on her. He claimed she was actually in love with him, and wanted to leave her husband. It was totally absurd. He stopped coming to our meetings, he gave up his job on the ferry, and we thought he'd disappeared for good. I simply told the rest of the congregation that he'd moved away from town, and was too shy to say goodbye. It was a great relief for Louise, of course. But then about three months ago, it all started again. One evening Louise noticed him standing on the street outside their house. It was a terrible shock for her, naturally. He started pestering her all over again. I have to admit, Inspector Wallander, that we did actually consider calling in the police. Now, of course, I'm sorry we didn't. It is all too possible that there is no connection whatsoever. But I begin to wonder more and more as the days pass."

At last, thought Wallander. Now I have something to get my teeth into. Even if I don't understand what this has got to do with black fingers, blown-up radio transmitters and very unusual handguns. But I have a starting point, a lead to follow.

"What's the man called?"

"Stig Gustafson."

"Do you know his address?"

"No. I've got his social security number, though. He fixed the church's heating system on one occasion, and we paid him." Tureson went over to a desk and leafed through a file. "570503–0470," he said.

Wallander closed his notebook. "You were right to tell me about this," he said. "I'd have found out about it sooner or later, anyway. This way, we save time."

"She's dead, isn't she?" Tureson suddenly said.

"I don't know," Wallander said. "To be absolutely honest with you, I just don't know the answer to that question."

Wallander shook hands with the minister and left the church. It was 12.15 p.m.

He almost ran to his car and drove straight to the station. He hurried up to his office in order to summon his colleagues to a meeting. Just as he was sitting down at his desk, the phone rang. It was Nyberg, who said he was still sifting through the ashes.

"Found something new?" Wallander said.

"No," Nyberg said. "But I've just realised what make the handgun is. The one we found the butt of."

"I'm writing it down," Wallander said, taking out his notebook.

"I was right when I said it was an unusual pistol and I doubt if there are more than a very few of them in this country."

"So much the better," Wallander said. "Makes it easier to trace."

"It's a 9mm Astra Constable," Nyberg said. "I saw one at a gun show in Frankfurt once, some time ago. I've got a pretty good memory for guns."

"Where is it made?"

"That's what so odd about it," Nyberg said. "As far as I know, it's only manufactured legally in one country."

"Which?"

"South Africa."

Wallander put his pen down. "South Africa?"

"Yes."

"Why's that?"

"I can't tell you why a particular gun is popular in one country but not in another. It just is."

"Damn it. South Africa?"

"There's no denying it gives us a possible link to the finger we found."

"What's a South African pistol doing in this country?"

"That's your job to find out," Nyberg said.

"OK," Wallander said. "It's good that you called me right away. We'll talk about this again later."

Wallander got out of his chair and went to the window. A long two minutes later, he had made up his mind. They would give priority to finding Louise Åkerblom and checking out Gustafson. Everything else would have to take second place for the time being.

This is as far as we've got, Wallander thought, 117 hours after Louise Åkerblom disappeared.

CHAPTER SIX

Peter Hanson was a thief. He was not a particularly successful criminal, but he usually managed to execute the assignments allocated to him by his employer and customer, a fence in Malmö called Morell.

That very day, the morning of Walpurgis Eve, April 30, Morell's stock was at a pretty low ebb with Hanson. He planned to take the day off, like everyone else, and maybe treat himself to a trip to Copenhagen. Late the previous evening, however, Morell called to say he had an urgent job for him.

"I want you to get hold of four water pumps," Morell said. "The old-fashioned sort. The ones you can see outside every cottage in the countryside."

"Surely it can wait until after the holiday," Hanson said. He was asleep when Morell called, and he did not like being woken up.

"It can't wait," Morell said. "I have a customer who lives in Spain, and he's driving there the day after tomorrow. He wants those pumps in the car with him. He sells them to other Swedish émigrés down there. They pay good money to have old Swedish water pumps outside their haciendas. It's nostalgia."

"How the hell am I going to get hold of four water pumps?" Hanson said. "Have you forgotten it's a holiday? Every summer cottage will be occupied tomorrow."

"That's your problem," Morell said. "Start early enough and you'll manage it." Then he turned threatening. "If you don't, I'll be forced to go through my papers and work out how much your brother owes me."

Hanson slammed down the phone. He knew Morell would take that as a positive reply. As he had been woken up and would not be able to get to sleep again for ages, he got dressed and drove down to town from Rosengård, where he lived. He went into a bar and ordered a beer.

Hanson had a brother called Jan-Olof. He was Hanson's big misfortune in life. Jan-Olof played the ponies at Jägersro, at the toto, and occasionally also at other trotting tracks up and down the country. He did a lot of betting, and he did it badly. He lost more than he could afford, and ended up in Morell's hands. As he could not provide any guarantees, Hanson had been forced to step in as a living guarantee.

Morell was first and foremost a fence. In recent years, however, he had realised that, like all other businessmen, he would have to make up his mind how to develop his activities. Either he would have to specialise and concentrate on a smaller field, or he could broaden his base. He chose the latter.

Although he had a big network of customers who could give very precise information about the goods they ordered, he decided to go in for loan-sharking as well. That way, he reckoned he could increase his turnover considerably.

Morell had just turned 50. After 20 years in the fraud business, he had changed course and since the end of the 1970s had built up a successful receiving business all the way across southern Sweden. He had about two dozen thieves and drivers on his secret payroll, and every week truckloads of stolen goods would be transported to his warehouse in the Malmö free port, ready for moving on to importers overseas. He collected stereos, televisions, and mobile telephones from Småland. Caravans of stolen cars came rolling up from Halland and were passed on to expectant buyers in Poland and, nowadays, the former East Germany. He could see an important new market ready to be opened up in the Baltic states, and he had already delivered a few luxury cars to Czechoslovakia as well. Hanson was one of the least significant cogs in his organisation. Morell was still doubtful about how good he was, and used him mostly for one-off deals. Four water pumps was an ideal assignment for him.

That was why Hanson was sitting in his car cursing on the morning of Walpurgis Eve. Morell had ruined his holiday. He was also worried about the assignment. There were too many people on the move for him to be confident of being undisturbed.

He had been born in Hörby, and knew Skåne inside out. There was hardly the tiniest of side roads in this part of the country he had not been on, and his memory was good. He had been working for Morell for four years now, ever since he was 19. He sometimes thought about all the things he had loaded into his rusty old van. He once rustled two young bulls. Orders for pigs were common around Christmas time. Several times he had acquired tombstones, and wondered what kind of a sick person commissioned such a theft. He had carried off front doors while the house owner was asleep upstairs, and dismantled a church spire with the assistance of a crane operator brought in for the purpose. Water pumps were run of the mill, as it were, but it was an unfortunate choice of day.

He decided to start in the area to the east of Sturup Airport. He banished all thought of Österlen. Every single country cottage would be occupied today. If he was going to make it, he'd have to concentrate on the area between Sturup, Hörby, and Ystad. There were quite a few empty houses around there.

Just beyond Krageholm, on a little dirt road which wound through the woods and eventually hit the main road at Sövde, he found his first pump. The house had almost collapsed and was well hidden from view. The pump was rusty, but intact. He started working it loose from the wooden base with a crowbar, but the wood was rotten. He dropped the crowbar and tugged at the pump, easing it away from the boards over the well itself. He began to think that maybe it wouldn't be impossible to find four pumps after all. Three more deserted houses, and he could be back in Malmö by early afternoon. It was still only 8.10 a.m. Perhaps he could nip over to Copenhagen in the evening after all.

At last he broke loose the rusty pump. As a result, the boards crumbled and fell away. He glanced down into the well.

There was something down there in the darkness. Something light yellow. He realised to his horror that it was a human head with blonde hair. There was a woman lying there. A corpse doubled up, twisted, deformed.

He dropped the pump and ran away. He drove off at a crazy speed, getting away from the deserted house as fast as possible. After a few kilometres, just before he got to Sövde, he braked, opened the car door, and threw up.

Then he tried to be calm. He knew he had not imagined it. There was a woman down the well. A woman lying in a well must have been murdered, he thought.

Then it occurred to him he'd left his fingerprints on the water pump he'd broken off. His fingerprints were in the files. Morell, he thought, confused. Morell's the man to sort this one out.

He drove through Sövde, far too fast, then took a left turn south, towards Ystad. He would drive back to Malmö and let Morell see to everything. The man leaving for Spain would have to go without his pumps.

Just before he got to the turning to the Ystad rubbish dump, his journey came to an end. As he tried to light a cigarette with shaking hands he went into a skid, and could only partially correct it. The van crashed into a fence, smashed through a row of letter boxes, and came to a halt. Hanson was wearing a seat belt, which prevented him from hurtling through the windscreen. Even so, the crash dazed him, and he remained in his seat, in shock.

A man mowing his lawn had seen what happened. He first ran over the road to make sure nobody had been badly injured, then he hurried back to his house, called the police, and stood by the car to make sure the man behind the wheel did not try to run away. He must be drunk, he assumed. Why else would he lose control on a stretch of straight road?

A quarter of an hour later, a patrol car arrived from Ystad. Peters and Norén, two of the most experienced officers in the district, had taken the call. Once they had established that no-one was injured, Peters started directing traffic past the scene of the accident, while Norén sat beside Hanson in the back of the police car, to try and find out what happened. Norén made him blow into the breathalyser, but the result was negative. The man seemed very confused, and not in the least interested in explaining how the accident happened. Norén was starting to think that perhaps the man was mentally unbalanced. He was talking disjointedly about water pumps, a fence in Malmö, and an empty house with a well.

"There's a woman in the well," he said.

"Oh, yes," Norén said. "A woman in a well?"

"She was dead."

Norén suddenly felt uneasy. What was the man trying to say? That he'd found a dead woman in a well at a deserted house?

67

Norén told him to stay in the car. Then he walked into the road where Peters was keeping the traffic moving, waving on inquisitive drivers who slowed down or showed signs of stopping.

"He claims he found a dead woman in a well," Norén said. "With blonde hair."

Peters dropped his arms to his side. "Mrs Åkerblom?"

"I don't know. I don't even know if it's true."

"Get hold of Wallander," Peters said. "Right away."

The mood among the detectives in the Ystad police station this Walpurgis Eve morning was expectant. They had gathered in the conference room at 8 a.m., and Björk rushed through the business. He had other things besides a missing woman to think about on a day like this. It was traditionally one of the most unruly days in the whole year, and there was a lot to do in preparation for the fun and games they could expect that evening and into the night.

The meeting was devoted to Stig Gustafson. Wallander had set his troops looking for the former marine engineer all Wednesday afternoon and evening. When he reported on his conversation with Pastor Tureson, everybody thought they were on the threshold of a breakthrough. The severed finger and the blown-up house would have to wait. Martinsson had even suggested that it was pure coincidence after all. That there simply was no connection between the incidents.

"This kind of thing has happened before," he said. "We've raided an illegal home distillery, and found an Aladdin's cave in a neighbour's house when we stopped to ask the way."

By Thursday morning they still had not found out where Gustafson lived.

"We have to crack this today," Wallander said. "Maybe we won't find him. But if we get his address, we can establish whether he's left in a hurry."

At that very moment, the telephone rang. Björk grabbed the receiver, listened briefly, then handed it to Wallander.

"It's Norén," he said. "He's at a car accident somewhere outside of town."

"Somebody else can take it," Wallander said, annoyed.

He took the receiver nevertheless, and listened to what Norén had to say. Martinsson and Svedberg were well acquainted with Wallander's reactions and adept at picking up the slightest change in his mood, and they could see at once that this call was important.

Wallander replaced the receiver slowly, and looked at his colleagues. "Norén's at the junction with the road leading to the rubbish dump," he said. "A car that has driven through a row of letter boxes. The driver of the car claims he's found a dead woman stuffed down a well."

They waited anxiously to hear what Wallander had to say next.

"If I understood it rightly," Wallander said, "this well is less than five kilometres from the property Louise Åkerblom was going to look at. And even closer to the pond where we found her car."

There was a moment's silence. Then they all got to their feet at the same time.

"Do you want a full-scale call-out right away?" Björk said.

"No," Wallander said. "We've got to get it confirmed first. Norén warned us not to get over-excited. The man sounds seriously confused."

"So would I have been," Svedberg said. "If I'd found a dead woman in a well and then driven off the road."

"Exactly what I was thinking," Wallander said.

They left Ystad in patrol cars. Wallander had Svedberg with him, and Martinsson had a car to himself. When they got to the northern exit road, Wallander switched on the siren. Svedberg stared at him in surprise.

"There's hardly any traffic," he said.

"Even so," Wallander said.

They stopped at the turning to the rubbish dump, put the ashen Hanson in the back seat, and followed his directions.

"It wasn't me," he said, over and over again.

"Who did what?" Wallander said.

"I didn't kill her," he said.

"What were you doing there, then?"

"I was only going to steal the pump."

Wallander and Svedberg exchanged glances.

"Morell called late last night and ordered four water pumps, but I didn't kill her."

Wallander was lost. The penny suddenly dropped for Svedberg, and he explained. "There is a fence in Malmö, name of Morell. He's notorious, and our colleagues in town have never been able to pin anything on him."

"Water pumps?" Wallander was suspicious.

"Antique value," Svedberg said.

They turned into the drive in front of the house. Wallander had time to register that it looked like a lovely day for the holiday. There wasn't a cloud in the sky, not a puff of wind, and it must be at least 20°C, even though it was only 9 a.m.

He contemplated the well and the broken-off pump beside it. Then he took a deep breath, walked to the well, and looked down.

Martinsson and Svedberg waited in the background with Hanson.

Right away Wallander could see that it was Louise Åkerblom. Even in death, there was a fixed smile on her face. He suddenly felt very ill. He turned away quickly and squatted on his haunches.

Martinsson and Svedberg approached the well. Both of them jerked back violently.

"Damn," Martinsson said.

Wallander swallowed and forced himself to breathe deeply. He thought of Louise Åkerblom's daughters. And of Robert Åkerblom. He wondered how they would be able to keep on believing in a good, all-powerful God when their mother and wife had been murdered and dropped into a well.

He stood up and went back to the well.

"It's her," he said. "No doubt about it."

Martinsson ran to his car, called Björk, and requested a full-scale call-out. They would need the fire brigade to get Louise Åkerblom's body out of the well. Wallander sat down with Hanson on the dilapidated veranda, and listened to his story. Occasionally he asked questions. He knew that Hanson was telling the truth. The police had reason to be grateful that he had set out that morning to steal old water pumps. If he hadn't, it might have been a long time before they found Louise Åkerblom.

"Take his personal details," Wallander said to Svedberg, when he had finished with Hanson. "And let him go. But make sure this Morell backs up his story. Who's the prosecutor on duty?" Wallander wondered.

"I think Björk said it was Åkeson," Svedberg said.

"Get hold of him," Wallander said. "Tell him we've found her and that it's murder. I'll give him a report later this afternoon."

"What do we do about Gustafson?" Svedberg said.

"You'll have to keep on looking for him by yourself for the time being," Wallander said. "I want Martinsson to be here when we get her up and make the first examination."

"I'll be only too glad to miss that," Svedberg said.

He drove off in one of the cars.

Wallander took a few more deep breaths before approaching the well once more. He did not want to be on his own when he told Åkerblom where they had found his wife.

It took the same two young firemen who had dragged the pond two hours to get Louise Åkerblom's corpse out of the well. They pulled her up using a rescue harness, and put the body in an investigation tent that had been pitched alongside the well. As they were pulling up the body, Wallander could see how she had died. She had been shot in the forehead. Once again he was struck by the thought that nothing in this investigation was straightforward. He still had not met Stig Gustafson, if he really was the one who killed her. But would he have shot her from the front? There was something that didn't add up.

He asked Martinsson for his first reaction.

"A bullet straight into the forehead," Martinsson said. "That doesn't make me think of uncontrolled passion or unrequited love. It makes me think of a cold-blooded execution."

"Exactly what I was thinking," Wallander said.

The firemen pumped the water out of the well. Then they went down again, and when they came back up they had with them Louise Åkerblom's handbag, her briefcase, and one of her shoes. The other was still on her foot. The water was pumped into a hastily constructed plastic pool. Martinsson found nothing else of interest when they filtered it.

The firemen went down to the bottom of the well one more time. They shone powerful lamps all around, but found nothing apart from what turned out to be the skeleton of a cat.

The doctor looked pale when she emerged from the tent.

"It's terrible," she said to Wallander.

"Yes," he said. "We know the key thing, namely that she was shot. I want the pathologists in Malmö to find out two things for me right away: first the bullet, second a report on any other injuries which might suggest she had been beaten or held prisoner. Anything you can find. And of course, whether she's been subjected to sexual assault."

"The bullet's still in her head," the doctor said. "There is no exit hole."

"One other thing," Wallander said. "I want her wrists and ankles examined. I want to know if there is any sign of her having been put in handcuffs."

"Handcuffs?"

"That's right," Wallander said. "Handcuffs."

Björk had been staying in the background while they worked to lift the corpse out of the well. Once the body had been placed on a stretcher and driven off to the hospital in an ambulance, he took Wallander aside.

"We have to inform her husband," he said.

We? Wallander thought. You mean, I'll have to do it.

"I'll take Pastor Tureson with me," he said.

"You'll have to try and find out how long it will take him to inform all her close relatives," Björk said. "I'm very much afraid we won't be able to keep this quiet for very long. And then, I really don't under-stand how you could just let that thief go. He can run to some evening tabloid or other and earn himself a fortune if he spills the beans on this story."

Wallander was irritated by Björk's niggling tone. On the other hand, he had to admit that there was a very real risk.

"Yes," he said. "That was stupid. My fault."

"I thought it was Svedberg who let him go," Björk said.

"It was Svedberg," Wallander said. "But it's my responsibility in any case."

"Please don't be angry with me for saying this," Björk said.

Wallander shrugged. "I'm angry at whoever did this to Louise Åkerblom," he said. "And to her daughters. And to her husband."

They sealed off the house and grounds, and the investigation continued. Wallander got into his car and called Pastor Tureson, who answered more or less right away. Wallander told him what they had found. Tureson was silent for quite some time before answering. He said he would wait for Wallander outside the church.

"Will he break down?" Wallander said.

"He has faith in God," Pastor Tureson said.

We'll see about that, Wallander thought. We'll see if that's enough. But he said nothing.

Pastor Tureson was standing on the street, his head bowed.

Wallander found it difficult to collect his thoughts as he drove into town. There was nothing he found more difficult than telling relatives that someone in their family had died. There was no real difference whether the death was caused by an accident, a suicide or a violent crime. No matter how hard he tried to express himself carefully and considerately, his words were cruelty itself. It had occurred to him that he was the ultimate herald of tragedy. He remembered what Rydberg, his friend and colleague, had said a few months before he died. "There will never be an appropriate way for a policeman to tell somebody of a sudden death. That's why we have to do it ourselves, and never delegate the job to anybody else. We're probably more resilient than the others – we've seen more of what nobody ought ever to see."

On the way into town he had also the persistent feeling that something was utterly wrong, absolutely incomprehensible; the whole investigation was totally misguided, and some explanation or other must soon come to light. He would ask Martinsson and Svedberg straight out if they felt as he did. Was there a possible link between that black finger and Louise Åkerblom's disappearance and death? Or was it just a combination of coincidences?

There might also be a third explanation, he thought: that somebody had manufactured the confusion.

But why had this death taken place at all? he asked himself. The only motive we have been able to find so far is unrequited love. But it is a pretty big step from there to a charge of murder. Not to mention murder so cold-blooded that the car was hidden in one place and the body several kilometres away.

Maybe we haven't found a single stone worth turning over, he thought. What do we do if we find that Stig Gustafson is not worth following up?

He thought of the handcuffs. Of Louise Åkerblom's constant smile. Of the happy family that had been destroyed. But was it the image that had collapsed? Or was it the reality? Pastor Tureson got into the car. He had tears in his eyes. Wallander immediately felt a lump in his throat.

"We've found her at an empty house some way outside of Ystad. I can't tell you any more, for the time being," Wallander said.

"How did she die?"

Wallander thought for a moment before replying. "She was shot," he said.

"I have one more question," Tureson said. "Apart from wanting to know who could have carried out such a crazy act. Did she suffer a lot before she died?"

"I don't know yet," Wallander said. "But even if I did know, I would tell her husband that death came very quickly, and hence painlessly."

They drew up outside the house. On the way to the church Wallander had stopped at the station and taken his own car. He did not want to arrive in a police car.

Åkerblom answered almost as soon as they rang the doorbell. He's seen us, Wallander thought. The moment a car brakes in the street outside, he hurries to the nearest window to see who it is.

He ushered them into the living room. Wallander listened to see if there was any noise. The two girls did not appear to be home.

"I'm afraid I have to tell you your wife is dead," Wallander said. "We've found her at an abandoned house some way outside of town. She was murdered."

Åkerblom stared at him, his face motionless. It seemed he was waiting for more.

"I very much regret this," Wallander said. "But the best I can do is to tell you exactly how it is. I'm afraid I shall also have to ask you to identify the body. But that can wait. It doesn't need to be done today. And it would be all right if Pastor Tureson were to do it."

Åkerblom kept on staring at him.

"Are your daughters at home?" Wallander said, cautiously. "This must be awful for them."

He turned to Tureson, appealing for help.

"We'll do all we can to help," Tureson said.

"Thank you for letting me know," Åkerblom said, all of a sudden. "All this uncertainty has been so difficult to bear."

"I am terribly sorry things have turned out so badly," Wallander said. "All of us on the case were hoping it would be otherwise."

"Who?" Åkerblom said.

"We don't know," Wallander said. "But we shall not rest until we do know."

"You'll never know," Åkerblom said.

Wallander looked at him inquiringly. "Why do you think that?" he said.

"Nobody could have wanted to kill Louise," Åkerblom said. "So how could you possibly find whoever is guilty?"

Wallander did not know what to say. Åkerblom had put his finger on their biggest problem.

A few minutes later he stood up. Tureson accompanied him into the hall. "You have a few hours in which to contact all the closest relatives," Wallander said. "Call me if you can't locate them. We won't be able to keep the news to ourselves for very long."

"I understand," Tureson said.

Then he lowered his voice. "Stig Gustafson?" he asked.

"We're still looking," Wallander said. "We don't know if it is him."

"Have you any other leads?"

"Could be," Wallander said, "but I'm afraid I can't answer that either."

"For technical reasons?"

"Exactly."

Wallander could see that Tureson had one more question. "Well," he said. "Fire away!"

Tureson lowered his voice so far that Wallander could hardly hear what he was saying. "Rape?" he said.

"We don't know that yet," Wallander said.

Wallander felt a strange mixture of hunger and uneasiness when he left the Åkerbloms' house. He stopped on the Österleden highway and struggled to eat a hamburger. He couldn't remember when he had last eaten. Then he hurried to the police station. When he got there he was met by Svedberg, who informed him that Björk had been forced to improvise a press conference at short notice. As he knew Wallander was busy informing relatives of Louise Åkerblom's death and he didn't want to disturb him, he had enlisted the help of Martinsson.

"Can you guess how the news leaked out?" he asked.

"Yes," Wallander said. "Peter Hanson?"

"Wrong! Try again!"

"One of us?"

"Not this time. It was Morell. He saw the chance to squeeze some money from one of the evening papers if he tipped them off. He's obviously a real bastard. At least the force in Malmö have something to pin on him now. Commissioning somebody to steal four water pumps is a criminal offence."

"He'll only get probation," Wallander said.

They went to the canteen and poured a mug of coffee each.

"How did Åkerblom take it?" Svedberg said.

"I don't know," Wallander said. "It must feel as if half your life has been taken away. No-one can imagine what it's like unless they've been through something similar. I can't. All I can say just now is that we'll have to have a meeting as soon as the press conference is over. I'll be writing a summary in my office until then."

"I will try to put together an overview of the tip-offs we've had," Svedberg said. "Somebody might have seen Mrs Åkerblom on Friday with a man who could be Stig Gustafson."

"Do that," Wallander said. "And let us have all you know about that man."

The press conference dragged on for an hour and a half. By then Wallander had tried to compose a summary under various headings and draw up a plan for the next phase of the investigation.

Björk and Martinsson were exhausted when they came to the meeting which was in Björk's room.

"Now I understand how you usually feel," said Martinsson, flopping down into a chair. "The only thing they didn't ask about was the colour of her underwear."

Wallander reacted angrily. "That was unnecessary," he said.

Martinsson opened his arms wide in apology.

"I'll try and give you a summary," Wallander said. "We know how it all started, so I'll skip that bit. Anyway, we've found Louise Åkerblom. She's been shot through the forehead. My guess is that she was shot at close range. But we'll know for sure later. We don't know if she was subjected to sexual assault. Nor do we know if she was ill-treated or held prisoner, or indeed where she was killed. Nor when. But we can be sure she was dead when she was put down that well. We've also found her car. It's essential we get a preliminary report from the hospital as soon as possible. Not least as to whether there was a sexual assault. Then we can start checking up on known offenders."

Wallander took a slurp of coffee before continuing.

"As for motive and murderer, we only have one track to follow so far," he said. "The engineer Stig Gustafson, who's been persecuting her and pestering her with hopeless declarations of love. We haven't found him yet. You know more about that, Svedberg. You can also give us a summary of the tip-offs we've had. Further complications in this investigation are the severed black finger and the house that blew up. Things have been made no clearer by the fact that Nyberg found the remains of a sophisticated radio transmitter in the ashes, and the butt of a handgun used mainly in South Africa, if I understood him properly. In one sense the finger and the pistol are linked by that fact. Not that it helps much. We still don't know if the murder and the explosion are connected."

Wallander was finished, and looked at Svedberg, who was leafing through the stack of papers he had in front of him. "I'll start with the tip-offs," he said. "I'm thinking of writing a book one of these days called *People Who Want to Help the Police*. It'll make me a rich man. As usual we've had curses, blessings, confessions, dreams, hallucinations, and a handful of sensible tips. As far as I can see, though, there's only one of immediate interest. The warden of the Rydsgård estate is quite certain he saw Louise Åkerblom driving past last Friday afternoon. The time is about right. That means we know which route she took. Apart from that there's very little of interest. We do know, of course, it's often a day or two before the best tip-offs come in. They come from sensible people who hesitate before getting in touch. As for Gustafson, we haven't managed to discover where he's moved to. But he's supposed to have an unmarried female relative in Malmö. Unfortunately we don't know her first name. The Malmö telephone directory is full of Gustafsons, as you would expect. We'll just have to get down to it and divide the list between us. That's all I have to say."

Wallander sat in silence for a moment. Björk looked expectantly at him. "Let's concentrate our efforts," Wallander said, at length. "We have to find Gustafson, that's the first priority. If the only lead we have is that relative in Malmö, then that's the one we'll have to follow up. Everybody in this station who's capable of picking up a phone will have to help. I'll join in and assist with the telephoning, as soon as I've dealt with the hospital." Then he turned to Björk. "We'd better keep going all evening," he said. "It's essential."

Björk nodded in agreement. "Do that," he said. "I'll be around if there's anything important."

Svedberg began organising the hunt for Gustafson's relative in Malmö, and Wallander went back to his office. Before calling the hospital, he rang his father. It was a long time before he answered. He must have been in his studio, painting. Wallander could hear right away that he was in a bad mood.

"Hello! It's me," he said.

"Who's me?" his father said.

"You know perfectly well who it is," Wallander said.

"I've forgotten what your voice sounds like," his father said.

Wallander gritted his teeth and resisted the temptation to slam down the receiver. "I'm busy," he said. "I've just found a murdered woman in a well. I won't be able to get out to your place today. I hope you'll understand."

"I can see you can't do that," he said. "It sounds unpleasant."

To his astonishment, his father sounded friendly.

"It is," Wallander said. "I just want to wish you a pleasant evening. And I'll try and come out tomorrow."

"Only if you get time," his father said. "I can't go on talking any longer right now."

"Why not?"

"I'm expecting a visitor."

Wallander could hear he'd been cut off. He was left sitting there with the receiver in his hand.

A visitor, he thought. So Gertrud Anderson goes around to see him even when she's not working? I must make time to go and see him soon, he thought. It would be a complete disaster if he married her.

He got up and went to see Svedberg. He collected a list of names and telephone numbers, returned to his office, and dialled the first on the list. At the same time he remembered that he had to contact the prosecutor during the afternoon.

At 4 p.m. they still hadn't traced Gustafson's relative. At 4.30 p.m. Wallander called Åkeson at home. He reported on what had happened so far, and told him that they would now make it their priority to find Stig Gustafson. The prosecutor had no objections. He asked Wallander to let him know if anything developed during the evening.

At 5.15 p.m., Wallander fetched his third list of names from Svedberg. Still no luck. Wallander groaned at the thought of it being Walpurgis Eve. A lot of people had gone away for the holiday.

Nobody answered at the first two numbers he called. The third was to an elderly lady who was quite sure there was no-one called Stig in her family.

Wallander opened the window, and could feel a headache coming on. He went back to the phone and dialled the fourth number. He let it go on ringing for quite a while, and was just about to replace the receiver when somebody answered. He could hear it was a young woman on the other end. He explained who he was and what he wanted to know.

"Sure," the young woman said, whose name was Monica. "I have a half-brother called Stig. He's a marine engineer. Has something happened to him?"

Wallander could feel all his exhaustion and dissatisfaction falling away at a stroke. "No," he said. "But we'd like to get in touch with him as soon as possible. Do you know where he lives?"

"Of course I know where he lives," she said. "In Lomma. But he's not at home."

"Where is he, then?"

"He's been on holiday in Las Palmas. He'll be home tomorrow. He's due in Copenhagen on a 10 a.m. flight. I think he's on a Spies package tour."

"Excellent," Wallander said. "I'd be grateful if you could give me his address and phone number."

She told him. He apologised for disturbing her evening, and hung up. Then he rushed into Svedberg's office, collecting Martinsson on the way. No-one knew where Björk was.

"We'll go to Malmö ourselves," Wallander said. "Our colleagues in town can assist. Run a check at the passport control on everybody disembarking from the various ferries. Björk will have to fix that."

"Did she say how long he'd been away?" Martinsson said. "If he had a week's vacation, that would mean he'd left last Saturday."

They looked at one another. The significance of Martinsson's point was obvious.

"I think you should go home now," Wallander said. "At least some of us ought to have had a good night's sleep before tomorrow. Let's meet here at 8 a.m. Then we'll drive to Malmö."

Martinsson and Svedberg went home. Wallander reached Björk, who promised to call his counterpart in Malmö and arrange things according to Wallander's wishes.

At 6.15 p.m. Wallander called the hospital. The doctor was only able to give vague answers. "There are no injuries on the body other than those that would have resulted from her being dropped into the well," she said. "Superficially, it doesn't look as though there was any sexual assault. I'll have to come back to that, though. I can't see any marks on her wrists or ankles."

"That's fine," Wallander said. "Thanks. I'll be in touch again tomorrow."

Then he left the police station. He drove out to Kåseberga and sat for a while on the hill top, staring out to sea. He was at home soon after 9 p.m.

CHAPTER SEVEN

At dawn, just before he woke up, Wallander had a dream that one of his hands was black. He had not put on a black glove. It was his skin that had grown darker until his hand was like an African's.

In his dream Wallander wavered between reactions of horror and satisfaction. Rydberg, his former colleague who had been dead for nearly two years, looked disapprovingly at the hand. He asked Wallander why only one of them was black.

"Something will have to happen tomorrow as well," Wallander said in his dream.

When he woke up and recalled the dream, he lay in bed wondering about the reply he gave Rydberg. What did he mean by that?

Then he got up and looked out of the window. May 1st in Skåne this year was cloud-free and sunny, but very windy. It was 6 a.m.

Although he had only slept for two hours, he did not feel tired. That morning they would get an answer to the question of whether Stig Gustafson had an alibi for Friday afternoon the previous week, when Louise Åkerblom had most probably been murdered.

If we can solve the crime today, it will have been surprisingly simple, he thought. The first few days we had nothing to go on. Then everything started to happen very quickly. A criminal investigation seldom follows regular day-to-day rhythms. It has its own life, its own energy. The clocks of a criminal investigation distort time, sometimes standing still, sometimes racing forward. No-one can know in advance.

They met at 8 a.m. in the conference room, and Wallander set the ball rolling. "There's no need for us to interfere in what the Danish police are doing," he said. "If what his half-sister says is to believed, Stig Gustafson will land on a Scanair flight to Copenhagen at 10 a.m. You can check that, Svedberg. Then he has three possible ways of getting to Malmö. The ferry to Limhamn, the hydrofoil, or the SAS hovercraft. We'll be keeping an eye on all three."

"An old marine engineer will probably take the big ferry," Martinsson said.

"He might have had enough of boats," Wallander said. "We'll have two men at each spot. He's to be taken firmly and informed of the reasons. A certain amount of caution would no doubt be appropriate. Then we'll bring him here. I thought I would start talking to him."

"Two men seems on the low side," Björk said. "Shouldn't we have a patrol car in the background, at least?"

Wallander agreed that this was a wise precaution.

"I've talked to our colleagues in Malmö," Björk said. "We'll get all the help we need. Decide for yourselves what signal the immigration people should give you when he shows up."

Wallander looked at his watch. "If that's all, we'd better get going," Wallander said. "It's best if we get to Malmö in good time."

"The flight could be delayed," Svedberg said. "Wait until I've checked."

Fifteen minutes later, he informed them that the plane from Las Palmas was expected at Kastrup at 9.20 a.m. "It's taken off," Svedberg said. "And they have a tailwind."

They drove to Malmö immediately, talked to their colleagues there, and divided up the assignments. Wallander allocated himself to the hovercraft terminal, with a young officer named Engman, who was still wet behind the ears. He had taken the place of Näslund, with whom Wallander had worked for many years. Näslund was from the island of Gotland, and couldn't wait for an assignment at home. When a vacancy occurred in the Visby force, he did not hesitate to go for it. Wallander missed him, especially his unfailing good humour.

Martinsson, with one other officer, was taking care of Limhamn, and Svedberg was to keep an eye on the hydrofoils. They were in touch by phone. Everything was set by 9.30 a.m. Wallander managed to arrange for coffee to be delivered to himself and the trainee by colleagues at the terminal.

"This is the first murderer I've ever hunted," Engman said.

"We don't know if he's our man," Wallander said. "In this country a man is innocent until he's proven guilty. Never forget that."

He was uncomfortable about the critical tone of his voice. He thought he'd better make up for it by saying something kind. But he couldn't think of anything.

Svedberg and his colleague made an undramatic arrest at the hydrofoil terminal. Gustafson was a small man, thin, balding, sunburnt after his holiday. Svedberg told him he was suspected of murder, put the cuffs on him and announced he was being taken to Ystad.

"I don't know what you're talking about," Gustafson said. "Why do I have to be handcuffed? Why are you taking me to Ystad? Who am I supposed to have murdered?"

Svedberg registered that he seemed genuinely surprised. The thought struck him that marine engineer Gustafson might be innocent.

By the time Wallander was sitting opposite Gustafson in an interview room at the Ystad police station, he had already informed Åkeson of the arrest. He started by asking if Gustafson would like a cup of coffee.

"No," he said. "I want to go home. And I want to know why I'm here."

"I want to talk to you," Wallander said, "and the answers I get will decide whether or not you can go home."

He wrote down Gustafson's details, noted that his middle name was Emil, and that he was born in Landskrona. The man was obviously nervous, and Wallander could see he was sweating at the roots of his hair. But that did not necessarily mean anything. Police phobia is just as real as snake phobia.

Then the real interrogation started.

"You are here to answer questions about a brutal murder," Wallander said. "The murder of Louise Åkerblom."

Wallander saw the man stiffen. Had he not counted on the body being found so soon? Wallander wondered. Or is he genuinely surprised?

"Mrs Åkerblom disappeared last Friday," he said. "Her body was found a few days ago. She was probably murdered during the latter part of Friday. What have you to say to that?"

"Is it the Louise Åkerblom I know?" Gustafson said.

Wallander could see he was scared now. "Yes," he said. "The one you got to know through the Methodists."

"She has been killed?"

"Yes."

"That's unspeakable!"

Wallander immediately began to feel a gnawing sensation in his stomach, and knew something was wrong, absolutely damned wrong. Gustafson's shock and astonishment seemed completely genuine. Mind you, Wallander knew from his own experience that there were people guilty of the most horrific crimes you could think of who nevertheless had the ability to appear innocent.

All the same, he could feel that gnawing sensation. Had they been following a trail that was cold from the start?

"I want to know what you were doing last Friday," Wallander said. "Start by telling me about the afternoon."

The answer he got surprised him.

"I was with the police," said Gustafson.

"The police?"

"Yes. In Malmö. I was flying to Las Palmas the next day. And I'd just discovered that my passport had run out. I was at the station in Malmö, getting a new passport. The office was already closed by the time I got there, but they were nice and helped me anyway. I got my passport at 4.00 p.m."

From that moment Stig Gustafson was out of the picture. Even so, Wallander didn't want to let go. He had a pressing need to solve this case as soon as humanly possible. Anyway, it would have been dereliction of duty to allow the interrogation to be governed by his feelings.

"I parked at Central Station," Gustafson said. "Then I went to the bar for a beer."

"Is there anybody who will testify that you were in that bar at that time?"

Gustafson thought for a moment. "I don't know," he said eventually. "I was on my own. Maybe one of the barmen will remember me? I'm not exactly a regular customer."

"How long were you there?" Wallander said.

"An hour, maybe. No longer."

"Until about 5.30 p.m.? Is that right?"

"I suppose so. I'd planned to go to Systemet before they closed."

"Which one?"

"The one behind the NK department store. I don't know the name of the street."

"And you went there?"

"I just bought a few beers."

"Will anyone remember you there?"

"The man who served me had a red beard," Gustafson said. "But I might still have the receipt. There's the date on those receipts, isn't there?"

"Go on," Wallander said, nodding.

"Then I collected the car," Gustafson said. "I was going to buy a suitcase at the B&W superstore, out at Jägersro, but they were too expensive. I thought I could manage with my old one. It was a disappointment."

"What did you do next?"

"I had a hamburger at the McDonald's. But the servers are only kids. I don't suppose they'll remember anything at all."

"Young people often have good memories," Wallander said, thinking of a young bank teller who had been extremely helpful in an investigation a year or so back.

"I've just remembered something else," Gustafson said. "Something that happened while I was at the bar."

"Go on."

"I went down to the toilet. I stood there talking to a man for a couple of minutes. He was complaining that there weren't any paper towels to dry your hands on. He was a bit drunk. Not too much. He said his name was Forsgård and he ran a garden centre at Höör."

Wallander made a note. "We'll follow that up," he said. "If we go back to McDonald's at Jägersro, that would have been about 6.30 p.m., right?"

"That's probably about right."

"What did you do next?"

"I went to Nisse's to play cards."

"Who's Nisse?"

"An old carpenter I used to have as a shipmate for many years. His name's Nisse Strömgren. Lives on Föreningsgatan. We play cards now and then. A game we learned in the Middle East. It's pretty complicated. But fun once you know it. You have to collect jacks."

85

"How long were you there?"

"It was probably near midnight by the time I went home. A bit too late, as I was going to have to get up so early. The bus was due to leave at 6 a.m. from the Central Station. The bus to Kastrup, that is."

Wallander nodded. Gustafson has an alibi, he thought. If what he says is true. And if Louise Åkerblom really was killed last Friday. Right now there were not sufficient grounds to arrest Gustafson. The prosecutor would never agree to it.

And it's not him, Wallander thought. If I start pressing him on his persecution of Louise Åkerblom, we'll get nowhere.

He stood up.

"Wait here," he said and left the room.

They gathered in the conference room and listened gloomily to Wallander's account.

"We'll check up on what he said," Wallander said. "But to be honest, I no longer think he's our man. This was a blind alley."

"I think you're jumping the gun," Björk said. "We don't even know for sure she really did die on Friday afternoon. Gustafson could in fact have driven from Lomma to Krageholm after leaving his card-playing buddy."

"What could have kept Louise Åkerblom out until that time?" Wallander said. "Don't forget she left a message on her answering machine to say she'd be home by 5 p.m. Something happened before 5 p.m."

Nobody spoke. Wallander looked around.

"I'll have to talk to the prosecutor," he said. "If nobody has anything to say, I'm going to let Gustafson go."

Nobody had any objection. Wallander walked across to the other end of the police station, where the prosecution authorities had their offices. He gave Per Åkeson a resumé of the interrogation. Every time Wallander visited his office, he was struck by the astonishing disorder all around him, papers stacked haphazardly on desks and chairs, the wastepaper basket was overflowing. But Åkeson was a skilful prosecutor. Moreover, no-one had ever accused him of losing a single paper of significance.

"We can't hold him," he said when Wallander had finished. "I take it you can check his alibi pretty quickly?"

"Yes," Wallander said. "To tell you the truth, I don't think he did it."

"Do you have any other leads?"

"It's all very vague," Wallander said. "We wondered if he might have hired somebody else to kill her. We'll make a thorough check this afternoon before we go any further. But we have no other individual to go after. We'll have to keep going on a broad front for the time being. I'll keep in touch."

Åkeson nodded, and stared at Wallander, frowning.

"How much sleep are you getting?" he said. "Or rather, how little? Have you seen yourself in a mirror? You look awful!"

"That's nothing compared to how I feel," Wallander said, getting to his feet.

He went back down the corridor, opened the door to the interview room, and went in.

"We'll arrange transport to take you to Lomma," he said. "But you can bet we'll be in touch again."

"Am I free?" Gustafson said.

"You've never been anything else," Wallander said. "Being questioned isn't the same as being accused."

"I didn't kill her," Gustafson said. "And I can't understand on what grounds you could think I did."

"Really?" Wallander said. "Though you've been chasing after her on and off?"

Wallander saw a shadow of unease flit over Gustafson's face. Just so he knows we know. He walked with Gustafson to the reception, and organised his lift home. I won't be seeing him again, he thought. We can write him off.

After an hour for lunch, they reassembled in the conference room. Wallander had been home for some sandwiches in his kitchen.

"Where are all the honest thieves nowadays?" Martinsson said with a sigh. "This case seems to have come out of a novel. All we have is a woman from a free church, dead and dumped in a well. And a black finger."

"I agree with you," Wallander said. "We can't get away from that finger, no matter how much we'd like to."

"There are too many loose ends flying around out of control," Svedberg said, scratching his bald head in irritation. "We have to collect

87

everything we have. And we must do it now. Otherwise we'll never get anywhere."

Wallander could detect indirect criticism of the way he was leading the investigation, but he had to concede even now that it was not entirely unjustified. There was always a danger of concentrating too soon on a single line of investigation. Svedberg's imagery reflected all too accurately the confusion he felt.

"You're right," Wallander said. "Let's see how far we've come. Louise Åkerblom is murdered. We don't know exactly where and we don't know who did it. But we do know roughly when. Not far from where we found her, a house that had been unoccupied for a year explodes. In the ruins of the fire, Nyberg finds parts of a sophisticated radio transmitter and the remains of a pistol butt. The pistol is manufactured in South Africa. In addition, we find a black finger in the drive outside the house. Then somebody tries to hide Louise Åkerblom's car in a pond. It's pure coincidence we find it as quickly as we do. The same goes for her body. She was shot in the middle of her forehead, and the killing calls to mind an execution. I rang the hospital before this meeting. There are no signs of sexual assault. She was just shot."

"We have to find more evidence," Martinsson said. "About the finger, the radio transmitter, the pistol. The lawyer in Värnamo, the one who was looking after the house, has to be contacted immediately. Obviously, there must have been somebody in the house."

"We'll sort out who does what before we close," Wallander said. "I just have two more thoughts I'd like to put forward."

"We'll kick off with them," Björk said.

"Who could possibly have wanted to shoot Louise Åkerblom?" Wallander said. "A rapist would have been a possibility. But she was not raped. There are no signs of her being beaten or held prisoner. She has no enemies. That all makes me wonder if the whole business could have been a mistake. She was killed instead of somebody else. The other possibility is that she happened to witness something she should not have seen or heard."

"The house could fit in there," Martinsson said. "It wasn't far from the property she was to look at. Something has definitely been going on in that house. She might have seen something, and been shot. Peters and Norén went to the house she was going to examine. The one that belongs to a widow by the name of Wallin. They both said it was easy to get lost on the way there."

Wallander nodded. "Go on," he said.

"There's not much more to say," Martinsson said. "For some reason or other, a finger gets cut off. Unless that happened when the house blew up. But it doesn't look that way. An explosion like that turns a man into pulp. The finger was whole."

"I don't know much about South Africa," Svedberg said. "Except that it's a racist country with lots of violence. Sweden has no diplomatic relations with South Africa. We don't even play tennis or do business with them. Not officially, at least. What I can't for the life of me understand is why something from South Africa should end up in Sweden. You'd think Sweden would be the last place to be involved."

"Maybe that's exactly why," Martinsson said.

Wallander homed in on Martinsson's comment immediately. "What do you mean?"

"Nothing," Martinsson said. "I just think we have to start thinking in a different way if we're going to get anywhere with this case."

"I agree entirely," Björk said, interrupting the exchange. "I want a written report on this business from every one of you by tomorrow. Let's see if a little quiet contemplation might get us somewhere."

They divided up the assignments among themselves. Wallander took over the lawyer in Värnamo from Björk, who was going to concentrate on producing a preliminary report on examinations of the finger.

Wallander dialled the number of the lawyer's office, and asked to speak to Mr Holmgren on urgent business. There was such a long delay before Holmgren answered that Wallander grew annoyed.

"I am calling about the property you are looking after in Skåne," he said. "The house that burned down."

"Inexplicable," Holmgren said. "But I have checked to make sure the insurance policy arranged by the late owner covers the incident. Do the police have any explanation for what happened?"

"No," Wallander said. "But we're working on it. I have some questions I need to ask you on the telephone."

"I hope this won't take long," the lawyer said. "I'm very busy."

"If you can't take the questions by telephone, the police in Värnamo will have to take you down to the station," Wallander said, "and you can answer them there."

There was a pause before the lawyer responded. "OK, fire away. I'm listening."

"We're still waiting for a fax with the names and addresses of the heirs to the estate."

"I'll make sure that's sent."

"I wonder who is directly responsible for the property."

"I am. I'm not sure what you are asking."

"A house needs attention. Roof tiles need replacing, mice need keeping under control. Do you do that as well?"

"One of the beneficiaries of the estate lives in Vollsjö. He looks after the house. His name is Alfred Olsson."

Wallander took down his address and telephone number.

"So the house has been empty for a year?"

"For more than a year. There's been some disagreement as to whether it should be sold or not."

"In other words, nobody's been living in the house?"

"Of course not."

"Are you quite sure?"

"I don't understand what you're getting at. The house has been boarded up. Alfred Olsson has been calling me at regular intervals to report that all is in order."

"When did he call last?"

"How on earth am I supposed to remember that?"

"You tell me, but I'd like an answer to my question."

"Some time around New Year's, I believe. But I can't swear to it. Why is that important?"

"Everything is important for the moment. But thank you for the information."

Wallander hung up, opened his telephone directory, and checked Alfred Olsson's address. Then he got up and grabbed his jacket.

"I'm off to Vollsjö," he said as he passed the door to Martinsson's office. "There's something odd about the house that blew up."

"There's something even more odd about it," Martinsson said. "I was just talking to Nyberg. He says that the radio transmitter may have been made in Russia."

"Russia?"

"That's what he said."

"Another country," Wallander said. "Sweden, South Africa, Russia. Where's it all going to end?"

Half an hour later, he arrived at Alfred Olsson's address. It was a relatively modern house, very different from the houses that must have first been built in that street. Three Alsatians started barking frenziedly as Wallander got out of his car. It was 4.30 p.m., and he was feeling hungry.

A man in his forties opened the door and came out onto the steps in his stockinged feet. His hair was in a mess, and as Wallander approached he could smell alcohol.

"Alfred Olsson?"

The man nodded.

"I'm from the police in Ystad."

"Oh, hell!" the man said even before Wallander had given his name.

"Excuse me?"

"Who's squealed? Is it that shit Bengtson?"

Wallander thought rapidly. "I can't comment on that," he said. "The police protect all their informers."

"It's got to be Bengtson. Am I under arrest?"

"We can talk about that," Wallander said.

Olsson let Wallander into his kitchen. He detected the faint but unmistakable smell of fusel oil. Olsson was running an illegal still, and must have assumed Wallander had come to arrest him.

The man sank onto a kitchen chair and was scratching his head. "Just my luck," he sighed.

"We'll talk about the moonshine later," Wallander said. "There's something else I want to talk about."

"What?"

"The property that burned down."

"I know nothing about that," the man said.

Wallander noticed immediately that he was alarmed. "You know nothing about what?"

The man lit a crumpled cigarette with trembling fingers. "I'm really a paint sprayer," he said. "But I can't face starting work at 7 a.m. every

91

morning. So I thought I might as well rent out that little shack, if anybody was interested. I mean, I want to sell the thing, but the family's making such a damned fuss."

"Who was interested?"

"Some fellow from Stockholm. He'd been driving around the area, looking for something suitable. He found the house and liked the location. I'm still wondering how he managed to trace it to me."

"What was his name?"

"He said he was called Nordström. I took that with a pinch of salt, though."

"Why?"

"He spoke good Swedish, but he had a foreign accent. You show me a goddamned foreigner called Nordström!"

"But he wanted to rent the house?"

"Yeah. And he paid well. I was gonna get 10,000 kronor a month. You don't turn your nose up at a deal like that. It wasn't doing anybody any harm, I thought. I get a bit of a reward in return for looking after the house. No need for the heirs or Holmgren in Värnamo to know anything about it."

"For how long was he going to rent the house?"

"He came at the beginning of April. Said he wanted it till the end of May."

"Did he say what he was going to use it for?"

"For people who wanted to be left in peace to do some painting."

"Painting?" Wallander thought of his father.

"Artists, that is. And he offered cash up front. Damn right I was going to take it."

"Did you see him again?"

"Never. It was a sort of unspoken condition. That I should keep my nose out of it. And I did. He got the keys, and that was that."

"Have you got the keys back?"

"No. He was going to mail them to me."

"And you have no address?"

"No."

"Can you describe him?"

"He was extremely fat."

"Anything else?"

"How the hell do you describe a fat guy? He was balding, red-faced, fat. And when I say fat, I do mean fat! He was like a barrel."

Wallander nodded.

"Have you any of the money left?" he asked, thinking of possible fingerprints.

"Not an öre. That's why I started distilling again."

"If you stop that as of today, I won't take you in to Ystad," Wallander said.

Olsson could hardly believe his ears.

"I mean what I say," Wallander said. "But I'll check up that you really have stopped. And you must pour away everything you've made already."

The man was sitting open-mouthed at the kitchen table when Wallander left. Dereliction of duty, he thought. But I haven't time to bother with moonshiners just now.

He drove back towards Ystad, and without really knowing why, he turned into the car park by Krageholm Lake. He got out of the car and walked down to the water's edge.

There was something about this investigation, about the death of Louise Åkerblom, that scared him. As if the whole thing had barely started yet. I am afraid, he thought. It's as if that black finger was pointing straight at me. I'm in the middle of something I can't understand.

He sat down on a rock, even though it was damp. All of a sudden his weariness and depression threatened to overwhelm him. With a sigh even he thought was pathetic, he decided he was as much at sea with his own life as he was with the search for Louise Åkerblom's murderer.

Where do I go from here? he said to himself. I don't want anything to do with ruthless killers, with no respect for life. I don't want to get involved in a kind of violence that will be incomprehensible to me as long as I live. Maybe the next generation of policemen in this country will have a different kind of experience and have a different view of their work. But it's too late for me. I'll never be any different from what I am, a pretty good policeman in a medium-sized Swedish police district.

He stood up and watched a magpie launching itself from a treetop.

All questions remain unanswered in the end, he thought. I devote my life to trying to catch and then put away criminals guilty of various crimes. Sometimes I succeed, often I don't. But when one of these days I pass away, I'll have failed in the biggest investigation of all. Life will still be an insoluble riddle.

I want to see my daughter, he thought. I miss her so much at times, it hurts. I have to find a black man missing a finger, especially if he's the one who killed Louise Åkerblom. I need to know: *why* did you kill her?

I must follow up on Stig Gustafson, not let him slide out of the picture too soon, though I'm sure already that he's innocent.

He walked back to his car.

The fear and repugnance would not go away. The finger was still pointing at him.

The Man from Transkei

CHAPTER EIGHT

You could hardly see the man squatting in the shadow of the wrecked car. He did not move a muscle, and his black face was indistinguishable from the dark bodywork.

He had chosen his hiding place carefully. He had been waiting since early afternoon, and now the sun was beginning to sink beyond the dusty silhouette of the suburban ghetto that was Soweto. The dry, red earth glowed in the setting sun. It was April 8, 1992.

He had travelled a long way to get to the meeting place on time. The white man who sought him out had said he would have to set off early. For security reasons they preferred not to give him a precise pick-up time. All he was told was that it would be shortly after sunset.

Only 26 hours had passed since the man who introduced himself as Stewart had stood outside his home in Ntibane. When he heard the knock at the door, he thought at first it was the police from Umtata. Seldom a month went by without a visit from them. As soon as a bank robbery or a murder took place, there would be an investigator from the Umtata homicide squad at his door. Sometimes they would take him in to town for questioning, but usually they accepted his alibi, even if it was no more than that he'd been drunk in one of the local bars.

When he emerged from the corrugated iron shack that was his home, he did not recognise the man standing in the bright sunlight.

Victor Mabasha could tell right away that the man was lying. He could have been called many names, but not Stewart. Although he spoke English, Mabasha could hear from his pronunciation that he was of Afrikaner origin.

Mabasha was asleep in bed when the knock came. It was afternoon. He made no attempt to hurry as he got up, put on a pair of trousers, and opened the door. He was getting used to not being wanted for any thing important nowadays. It was usually somebody he owed money to. Or somebody stupid enough to think he could borrow money from him. Unless it was the police. But they didn't knock. They hammered on the door. Or forced it open.

The man claiming to be Stewart was about 50. He wore an ill-fitting suit and was sweating. His car was parked under a baobab tree on the other side of the road. Mabasha noticed the plates were from Transvaal. He wondered why he had come so far, all the way to Transkei province, in order to meet him.

The man did not ask to come in. He just handed over an envelope and said somebody wanted to see him on important business on the outskirts of Soweto the following day.

"All you need to know is in the letter," he said.

Some children were playing with a buckled hubcap outside the hut. Mabasha yelled at them to go away, and they disappeared immediately.

"Who?" Mabasha said.

He mistrusted all white men. But most of all he mistrusted white men who lied so badly, and made things worse by thinking he would be satisfied with an envelope.

"I can't tell you that," Stewart said.

"There's always somebody wanting to see me," Mabasha said. "Question is, do I want to see him?"

"It's all in the envelope."

Mabasha held out his hand and took the thick, brown envelope. He could feel that there was a thick bundle of money in there. That was both reassuring and worrying. He needed money. But he did not know why he was being given it. That made him uneasy. He had no desire to get involved in something he knew too little about.

Stewart wiped his face and bald head with a soaking handkerchief. "There's a map," he said. "The meeting place is marked. It's close to Soweto. You haven't forgotten the layout there?"

"Everything changes," Mabasha said. "I know what Soweto looked like eight years ago, but I have no idea what it looks like today."

"It's not in Soweto itself," said Stewart. "The pickup point is on a feeder road to the Johannesburg motorway. Nothing has changed out there. You'll have to leave early tomorrow morning if you're going to make it in time."

"Who wants to see me?" Mabasha asked again.

"He prefers not to give his name," said Stewart. "You'll meet him tomorrow."

Mabasha shook his head slowly and handed back the envelope.

"I want a name," he repeated. "If I don't get a name, I won't ever be there."

The man hesitated. Mabasha stared fixedly at him. After a long pause, Stewart seemed to realise that Mabasha meant what he said. He looked around. The kids had gone away. It was 50 or so metres to Mabasha's nearest neighbours, who lived in a corrugated iron shack just as dilapidated as his own. A woman was pounding corn in the swirling dust outside the front door. Goats searched for blades of grass in the parched red earth.

"Jan Kleyn," he said in a low voice, pressing the envelope back into Mabasha's hand. "Kleyn wants to see you. Forget I ever said that. But you've got to be on time."

Then he turned and went back to his car. Mabasha stood watching him disappear trailing a cloud of dust. He was driving far too fast. Mabasha thought that was typical of a white man who felt insecure and exposed when he entered a black township. For Stewart it was like entering enemy territory. And it was. He grinned at the thought. White men were scared men. Then he wondered how Kleyn could stoop so low as to use a messenger like that. Or might it be another lie of Stewart's? Maybe it wasn't Kleyn who sent him? Maybe it was somebody else?

The kids playing with the hubcap were back. He went back into his hut, lit the kerosene lamp, sat on the rickety bed, and slit open the envelope. From force of habit he opened it from the bottom up. Letter bombers nearly always placed their detonators at the top of the envelope. Few people expecting a bomb through the mail opened their letters the normal way.

The envelope contained a map, carefully drawn by hand in black India ink. A red cross marked the meeting place. He could see it in his mind's eye. Impossible to go wrong. Apart from the map there was a bundle of red 50-rand bills in the envelope. Without counting, Mabasha knew there were 5,000 rand. That was all. No message saying why Kleyn wanted to see him.

Mabasha put the envelope on the mud floor and stretched out on the bed. The blanket smelled mouldy. A mosquito buzzed around his face. He turned his head and contemplated the kerosene lamp.

Kleyn wants to see me, he thought. It's been two years since the last time. And he said then he never wanted anything to do with me again. But now he wants to see me. Why?

He sat up on the bed and looked at his wristwatch. If he was going to be in Soweto the next day, he'd have to take the bus from Umtata this evening. Stewart was wrong. He couldn't wait until tomorrow morning. It was 900 kilometres to Johannesburg.

He had no decisions to make. Having accepted the money, he would have to go. He had no desire to owe Kleyn 5,000 rand. That would be tantamount to signing his own death warrant. He knew Kleyn well enough to be aware that nobody who crossed him got away with it.

He took out a bag tucked under the bed. As he did not know how long he was going to be away, or what Kleyn wanted him to do, he just packed a few shirts, underpants and a pair of sturdy shoes. If the assignment was going to be a long one, he would have to buy whatever clothes he needed. Then he carefully detached the back of the bed frame. His two knives were coated in grease and wrapped in plastic. He wiped away the grease and took off his shirt. He took down the specially made knife belt from a hook in the ceiling and buckled it around his waist, noting with satisfaction that he could still use the same hole. Although he had spent several months until his money ran out drinking beer, he had not put on weight. He was in good shape still, though he would soon be 31.

He put the knives in their sheaths, after testing the edges with his finger tips. He needed only to press slightly to draw blood. Then he removed another part of the bed frame and produced his pistol: that, too, was greased with coconut fat and wrapped in plastic. He sat on the bed and cleaned the gun meticulously. It was a 9mm Parabellum. He loaded the magazine with special ammunition that could only be had from an unlicensed arms dealer in Ravenmore. He wrapped two spare magazines inside one of his shirts in the bag. Then he strapped on his shoulder holster and inserted the pistol. Now he was ready to meet Kleyn.

He locked the shack with the rusty padlock, and started walking to the bus stop a few kilometres down the road to Umtata.

*

He screwed up his eyes and gazed at the red sun rapidly setting over Soweto, remembering the last time he was there eight years ago. A businessman there had given him 500 rand to shoot a competitor. As usual, he had taken all possible precautions and had a detailed plan. But it had gone wrong from the very start. A police patrol happened to be passing, and he fled Soweto as fast as his feet could carry him. He had not been back since.

The African dusk was short. Suddenly, he was surrounded by darkness. In the distance he could hear the roar of traffic on the motorway headed for Johannesburg and, in the other direction, Durban. A police siren was wailing in the far distance, and it occurred to him that Kleyn must have a very special reason for contacting him of all people. There are lots of assassins ready to shoot anyone you name for 1,000 rand. But Kleyn had paid him 5,000 rand in advance, and that could not be only because he was considered the best and most cold-blooded professional killer in all of South Africa.

His thoughts were interrupted by the sound of a car peeling off from the motorway. Soon afterwards, he saw headlights approaching. He moved further back into the shadows, and drew his pistol. He released the catch with a flourish.

The car came to a halt where the exit road petered out. The headlights lit up the dusty bushes and the wrecked car. Mabasha waited in the shadows. He was on tenterhooks now.

A man got out of the car. Mabasha could see at once that it was not Kleyn. He had not really expected to see him. Kleyn sent others to summon the people he wanted to talk to. Mabasha slipped soundlessly around the wreck and worked his way in a circle behind the man. The car had stopped exactly where he thought it would, and he had practised the flanking movement to be sure of doing it silently.

He stopped behind the man, and pressed the pistol against his head. The man started.

"Where's Kleyn?" Mabasha said.

The man turned his head carefully. "I'll take you to him," he said. Mabasha could hear he was scared.

"Where is he exactly?"

"On a farm near Pretoria. In Hammanskraal."

Mabasha knew right away this was not a trap. He had done business with Kleyn once before in Hammanskraal. He put his pistol back into its holster.

"We'd better get started, then," he said. "It's 100 kilometres to Hammanskraal."

He sat in the back seat. The man at the wheel did not speak. The lights of Johannesburg rolled by as they drove past on the motorway to the north of the city. Every time he found himself in the vicinity of the city he could feel a raging hatred welling up inside him. It was like a wild animal constantly following him around, constantly appearing and reminding him of things he would rather forget.

Mabasha had grown up in Johannesburg. His father was a miner, rarely at home. For many years he had worked in the diamond mines at Kimberley, and later in the mines to the north-east of Johannesburg, in Verwoerdburg. At the age of 42, his lungs collapsed. Mabasha could still remember the horrific rattling noise his father made as he struggled to breathe during the last year of his life, a look of terror in his eyes. During those years his mother tried to keep the house going and take care of her nine children. They lived in a slum, and Mabasha remembered his childhood as one long, drawn-out, and apparently endless humiliation. He rebelled against it all from an early age, but his protest was misguided and erratic. He joined a gang of young thieves, was arrested, and beaten up in a prison cell by white policemen. That merely increased his bitterness, and he returned to the streets and a life of crime. Unlike many of his comrades, he went his own way when it came to surviving the humiliation. Instead of joining the black awareness movement that was in its early stages, he went the opposite way. Although it was white oppression that had ruined his life, he decided the only way to get by was to remain on good terms with the whites. He started off by thieving for white fences, in return for their protection. Then one day, not long after his 20th birthday, he was offered 1,200 rand to kill a black politician who had insulted a white store owner. Mabasha did not hesitate. This was final proof that he had sided with the whites. His revenge would always be that they did not understand how deep his contempt for them was. They thought he was a simple *kaffir* who knew how blacks should behave in South Africa. But deep down, he hated the whites and that was why he ran their errands.

Sometimes he read in the newspapers that one of his former companions had been hanged or given a long prison sentence. He could feel sorry for what had happened to them, but he never doubted that he had chosen the right way to survive and maybe in the end start to build a life for himself outside the slums.

When he was 22, he met Kleyn for the first time. Although they were the same age, Kleyn treated him with superior contempt.

Kleyn was a fanatic. Mabasha knew he hated blacks and thought they were animals to be controlled by the whites. Kleyn had joined the fascist Afrikaner Resistance Movement at an early age, and in just a few years reached a senior position. But he was no politician; he worked in the background, and did so from a post he held in NIS, the South African state intelligence service. His biggest asset was his ruthlessness. As far as he was concerned, there was no difference between shooting a black and killing a rat.

Mabasha both hated and admired Kleyn. Kleyn's absolute conviction that the Afrikaners were a chosen people combined with a total disregard for death impressed him. He always seemed to have his thoughts and emotions under control. Mabasha tried in vain to find a weakness in Kleyn, but there was no such thing.

On two occasions he carried out murders for Kleyn. He performed satisfactorily. Kleyn was pleased. But although they met regularly at that time, Kleyn had never once shaken his hand.

The lights of Johannesburg faded behind them. Traffic on the motorway to Pretoria thinned out. Mabasha leaned back in his seat and closed his eyes. He would soon discover what had changed Kleyn's decision that they should never meet again. Against his will, he could feel his own excitement building. Kleyn would not have sent for him unless it was a matter of great importance.

The house was on a hill about ten kilometres outside Hammanskraal. It was surrounded by high fences, and Alsatians roamed loose to ensure that no unauthorised persons gained entry.

That evening two men were sitting in a room full of hunting trophies, waiting for Mabasha. The curtains were drawn, and the servants had been sent home. The two men were sitting on either side of a table covered by a green felt cloth. They were drinking whisky and talking in low voices, as if there might have been someone listening despite all the precautions.

One of the men was Kleyn. He was extremely thin, as if recovering from a serious illness. His face was angular, resembling a bird on the lookout. He had grey eyes, thin blond hair, and was wearing a dark suit, a white shirt and a blacktie. When he spoke, his voice was hoarse, and his way of expressing himself restrained, measured.

The other man was his opposite. Frans Malan was tall and fat. His belly hung over his waistband, his face was red and blotchy, and he was sweating copiously. To all outward appearances they were an ill-matched couple, waiting for Mabasha to arrive that evening in April, 1992.

Kleyn glanced at his wristwatch.

"Another half-hour and he'll be here," he said.

"I hope you're right," Malan said.

Kleyn started back, as if somebody had suddenly pointed a gun at him. "Am I ever wrong?" he said. He was still talking in a low voice. But the threat was unmistakable.

"Not yet," Malan said. "It was just a thought."

"You're thinking the wrong thoughts," Kleyn said. "You waste your time worrying unnecessarily. Everything will go according to plan."

"I have to hope so," Malan said. "My superiors would put a price on my head if anything went wrong."

Kleyn smiled at him. "I would commit suicide," he said. "But I have no intention of dying. When we have recovered all we have lost during the last few years, I will withdraw. But not until then."

Kleyn had enjoyed an astonishing career. His uncompromising hatred of everyone who wanted to put a stop to Apartheid policies in South Africa was well known, or notorious, depending on one's point of view. Many dismissed him as the most dangerous madman in the Afrikaner Resistance Movement. But those who knew him were aware that he was a cold, calculating man whose ruthlessness never pushed him into rash actions. He described himself as a "political surgeon", whose job was to remove tumours forever threatening the healthy body of South Afrikanerdom. Few people knew he was one of the NIS's most efficient operatives.

Frans Malan had been working more than ten years for the South

African army, which had its own intelligence department. He had been an officer in the field, and led secret operations in Southern Rhodesia and Mozambique. When he suffered a heart attack at the age of 44, his military career came to an end. But his views and his abilities led to his being immediately redeployed in the security service. His assignments were varied, ranging from planting bombs in the cars of opponents of Apartheid to the organisation of terrorist attacks on ANC meetings and their delegates. He was also a member of the Afrikaner Resistance Movement. But like Kleyn's, his role was behind the scenes. They had worked out a plan together, which was to be realised that very evening with the arrival of Mabasha. They had been discussing what had to be done for many days and nights. Eventually, they reached an agreement. They put their plan before the secret society that was never known as anything other than the Committee.

It was the Committee that gave them their current assignment.

It all started when Nelson Mandela was released from the prison cell he had occupied on Robben Island for nearly 30 years. As far as Kleyn, Frans Malan, and all other right-thinking Afrikaners were concerned, the act was a declaration of war. President de Klerk had betrayed his own people, the whites of South Africa. The Apartheid system would collapse unless something drastic was done. A number of highly placed Afrikaners, among them Kleyn and Malan, realised that free elections would inevitably lead to black majority rule. That would be a catastrophe, doomsday for the right of the chosen people to rule South Africa as they saw fit. They discussed many different courses of action before deciding what needed to be done.

The decision had been made four months earlier. They met in this very house, which was owned by the South African army and used for conferences and meetings that required privacy. Officially neither NIS nor the military had any links with secret societies. Their loyalty was formally bound to the sitting government and the South African constitution. But the reality was different. Just as when the Broederbond was at its peak, Kleyn and Malan had contacts throughout South African society. The operation they had planned on behalf of the Committee and were now ready to set in motion had its roots in the high command of the South African army, the Inkatha movement that opposed the ANC, and among high-placed businessmen and bankers.

They had been sitting in the same room as they found themselves in now, at the table with the green baize cloth, when Kleyn had suddenly asked them a question.

"Who is the single most important person in South Africa today?"

It did not take Malan long to realise to whom Kleyn was referring.

"Try a little thought experiment," Kleyn went on. "Imagine him dead. Not from natural causes. That would only turn him into a martyr. No, imagine him assassinated."

"There would be uproar in the black townships on a scale far in excess of anything we have seen so far. General strikes, chaos. The rest of the world would isolate us even further."

"One more step. Let's suppose it could be demonstrated that he was murdered by a black man."

"That would increase the confusion. Inkatha and the ANC would go for each other in an all-out war. We could sit watching with our arms crossed while they annihilated each other with their machetes and axes and spears."

"Right. But think yet one step more. That the man who murdered him was a member of the ANC."

"The movement would collapse in chaos. The crown princes would slit each other's throats."

Kleyn nodded enthusiastically. "Right. Think further!"

Malan pondered for a moment before responding. "In the end, no doubt, the blacks would turn on the whites. And since the black political movement would be on the brink of collapse and anarchy by this point, we'd be forced to send in the police and the army. The result would be a brief civil war. With a little careful planning we should be able to eliminate every black of significance. Whether the watching world liked it or not, it would be forced to accept that it was the blacks who started the war."

Kleyn nodded.

Malan gazed expectantly at the man opposite him. "Are you serious about this?" he said.

"Serious?"

"That we should actually kill him?"

"Of course I'm serious. The man will be liquidated before next summer. I'm thinking of calling it Operation Steenbok."

"Why?"

"Everything has to have a name. Have you ever shot an antelope? If you hit it in the right spot, it jumps into the air before it dies. That's the jump I'm going to offer to the greatest enemy we have."

They sat up until dawn. Malan could not help admiring the meticulous way in which Kleyn had thought the whole thing through. The plan was daring without unnecessary risks. When they walked out onto the veranda at dawn to stretch their legs, Malan voiced one last objection.

"Your plan is excellent," he said. "I can see only one possible snag. You are relying on Mabasha not to let us down. You are forgetting that he's a Zulu. They are like the *Boere* in some respects, Zulus. Their loyalty is to themselves, in the last resort, and the ancestors they worship. You are placing an enormous amount of faith in a black man. You know they can never feel the same loyalty as we do. Presumably you are right. He will become a rich man. Richer than he could ever have dreamed. But still, the plan means we are relying on one black man."

"You can have my answer right away," Kleyn said. "I don't trust anybody at all. Not completely, at least. I trust you. But I'm aware that everybody has a weak point somewhere or other. I replace this lack of trust by being extra cautious. That naturally applies to Mabasha as well."

"The only person you trust is yourself," Malan said.

"Yes. You'll never find the weak point I'm speaking of in me. Of course, Mabasha will be under constant watch. And I'll make sure he knows that. He'll get some special training by one of the world's leading experts on assassination. If he lets us down, he will know he can look forward to a slow and painful death, so awful he'd wish he'd never been born."

When the car came to a halt outside the house on the hill, Malan tethered the dogs. Mabasha, terrified of Alsatians, remained in the car until he was certain he would not be attacked. Kleyn was on the veranda to receive him. Mabasha could not resist the temptation to hold out his hand. But Kleyn ignored it and asked how the journey had been.

"When you're sitting in a bus all night, you have time to think up any number of questions," Mabasha said.

"Excellent," Kleyn said. "You'll get all the answers you need."

"Who decides that?" Mabasha said. "What I need or don't need to know?"

Before Kleyn could reply, Malan emerged from the shadows. He did not offer his hand either.

"Let's go inside," Kleyn said. "We have a lot to talk about, and time is short."

"I'm Frans," Malan said. "Put your hands up over your head."

Mabasha did not protest. It was one of the unwritten rules that you gave up your weapons before negotiations could begin. Malan took the pistol and then examined the knives.

"They were made by an African armourer," Mabasha said. "Excellent both for close combat and throwing."

They sat down at the table with the green baize cloth. The driver went to make coffee in the kitchen.

Mabasha waited. He hoped the two men would not notice how tense he was.

"A million rand," Kleyn said. "Let's start at the end this once. I want you to bear in mind the whole time how much we're offering you for the job we want you to do for us."

"A million can be a lot or very little," Mabasha said. "It depends on the circumstances. And who is 'we'?"

"Save your questions for later," Kleyn said. "You know me, you know you can trust me. You can regard Frans, sitting opposite you, as an extension of my arm. You can trust him as you can trust me."

Mabasha nodded. He understood. The game had started. Everybody was assuring everybody else how reliable they were. In truth, nobody trusted anybody but themselves.

"We thought we'd ask you to do a little job for us," Kleyn said, making it sound to Mabasha's ears as though he was asking him to get a glass of water. "Who 'we' are in this context doesn't matter as far as you're concerned."

"A million rand," Mabasha said. "Let's assume that's a lot of money. I take it you want me to kill somebody for you. A million is too much for such an assignment. So let's assume it's too little – what's the explanation?"

"How the hell can a million be too little?" Malan said, in annoyance.

"Let's just say it's good money for an intense but brief assignment," Kleyn said.

"You do want me to kill somebody," Mabasha said.

Kleyn looked at him for a long time before replying. Mabasha suddenly felt as if a cold wind was blowing through the room.

"That's right," Kleyn said, slowly. "We do."

"Who?"

"You'll find out when the time is ripe."

Mabasha suddenly felt uneasy. It ought to be the obvious first move, giving him the most important piece of information. Who he would be aiming his gun at.

"This is a very special assignment," Kleyn said. "It will involve travel, perhaps a month of preparations, rehearsals, and extreme caution. I will only say that it's a man we want you to eliminate. An important man."

"A South African?"

Kleyn hesitated for a moment before replying. "Yes," he said. "A South African."

Mabasha tried to work out who it could be. And who was this fat, sweaty man sitting hunched up in the shadows on the other side of the table? Mabasha had a vague feeling he recognised him. Had he met him before? If so, in what connection? Had he seen his photograph in a newspaper? He searched his memory frantically, but in vain.

The driver put out some cups and saucers, and placed the coffee pot on a mat in the middle of the green cloth. Nobody said a word until he had left the room and closed the door behind him.

"In about ten days we want you to leave South Africa," Kleyn said. "In the meantime you'll go back to Ntibane. Tell everybody you know there you're going to Botswana to work for an uncle who has an iron-monger's store in Gaborone. You'll be receiving a letter postmarked in Botswana, offering you a job. Show people this letter as often as you can. On April 15, in a week, you'll take the bus to Johannesburg. You'll be picked up at the bus station and spend the night in an apartment, where you'll meet me in order to receive your final instructions. The next day you'll fly to Europe, and then on to St Petersburg. Your passport will say you're from Zimbabwe, and you'll have a new name.

You can choose one yourself. You'll be met at the airport in St Petersburg. You'll go by train to Finland, and go from there to Sweden by boat. You'll stay in Sweden for a few weeks. You'll meet somebody there who will give you your most important instructions. On a date as yet unfixed you'll return to South Africa. I'll take over responsibility for the final phase. It'll be all over by the end of June at the latest. You can collect your money wherever you like in the world. You'll be paid an advance of 100,000 rand as soon as you've agreed to carry out the assignment."

Kleyn now stared intently at him. Mabasha wondered if his ears had deceived him. St Petersburg? Finland? Sweden? He tried to picture a map of Europe, but he could not.

"One question," he said after a while. "What's this all about?"

"It shows we are cautious and meticulous," Kleyn said. "You ought to appreciate that, because it's a guarantee for your own safety."

"I can look after myself," Mabasha said, dismissively. "But let's start from the beginning. Who'll be meeting me in St Petersburg?"

"As you may know, the Soviet Union has undergone big changes these last few years," Kleyn said. "Changes we're all very pleased about. On the other hand, it has meant that a lot of very efficient people are out of a job. Including officers in the old KGB. We get a steady stream of enquiries from these people, wondering if we're interested in their skills and experience. In some cases there's no limit to what they'll do to get a residence permit in our country."

"I'm not working with the KGB," Mabasha said. "I don't work with anybody. I'll do whatever I have to do, and I'll do it alone."

"Quite right, too," Kleyn said. "You will be working on your own. But you'll get some very useful tips from our friends in St Petersburg. They're good."

"Why Sweden?"

Kleyn took a sip of coffee. "A fair question, and a natural one to ask," he said. "In the first place, it's a diversionary measure. Nobody in this country who's not closely involved has any idea what's going on, but it's a good idea to put out a few smokescreens. Sweden is a neutral, insignificant country, and has always been aggressively opposed to our social system. It would never occur to anybody that the lamb would hide away in the wolf's lair. Second, our friends in St Petersburg have

110

good contacts in Sweden. It's easy to get into the country because the border controls are pretty casual, if indeed there are any at all. Many of our Russian friends have already established themselves in Sweden, with false names and false papers. Third, we have some reliable friends who can arrange appropriate living quarters for us in Sweden. But most important of all, perhaps, is that you keep well away from South Africa. There are far too many people interested in knowing what a fellow like me is up to. A plan can be exposed."

Mabasha shook his head. "I have to know who it is I'm going to kill," he said.

"When the time is ripe," Kleyn said. "Not before. I'll conclude by reminding you of a conversation we had nearly eight years ago. You said then that it's possible to kill anybody at all, provided you plan it properly. The bottom line is that nobody can get away. And now I'm waiting for your answer."

That was the moment it dawned on Mabasha whom he was going to kill. The thought sent him reeling. But it all fitted. Kleyn's irrational hatred of blacks, the increasing liberalisation of South Africa. An important man. They wanted him to shoot President de Klerk.

His first reaction was to say no. It would be taking too big a risk. How could he possibly get past all the bodyguards surrounding the President night and day? How could he possibly escape afterwards? President de Klerk was a target for an assassin who was prepared to die in a suicide attack.

At the same time he could not deny he still believed what he had said to Kleyn. Nobody in the world was immune from a skilled assassin. And a million rand. Mind-boggling. He couldn't refuse.

"An advance of 300,000," he said. "I want it in a London bank by the day after tomorrow at the latest. I want the right to refuse to go along with the final plan if I consider it to be too risky. In that case you would have the right to require me to work out an alternative. In those circumstances I'll take it on."

Kleyn smiled. "Excellent," he said. "I knew you would."

"I want my passport made out in the name of Ben Travis."

"Of course. A splendid name. Easy to remember."

There was a plastic file on the floor next to Kleyn's chair. He took out a letter postmarked in Botswana and handed it to Mabasha.

"There's a bus to Johannesburg from Umtata at 6 a.m. on April 15. That's the one we want you to take."

Kleyn and the man who said his name was Frans got to their feet.

"We'll take you home by car," Kleyn said. "As time is short, you'd better go tonight. You can sleep on the journey."

Mabasha nodded. He was in a hurry to get home. A week was not long for him to sort out all the things he needed to do. Such as finding out who this Frans really was. Now his own safety was on the line. It needed all his concentration.

They parted on the veranda. This time Mabasha did not hold out his hand. His weapons were returned to him, and he got into the back seat of the car.

President de Klerk, he thought. Nobody can escape. Not even you.

Kleyn and Malan remained on the veranda, watching the car lights disappear.

"I think you're right," Malan said. "I think he'll do it."

"Of course he'll do it," Kleyn said. "Don't I always choose the best?"

Malan gazed up at the stars. "Do you think he realised who the target was?"

"I think he guessed it was de Klerk," Kleyn said. "That would be the obvious person."

Malan turned from the stars and looked at Kleyn. "That was what you wanted him to do, wasn't it? Guess?"

"Of course," Kleyn said. "And now we'd better go our separate ways. I have an important meeting in Bloemfontein tomorrow."

On April 17 Mabasha flew to London under the name of Ben Travis. By then he knew who Frans Malan was. That had also convinced him the target was President de Klerk. In his suitcase he had a few books on de Klerk. He would have to find out as much about him as possible.

The following day he flew to St Petersburg. He was met there by a man called Konovalenko.

Two days later a Finland ferry pulled into the docks in Stockholm. After a long car journey south, he came to a remote cottage late in the evening. The man driving the car spoke excellent English, even though he did have a Russian accent.

On Monday, April 20 Mabasha woke at dawn. He went out into the yard to relieve himself. A mist lay motionless over the fields. He shivered in the chilly air. Sweden, he thought. You are welcoming Ben Travis with fog, cold, and silence.

CHAPTER NINE

Pik Botha was first to notice the snake.

It was almost midnight and most members of the government had said goodnight and withdrawn to their bungalows. The only ones left around the campfire were President de Klerk, Foreign Minister Botha, Home Secretary Vlok and his private secretary, plus a few of the security men. They were all officers handpicked by the President and his cabinet. They had all pledged special oaths of allegiance and secrecy to de Klerk personally. Further away, barely visible from the campfire, some black servants were hovering in the shadows.

It was a green mamba, and difficult to see as it lay motionless at the edge of the flickering light. The foreign minister would probably never have noticed it had he not bent down to scratch his ankle. He started when he saw the snake, then just sat motionless. He had learned early in life that a snake can only see and attack moving objects.

"There is a poisonous snake two metres from my feet," he said in a low voice.

President de Klerk was deep in thought. He had adjusted his deck chair so that he could stretch out. As usual he was sitting some distance from his colleagues. It had struck him some time ago that his ministers never placed their chairs too close to him when they were gathered around the campfire, presumably to show their respect. That suited him fine. President de Klerk was a man who often felt a burning necessity to be on his own.

The foreign minister's words slowly sunk in, dissolving his thoughts. He turned to look at his foreign minister's face in the light of the dancing flames.

"Did you say something?" he said.

"There is a green poisonous snake by my feet," Botha said again. "I don't think I've ever seen such a big mamba."

President de Klerk sat up slowly in his chair. He hated snakes. He had an almost pathological fear of crawling animals in general. At the presidential residence, the servants knew they had to search every nook and cranny every day for spiders, beetles or any other insects. The same applied to those who cleaned the President's office, his cars and the cabinet offices.

He slowly craned his neck and located the snake. He felt sick immediately.

"Kill it," he said.

The home secretary had fallen asleep in his deck chair, and his private secretary was listening to music on his headphones. One of the bodyguards slowly drew a knife from his belt, and struck at the snake with unerring accuracy. The mamba's head was severed from its body. The bodyguard picked up the snake's body, still thrashing from side to side, and flung it into the fire. To his horror de Klerk saw how the snake's head, still lying on the ground, was opening and closing its mouth, displaying its fangs. He was overcome by dizziness, as if about to faint. He leaned back quickly in his chair and closed his eyes.

A dead snake, he thought. But its body is still writhing away, and anyone not in the know would think it was still alive. That's just what it's like here, in my country, my South Africa. A lot of the old ways, things we thought were dead and buried, are still alive. We're not just fighting alongside and against the living, we've also got to fight those who insist on coming back to life to haunt us.

Every four months or so President de Klerk took his ministers and selected secretaries to a camp at Ons Hoop, just south of the border with Botswana. They stayed for a few days, and all business was conducted very openly. Officially, the President and his cabinet gathered away from the public eye to consider important matters. De Klerk had introduced this routine when he first came to office as head of state. Now he had been President for nearly four years, and some of the government's key decisions had been made in the informal atmosphere, around the campfire, at Ons Hoop. The camp had been built with government money, and de Klerk had no difficulty in justifying its existence. It seemed he and his assistants thought more liberal and perhaps also more daring thoughts while sitting around the campfire under the night sky, enjoying the scents of ancient Africa. De Klerk sometimes thought it was their *Boere* blood coming to the fore. Free men, always linked with nature, who could never quite get used to a modern era, to air-conditioned studies and cars with bulletproof windows. Here in Ons Hoop they could enjoy the mountain horizon, the unending plains, and not least a roast over an open fire. They could have their discussions without feeling hounded by time, and de Klerk felt it had produced results.

Pik Botha watched the snake being consumed by the fire, then turned his head and saw de Klerk was sitting with his eyes closed. He knew that meant the President wanted to be left alone. He shook the home secretary gently by the shoulder. Vlok woke with a start. When they stood up, his secretary quickly switched off his music and collected the papers that were lying under his chair.

Pik Botha hung back after the others had disappeared, escorted by a servant with a lamp. It sometimes happened that the President wanted to exchange a few words with his foreign minister in confidence.

"I think I'll be going, then," Botha said.

De Klerk opened his eyes and looked at him. That particular night he had nothing to discuss with Botha.

"You do that," he said. "We need all the sleep we can get."

Botha wished him good night and left the President on his own.

De Klerk would sit there alone for a while, thinking through the discussions that had taken place that day and evening. When they went out to the camp at Ons Hoop, it was to discuss overall political strategies, not routine government affairs. In the light of the campfire, they would talk about the future of South Africa, never about anything else. It was here they had developed the strategy for how the country would change without the whites losing too much influence.

But on that night, April 27, 1992, de Klerk was waiting for a man he wanted to meet by himself, without even his foreign minister, his most trusted colleague in the government, knowing about it. He nodded to one of the bodyguards, who disappeared immediately. When the guard returned a few minutes later, he had with him a man in his forties, dressed in a plain khaki suit. He greeted de Klerk and moved one of the deck chairs closer to the President. At the same time de Klerk gestured to the bodyguards that they should withdraw. He wanted them close by, but not within earshot.

There were four people de Klerk trusted in this life. First of all his wife. Then his foreign minister, Pik Botha. And there were two others. One of them was sitting right now in the chair beside him. His name was Pieter van Heerden, and he worked for the South African intelligence service, NIS. But even more important than his work for the security of the republic was the fact that van Heerden played the role of special informer and messenger to de Klerk, bringing him news of the state of the nation. From Pieter van Heerden, de Klerk received regular reports about what was foremost in the minds of the military high command, the police, the other political parties, and the internal organisations of NIS. If a military coup was being planned, if a conspiracy was under way, van Heerden would hear of it and immediately inform the President. Without van Heerden, de Klerk would be missing a pointer to the forces working against him. In his private life and in his work as an intelligence officer, van Heerden played the role of a man openly critical of President de Klerk. He performed skilfully, always well balanced, never exaggerated. No-one had ever suspected him of being the President's personal messenger.

De Klerk was aware that by enlisting the aid of van Heerden, he was compromising the confidence he placed in his own cabinet. But he could see no other way of guaranteeing himself the information he considered essential to carry out the huge changes South Africa needed to avoid a national catastrophe.

This was not least associated with the fourth person in whom de Klerk placed absolute trust. Nelson Mandela. The leader of the ANC, the man who had been imprisoned for 27 years on Robben Island, who had been incarcerated for life at the beginning of the 1960s for alleged but never proven acts of sabotage.

President de Klerk had few illusions. He could see that the only two people who together could prevent a civil war from breaking out and the bloodbath that would inevitably follow were himself and Mandela. Many a time he had prowled sleepless through the presidential residence at night, gazing at the lights from the city of Pretoria, and thinking how the future of South Africa would depend on the compromise he and Mandela would with good fortune be able to reach.

He could speak quite openly with Mandela. He knew that feeling was mutual. They were very different in character and temperament. Mandela was a truth seeker with philosophical leanings, who used those characteristics to enhance the decisiveness and practical drive he also possessed. President de Klerk lacked that philosophical dimension. He would head straight for a practical solution to every problem. For him the future of the republic lay in changing political realities, and constant choices between what was possible to achieve and what was not. But between these two men with such different qualities and experience was a level of trust which could only be destroyed by open betrayal. That meant they never needed to disguise their differences of opinion, never needed to resort to unnecessary rhetoric when talking to one another. But it also meant they were fighting on two different fronts at the same time. The white population was split, and de Klerk knew that everything would collapse if he could not manage to make progress bit by bit, by means of compromises that could be accepted by a majority of the white population. He would never manage to persuade the ultra-conservative right. Nor would he ever convince the racist members of the officer class in the army and the police force. But he had to ensure they did not become too powerful.

President de Klerk knew Nelson Mandela had similar problems. The blacks were also divided among themselves. Not least between the Inkatha movement, dominated by the Zulus, and the ANC. This meant they could come together in an understanding of each other's difficulties, but at the same time they need never deny the disunity that existed.

Van Heerden was a provider of the information de Klerk needed to have. He knew it was necessary to stay close to his friends, but to stay even closer to his enemies and their thoughts.

They normally met once a week in de Klerk's office, often late on Saturday afternoons. But on this occasion, van Heerden had requested an urgent meeting. At first de Klerk had been unwilling to let him come to the camp. It would be difficult to meet him there without someone in the government finding out. But van Heerden had been unusually persistent. The meeting could not be put off until de Klerk returned to Pretoria. At that point de Klerk had given way. He knew van Heerden was thoroughly cold-blooded and disciplined, and would never act impulsively; he must have something of exceptional importance to share with the President.

"We're alone now," de Klerk said. "Pik found a poisonous snake right by his feet just a few minutes ago. I wondered for a moment if it might have been fitted with a recording device."

Van Heerden smiled. "We haven't started to employ poisonous snakes as informers yet," he said. "Maybe we'll have to one of these days. Who knows?"

De Klerk looked at him searchingly. What was so important that it couldn't wait?

Van Heerden moistened his lips before starting to speak. "A plot to assassinate you is at an advanced planning stage," he said. "There is absolutely no shadow of a doubt that this is a serious threat. To yourself, to government policy in general, and in the long run to the whole nation."

Van Heerden paused. He was used to de Klerk firing questions at him. But on this occasion de Klerk did not say a word. He merely stared attentively at his messenger.

"I'm still short of information about much of the detail," van Heerden said. "But I'm aware of the main thread, and that's serious enough. The plotters have links with the military high command, and with extreme conservative circles, notably the Afrikaner Resistance Movement. We should not forget that many conservatives, most of them in fact, are not members of any political organisation. In addition there are signs that foreign terrorist experts, primarily from the KGB, are involved."

"There's no such thing as the KGB any more," de Klerk said, interrupting him. "At least, not in the form we are familiar with."

"There are unemployed KGB officers, though," van Heerden said. "As I have told you before, Mr President, we are frequently approached by officers of the former Soviet intelligence service, offering us their services for some future occasion."

"A conspiracy always has a hard core," de Klerk said, after a while. "One or more people, usually very few, in the background, very much in the background, pulling the strings. Who are they?"

"I don't know," van Heerden said. "And that worries me. There's somebody in the military intelligence service called Frans Malan – you can be quite sure he's involved. He has been careless enough to store some material connected with the conspiracy in his computer files, without blocking them. I noticed it when I asked one of my trusted colleagues to run a routine check."

If only people knew, de Klerk thought. It's reached a hitherto unthinkable point where security service members spy on one another, hack their way into one another's computer files, have reason to suspect one another of treachery.

"Why just me?" de Klerk said. "Why not Mandela as well?"

"It's too soon to say," van Heerden said. "But of course, it's not difficult to imagine what effect a successful assassination attempt on you would have in the current circumstances."

De Klerk raised his hand. Van Heerden did not need to spell it out. De Klerk could picture only too clearly the resulting catastrophe.

"There is another detail which worries me," van Heerden said. "We keep a watch on a number of known murderers, both black and white. People who are prepared to kill anybody at all if the contract is right. I think I'm right in claiming that our precautionary measures against possible attacks on politicians are quite efficient. Yesterday I received a report from the security police in Umtata saying that a certain Victor Mabasha paid a visit to Johannesburg a few days ago. When he returned to Ntibane, he had a lot of cash with him."

De Klerk made a face. "That sounds a bit circumstantial," he said.

"I'm not so sure about that," van Heerden said. "If I were planning to kill the President of this country, I would probably choose Mabasha to do it."

De Klerk raised his eyebrows. "Even if you were going to assassinate Nelson Mandela?"

"Oh, yes."

"A black contract killer?"

"He is very good."

De Klerk got up from his deck chair and poked away at the fire, which was dying out. He did not have the strength just now to absorb what constituted a good contract killer. He put a few branches on the fire, and stretched his back. His bald head glittered in the light from the fire, which flamed up once more. He looked up at the sky and contemplated the Southern Cross. He felt very tired. Nevertheless, he tried to come to terms with what van Heerden had said. A conspiracy was more than plausible. He had often imagined being killed by an assassin sent by furious white *Boere* who were forever accusing him of selling out and handing their country over to the blacks. Of course, he also wondered what would happen if Mandela were to die, irrespective of whether it was a natural or an unnatural death. Nelson Mandela was an old man. Even if he did have a strong constitution, he had spent nearly 30 years in jail.

De Klerk went back to his chair. "You'll have to concentrate on exposing this conspiracy," he said. "Use whatever means you like. Money is no problem at all. Get in touch with me at any time of day or night if something significant happens. For the moment, there are two measures that must be taken, or at least considered. One is perfectly obvious, of course: my guard will have to be intensified as discreetly as possible. I'm rather more doubtful about the other one."

Van Heerden suspected what the President had in mind. He waited for him to continue.

"Shall I tell him, or shan't I?" wondered de Klerk. "How will he react? Or should I wait until we know a bit more?"

Van Heerden knew de Klerk was not asking him for advice. The questions were directed towards himself. The answers would also be his own.

"I'll think about it," said de Klerk. "We live in the most beautiful country on earth. But there are monsters lurking in the shadows. I sometimes wish I could see into the future. I'd like to be able to. But to be honest, I don't know if I dare."

The meeting was over. Van Heerden vanished into the shadows.

De Klerk sat staring into the fire. He was really too tired to make a decision. Should he inform Mandela of the conspiracy, or should he wait? He remained by the fire, watching it die down. At last he made up his mind. He would say nothing to his friend just yet.

CHAPTER TEN

Mabasha had been trying in vain to dismiss what happened as just a bad dream. The woman outside the house had never existed. Konovalenko, the man he was forced to hate, did not kill her. It was just a dream that a spirit, a *sangoma*, had poisoned his mind with, to make him unsure, and possibly unable to carry out his assignment. It was the curse hanging over him because he was a black South African, he was aware of that. Not knowing who he was, or what he was allowed to be. A man who ruthlessly wallowed in violence one minute, and the next minute failed to understand how anybody could kill a fellow human being. He realised the spirits had set their singing hounds on him. They were watching over him, keeping tabs on him; they were his ultimate guardians, infinitely more watchful than Kleyn could ever be . . .

From the very start everything had gone wrong. He instinctively disliked and mistrusted the man who met him at the airport outside St Petersburg.

He was devious. Plus, Anatoli Konovalenko was racist. On several occasions Mabasha had come close to throttling him and telling him that he knew what Konovalenko was thinking: that he was just a *kaffir*, an inferior being.

But he controlled himself. He had an assignment, and that had to come before anything else. Yet the violence of his own reaction surprised him. He had been surrounded by racism all his life. In his own way, he had learned to live with it. So why did he react like this to Konovalenko? Perhaps he could not accept being regarded as inferior by a white man who did not come from South Africa?

The journey from Johannesburg to London, and then on to Russia, had gone without a hitch. He sat awake on the night flight to London, looking out into the darkness. Occasionally he thought he could see fires blazing away in the darkness far below, but he realised it was his imagination. It was not the first time he had left South Africa. He had killed an ANC representative in Lusaka, and on another occasion he had been in what was then Southern Rhodesia as part of a team that had attempted to assassinate the revolutionary leader Joshua Nkomo. That was the only time he had failed. And that was when he decided he would only work alone in the future.

Yebo, yebo, never, ever again would he subordinate himself. As soon as he was ready to return to South Africa from this freezing cold Scandinavian land, Konovalenko would be no more than an insignificant detail in the bad dream that his *sangoma* had poisoned him with. Konovalenko was an insignificant puff of smoke that would be chased out of his body. The holy spirit hidden in the howls of the singing hounds would chase him away. His poisoned memory would never again need to worry about the arrogant Russian with grey, worn-down teeth.

Konovalenko was small and sturdy. He barely came up to Mabasha's shoulders. (But there was nothing wrong with his head, something Mabasha had established right away.) It was not surprising, of course. Kleyn would never be satisfied with anything less than the best on the market.

On the other hand, Mabasha could never have imagined how brutal Konovalenko was. Of course, he recognised that a senior officer in the KGB, whose specialty had been liquidating infiltrators and deserters would have few scruples. But as far as Mabasha was concerned, unnecessary brutality was the sign of an amateur. A contract killing should be carried out *mningi checha*, very fast and without unnecessary suffering for the victim.

They left St Petersburg the day after Mabasha arrived. The ferry passage to Sweden was so cold that he spent the whole voyage in his cabin, wrapped in a blanket. Before their arrival in Stockholm Konovalenko gave him a new passport and his instructions. He discovered he was now a Swedish citizen named Shalid.

"You used to be a stateless Eritrean exile," Konovalenko said. "You came to Sweden at the end of the 1960s, and were granted citizenship in 1978."

"Shouldn't I at least speak a few words of Swedish after more than 20 years?" Mabasha said.

"It'll be enough to be able to say thank you, *tack*," Konovalenko said. "No-one will ask you anything."

Konovalenko was right.

To Mabasha's great surprise, the young Swedish passport officer had done no more than glance casually at his passport before returning it. Could it really be as simple as this to travel into and out of a country? He began to understand why the preparations for his assignment were happening so far away from South Africa.

Even if he distrusted – no, positively disliked – the man who was to be his instructor, he was impressed by the invisible organisation behind him. A car was waiting for them at the docks, the keys were on the left rear wheel. As Konovalenko didn't know his way out of Stockholm, another car led them out as far as the south-bound highway before disappearing. It seemed to Mabasha that the world was being run by secret organisations and people like his *sangoma*. The world was shaped and changed in the underworld. People like Kleyn were mere messengers. Just where Mabasha fitted into this secret organisation, he had no idea. He wasn't sure he wanted to know.

They drove through the Swedish countryside. Here and there Mabasha glimpsed patches of snow through the conifer trees. Konovalenko did not drive especially fast, and said practically nothing as he drove. That suited Mabasha, as he was tired after the long journey. He kept falling asleep in the back seat, and immediately his spirit would start talking to him. The singing hound howled away in the darkness of his dreams, and when he opened his eyes he was not at all sure where he was. It was raining non-stop. Everything seemed clean and orderly. When they stopped for a meal, Mabasha had the feeling that nothing could ever go wrong in this country.

But there was something missing. Mabasha tried, but in vain, to determine what it was. The countryside they were travelling through filled him with a nostalgic longing.

The journey took all day.

"Where are we making for?" Mabasha said after they had been in the car for three hours. Konovalenko waited several minutes to reply. "We're headed south," he said. "You'll see when we get there."

*

The evil dream of his *sangoma* was still some way off. The woman had not yet entered the yard, and her skull had not yet been shattered by the bullet from Konovalenko's pistol. Mabasha had no thoughts beyond doing what Kleyn was paying him to do. Part of the assignment was to listen to what Konovalenko had to say to him. According to Mabasha's imagination the spirits, both good and bad, had been left behind in South Africa, in the mountain caves near Ntibane. The spirits never left the country, never crossed borders.

They arrived at the farmhouse, well off the main roads, at 8 p.m. Even in St Petersburg Mabasha had noted with surprise that dusk and night were not as in Africa. It was light when it should have been dark, and dusk did not drop down over the earth like the heavy fist of night; it wafted down slowly like a leaf floating on an invisible breath of air.

They carried the few bags into the house and installed themselves in their separate bedrooms. The house was comfortably warm. That too must have been thanks to the perfectionism of the discreet organisation. They would have assumed a black man would freeze to death in polar regions like this. And a man who is cold, like a man who is hungry or thirsty, would be unable to do or learn anything.

The ceilings were low. Mabasha could barely fit under the exposed roof beams. He wandered around the house and noticed a strange smell of furniture, carpets and wax polish. But the smell he missed most was that of an open fire.

Africa was a long way away. It occurred to him that making him feel the distance might be intentional. This is where the plan was to be tested, retested, and perfected. Nothing should be allowed to interfere; nothing should arouse thoughts of what might be in store later.

Konovalenko produced frozen meals from a big freezer. Mabasha realised he should check this out later to see how many portions were stored there; that way he could calculate how long he was expected to stay in the house.

Konovalenko opened his bags and took out a bottle of Russian vodka. He offered Mabasha a glass as they sat at the dining table, but he declined. He always cut down his drinking when he was preparing for an assignment: one beer a day, two at the most. But Konovalenko drank heavily and was clearly drunk even the first evening. This presented Mabasha with an obvious advantage. If he needed to, he could exploit Konovalenko's weakness for alcohol.

The vodka loosened Konovalenko's tongue. He started talking about paradise lost, the KGB during the 1960s and 70s, when they held undisputed sway over the Soviet empire and no politician could be sure that the KGB did not have extensive files on their secrets. Mabasha thought the KGB might have replaced the *sangoma* in this Russian empire, where no citizen was allowed to believe in holy spirits except in secrecy.

To Mabasha it seemed that a society which attempted to put the gods to flight would be doomed. The *amakosi* know this in my homeland, and hence our gods have not been threatened by Apartheid. They can live freely and have never been subjected to the pass laws; they have always been able to move around without being humiliated. If our holy spirits had been banished to remote prison islands, and our singing hounds chased into the Kalahari Desert, not a single white man, woman or child would have survived in South Africa. All of them, Afrikaners as well as Englishmen, would have been annihilated long ago and their miserable skeletons buried in the red soil. In the old days, when his ancestors were still fighting against the white intruders, the Zulu warriors used to cut off their fallen victims' lower jaw. An *impi* returning from a victorious battle would bring with him these jawbones as trophies to adorn the temple entrances of their tribal chiefs. Now it was the gods who were on the front line against the whites, and they would never submit.

The first night in the strange house, Mabasha enjoyed a dreamless sleep. He shed the lingering after-effects of his journey, and when he woke at dawn he felt entirely rested and restored. Somewhere in the background he could hear Konovalenko snoring. He got up, dressed, and searched the house. He did not know what he was looking for, but Kleyn seemed always present, his watchful eye was ever on him.

In the attic, which surprisingly smelled vaguely of corn, reminiscent of sorghum, he found a radio transmitter. Mabasha was no expert on advanced electronics, but he had no doubt this equipment was capable of transmitting to and receiving messages from South Africa. He continued his search, and eventually found what he was looking for – in the form of a locked door at one end of the house. Behind that door was the reason he had undertaken this long journey.

He went outside and urinated in the yard. He had the impression his urine had never been so yellow. It must be the food, he thought. This strange, unspiced food. The journey. And the spirits struggling in my dreams. Wherever I go, I take Africa with me.

There was a mist lying motionless over the countryside. He walked round the house, and came upon a neglected orchard where he could recognise only a few of the trees. All was silent, and it seemed to him he might have been somewhere else – possibly even somewhere in Natal on a June morning.

He felt cold, and went back into the house. Konovalenko was making coffee in the kitchen, dressed in a red tracksuit. When he turned his back to Mabasha, he saw that it had CCCP embroidered on it.

The work started after breakfast. Konovalenko unlocked the door to the secret room. It was empty, apart from a table and a very bright ceiling light. On the table were a rifle and a pistol, but what makes they were Mabasha could not say. His first impression was that the rifle looked awkward.

"This is one of our prize products," Konovalenko said. "Effective, but not exactly sleek. The starting point was a run-of-the-mill Remington 375 HH. But our KGB technicians refined the weapon until it reached a state of perfection. You can pick off whatever you like up to 800 metres. The only things to rival the laser sights are on the American army's most guarded secret weapons. Unfortunately, we were never able to use this masterpiece in any of our assignments. In other words, you have the honour of introducing it to the world."

Mabasha approached the table and examined the rifle.

"Feel it," Konovalenko said. "From this moment on, you will be inseparable."

Mabasha was surprised how light the rifle was, but when he raised it to his shoulder, it felt well balanced and stable.

"What type of ammunition?"

"Superplastic," Konovalenko said. "A specially prepared variation of the classic Spitzer prototype. The bullet will travel fast over a long distance. The pointed version is better at overcoming air resistance."

Mabasha put the rifle on the table and picked up the pistol. It was a 9mm Glock Compact. He had read about this weapon in various magazines, but he had never held one.

"I think standard ammunition will be OK in this case," Konovalenko said. "No point in overdoing things."

"I'll have to get used to the rifle," Mabasha said. "That'll take time if the range is going to be nearly a kilometre. But where can you find such a training range that's sufficiently private?"

"Here," Konovalenko said. "This house has been carefully chosen."

"By whom?"

"Those whose job it was," Konovalenko said.

Questions not triggered directly by what Konovalenko said annoyed him. "There are no neighbours around here, and the wind blows all the time. Nobody will hear a thing. Let's go back to the living room. Before we start working I want to review the situation with you."

They sat opposite each other in two old, worn leather chairs.

"It's very simple," Konovalenko said. "First, this liquidation will be the most difficult of your career. Not only because there's a technical complication, the distance, but second and most important, because failure is simply not an option. You will have only one opportunity. The final plan will be decided at very short notice. You will have only a little time to get everything organised, and no time for hesitation or contemplating alternatives. The fact that you have been chosen doesn't only mean you are thought to be skilful and cold-blooded. You also work best on your own. In this case you'll be more alone than you've ever been. Nobody can help you, nobody will acknowledge you, nobody will support you. Third, there is a psychological dimension to this assignment which shouldn't be underestimated. You won't discover who your victim is until the very last moment. You will need to be totally cold-blooded. You know that the person you are going to liquidate is a figure of the first rank. That means you're spending a lot of time wondering who it is. But you won't know almost until you've got your finger on the trigger."

Mabasha was irritated by Konovalenko's patronising tone. For a fleeting moment he wanted to tell him he already knew who the victim would be. But he said nothing.

"I can tell you, we had you in the KGB records," Konovalenko said with a smile. "If my memory serves me right we had you down as a useful lone wolf. Unfortunately we can no longer check that because all the archives have been destroyed or are in a state of chaos."

Konovalenko fell silent and seemed to be reflecting on the proud secret service organisation that no longer existed. But the silence didn't last long.

"We don't have much time," Konovalenko said. "That doesn't need to be a negative factor. It will force you to concentrate. The days will be divided between target practice with the rifle, psychological exercises, and working on the various possible liquidation scenarios. Moreover, I gather you are not used to driving. I'll be sending you out in a car for a few hours every day."

"They drive on the right in this country," Mabasha said. "In South Africa we drive on the left."

"Exactly," Konovalenko said. "That should help sharpen your reflexes. Any questions?"

"Lots of questions," Mabasha said. "But I realise I'll only get answers to a few of them."

"Quite right," Konovalenko said.

"How did Kleyn get hold of you? He hates communists. And as a KGB man, you were a communist. Maybe you still are."

"You don't bite the hand that feeds you," Konovalenko said. "Being a member of a secret security service is a question of loyalty to the people in power. You could of course find a few ideologically sound communists in the KGB at any given time. But the vast majority were professionals who carried out the assignments given them."

"That doesn't explain your contact with Kleyn."

"If you suddenly lose your job, you start looking for work," Konovalenko said. "Unless you prefer to shoot yourself. South Africa has always seemed to me and to many of my colleagues a well-organised and disciplined country. Never mind the uncertainty there now. I offered my services through channels that already existed between our respective intelligence agencies. Evidently, I had the qualifications to interest Mr Kleyn. We made a deal. I agreed to take care of you for a few days – for a price."

"How much?"

"No money," Konovalenko said. "But do I get the possibility of emigrating to South Africa and certain guarantees regarding the possibility of work in the future."

Importing murderers, Mabasha thought. But of course, that is a clever thing to do from Kleyn's point of view. I might well have done the same myself.

Konovalenko sprang from the leather chair with surprising agility.

"The mist has dispersed," he said. "The wind is up. We should start getting acquainted with the rifle."

Mabasha would recall the days that followed in the isolated house where the wind was always keening as a long-drawn-out wait for a catastrophe that was bound to happen. Yet when it actually came, it was not in the form he had expected. Everything ended up in chaos, and even when he was making his escape he still did not understand what had happened.

The days appeared to be going according to plan. Mabasha quickly mastered the rifle. He practised shooting in prone, sitting, and standing positions in a vast field behind the house. At the end of the field there was a sandbank against which Konovalenko had set targets. Mabasha shot at footballs, cardboard faces, an old suitcase, a radio, saucepans, coffee trays and other objects he couldn't even identify. Every time he pulled the trigger, he was given a report on the outcome via a walkie-talkie, and made very slight adjustments to the sights. Slowly, the rifle began to obey Mabasha's commands.

The days were divided into three sections, separated by meals prepared by Konovalenko. Mabasha was persuaded that Konovalenko knew exactly what he was doing, and was very good at passing on what he knew. Kleyn had chosen the right man.

The feeling of imminent catastrophe came from another direction altogether. It was Konovalenko's attitude towards him, the black contract killer. For as long as he could bear to, Mabasha overlooked the scornful tone of everything Konovalenko said, but in the end it was more than he could tolerate. When his Russian master drank too much vodka after dinner, his contempt became blatant. There were never any direct racial aspersions to give Mabasha an excuse to react. But that only made things worse.

If things went on like this he would be provoked to kill Konovalenko, even though doing so would make his situation impossible.

When they were sitting in their leather armchairs for the psychological sessions, Mabasha noticed that Konovalenko assumed he was totally ignorant about the most basic human reactions. As a means of defusing his growing hatred, Mabasha decided to play the role he had been given. He pretended to be stupid, made the most irrelevant comments he could think of, and observed how delighted Konovalenko was to see his prejudices confirmed.

At night, the singing hounds howled in his ears. Sometimes he woke up and imagined Konovalenko leaning over him with a gun in his hand, but there was never anybody there, and he would lie awake until dawn.

The only breathing space he had were his daily car rides. There were two cars in an outbuilding, one of which, a Mercedes, was meant for him. Konovalenko used the other car for errands, whose purpose he never alluded to.

Mabasha drove around on minor roads, found his way to a town called Ystad and explored some roads along the coast. These excursions helped him to hold out. One night he left his room and counted the portions of frozen food in the freezer: they would be one more week in this isolated place.

I'll have to put up with it, he thought. Kleyn requires me to suffer whatever I have to suffer to earn my million rand.

He assumed Konovalenko was in daily touch with South Africa, and that the transmissions were made while he was out in the car. He was also confident that Konovalenko would be sending only good reports to Kleyn.

But the feeling of impending disaster would not abate. Every hour that passed brought him closer to breaking point, to the moment when his nature would require him to kill Konovalenko. He would be forced to do it so as not to offend his ancestors, and not to lose his self-respect.

But it did not happen as he had expected.

They were in the living room one day at about 4 p.m., and Konovalenko was talking about the problems and opportunities associated with carrying out a liquidation from various kinds of rooftops.

Suddenly he stiffened. At the same time, Mabasha heard a car approaching and coming to a halt. They sat motionless, listening. A car door opened, then shut. Konovalenko, who always carried his pistol, a simple Luger, in one of his tracksuit pockets, rose quickly to his feet and slipped the safety catch.

"Move so you can't be seen from the window," he said.

Mabasha did as he was told. He crouched down by the open fire. Konovalenko carefully opened a door into the overgrown orchard, closed it behind him, and was gone.

Mabasha did not know how long he had been crouching behind the fire. But he was still there when the pistol shot rang out like the crack of a whip. He straightened up cautiously and looked out of a window at Konovalenko bending over something at the front of the house. He went out.

There was a woman lying on her back on the damp gravel. Konovalenko had shot her through the head.

"Who is she?" Mabasha said.

"How should I know?" Konovalenko said. "But she was alone in the car."

"What did she want?"

Konovalenko shrugged and replied as he closed the dead woman's eyes with his foot. Mud from the sole of his shoe stuck to her face. "She asked for directions," he said. "She must have taken a wrong turning."

Mabasha could never decide whether it was the bits of mud from Konovalenko's shoe on the woman's face, or the fact that she had been killed just for asking directions that finally settled his resolve to kill Konovalenko. Now he had one more reason: the man's unrestrained cruelty.

Killing a woman for asking the way was something he would never be able to do. Nor could he close a dead person's eyes by putting his foot on their face.

"You're crazy," he said.

Konovalenko raised his eyebrows in surprise. "What else could I have done?"

"You could have said you didn't know where the road was that she was looking for."

Konovalenko put his pistol back in his pocket. "You still don't understand," he said. "We don't exist. We'll be disappearing from here in a few days, and everything must be as if we had never been here."

"She was only asking directions," Mabasha said again, and he could feel he was starting to sweat with excitement. "There has to be a reason for killing a human being."

"Get back in the house," Konovalenko said. "I'll take care of it."

He watched from the window as Konovalenko backed the woman's car up to the body and put it in the boot before driving off.

He was back again in barely an hour. He came walking along the dirt track.

"Where is she?" Mabasha said.

"Buried," Konovalenko said.

"And the car?"

"Also buried."

"That didn't take long."

Konovalenko put the coffee pot on the stove. He turned to Mabasha with a smile. "Something else for you to learn," he said. "No matter how well organised you are, the unexpected is always liable to happen. But that's precisely why such detailed planning is necessary. If you are well organised, you can improvise. If not, the unexpected intervention is liable to cause confusion."

Konovalenko turned back to the coffee pot.

I'll kill him, Mabasha thought. When all this is over, when we're ready to go our separate ways, I'll kill him. There's no going back now.

That night he could not sleep. Through the wall, he could hear Konovalenko snoring. Kleyn will understand, he thought. He is like me. He wants everything to be clear cut and well planned. He hates brutality, hates senseless violence. By my killing President de Klerk he wants to put an end to all the pointless killing in South Africa today. A monster like Konovalenko must never be granted asylum in our country. A monster must never be given permission to enter paradise on earth.

Three days later Konovalenko announced they were ready to move on. "I've taught you all I can," he said. "And you've mastered the rifle. You know how to think once you're told who will soon be in the cross hairs of your sights. You know how to think when you're planning the final details of the assassination. It's time for you to go back home."

"There's one thing I've been wondering," Mabasha said. "How am I going to get the rifle to South Africa with me?"

"You won't be travelling together, of course," Konovalenko said, not bothering to disguise his contempt for what seemed to him such an

133

idiotic question. "We'll use another method of transport. You don't need to know what."

"I have another question," Mabasha said. "The pistol. I haven't even had a test shot, not a single one."

"You don't need one," Konovalenko said. "It's for you, if you fail. It's a gun that can never be traced."

Wrong, Mabasha thought. I'm never going to point that gun at my own head. I'm going to use it on you.

That evening Konovalenko got drunker than Mabasha had ever seen him. He sat across from him at the table, staring at him with bloodshot eyes.

What is he thinking about, Mabasha wondered. Has that man ever experienced love? If I were a woman, what would it be like to share a bed with him? The thought made him uneasy. He pictured the dead woman on the gravel.

"You have many faults," Konovalenko said, intuiting his train of thought, "but the biggest is that you are sentimental."

"Sentimental?" He knew what it meant. But he was not sure just what significance Konovalenko was attaching to the word.

"You didn't like me shooting that woman," Konovalenko said. "These last few days you've been absent-minded and you've been shooting badly. I'll point out this weakness in my final report to Kleyn. It worries me."

"It worries me to think that a man can be as brutal as you are," Mabasha said.

At that there was no turning back. He knew he was going to have to tell Konovalenko what he was thinking.

"You're dumber than I thought," Konovalenko said. "I guess that's the way black men are."

Mabasha let the words sink into his consciousness. Then he rose slowly to his feet. "I'm going to kill you," he said.

Konovalenko shook his head with a smile. "No, you're not," he said.

Mabasha drew the pistol and aimed it at Konovalenko. "You shouldn't have killed her," he said. "You degraded both me and yourself."

He saw that Konovalenko was scared.

"You're crazy," he said. "You can't kill me."

"There's nothing I'm better at than doing what needs to be done," Mabasha said. "Get up. Slowly. Hands up. Turn around."

Konovalenko did as he was told.

Mabasha had just enough time to register that something was wrong before Konovalenko flung himself to one side with prodigious speed. Mabasha pulled the trigger, but the bullet smashed into a bookcase. Where the knife came from he had no idea, but Konovalenko had it in his hand when he hurled himself at him, faster even than he could aim a second shot. Their combined weight broke a table beneath them. Mabasha was strong, but so was Konovalenko. Mabasha could see the knife being forced closer and closer to his face. Only when he managed to kick Konovalenko in the back did he loosen his grip. He had dropped the pistol. He thumped Konovalenko with his fist, but there was no reaction. Before he broke loose he felt a sudden stinging sensation in his left hand. His whole arm went numb. But he managed to grab Konovalenko's bottle of vodka, turn around and smash it over his head. Konovalenko collapsed and stayed down.

At the same moment Mabasha realised the index finger of his left hand had been sliced off and was hanging on to his hand by a thin piece of skin.

He staggered out of the house. He had no doubt he had smashed Konovalenko's skull. He looked at the blood pouring out of his hand. Then he gritted his teeth and tore off the scrap of skin. The finger fell onto the gravel. He went back into the house, wrapped a cloth round his bleeding hand, flung some clothes into his suitcase and then retrieved the pistol. He closed the door behind him, opened the doors of the outbuilding, started the Mercedes, and hurtled out of the driveway. He drove far too fast for the narrow dirt road. At one point he narrowly avoided a collision with a car coming in the other direction. Then he found his way onto a bigger road and forced himself to slow down.

My finger, he thought. It's for you, *sangoma*. Guide me home now. Kleyn will understand. He is a clever *nkosi*. He knows he can trust me. I shall do what he wants me to do. Even if I don't use a rifle that can be accurate over more than 800 metres. I shall do what he wants me to do and he'll give me a million rand. But I need your help now, *sangoma*. That's why I have sacrificed my finger.

*

135

Konovalenko sat in one of the leather chairs. His head was throbbing. If the bottle had hit his temple in front rather than from the side, he would have been dead. Now and then he pressed a handkerchief filled with ice cubes against his temple. He forced himself to think clearly despite the pain. This was not the first time Konovalenko had found himself in a crisis.

After an hour he had considered all the alternatives and knew what he was going to do. He looked at his watch. He could call South Africa twice each day and be in direct touch with Kleyn. There were 20 minutes to go before the next transmission. He went to the kitchen for more ice cubes.

When he called South Africa, using the radio transmitter, it took a few minutes before Kleyn came on the line. They used no names when they talked to each other.

Konovalenko reported what had happened. *The cage was open and the bird has disappeared. It hasn't managed to learn how to sing.*

It took a while for Kleyn to absorb what had happened. But once he had grasped the situation, his response was unequivocal. *The bird must be caught. Another bird will be sent as a substitute. More information about this later.*

When the conversation was over, Konovalenko felt satisfied. Kleyn had understood that he had done what had been asked of him.

"Try him out," he had said when they met in Nairobi to plan Mabasha's training. "Test his staying power, look for his weaknesses. We have to know if he really can hold out. There's too much at stake for anything to be left to chance. If he's not up to it, he'll have to be replaced."

Mabasha was not up to it, was Konovalenko's verdict. Behind the tough façade and skilled marksman was a dangerously sentimental African. Now it was Konovalenko's job to find and kill him. Then he would train the new candidate.

What he had to do next would not be all that easy. Mabasha was wounded, and he would be acting irrationally. But Konovalenko had no doubt he would succeed. His staying power was legendary during his KGB days. He was a man who never gave up.

He lay on the bed and slept for a few hours. As dawn broke he packed his bag and carried it out to the BMW.

Before he locked the front door he primed the detonator to blow up the house. When the explosion came, he would be a long way away.

He drove off a little after 6 a.m. He would be in Stockholm by late afternoon. There were two police cars by the junction with the E14. For a moment he was afraid that Mabasha had given himself up and betrayed Konovalenko's whereabouts, but no-one in the cars reacted as he drove past.

Kleyn called Malan at 7 a.m. on Tuesday. "We have to meet," he said briskly. "The Committee will have to meet as soon as you can arrange it."

"Has something happened?"

"Yes. The first bird wasn't up to the job. We'll have to find another."

CHAPTER ELEVEN

Konovalenko parked outside the apartment in a high-rise building in Hallunda late in the evening of Tuesday, April 28. He had taken his time on the journey from Skåne. He liked driving fast and the powerful BMW invited high speeds, but he had been careful to stay within the speed limits. Just outside Jönköping he observed that a number of motorists had been waved down at the side of the road by the police. As several of them had overtaken him, he assumed they had been caught in a radar speed trap.

Konovalenko had no respect at all for the Swedish police. He supposed that the basic reason for this was his contempt for the open, democratic Swedish society. Konovalenko hated democracy. It had robbed him of a large part of his life. It would take a very long time to establish – perhaps it would never become a reality – but he left Leningrad the moment he realised the old, closed Soviet society was past saving. The final straw was the failed coup in the autumn of 1991, when a number of top military officers and Politburo members of the old school tried to restore the former hierarchical system. But when the failure was plain for all to see, Konovalenko at once began planning his escape. He would never be able to live in a democracy, no matter how diluted a form it took. The uniform – the esprit de corps, the ideology – he had worn since he joined the KGB as a recruit in his twenties had become an outer skin as far as he was concerned. And he could not shed his skin. What would be left of him if he did?

He was not the only one to think like that. In those last years, when the KGB was subjected to severe reforms and the Berlin wall came down, he and his colleagues were forever discussing what the future would look like. It was one of the unwritten rules of the intelligence service that somebody would have to be held responsible when a totalitarian society started to crumble. Far too many citizens had been subjected to treatment by the KGB, far too many relatives were eager to exact vengeance for their missing or dead kin. Konovalenko had no desire to be hauled before the courts and treated like his former Stasi colleagues in the new Germany. He hung a map of the world on his office wall and studied it for hours. He was forced to grit his teeth and accept that he was not cut out for life in the late 20th century. He found it hard to imagine himself living in one of the brutal but highly unstable dictatorships in South America. Nor did he have any confidence in the home rule leaders who were still in power in some African states. On the other hand, he thought seriously about building a future in a fundamentalist Arab country. In some ways he was indifferent to the Islamic religion, and in other ways he loathed it. But he knew the governments ran both open and secret police forces with far-reaching powers. In the end, though, he rejected this alternative as well. He thought he would never be able to handle the transformation to such a foreign culture, no matter which Islamic state he selected. Besides, he did not want to give up drinking vodka.

He had also considered offering his services to an international security company. But he lacked the necessary experience: it was a world with which he was unfamiliar.

In the end, there was only one country he could contemplate. South Africa. He read whatever literature he could lay his hands on, but it was not easy to find much. Thanks to the authority that still attached to KGB officers, he managed to track down a few literary and political works. What he read confirmed his impression that South Africa would be a suitable place to build a future for himself. He was attracted by the racial discrimination, and could see how both the regular and secret police forces were well organised and wielded considerable influence.

He disliked coloured people, especially blacks. As far as he was concerned, they were inferior beings, unpredictable, usually criminal. Whether such views constituted prejudice, he had no idea. He just decided that was the way things were. But he liked the thought of having domestic servants and gardeners.

Anatoli Konovalenko was married, but he was planning a new life without Mira. He had tired of her years ago. She was no doubt equally tired of him. He never bothered to ask her. All they had left was a routine, devoid of substance, devoid of emotions. He compensated by indulging in regular affairs with women he met through his work.

Their two daughters were already living their own independent lives. No need to worry about them.

As the empire collapsed around him, he thought he would be able to melt into oblivion. Anatoli Konovalenko would cease to exist. He would change his identity, and perhaps also his appearance. His wife would have to cope as best she could on the pension she would receive once he was declared dead.

Most of his colleagues had organised their own emergency exits over the years, through which he could escape if necessary from a crisis situation. He had built up a reserve of foreign currency, and had a variety of identities at his disposal in the form of passports and other documents. He also had a number of contacts in top echelons in Aeroflot, the customs authorities, and the foreign service. Anybody belonging to the *nomenklatura* was like a member of a secret society. They were there to help each other, and as a group had the certainty that their way of life would not give way beneath them. That was until the unimaginable collapse actually took place.

Towards the end, just before he fled, everything happened very quickly. He contacted Kleyn, who was a liaison officer between the KGB and the South African intelligence service. They had met when Konovalenko was visiting the Moscow station in Nairobi – his first assignment in the African continent, in fact. Kleyn made it clear that Konovalenko's services could be useful to him and his country. He planted in Konovalenko's head visions of immigration and a comfortable future.

But it would take time. Konovalenko needed an intermediate port of call after leaving the Soviet Union. He decided on Sweden. Several colleagues had recommended it. Apart from the high standard of living, it was easy to cross the borders, and at least as easy to keep out of the public eye. There was also a growing colony of Russians, many of them criminals, organised into gangs, that had started to operate in Sweden. They were generally the first rats to abandon the sinking ship. The KGB had always had excellent relations with the Russian criminal classes. Now they could be mutually helpful in exile.

As he got out of the car he noticed that there were blemishes on the face even of this country, and it was supposed to be a model society. This grim suburb reminded him of Leningrad and Berlin. It looked as though future decay was built into the façades. And yet Vladimir Rykoff and his wife Tania had done the right thing when they settled in Hallunda. They could live here in the anonymity they desired.

That I desire, he thought, correcting himself.

When he first came to Sweden, he used Rykoff to help him settle in. Rykoff had been living in Stockholm since the beginning of the 1980s. He had shot a KGB colonel in Kiev by mistake and fled the country. Because he had a dark complexion and looked like an Arab, he travelled as a Persian refugee and was rapidly granted refugee status, though he did not speak a word of Persian. When in due course he was granted Swedish citizenship, he took back his own name. He was only an Iranian when he dealt with the Swedish authorities. In order to support himself and his supposedly Iranian wife, while he was still living in a refugee camp near Flen, he carried out a few simple bank robberies. This produced sufficient capital to start out with. He set up a settlement service for other Russian immigrants who were now making their way to Sweden, more or less legally, in increasing numbers. His somewhat unorthodox travel agency became well known, and there were times when he had more potential clients than he could cope with. He had a number of Swedish civil servants on his payroll, including at times people in the immigration office, and it all helped to give the agency its reputation of efficiency. He was sometimes irritated by how hard it was to bribe Swedish civil servants, but he generally managed it eventually, as long as he was discreet. Rykoff had also established the much appreciated custom of inviting all new arrivals to a genuine Russian dinner in his apartment at Hallunda.

It did not take Konovalenko long to grasp that behind the hard exterior, Rykoff was in fact a weak character and easily led. When Konovalenko made a pass at his wife and she proved to be far from unwilling, he soon had Rykoff where he wanted him. Konovalenko arranged his business so that Rykoff did all the legwork, all the boring and routine assignments.

When Kleyn contacted him and offered him the job of taking care of an African contract killer, it was Rykoff who dealt with all the practical arrangements. It was Rykoff who rented the house in Skåne, fixed the cars, and brought in the food supply. He dealt with the forgers and the weapon Konovalenko smuggled out of St Petersburg.

Konovalenko knew Rykoff had another virtue. He never hesitated to kill, when it was necessary.

Konovalenko took out his bag, locked the car, and took the lift to the fifth floor. He had a key, but he rang the doorbell instead. The signal was a sort of morse code version of the "Internationale".

Tania opened the door. She looked at him in surprise, seeing no sign of Mabasha, and alarmed at the bruise on his head.

"What happened?" she said. "Where's the African?"

"Is Vladimir here?" Konovalenko said, without troubling to answer her questions.

He handed her his bag and walked in. The apartment had four rooms and was furnished with expensive leather armchairs, a marble table, and the last word in stereo and video equipment. It was all very tasteless, and Konovalenko did not like living there. Right now, though, he had no alternative.

Rykoff emerged from the bedroom dressed in a silk robe. Unlike Tania, who was so slim, Rykoff looked as if he'd been given an order to get fat – an order he had been delighted to obey.

Tania prepared a meal and put a bottle of vodka on the table. Konovalenko told them as much as he thought they needed to know. He said nothing about the woman he had killed.

The thing that mattered was that Mabasha had suffered a mysterious breakdown. He had run away and had to be found and got rid of as rapidly as possible.

"Why didn't you do it in Skåne?" Rykoff said.

"There were certain difficulties," Konovalenko said.

Neither Rykoff nor his wife asked any more questions.

While he was driving to Stockholm, Konovalenko had thought about what had happened, and what needed to happen now. Mabasha had only one possibility of leaving the country. He would have to find Konovalenko. Konovalenko was the one with the passports and tickets; he was the one who could supply him with money. Mabasha would most probably make his way to Stockholm. He was indeed most likely there already. Konovalenko and Rykoff would be ready to find him.

Konovalenko drank a few glasses of vodka. But he did not get drunk, even if that was what he most wanted to do right now. He had an important job to do first. He had to call Kleyn on the Pretoria telephone number he was only allowed to use in case of absolute necessity.

"Go into the bedroom," he said to the Rykoffs. "Close the door and switch the radio on. I have to make a call, and I don't want to be disturbed."

He knew that both of them would listen if they had the chance and he wanted none of it. He needed to explain to Kleyn about the woman he had been forced to kill.

That would give him the perfect reason to imply that Mabasha's breakdown was to their advantage. It would be obvious that it was thanks to Konovalenko that the man's weakness had been exposed before it could do any damage. Killing the woman could have been another plus. It would be clear to Kleyn, if he did not know it already, that Konovalenko was ruthless. As Kleyn had said, when they were in Nairobi, this was the kind of person South Africa needed most right now. White people with a disregard for death.

Konovalenko dialled the number he had memorised as soon as he was given it in Africa. During his many years as a KGB officer he had always honed his powers of concentration and memory. He had to dial the string of numbers four times before they were picked up by the satellite over the equator and sent back to earth again.

The call was answered at once in Pretoria.

Konovalenko recognised the slow, hoarse voice.

He described what had happened. This time he used a new code. Mabasha was the entrepreneur. He had prepared himself thoroughly while driving up to Stockholm, and Kleyn did not once interrupt him. When Konovalenko was finished, there was silence. He waited.

"We'll send you a new entrepreneur," Kleyn said, in the end. "The first one must be dismissed immediately, of course. We'll be in touch when we know more about his successor."

Konovalenko replaced the receiver and knew the call had turned out as he hoped. He would be seen as having prevented a disaster in the final stages. He could not resist tiptoeing up to the bedroom door and listening. There was no sound apart from the radio.

He sat at the table and poured himself half a glass of vodka. Now he could afford to get drunk. Since he needed to be alone, he let the bedroom door stay closed.

He thought about taking Tania now to the room where he slept when he was there, but she would come later, in her own time.

He got up early, taking care not to disturb Tania. Rykoff was sitting in the kitchen over a cup of coffee. Konovalenko got a cup for himself and sat on the other side of the kitchen table.

"Victor Mabasha has got to die," he said. "Sooner or later he'll come to Stockholm. I have a strong feeling that he's already here. I cut him badly, I am pretty sure. He'll have a bandage or a glove on one hand. He'll look for the clubs in town where Africans go. He has no other alternative if he's going to track me down. And so you can start spreading the word today that there's a contract on an African with a wound on one of his hands: 100,000 kronor to anybody who can eliminate this man. Go and see all your contacts, all the Russian criminals you know. Don't mention any names. Just say the person issuing the contract is OK."

"That's a lot of cash," Rykoff said.

"You leave that to me," Konovalenko said. "Just do as I say. There's nothing to stop you earning the money yourself. Nor me, come to that."

Konovalenko would have no qualms about putting a pistol to Mabasha's head himself. But he knew that was hardly likely. Such good fortune would be too much to hope for.

"Tonight we can tour the clubs," he said. "By then the contract must have been issued so that everybody who ought to know about it has heard. I'd say you've plenty to do."

Rykoff got to his feet. Despite his flabbiness he was extremely effective, Konovalenko knew, when it mattered. Half an hour later Konovalenko stood at the window, watching him in the car park, getting into a Volvo that looked to be a more recent model than the one he had last seen him in. He's eating himself to death, Konovalenko thought. He gets his kicks from buying new cars. He'll die without experiencing the great pleasure of exceeding his own limitations. He's just a cow chewing its cud.

Konovalenko also had an important job to do that day. He had to raise 100,000 kronor. The question was, which bank to rob?

He went back to his bedroom and was tempted to slip back under the covers and wake Tania. But he resisted, and quickly and noiselessly got dressed.

He left the apartment in Hallunda shortly before 10 a.m. There was a chill in the air, and it was raining. He wondered where Mabasha was now.

At 2.15 p.m. on Wednesday, April 29, Anatoli Konovalenko robbed the Commercial Bank in Akalla. The raid took two minutes. He ran out of the bank, sprinted into the side street on the left and jumped into his car.

He reckoned he had got away with twice as much at least as he needed. If nothing else, he would treat himself and Tania to a gourmet dinner – once Mabasha was disposed of.

The road curved sharply to the right as he approached Ulvsundavägen. There were two police cars blocking the way. He slammed on the brakes. How had the police had time to set up a roadblock? It was no time at all since the bank alarm went off. How could they have known he would choose this route?

He checked his mirrors and heard the tyres squeal as he swung the car in reverse. A rubbish bin flew onto the pavement and his mudguard tore loose on a tree. Now there was no question of driving slowly any more. All that mattered was to lose his pursuers.

He heard the sirens behind him. He swore and wondered again how the trap could have been set out so rapidly. He also cursed the fact that he did not know his way around the district north of Sundbyberg. He had no idea what was the best way of escape.

He strayed into an industrial estate and soon found himself trapped on a one-way street. The police were still in pursuit, even though he had stretched the distance between them by jumping two sets of lights. He leaped out of the car, the carrier bag in one hand and his pistol in the other. When the first police car screeched to a halt he took aim and shattered the windscreen. He had no idea if he had hit anybody, but now he had the advantage he needed. They would not chase him until they had reinforcements.

He scrambled over a fence and into an enclosure that could have been either a dump or a building site. But he was lucky. As he reached the road on the other side, a car with a young couple in it drew up. They must have been looking for some place off the beaten track where they could be alone. Konovalenko did not hesitate. He crept up on the car from behind and thrust the pistol through the window at the man's head.

"Keep quiet, and do exactly what I say," he said in his broken Swedish. "Out of the car. Leave the keys."

The couple seemed completely paralysed. Konovalenko had no time to waste. He ripped open the door, dragged the driver bodily out of the car, jumped in behind the wheel, and looked at the girl in the seat next to him.

"Now I drive," he said. "You have one second to decide if you come with me or not."

She screamed and flung herself out of the car. Konovalenko drove off. Now he was no longer in a hurry. Sirens were approaching from all directions, but his pursuers could not know he had a new car.

Did I wound anybody? he wondered. I'll find out if I turn on the television tonight.

He left the car at the underground station in Duvbo and rode back to Hallunda. Neither Tania nor Vladimir were at home when he rang the doorbell. He let himself in with his own key, put the plastic bag on the dining table, and got out the vodka bottle. A few big swallows and he was calm again. It had gone well. If he had wounded or even killed a policeman, that would raise tensions throughout the city, but he could not see how that would put a stop to or even delay the liquidation of the African.

He counted the money; he had 162,000 kronor.

At 6 p.m. he turned on the television to see the early evening news. Only Tania was back by then, in the kitchen preparing dinner. The broadcast began with the story Konovalenko was waiting for. To his astonishment, he learned that the pistol shot intended only to shatter the windscreen had hit one of the policemen right where his nose met his forehead. He died instantly.

146

Then came a picture of the policeman Konovalenko had killed: Klas Tengblad, 26 years old, married with two small children.

The police had no clues beyond the fact that the killer had been alone, and was the man who had robbed the Akalla branch of the Commercial Bank just a few minutes previously.

Konovalenko made a face and moved to switch off the television. Just then he noticed Tania in the doorway, watching him.

"The only good policeman is a dead one," he said, punching the off button. "What's for dinner? I'm hungry."

Rykoff came home and sat down at the table just as Tania and Konovalenko were finishing their meal. "A bank robbery," he said. "And a policeman killed. A killer speaking broken Swedish. The town won't exactly be clear of police tonight."

"These things happen," Konovalenko said. "Have you spread the word about the contract?"

"There's not a single paid-up member of the underworld who won't know before midnight that there's a 100,000 kronor reward to be earned," Rykoff said.

Tania handed him a plate of food.

"Was it really necessary to kill a policeman, today of all days?" he said.

"What makes you think it was me who shot him?" Konovalenko said.

Rykoff shrugged his shoulders. "A masterly shot," he said. "A bank raid to raise the money for the contract. Foreign accent. It sounds pretty much like you."

"You're wrong if you think the shot was deliberate," Konovalenko said. "It was pure luck. Or bad luck, depending on how you look at it. But to be on the safe side I think you'd better go in to town on your own tonight. Or take Tania with you."

"There are a few clubs in the south of the city where Africans hang out," said Rykoff. "I thought I'd start there."

At 8.30 Tania and Vladimir drove to town. Konovalenko showered, then settled down to watch television. Every news broadcast had long items on the murdered policeman. There were no clues to follow yet.

Of course not, Konovalenko thought. I don't leave a trail.

He had fallen asleep in his chair when the telephone rang. Just one signal. Then another ring, seven signals this time. When it rang for the third time Konovalenko lifted the receiver. It was Rykoff using the code. The noise in the background suggested he was at a disco.

"Can you hear me?" Rykoff was shouting.

"I can hear you."

"I can hardly hear myself speak," Rykoff said. "But I've got news. Mabasha's here right now."

Konovalenko took a deep breath. "Has he seen you?"

"No. But he's on his guard."

"Is anybody with him?"

"He's on his own."

Konovalenko thought for a moment. It was 11.20 p.m. What was the best thing to do? "Give me the address," he said. "Wait for me outside with a layout of the club. Most important to know where all the emergency exits are."

"Will do," Rykoff said.

Konovalenko checked his pistol and put an extra magazine into his pocket. Then he went to his room and from a chest he took three tear gas grenades and two gas masks, which he put into the carrier bag he had used for the money from the bank raid.

Finally, he combed his hair in the bathroom mirror. This was part of the ritual he went through before setting out on any assignment that mattered as much as this one did.

At 11.45 p.m. he left the apartment and took a taxi into town. He asked to be taken to Östermalmstorg. He got out there, hailed another taxi, and headed for Söder. The disco was at number 45. Konovalenko directed the driver to number 60. He got out and walked slowly back the way the taxi had come.

Rykoff stepped out of the shadows. "He's still there," he said. "Tania has gone home."

"Let's get him, then," Konovalenko said.

Rykoff described the interior of the club.

"Exactly where is he?" asked Konovalenko when he could picture it.

"At the bar."

Konovalenko nodded. They donned the gas masks, took a while in

148

the shelter of their doorway still to get used to breathing through them, and cocked their weapons. They walked steadily to the club entrance. The street was empty. They negotiated the steps down to the black iron outer doors.

Rykoff flung them open and brushed the two startled doormen aside. Konovalenko primed the first grenade and tossed it along the floor by the bar.

CHAPTER TWELVE

Give me the night, sangoma. How shall I survive these nights full of light that prevents me from finding a hiding place? Why have you sent me to this strange land where people have been robbed of their darkness? I give you my severed finger, sangoma. I sacrifice a part of my body so you can give me back my darkness in return. But you have forsaken me. I am all alone. As lonely as the antelope no longer capable of escaping the hunting cheetah.

Mabasha experienced his flight as a journey made in a dream-like, weightless state. His soul seemed to be travelling on its own, invisible, somewhere close by. He thought he could feel his own breath on his neck. In the Mercedes, whose leather seats reminded him of the distant smell of antelope hides, there was nothing but his body, and above all his aching hand. His finger was gone, but was there even so, like a homeless pain in a strange land.

From the very beginning of his wild flight he had tried to make himself control his thoughts, act sensibly. I am a *zulu*, he kept repeating to himself, like a mantra. I belong to the undefeated warrior race, I am one of the Sons of Heaven. My forefathers were always in the front line when the *impis* attacked. We defeated the whites long before they hounded the bushmen into the endless wildernesses where they soon succumbed. We defeated them before they claimed our land was theirs. We defeated them at the foot of Isandlwana and cut off their jawbones to adorn the *kraaler* of our kings. I am a *zulu*, one of my fingers is lost. But I can endure the pain and I have nine fingers left, as many as the jackal has lives.

When he could bear it no longer he turned off into the forest on the first dirt track he saw, and came to a halt by a glistening lake. The water was so black, he thought at first it was oil. He sat there on a stone by the shore, unwound the bloodstained towel and forced himself to examine his hand. It was bleeding still. The pain was more in his mind than where the finger had been.

How was it possible for Konovalenko to be faster than he was? His momentary hesitation had defeated him. His flight, too, had been thoughtless. He had been like a bewildered child. His actions were unworthy, of himself and of Kleyn. He should have stayed put, and searched through Konovalenko's baggage, looking for air tickets and money. But all he did was to grab a few clothes and the pistol. He couldn't even remember the way he had come. He would never find the road back.

Weakness, he thought. I have never managed to overcome it, even though I have renounced all my loyalties, all the principles that possessed me as I grew up. I have been burdened with weakness as a punishment by my *sangoma*. She has listened to the spirits and let the hounds sing my song, a song of the weakness I shall never be able to overcome.

The sun never seemed to rest in this strange land; it had already climbed over the horizon. A bird of prey rose from a treetop and flapped its way over the mirror-like lake.

First of all he must sleep. A few hours, no more. He knew he did not need much sleep. Afterwards, his brain would be able to assist him once again.

At a time which seemed to him as far distant as the dim and distant past of his ancestors, his father, Okumana, the man who could make better spear tips than anyone else, had explained to him that there was always a way out of any situation, as long as one was alive. Death was the last hiding place. That was something to keep in reserve until there was no other way of avoiding an apparently insuperable threat. There were always escape routes that were not immediately obvious, and that was why humans, unlike animals, had a brain. To look inward, not outward. Inward, towards the secret places where the spirits of one's ancestors were waiting to act as a man's guide through life.

Who am I? he thought. A human being who has lost his identity is no longer a human being. He is an animal. That's what has happened to me. I started to kill people because I myself was dead. When I was a child and saw the signs, the accursed signs telling the blacks where they were allowed to go and what existed exclusively for the whites, I started to be diminished even then. A child should grow, grow bigger; but in my country a black child had to learn how to grow small and smaller. I saw my parents succumb to their own invisibility, their own accumulated bitterness. I was an obedient child and learned to be a nobody among nobodies. Apartheid was my real father. I learned what no-one should need to learn. To live with falsehood, contempt, a lie elevated to the only truth in my country. A lie enforced by the police and laws, but above all by a flood of white water, a torrent of words about the natural distinctions between white and black, the superiority of white civilisation. That superiority turned me into a murderer, *sangoma*. And I can believe this is the ultimate consequence of learning to grow smaller as a child. For what has this Apartheid, this falsified white superiority been but a systematic plundering of our souls? When our despair exploded in furious destruction, the whites failed to see the despair and hatred which is so boundlessly greater. All the things we have been carrying around inside us. It is inside myself that I see my thoughts and feelings being split asunder as if with a sword. I can manage without one of my fingers. But how can I live without knowing who I am?

He came to with a start. He had almost fallen asleep. In the borderlands of sleep, half dreaming, thoughts he had long since forgotten returned to him.

He remained on the stone by the lake for a long time.

The memories found their own way into his head. He had no need to summon them.

Summer, 1967. He had just passed his sixth birthday when he discovered a talent that set him apart from the other children he used to play with in the dusty slum in the suburbs of Johannesburg. They had made a ball out of paper and string, and he had far more skill with it than any of his friends. He could work miracles with the ball: this discovery led to his first great dream. He would be the best rugby player in South Africa.

It brought him untold joy. He thought the spirits of his forefathers had been good to him. He filled a bottle with water from a tap and sacrificed it to the red earth.

One day that summer a white liquor salesman stopped his car in the dust where Victor and his friends were playing with the paper-and-string ball. The man behind the wheel sat for a long time watching the black boy with the phenomenal ball control.

When once the ball rolled close to the car, Victor approached gingerly, bowed to the man and picked up the ball.

"If only you'd been born white," the man said. "I've never seen anybody handle a ball like you do. It's a pity you're black."

He watched an aeroplane sketching a white streak across the sky.

I don't remember the pain, he thought. But I must have felt it, even then. Or did I simply not react because it was so far ingrained in me as a six-year-old that injustice was our heritage? By the time he was 16, everything had changed.

June 1976. Soweto. More than 15,000 students were gathered outside Orlando West Junior Secondary School. He did not really belong in that assembly. He lived on the streets, lived the obscure but increasingly skilful, increasingly ruthless, life of a thief. At that time he was still only robbing blacks, but his eyes were by then drawn to the white residential areas where it was possible to pull off big robberies. He was carried along by the tide of young people, and shared their fury over the government's ruling decree that all education would in future be conducted in the hated language of the *Boere*. He could remember still the young girl clenching her fist and yelling at the President, who was not present, "Vorster! You speak *zulu*, then we'll speak Afrikaans!" He was in turmoil. The drama of the situation as the police charged, beating people with their *sjamboks*, did not affect him until he was hit himself. He had taken part in the stone-throwing, and his ball skills had not deserted him. Nearly every throw hit home; he saw a policeman clutch at his cheek and blood pour out between his fingers, and he remembered the man in the car and what he had said as Victor bent down to pick up his paper ball. Then he was caught, and the lashes from the whips dug deeply into his skin, the pain penetrated his inner self. He remembered one policeman above all the others, a powerful red-faced man smelling of stale alcohol. He had detected a gleam of fear in his eye. At that moment he realised he was the stronger, and from then on the white man's terror would always fill him with boundless contempt.

He was woken from his reverie by a movement on the other side of the lake. It was a rowing boat coming slowly in his direction. A man was rowing with lazy strokes. The sound from the rowlocks reached him despite the distance.

He got up from his stone, staggered in a sudden fit of dizziness, and knew he would have to find a doctor. He had always had thin blood, and once he started bleeding, it took an age to stop. He must find something to drink too. He sat in the car and started the engine. He had enough petrol for an hour's driving at most.

It took him all of 45 minutes to get to a town called Älmhult. He wondered how the name was pronounced. He stopped at a petrol station. Konovalenko had given him money for petrol earlier on. He had two 100-kronor notes left, and knew how to operate the automatic dispenser. His hand was an agonising impediment, and it was attracting attention. An old man offered to help him. Mabasha could not understand what he said, but nodded and tried to smile. He used one of the 100-kronor notes and saw it was only enough for just over ten litres. But he needed something to eat and above all he needed to quench his thirst. He mumbled his thanks to the man who helped him and drove the car away from the pump. He bought some bread and two large bottles of Coca-Cola. That left him with 40 kronor. There was a map on the counter, and he tried in vain to find Älmhult.

He went back to the car and bit off a large chunk of bread. He drank a whole bottle of Coca-Cola. He tried to make up his mind what to do. Where could he find a doctor or a hospital? He had no money to pay for treatment anyway. The hospital staff would refuse to treat him. He knew what that meant. He would have to commit a robbery. The pistol in the glove compartment was his only means of survival.

He left the little town behind him and drove on through the endless forest. I hope I don't need to kill anyone, he thought. I don't want to kill anyone until I have completed my assignment, until I have shot de Klerk.

*

The first time I killed a human being, *sangoma*, I was not alone. I still can't forget it, even if I have difficulty in remembering other people I killed later. It was on a morning in January, 1981, in the cemetery at Duduza. I remember the cracked gravestones, *sangoma*, I remember thinking I was walking across the roof of the abode of the dead. We were going to bury an old man that morning. I think he was my father's cousin. There were other burials going on elsewhere in the cemetery. There was a disturbance somewhere: a funeral procession was breaking up. I saw a young girl running among the memorial stones, running like a hunted deer. She *was* being hunted. Somebody yelled that she was a white man's informer, a black girl working for the police. She was caught, she screamed; her despair was greater than anything I had ever seen before. But she was stabbed, clubbed, and lay between the graves, still alive. Then we started gathering dry sticks and clumps of grass we pulled up from between the gravestones. I say "we", because I was suddenly involved in what was happening. A black woman passing information to the police – what right had she to live? She begged for her life, but her body was soon covered in dry sticks and grass and we burned her alive as she lay there. She tried in vain to get away from the flames, but we held her down until her face turned black. She was the first human being I killed, *sangoma*, and I have never forgotten her for in killing her I killed also myself. Racial segregation had triumphed. I had become an animal, *sangoma*. There was no turning back.

His hand started hurting again. Mabasha tried to hold it motionless to reduce the pain. The sun was still very high in the sky, and he did not bother to look at his watch. He had a long time to sit in the car with his thoughts for company.

I have no idea where I am, he thought. I know I'm in Sweden. But that's all. Perhaps that's what the world is really like. No here, no there. Only a now.

Eventually the strange, barely noticeable dusk descended. He loaded his pistol and tucked it into his belt. He no longer had his knives. But then, he was determined that he was not going to kill anybody, if he could possibly avoid it.

Soon he would have to fill the petrol tank. He had no money and

155

he needed to solve that problem – and without, he said to himself, over and over, killing anyone.

A few kilometres further on he came upon a store open late. He stopped, switched off the engine and waited until all the other customers had gone. He released the safety catch on his pistol, got out of the car and went quickly inside. There was an old man behind the counter. Mabasha pointed at the cash register with his pistol. The man tried to say something, but Mabasha fired a shot into the ceiling and pointed again. With trembling hands the man opened the till. Mabasha switched the pistol to his injured hand and, leaning forward, grabbed all the cash he could see. Then he turned and hurried out of the store.

He didn't see the man behind the counter collapse on the floor. As he fell, his head smacked hard against the concrete floor. The man was dead. His heart had not been able to cope with the shock. Afterwards, they would decide that the thief had knocked him down.

As Mabasha ran out of the store, his bandage caught in the door handle. He had no time gently to untangle it, so he gritted his teeth against the pain and jerked his hand free.

Then he saw a girl staring at him. She was perhaps 13, and wide-eyed. She stared at his bloodstained hand.

I'll have to kill her, he thought. There can't be any witnesses. He drew his pistol and aimed it at her, but he couldn't bring himself to shoot her. He ran to the car and drove away.

He knew he would have the police after him now. They would start looking for a black man with a wounded hand. The girl he hadn't killed would talk. He gave himself four hours at the most before he would be forced to change cars.

He stopped at an unmanned petrol station and filled his tank. He followed a signpost for Stockholm. Somewhere along the way he would have to sleep. He hoped he could find another lake with still, black water.

He found one south of Linköping. He had changed cars by then. He turned into a motel near Huskvarna and managed to crack the door lock and short-circuit the ignition of another Mercedes. He drove on until his strength ran out. Still south of Linköping, just before midnight, he turned onto a minor road, then onto a smaller one still, and eventually came upon a lake stretched out before him, its surface like black glass. He got into the wide rear seat, curled up, and fell asleep.

He awoke with a start. It was almost 5 a.m. He could hear a bird singing in a way he had never heard before. He continued his journey northwards. Shortly before 11 a.m. he was in Stockholm.

It was Wednesday, April 29, the day before Walpurgis Eve.

CHAPTER THIRTEEN

Three masked men appeared as dessert was being served. They fired 300 rounds from automatic weapons and then ran out to a waiting car.

After a moment of silence the restaurant was filled with the screams of the wounded and the terrified.

It had been the annual meeting of the venerable wine-tasting club of Durban. The dining committee had most carefully considered security before deciding to hold the banquet at the golf club in Pinetown. Pinetown had so far escaped the violence that was increasingly widespread in Natal. Moreover, the restaurant manager had undertaken to double the usual security for the evening. But the guards were struck down before they could raise the alarm. The fence surrounding the restaurant had been broken through with wire-cutters. The assailants had also managed to throttle an Alsatian.

There were 50 people in the restaurant when the men burst in. The membership of the wine-tasting club was exclusively white. There were five black waiters, four men and one woman. The black chefs and kitchen hands fled through the back door with the Portuguese head chef the instant the shooting started.

When order was restored, nine people lay dead among the upturned tables and chairs, the shattered crockery, and fallen chandeliers. Seventeen more were seriously wounded, and all the elderly survivors were in shock, among them an old lady who would later die from a heart attack.

Dozens of wine bottles had been smashed. The police had a hard time distinguishing blood from red wine.

Chief Inspector Samuel de Beer from the Durban homicide squad was one of the first to reach the restaurant. He had with him Inspector Harry Sibande, who was black. Although de Beer made no attempt to conceal his racial prejudice, Sibande had learnt to tolerate it. This was due not least to the fact that Sibande had realised long ago that he was a much better policeman than de Beer could ever be.

They surveyed the devastation, and watched the wounded being carried to the ambulances.

The badly shocked witnesses who remained did not have much to say. There had been three men, all masked. But their hands were black. De Beer called Intelligence in Pretoria. They promised him that the army's special unit for political assassinations and terrorist actions would place an experienced investigator at his disposal first thing in the morning.

President de Klerk was informed about the incident shortly before midnight. His foreign minister, Pik Botha, could tell that de Klerk was annoyed at being disturbed.

"Innocent people get murdered every day," he said. "What's so special about this incident?"

"The scale," the foreign minister said. "It's too big, too crude, too brutal. There'll be a violent reaction within the party unless you make a very firm statement tomorrow morning. I'm convinced that the ANC leadership, presumably Mandela himself, will condemn what's happened. It won't look good if you have nothing to say."

Botha was one of the very few who had President de Klerk's ear. The President generally acted on his advice.

"I'll do as you suggest," de Klerk said. "Put something together, please. See that I get it by 7 a.m."

Later that evening, Malan took a call from his colleague in NIS, Kleyn. Both of them had been told of the massacre in Pinetown. Both reacted with dismay and disgust. They played their roles like the old hands they were. The Pinetown massacre was part of a strategy to raise the level of insecurity across the country. At the end of it all, the final link in a chain of increasingly frequent and serious attacks and murders, was the liquidation the Committee had ordained.

Kleyn called Malan about an entirely different matter, however. He had discovered earlier in the day that someone had hacked into his private computer files at work. After a few hours of pondering and a process of elimination, he had worked out who it must be that was keeping them under scrutiny. He also realised the discovery was a vital threat to their immediate plans.

They never used their names when they telephoned each other. They recognised each other's voices. If they ever had a bad line, they had a code to identify themselves.

"We have to meet," Kleyn said. "You know where I'm going tomorrow?"

"Yes."

"Be sure you do the same," Kleyn said.

Malan had been told that a Captain Breytenbach would represent his own secret unit in the investigation of the massacre, but he only needed to call Breytenbach to ensure that he could take the assignment himself. Malan had a dispensation to alter any assignment without the need to consult his superiors.

"I'll be there," he said. That was the end of the conversation. Malan called Captain Breytenbach and told him that he would be flying to Durban himself in the morning. Then he considered what could have upset Kleyn. It must have something to do with the major operation. He just hoped their plans were not unravelling.

At 4 a.m. on May 1, Kleyn skirted Johannesburg and soon joined the E3 highway to Durban. He expected to get there by 8 a.m. He enjoyed driving. He could have had a helicopter take him to Durban, but the journey would have been over too quickly. Alone in the car, with the countryside flashing past, he would have time to reflect.

He expected the problems in Sweden would be swiftly solved. For some days he had been wondering if Konovalenko really was as skilful and cold-blooded as he had counted on. Had he made a mistake employing him? He decided not. Konovalenko would do whatever was necessary. Mabasha would soon be dealt with. Indeed, it might have happened already. A man called Tsiki, number two on his original list, would take his place and Konovalenko would give him the same training.

The only thing that still struck Kleyn as odd was the incident that brought on Mabasha's breakdown. How could a man with his background react in such a volatile way to the death of a total stranger, this Swedish woman? Had there been a weak point of sentimentality in him after all? In that case it was a good job they found out in time. If they hadn't, there was no knowing what might have happened when Mabasha had his victim in his sights.

He brushed all thought of Mabasha aside and concentrated instead on the surveillance he had uncovered. There were no incriminating details, no names in his computer files. A skilful intelligence specialist would, even so, be able to draw certain conclusions, chief among which would obviously be that preparations were well advanced for a dramatic assassination that would have far-reaching political consequences.

He concluded that he had been lucky. He had discovered the penetration of his computer files in time, and would be able to take the neecessary precautions.

Colonel Malan climbed aboard the helicopter at the army airfield near Johannesburg. It was 7.15 a.m.; he would be in Durban by about 8 a.m. He nodded to the pilots, fastened his seat belt, and contemplated the ground below as they rose into the sky.

He gazed thoughtfully at the African township they were flying over. He could see the ramshackle houses, the smoke from the fires.

How could those people defeat us? All we need is to be stubborn and show them we mean business. It will cost blood, even white blood, as in Pinetown last night. But continued white rule in South Africa would not come without cost. It required sacrifices.

He leaned back, closed his eyes, and tried to sleep.

Soon he would discover what had been so disconcerting to Kleyn.

They reached the cordoned-off restaurant in Pinetown within ten minutes of each other. They spent a little over an hour in the blood-stained rooms, together with the local investigators led by Inspector de Beer. The attackers had done a good job. They had expected the death toll to be higher than nine, but that was of minor importance. The killing of the innocent wine-tasters had had the expected effect. Blind fury and demands for revenge from the whites had already been forthcoming. Kleyn heard both Mandela and President de Klerk on his car radio condemning the incident. De Klerk even threatened the killers with violent revenge.

"Is there any trace of who may have carried out this monstrous attack?" Kleyn said.

"Not yet," de Beer said. "We haven't even found anyone who saw the escape car."

"The government should offer a reward right away," Malan said. "I shall ask the Minister of Defence to propose that at the next cabinet meeting."

As he spoke there came the sound of a disturbance on the street, where a crowd of whites had gathered. Many of them were brandishing shotguns or rifles, and blacks who saw the crowd turned off and went another way. The restaurant door burst open and a white woman in her 30s barged in. She was dishevelled and hysterical. When she saw Inspector Sibande, the only black man on the premises, she drew a pistol and fired a shot in his direction. Harry Sibande managed to take refuge behind an upturned table. But the woman kept on going, still firing the pistol which she held stiffly in both hands. All the time she was screeching in Afrikaans that she would avenge her brother who had been killed in the massacre. She would not rest, she cried, until every last *kaffir* had been executed.

De Beer came up behind her and hammered the weapon from her grasp. Then he led her outside. Sibande stood up behind the table. He was shaken. One of the bullets had penetrated the table top and torn through the sleeve of his uniform.

Kleyn and Malan had observed the incident. It happened very quickly, but both of them were thinking the same thing. The white woman's reaction was exactly what the previous night's slaughter had been intended to provoke. Only on a larger scale.

De Beer returned, wiping sweat and blood from his face. "You can't help but sympathise with her," he said. Sibande said nothing.

Kleyn promised to supply all the assistance de Beer thought he needed. They concluded the conversation by assuring one another that the culprits of this terrorist outrage must and would be quickly run to ground. They left the restaurant together and drove in Kleyn's car out of Pinetown. They went north along the N2 and turned towards the sea at a sign for Umhlanga Rocks. Kleyn pulled up at a little seafood restaurant on the oceanfront. They would be undisturbed here. They ordered langoustine and drank mineral water. Malan took off his jacket and hung it up.

"According to my information, de Beer is an outstandingly incompetent detective," he said. "His *kaffir* colleague is supposed to be much brighter. Persistent as well."

"Yes, that's what I've heard," Kleyn said. "The investigation will go around and around in circles until all the relatives have tired of pursuing it."

He put his knife down and wiped his mouth with a napkin.

"Death is never pleasant," he went on. "Nobody causes a bloodbath unless it's really necessary. On the other hand, there are no winners, only losers. Nor are there any victors without sacrifices. I suppose I'm basically a very primitive Darwinist. Survival of the fittest. When a house is on fire, no-one asks where the fire started before putting it out."

"What'll happen to the three men?" Malan said. "I don't remember seeing what was decided."

"Let's take a walk when we've finished eating," Kleyn said with a smile. Malan knew that was the nearest he would get to an answer for the time being.

Over coffee Kleyn started to explain the reason for this meeting with Malan. "As you know, those of us who work undercover for whichever intelligence organisation live by certain unwritten rules and assumptions," he said. "One of them is that we keep an eye on everybody else. The trust we place in our colleagues has to be limited. We all take our own measures to ensure our personal security. We make sure nobody trespasses too far into our territory. We lay a minefield around us, and we do so because everybody else does the same. In this way we strike a balance, and everybody can get on with his job. Unhappily, I find that somebody has been taking an interest in my computer files. Somebody has obviously been given the job of checking me out. That assignment can only have come from very high up."

Malan turned pale. "Have our plans been compromised?"

Kleyn regarded him with eyes as cold as ice. "I am not as careless as that. Nothing in my computer files could reveal the plan. There are no names, nothing. On the other hand, one has to accept that a sufficiently intelligent person could draw conclusions which might point him in the right direction. That makes it serious."

"It will be difficult to find out who it is," Malan said.

"Not at all. I already know who it is."

Malan stared at him in astonishment.

"I started to find my way forward by going backward," Kleyn said. "That's often an excellent way of getting results. I asked myself where the assignment could have come from. It didn't take long to see that there are only two persons who can really be interested in finding out what I'm up to. The President and the Foreign Minister."

Malan wanted to say something.

"Let me go on," Kleyn said. "Think for a moment and you'll see that's obvious. There is a fear of conspiracy in this country, and rightly so. De Klerk has every reason to be afraid of the current of opinion in some parts of the military high command. Nor can he be sure of the loyalty of those in charge of the state intelligence service. There's a lot of uncertainty in the country today. Not much can be taken for granted. That means there's no limit to the amount of information that needs to be collected. There's only one member of the cabinet the President can trust absolutely, and that is Pik Botha. All I needed to do was to go through the feasible candidates for the role of secret messenger to the President. For reasons I don't need to go into, it soon boiled down to a shortlist of one: Pieter van Heerden."

Malan had met him on several occasions. "I take van Heerden to be very intelligent," he said.

"Quite right," Kleyn said. "He's a very dangerous man, an enemy who deserves our respect. Unfortunately, he's not a well man."

Malan raised an eyebrow. "Not well?"

"Some difficulties solve themselves. I happen to know that he's booked into a private hospital in Johannesburg next week for a minor operation. He has prostate problems."

Kleyn took a slurp of coffee.

"He'll never leave that hospital," he said. "I'll take care of that myself. After all, it's me he was trying to get at. They were my computer files he hacked into."

They sat in silence while a black waiter cleared the table.

"I've solved the problem myself," Kleyn said when they were alone again. "But I wanted to tell you about it for one reason, and one reason only. You must also be very careful. In all probability there's someone looking over your shoulder as well."

"It's good that I know," Malan said. "I'll double-check my security procedures."

The waiter reappeared, and Kleyn paid.

"You had a question," Kleyn said. "Let's take a little walk."

They took a path above the beach.

"Tsiki will be ready to fly out within ten days," Kleyn said.

"And Mabasha?"

"Presumably dead by now. I'm expecting Konovalenko to get in touch tonight, tomorrow at the latest."

"We've heard a rumour from Cape Town that there'll be a big meeting there on June 12," Malan said. "I'm investigating to see whether that could be a suitable opportunity."

Kleyn stopped. "That could be an excellent time," he said.

"I'll keep you informed," Malan said.

Kleyn stood looking down to the sea. Malan followed his gaze. Below them was a car upside down in the sand.

"The car has evidently not yet been traced," Kleyn said. "When they find it, they'll discover three black men aged about 25. They were shot and then the car was tipped onto the beach. This was where they were to get their money."

They turned and retraced their steps. Malan did not bother to ask who had carried out the executions. There were some things he would rather not know.

Kleyn avoided the highway back to Pretoria. He preferred to take roads with less traffic through Natal. He was in no hurry, and felt the need to assess how things stood. There was a lot at stake, for himself, for his fellow conspirators, and not least for all the white citizens of South Africa.

Sometimes Kleyn was scared by his own lack of feelings. He knew he was what was often called a fanatic, but he knew of no other life he would rather lead. There were two things, however, that made him unsettled. One was the recurring nightmare he had, in which he found himself trapped in a world populated exclusively by black people. He could no longer speak. What came out of his mouth were words transformed into animal noises. He sounded like a laughing hyena.

The other was that nobody knew how much time they had left. It was not that he wanted to live for ever, but he did want to live long enough to see white South Africans secure their threatened dominion. Then he could die. Not before. He made his way home by way of

Witbank and stopped for dinner at a little restaurant there. By then he had thought through the plan one more time, all the assumptions and all the pitfalls. He felt at ease. Everything would go according to plan. Maybe Malan's June 12 meeting in Cape Town would be the best opportunity.

He turned into the drive leading to his big house on the outskirts of Pretoria just before 11 p.m. His black night porter opened the gate for him. The last thing he thought about before falling asleep was Mabasha. Only with difficulty could he remember what he had looked like.

CHAPTER FOURTEEN

Feelings of uneasiness, of insidious fear, were nothing new to him. Moments of excitement and danger were a natural part of his work in the intelligence service. But he felt more defenceless in the face of his anxiety, now that he was in a hospital bed, waiting to be operated on.

Brenthurst Clinic was situated in the north Johannesburg suburb of Hillbrow. He might have chosen a more expensive alternative, but Brenthurst suited him. It was renowned for its high standards and the level of care was beyond reproach. On the other hand, the private rooms were not at all luxurious. Indeed, the whole building was rather shabby.

Van Heerden was well off without being rich, and he did not like ostentation. On holiday, he made a point of not staying at luxury hotels, which just made him feel surrounded by that special kind of emptiness a certain class of white South Africans seemed to wallow in.

Van Heerden was in a room on the second floor. He heard laughter in the corridor, and then a tea trolley rattle past. He looked out of the window. A solitary pigeon stood guard on the roof next door. Behind it the sky was the dark shade of blue he was so fond of. The brief African dusk would soon be over. His uneasiness increased as darkness gathered.

It was Monday, May 4. The next morning, at 8 a.m., two senior and renowned specialists would perform the straightforward surgery that was supposed to cure the urinary problems he had been having. He was not fearful about the operation. His own doctor had convinced him the operation was routine. He would be discharged in a matter of days, and in another week or so he would have forgotten all about it.

There was something else. It was partly to do with his illness. He was 36 years old, but he suffered from a physical complaint which normally afflicted men in their sixties. He wondered if he were already burned out, if he had aged so prematurely and so dramatically. Working for NIS was demanding; that had been clear to him for a long time. Being the President's special messenger also increased the pressure he had anyway to live with. But he kept himself in good shape, he did not smoke, and he very seldom touched alcohol.

What continually assailed him, and was no doubt an indirect cause of his illness, was the feeling that there was nothing he could do about the state his country was in.

Van Heerden grew up in Kimberley, and had been surrounded since birth by the Afrikaner traditions. His family's neighbours were Afrikaners, as were his schoolfriends and his teachers. His father had worked for de Beers, the company that controlled the production of diamonds in South Africa. His mother had assumed the traditional role of *Boere* housewife, subservient to her husband and dedicated to the task of raising their children and teaching them a fundamentally religious view of the order of things. She devoted all her time and energy to Pieter and his four siblings. Until he was 20 and in his second year at Stellenbosch University, he had never questioned the life he led. He was not tempted to follow in his father's footsteps and devote his life to mining. As he did not think he possessed any special talents and cherished no startling future ambitions, he studied law and found it suited him, even if he did not distinguish himself.

One day he was persuaded by a fellow student to visit a black township not far from Cape Town. Recognising that times, like it or not, were changing, a small number of students were driven by curiosity to visit black suburbs. The radicalism claimed by the few liberal students at Stellenbosch University was active. For the first time these young Afrikaners were forced to see things as they were.

It was a shocking experience for van Heerden. He became aware of the wretched and humiliating circumstances in which the blacks lived. The contrast between the park-like neighbourhoods where the whites lived and the black shanty towns was heart-rending. He became introverted and withdrew from the company of his friends. Looking back long afterwards, it seemed to him it was like the unmasking of a skilful fake. But this was not a painting on a wall with a false signature. The whole of his life so far had been a lie. Even his memories now seemed to him distorted and untrue. He had a black nanny as a child. One of his earliest and most secure childhood memories was the way she lifted him in her strong arms and clutched him to her breast. Now he realised that she must have hated him. That meant it was not only the whites who were living in a false world. The same applied to the blacks who, to survive, were forced to conceal the hatred engendered by the injustice they constantly suffered. And this in a country that had belonged to them. The whole basis on which his life was built, with rights given by God, nature and tradition, had proved to be a morass. His conception of the world, which he had never questioned, was founded on shameful inequity. And he discovered all this in the black township of Langa, situated as far from exclusively white Cape Town as the architects of Apartheid had considered appropriate.

This discovery affected him more deeply than it did most of those he had accompanied. What for him had been a severe trauma was more like a sentimental episode for them. Whereas he thought he could see an impending apocalyptic catastrophe, his friends set about organising collections of cast-off clothing.

He took his final examinations without having come to terms with his experience. Once, when he went home to Kimberley during a holiday, his father had a fit of rage when Pieter told him about his visit to the black township. It dawned on him that his innermost thoughts were like himself – increasingly homeless.

After graduation he was offered a position in the Department of Justice in Pretoria. He accepted it without hesitation. He had proved his worth after a year, and one day was asked whether he would consider working for the intelligence service. By that time he had learned to live with his trauma, as he had been unable to find any way of solving it. His division was reflected in his personality. He could play the part of the right-thinking and convinced Afrikaner who did and said what was expected of him; but deep down, the sense of impending catastrophe was growing stronger. There was no-one he could talk to, and he lived an increasingly solitary life.

His work for NIS had many advantages. Not least was the insight he was able to get into the political process of which the general public had only a vague conception.

When Frederik de Klerk became President and made his public declaration to the effect that Nelson Mandela would be released and that the ANC would no longer be banned, it seemed to him there might yet be a possibility of averting havoc. The shame of Apartheid would never pass; but perhaps there could be a future for South Africa after all?

Van Heerden had immediately held President de Klerk in the highest regard. He knew many people who branded him a traitor, but as far as he was concerned, de Klerk was a saviour. When he was picked to be the President's contact man, he felt proud. A mutual trust rapidly developed. For the first time in his life van Heerden was sure he was doing something significant. By passing on to the President information which was sometimes not intended for his ears, van Heerden was helping those forces bent on creating a new South Africa, a country free of racial oppression.

He thought about that as he lay in bed at the clinic. Not until South Africa had been transformed, with Mandela its first black President, would the malaise within him disappear.

The door opened and Marta, one of the black nurses, came in. "Mr Plitt just called," she said. "He'll be here in about half an hour to give you a lumbar puncture."

Van Heerden looked at her in surprise. "Lumbar puncture? Now?"

"I think it's odd as well," Marta said. "But that's what he said. I was to tell you to lie on your left side right away. Best to do as you're told. The operation's in the morning. Mr Plitt's bound to know what he's doing."

Van Heerden smiled. He had every confidence in his specialist. All the same, he couldn't help thinking it was a strange time to do a lumbar puncture.

Marta helped him to lie as he was supposed to.

"Mr Plitt said you were to lie absolutely still. You shouldn't move at all."

"I always do what the doctors tell me," van Heerden said. "I usually do what you tell me, too, don't I?"

"We don't have any problems with you," Marta said. "I'll see you tomorrow, after the operation. I'm off tonight."

She went out, and van Heerden thought about the bus journey of an hour or more she had ahead of her. He did not know where she lived.

He was almost asleep when he heard the door open. It was dark in the room; only his bedside lamp was on. He could see the doctor's reflection in the window pane as he entered the room.

"Good evening," van Heerden said, without moving.

"Good evening, Pieter van Heerden," he heard a voice reply.

It was not the voice he expected. It took a few seconds before it dawned on him who was standing behind him. He turned over at once.

Kleyn knew the doctors at the Brenthurst Clinic seldom wore white coats when visiting patients. He knew everything he needed to know about the hospital routines. It had been very simple to arrange a situation in which he could pass as a doctor. They regularly traded shifts. They didn't even need to work at the same hospital. Moreover, doctors frequently called on their patients at unusual times. This was especially true before or after an operation. Once he had established when the nursing staff changed shifts, his plan was straightforward. He parked a borrowed van at the front of the hospital, walked through reception and showed the security guard an identity card issued by a transport firm often used by hospitals and laboratories.

"I'm here for a blood sample," he said. "A patient on Ward Nine."

"Do you know your way?" the guard asked him.

"I've been there before," Kleyn said, pressing the lift button. That was true. He had been to the clinic during the morning the previous day, carrying a basket of fruit. He pretended to be visiting a patient on Ward Nine. He knew exactly how to get there.

The corridor was empty. He went straight to the room he knew van Heerden was in. At the far end of the corridor a night nurse was bent over a desk, reading. He opened the door quietly.

When van Heerden turned around in terror, Kleyn already had the silenced pistol in his right hand. In his left hand was a jackal skin that he had brought in a plastic bag attached to his shoulder harness.

Kleyn sometimes liked to introduce a touch of the macabre. In this case, too, the jackal skin would distract the detectives assigned to investigate the murder. An intelligence officer shot in a hospital would cause quite a stir in the Johannesburg homicide department. They would try to establish a link between the murder and the work van Heerden was doing. His link to the President would make it the more imperative to solve the murder. Kleyn had decided to plant a red herring. Black criminals sometimes amused themselves by introducing a ritual element into their crimes. That was especially true in cases of robbery with violence. They were not content with smearing blood on the walls. The killer often left some kind of symbol by the victim's side. A broken branch, or stones arranged in a certain pattern. Or an animal skin.

Kleyn had immediately thought of a jackal. As far as he was concerned, that was the role van Heerden had been playing: exploiting other people's work.

He observed van Heerden's horrified expression.

"The operation's been cancelled," Kleyn said, in a hoarse voice. Then he threw the jackal skin over van Heerden's face and pumped three bullets into his head. A stain spread down the pillow and onto the sheet. Kleyn put the pistol in its holster and buttoned his jacket. He opened the drawer in the bedside table. He took van Heerden's wallet, and left the room. He left the clinic as unobtrusively as he had come. The security guard was busy with a family of visitors when Kleyn came out of the lift and afterwards was unable to give a clear description of the messenger who had come for a blood sample. Not that he was thought to have been the man who had robbed and killed van Heerden.

Robbery with violence was how the police classified the attack, but President de Klerk was not convinced. As far as he was concerned, van Heerden's death had been his last communiqué. There was no longer any doubt about it. The conspiracy was a fact.

A Flock of Sheep in the Fog

CHAPTER FIFTEEN

On Monday, May 4, Inspector Wallander was ready to hand over responsibility for the investigation into Mrs Åkerblom's death to one of his colleagues. It was not because he believed their getting nowhere reflected badly on him as a policeman. It was something quite different: a feeling he had that was getting all the time stronger. It was that he couldn't drive himself to the necessary intensity of effort and concentration any more.

The investigation was completely stalled on Saturday and Sunday. It was the May Day holiday weekend, and people were away or unobtainable. It was practically impossible to get any response from the forensic people in Stockholm. The search there for the man who had shot a young policeman was obviously taking all their resources.

The investigation into Louise Åkerblom's death was wreathed in silence. Björk had been struck down by a severe attack of gallstones on Friday night and rushed to the hospital. Wallander went to see him early on Saturday to receive instructions.

When he got back from the hospital, Wallander sat down with Martinsson and Svedberg in the conference room at the station.

"Today and tomorrow Sweden is closed down," he said. "The results of the tests we're waiting for are not going to be here before Monday. We can use the next two days to go through the material we already have. I also think it would be a good idea for you, Martinsson, to show your face at home and spend some time with your family. Next week might be a bit busy. But let's keep our wits about us for a while this morning. I want us to go through the whole thing just one more time, right from the beginning. And I also want you both to answer me a question."

He paused for a moment before continuing.

"This isn't in accordance with police procedure, I know," he said, "but all through this investigation I've had the feeling there's something funny going on. I can't put it any clearer than that. What I want to know is, have either of you had the same feeling? That we were up against a crime that doesn't fit any of the usual patterns?"

"I've never seen anything quite like this," Martinsson said. "Of course, I don't have as much experience as you, Kurt. But I have to admit I'm baffled by the whole business. First we try to catch somebody who's carried out the horrific murder of a woman. The deeper we dig, the harder it is to understand why she's been murdered. In the end we come back to the feeling that her death is just an incident on the periphery of something quite other, something bigger. I didn't get much sleep this last week. That's unusual for me."

Wallander nodded and turned to Svedberg.

"What can I say?" he said, scratching his bald head. "Martinsson's already said it, better than I could put it. When I got home last night I made a list: *dead woman, well, black finger, blown-up house, radio transmitter, pistol, South Africa.* Then I sat staring at that list for an hour, as if it were a rebus. There just don't seem to be any connections and contexts in this investigation. I've never had such a feeling of trying to find my way in the pitch dark as I have in this case."

"That's what I wanted to hear," Wallander said. "It can't be insignificant that we all feel the same. Nevertheless, let's see if we can penetrate a bit of this darkness Svedberg describes."

For nearly three hours they went through the investigation. They agreed that they hadn't made any obvious mistakes, or overlooked anything. But nor had they found any new ways forward.

"The only real clue we have is a black finger," Wallander said, in summary. "We can be pretty sure the man who lost his finger was not alone, assuming he's the one who did it. The farmhouse was rented by Alfred Olsson to an African. We know that for sure. But we've no idea who this man is who calls himself Nordström and paid 10,000 kronor up front. Nor do we know what the house was used for. When it comes to the connection between these people and Louise Åkerblom or the house that was blown up, the radio transmitter, and the pistol, we have only theories we can't substantiate. There's nothing so dangerous as an investigation that invites guessing rather than logical thinking. The theory that seems most likely just now is that Louise Åkerblom happened to see something someone didn't want her to see. But what kind of people turn that into a reason for cold-blooded murder?"

They sat in silence, mulling over what he had said. The door opened and a cleaning lady peeked in.

"Not now," Wallander said.

She shut the door again.

"I think I'll spend the day going through the tip-offs we've had," Svedberg said. "If I need help, I'll let you know. I'm hardly going to have time for anything else."

"It might be as well to sort out Stig Gustafson once and for all," Martinsson said. "I can start by checking his alibi, in so far as that's possible on a day like today. If necessary I'll drive to Malmö. But first I'll try and track down that flower seller Forsgård he claims to have met in the toilets."

"This is a murder investigation," Wallander said. "Track these people down even if they're in their weekend cottages trying to get some peace and quiet."

They agreed to meet again at 5 p.m. to see where they were. Wallander got some coffee, went to his office and called Nyberg at home.

"You'll have my report on Monday," Nyberg said. "But you already know the most important parts."

"I still don't know why the house burned down. I don't know the cause of the fire."

"Maybe you ought to talk to the chief fire officer about that," Nyberg said. "He might have a good explanation. We're not ready yet."

"I thought we were working together," Wallander said, irritated. "Us and the fire service. But maybe there've been some new instructions I don't know about."

"It's just that we don't have an obvious explanation," Nyberg said.

"What do you think, then? What does the fire service think? What does Peter Edler think?"

"The explosion seems to have been so powerful that there's nothing left of the detonator. We've discussed the possibility of a series of explosions."

"No," Wallander said. "There was only one bang."

"I don't mean it quite like that," Nyberg said patiently. "You can set off ten explosions within a second if you're smart enough. We'd be talking about a chain with a tenth-of-a-second delay between each charge. But that increases the effect enormously. It has to do with the changed air pressure."

Wallander thought for a moment. "We would not be talking about a bunch of amateurs in that case?" he said.

"Not by any means."

"Could there be any other cause of the fire?"

"Hardly."

Wallander glanced at his papers before going on. "Can you say anything else about the radio transmitter?" he said. "There's talk that it was made in Russia."

"That's not just talk," Nyberg said. "I've had confirmation. I had help from the military."

"What do you make of that?"

"It's a mystery. The army is interested to know how it got here."

Wallander pressed ahead. "The pistol butt?"

"Nothing new on that."

"Do you have anything else?"

"Not really. The report won't spring any surprises."

Wallander brought the call to a close. Then he did something he'd made up his mind to do during that morning's meeting. He dialled the number of police headquarters in Stockholm and asked to speak with Inspector Lovén. Wallander had met him the previous year, while investigating the case of a raft carrying two bodies that was washed up at Mossby Beach. They had only worked together for a few days, but Wallander remembered him as a good detective.

"Inspector Lovén isn't available at the moment," the operator said.

"This is Inspector Wallander, Ystad. I have a message for him which has to do with the policeman who was killed."

"I'll see if I can find Inspector Lovén."

"It's urgent," Wallander said, but the line was cut.

It took Lovén twelve minutes to call back. "Wallander," he said. "I thought of you the other day, when I read about the murder of that woman. How's it going?"

"Slowly," Wallander said. "How about you?"

"We'll get him," Lovén said. "We always get the ones who kill one of ours in the end. You had something to tell us in that connection?"

"Could be," Wallander said. "It's just that the woman down here was shot through the head. Like Tengblad. I think it would be a good idea to compare the bullets."

"Right," Lovén said. "Don't forget, this fellow was shooting through a windscreen. Must have been hard to make out a face on the other side. And it's one hell of a shot if you can get somebody in the middle of the forehead when they're in a moving car. But I agree with you. We ought to make the comparison."

"Do you have a description?" Wallander said.

The reply came without a pause. "He stole a car from a young couple after the murder. Unfortunately they were so scared they've only been able to give us very muddled accounts."

"They didn't happen to hear him speak, did they?"

"That was the only thing they agreed on," Lovén said. "He had some sort of a foreign accent."

Wallander could feel his excitement growing. He told Lovén about his conversation with Alfred Olsson and about the man who had paid 10,000 kronor to rent an empty farmhouse in the middle of nowhere in Skåne. And about the black man's finger.

"We'll have to look into this," Lovén said. "Even if it does sound odd."

"The whole thing is extremely odd," Wallander said. "I could drive up to Stockholm on Monday. I believe that's where my black man is."

"Maybe he was mixed up in the tear gas attack on a discotheque."

Wallander vaguely remembered seeing something about that in the *Ystad Allehande*.

"What attack was that?"

"Somebody threw some tear gas grenades into a club in Söder," Lovén said. "A discotheque with lots of Africans among the clientele. We've never had any trouble there before. But we have now. Somebody fired a few shots as well."

"Take good care of those bullets," Wallander said. "Let's take a close look at them too."

"You think there's only one gun in this country?"

"No. But I'm looking for links."

"I'll set things in motion here," Lovén said. "Thanks for calling. I'll tell the people running the investigation you'll be here on Monday."

*

179

They gathered again at 5 p.m., and the meeting was very short. Martinsson had confirmed so much of Gustafson's alibi that he was well on the way to being excluded from the investigation. Wallander was doubtful, without being sure why. "Let's not let him go altogether," he said. "We'll go through all the evidence concerning him one more time."

Martinsson stared at him in surprise. "What exactly do you expect to find?"

Wallander shrugged. "I don't know. I'm just worried about letting him go too soon."

Martinsson was about to protest, but checked himself. He had great respect for Wallander's intuition.

Svedberg had worked his way through the stack of tip-offs the police had received so far. There was nothing that obviously threw new light on either Mrs Åkerblom's death or the blown-up farmhouse.

"You'd think somebody would have noticed an African missing a finger," Wallander said.

"Maybe he doesn't exist," Martinsson said.

"We've got the finger," Wallander said.

They agreed that Wallander should go to Stockholm. There could be a link, no matter how unlikely it seemed, between the murders of Louise Åkerblom and Tengblad.

They concluded the meeting by listing the heirs to the farmhouse.

"They can wait," Wallander said afterwards. "There's not a lot here that looks as if it will get us any further."

He sent Svedberg and Martinsson home and stayed behind in his office. He called Åkeson, the prosecutor, at home to give him a summary of where they stood.

"It's not good if we can't solve this quickly," Åkeson said.

They decided to meet first thing on Monday morning. Wallander could tell that Åkeson was afraid of being accused later of allowing a carelessly conducted investigation to go ahead. He switched off his desk lamp, and left the station. He drove down the long incline and turned into the hospital car park.

Björk was feeling better and expected to be discharged on Monday. Wallander gave him a report, and Björk too thought Wallander ought to go to Stockholm.

"This used to be a quiet district," he said as Wallander was getting ready to leave. "Nothing much used to happen here to attract attention. That's all changed."

"It's not just here," Wallander said. "You're remembering a whole different age."

"I'm getting old," Björk sighed.

"You're not the only one."

The words were still echoing in his ears as he left the hospital. It was nearly 6.30 p.m., and he was hungry. He did not feel like cooking at home, and he decided to eat out. He went home, took a shower, and changed. Then he called his daughter Linda in Stockholm. He let the phone ring for quite some time before he gave up. He went down to the basement and booked himself a time in the laundry room. Then he walked in to the town centre. The wind had dropped, but it was chilly.

Getting old, he thought to himself. I'm only 44 and I'm already feeling worn out.

His train of thought suddenly angered him. It was up to him and nobody else to decide if he was getting old before his time. He could not blame his work, nor his divorce – that was already five years ago. The only question was: how would he be able to change things?

He came to the square and wondered where he should eat. In a moment of extravagance, he decided on the Continental. He paused on Hamngatan to look at the display in the lamp shop, then continued to the hotel. He nodded to the girl at the front desk, recalling that she had been in the same class as his daughter.

The dining room was almost empty, and he nearly changed his mind. Sitting all by himself in a deserted dining room seemed like too much solitude. But he sat down anyway. He couldn't be bothered to start looking for somewhere to eat now.

I'll turn over a new leaf tomorrow, he thought, grimacing. He always put off the most important matters affecting his own life. When he was at work, on the other hand, he insisted on precisely the opposite approach. Always do the most important things first. He had a split personality.

He was studying the menu when a young waiter came over to his table and asked what he would like to drink. Wallander had an idea he recognised the boy, but he could not quite place him.

"Whisky," he said. "No ice. But a glass of water as well."

He emptied the glass at once, and immediately ordered another. He did not often drink to get drunk. But tonight he was not going to hold back.

When he got his third whisky, he remembered who the waiter was. A few years earlier Wallander had questioned him about a series of robberies and car thefts. He was later arrested and convicted.

So things have turned out all right for him, at least, he thought. And I'm not going to say anything. Maybe you could say things have gone better for him than they have for me?

He could feel the effects of the spirits already.

He drank a bottle of wine with his dinner, and two brandies with his coffee.

It was 10.30 p.m. when he left the restaurant. He was pretty drunk by then, but he had no intention of going home to lie down.

He crossed over to the taxi stand opposite the bus station and took a taxi to the only dance club in town. It was surprisingly full, and he had some difficulty finding a table near the bar. He ordered a whisky and went out on the dance floor. He was not a bad dancer, and always performed with a certain measure of self-confidence. Music from the Swedish hit parade made him maudlin. He generally fell in love with every woman he danced with. He always planned to take them back to his apartment afterwards. But the prospect was scuppered on this occasion when he began to feel queasy, barely managing to get outside before throwing up. He did not go back in, but staggered homewards instead. When he got back to his apartment, he stripped and stood naked in front of the hall mirror.

"Kurt Wallander," he said aloud. "This is your life."

Then he decided to call Baiba Liepa in Riga. It was 2 a.m. He dialled a wrong number first, and though he knew he shouldn't, he tried again and let it ring until eventually she answered.

And then he had no idea what to say. He could not find the English words he needed. He had obviously woken her up, and she had been frightened by the telephone ringing in the middle of the night.

He told her he loved her. She did not know what he meant at first. Once it had dawned on her, she also realised he was drunk, and Wallander knew the whole thing was a terrible mistake. He apologised for disturbing her and went straight into the kitchen and took a half bottle of vodka from the refrigerator. He still felt sick, but he forced the drink down.

He woke at dawn on the sofa in the living room. He had a king-size hangover. What he regretted most was the call to Baiba Liepa. He groaned at the thought of it, staggered into the bedroom, and sank into his bed. He forced his mind to go blank. It was late in the afternoon before he got up and made coffee. He sat in front of the television and watched one programme after another. He did not bother to call his father, nor did he try again to contact his daughter. At about 7 p.m. he heated up some fish *au gratin*, which was all he had in the freezer. Then he returned to the television. He tried to avoid thinking about last night's telephone call.

At 11 p.m. he took a sleeping pill and pulled the covers over his head. Everything will be better tomorrow, he thought. I'll call her again and explain everything. Or maybe I'll write a letter. Or something.

Monday, May 4, turned out to be very different from the day Wallander had anticipated. Everything seemed to happen all at once. He had just arrived at his office shortly after 7.30 p.m. when the telephone rang. It was Lovén in Stockholm.

"There's a word going around town," he said. "Talk of a contract on an African. He can be recognised first and foremost by the bandage he has on his left hand."

It was a second before it dawned on Wallander what kind of a contract Lovén was talking about.

"Oh, shit," he said.

"I thought that's what you would say," Lovén said. "If you can tell me when you'll arrive, we can drive out and pick you up."

"I don't know yet," Wallander said. "But it won't be before this afternoon. Björk, if you remember who that is, has gallstones. I have to sort things out here first. But I'll call as soon as I get things straightened out."

"We'll be waiting," Lovén said.

Wallander had just replaced the receiver when the telephone rang again. At the same time, Martinsson marched into the room waving a sheet of paper in his excitement. Wallander pointed to a chair, and answered the phone.

It was Högberg, the pathologist in Malmö, who had completed the preliminary autopsy on Louise Åkerblom's body. Wallander had dealt with him before, and knew the man was thorough. He pulled a notepad towards him and gestured to Martinsson to give him a pen.

"There is no apparent trace of rape," Högberg said. "Unless the attacker used a condom, and it all took place in peaceful fashion. Nor does she have any injuries to suggest there was any other kind of violence. Just the abrasions she must have suffered in the well. I couldn't find any sign of her having had handcuffs either on her wrists or on her ankles. All that happened to her is that she was shot."

"I need the bullet as soon as possible," Wallander said.

"You'll get it this morning, but it will be some time before you get the comprehensive report, you understand."

"Thank you for your efforts," Wallander said.

He hung up and turned to Martinsson. "Louise Åkerblom was not raped. So no sexual motives."

"So now we know," Martinsson said. "We also know the black finger is the index finger of a man's left hand. The man is probably about 30. It's all here in this fax from Stockholm. You wonder how can they be so precise."

"I've no idea," Wallander said. "But the more we know, the better. If Svedberg is around, I think we'd better have a meeting right away. I'm going to Stockholm this afternoon. I told Björk I'd hold a press conference at 2 p.m. You and Svedberg had better take care of that."

"Svedberg will be pleased when he hears that," Martinsson said. "Are you sure you can't travel a little later?"

"Positive," Wallander said, getting to his feet.

"I hear our colleagues in Malmö have brought Morell in," Martinsson said when they were out in the corridor.

Wallander stared at him. "Who?" he said.

"Morell. The fence in Malmö. The one with the water pumps."

"Oh, him," Wallander said absentmindedly. "That one."

He went out into reception and asked Ebba to book him a flight at about 3 p.m. He also asked her to reserve a room at the Central Hotel on Vasagatan, which wasn't too expensive. Then he went back to his office and reached for the receiver, intending to call his father, but had second thoughts. He did not want to risk getting into a bad mood. He would need all his powers of concentration today. Then he had a brain-wave. He would ask Martinsson to call Löderup later in the day, pass on messages to his father, and explain that he had been forced to go to Stockholm at short notice. That might persuade the old man that Wallander was up to his neck in important business.

The thought cheered him up. It could be a useful ploy for the future.

At 3.55 p.m. Wallander landed at Arlanda, where it was drizzling slightly. He passed through the hangar-like terminal and saw Lovén waiting for him outside the revolving doors.

Wallander had a headache. It had been a very intense day. He had spent nearly two hours with the prosecutor. Åkeson had many questions and querulous observations. Wallander wondered how to explain to a prosecutor that police officers were occasionally bound to rely on instinct when priorities had to be set. Åkeson was critical of the reports he had received so far. By the end of the meeting the atmosphere was tense between them. Before Peters drove Wallander to Sturup Airport, he had managed to stop at his apartment and pack some clothes into a bag. That was when he finally managed to reach Linda on the telephone. She was pleased to hear he was coming, he could hear that. They agreed he would call her that night, no matter how late it was.

Only when the plane had taken off did he realise how hungry he was. The SAS sandwiches were the first food to pass his lips that day.

As they drove to the police station at Kungsholmen, Wallander learned what Lovén could tell him about the hunt for Tengblad's killer. They obviously had no useful clues to follow up, and he could see the search was characterised by frustration. Lovén also managed to give him a summary of what had happened at the discotheque. It seemed to be either a heavy-handed prank or an act of revenge. No definite clues here, either. Wallander asked about the contract. As far as he was concerned, this was something new and frightening. Something that had only surfaced in the last few years, and then only in the three largest cities in the country. But before long it would be happening in his own back yard. Contracts were made between a customer and a professional killer, with the aim of murdering people. Pure and simple, a business deal: the ultimate proof that the brutalisation of society had reached unfathomable depths.

"We have people out there trying to get a line on what's actually at the bottom of this," Lovén said as they passed the northern cemetery on the way into Stockholm.

"I can't work it out," Wallander said. "It's like it was last year, when that raft came ashore. Nothing added up then, either."

"We'll have to hope our forensic people can come up with something," Lovén said. "They might be able to make something of the bullets." Wallander tapped his jacket pocket. He had with him the bullet that had killed Louise Åkerblom.

They drove into the underground garage and then took the lift straight up to headquarters, where the hunt for Tengblad's killer was being organised.

As Wallander entered the room, he was struck by the number of officers present. Fifteen or more were staring at him, and he thought about how different it was from Ystad.

Lovén introduced him, and Wallander took the chorus of mumbles as a greeting. A short, balding man in his fifties introduced himself as Stenberg, the officer in charge of the investigation.

Wallander suddenly felt nervous and badly prepared. Perhaps they might not understand his Scanian dialect. Nevertheless, he sat at the table and very concisely talked them through his investigation. He had to field a lot of questions, and it was obvious he was dealing with experienced detectives who were very quick to get to the heart of a case, locate the weak points, and plan the way forward.

The meeting lasted for more than two hours. When everyone was obviously beginning to run out of steam and Wallander had to ask for some aspirin, Stenberg gave a summary.

"We need a rapid response regarding the results of the ammunition analysis," he said. "If we can establish a link between the weapons used, then, if nothing else, we've succeeded in muddying the waters a bit more." One or two of the officers managed a smile, but most of them just sat staring into space.

It was nearly 8 p.m. by the time Wallander left the Kungsholmen police station. Lovén drove him to his hotel.

"Will you be OK?" Lovén said, as he dropped Wallander off.

"I have a daughter here in town," Wallander replied. "By the way, what's the name of that disco where they threw the tear gas grenades?"

"Aurora," Lovén said. "But I hardly think it's the sort of place for you."

"I'm sure it isn't," Wallander said.

Lovén drove off. Wallander picked up his key and resisted the temptation to look for a bar close to the hotel. The memory of Saturday night in Ystad was still all too raw. He took the lift to his room, showered, and changed his shirt. After an hour's catnap, he looked up the address of the Aurora in the telephone book. He left the hotel at 8.45 p.m. He asked himself several times whether he should call Linda before going out. In the end, he decided that his excursion to the Aurora should not take too long. Besides, Linda was a night owl. He crossed over towards Central Station, found a taxi and gave an address in the Söder district. Wallander gazed thoughtfully at the city as they drove through it. Somewhere out there was his daughter Linda, and somewhere else his sister Kristina. Hidden among all those houses and people was presumably also an African missing the index finger of his left hand.

He suddenly felt uneasy. It was as if he expected something to happen any minute. Something he'd better start worrying about right now. Louise Åkerblom's smiling face flashed across his mind's eye. What had she stumbled upon? he wondered. Had she time to realise she was going to die?

Steps led down from ground level to a black-painted iron door. Above it was a filthy red neon sign. Several of the letters had gone out. Wallander was moved to wonder why he had chosen to look at the place into which somebody had thrown tear gas grenades a couple of days ago. But he was to such an extent groping in the dark, he couldn't afford not to follow up every slightest chance of finding a black man with a bandaged hand. He went down the stairs, pushed open the door, and entered a dark room where at first he had difficulty seeing anything at all. He could barely hear the music coming from a loudspeaker attached to the ceiling. The room was full of smoke, and he thought at first he was the only one there. Then he made out some shadows in a corner with the whites of their eyes gleaming, and a bar counter slightly more illuminated than the rest of the room. When he was used to the light, he went to the bar and ordered a beer.

The barman had a shaven head. "We can manage on our own, thank you," he said. Wallander did not know what he was talking about.

"We can supply all the security cover we need ourselves," the man said.

"How do you know I'm a policeman?" he asked, wishing he hadn't even as the words crossed his lips.

"Trade secret," the barman said.

Wallander was starting to get angry. The man's arrogant self-assurance irritated him. "I have a few questions," he said. "Since you already know I'm a police officer, I don't need to show you my ID."

"I rarely answer questions," the barman said.

"You will this time," Wallander said. "God help you if you don't."

The man stared at Wallander in astonishment. "I might," he said.

"You get a lot of Africans in here," Wallander said.

"They just love this joint."

"I'm looking for a black man about 30, and there's something very special about him."

"Such as?"

"He's missing the index finger of his left hand."

Wallander did not expect the reaction he got. The barman burst out laughing.

"What's so funny about that?"

"You're the second one in two nights," the barman said. "There was a guy here last night wondering if I'd seen an African with his left hand in a bandage."

Wallander thought for a moment before going on. "What did you tell him?"

"No."

"No?"

"I ain't seen nobody missing a finger."

"Who was asking?"

"Never seen him before," he said, starting to wipe a glass.

Wallander suspected the man was lying. "I'll ask you one more time," he said. "But only once."

"I have nothing more to say."

"Who was doing the asking?"

"Like I said. No idea."

"Did he speak Swedish?"

"Sort of."

"What do you mean by that?"

"That he didn't sound like you and me."

Now we're getting somewhere, thought Wallander. "What did he look like?"

"Don't remember."

"There'll be hell to pay if you don't give me a straight answer."

"He looked kinda ordinary. Black jacket. Blond hair."

Wallander had the feeling the man was scared. "Nobody can hear us," he said. "I promise you I'll never repeat what you tell me."

"His name might have been Konovalenko," the man said. "The beer's on the house if you get out right now."

"Konovalenko?" Wallander said. "Are you sure of that?"

"How the hell can you be sure of anything in this world?" the barman said. "But one thing I am absolutely sure of: someone had hit him on the side of the head with a baseball bat." And that was as much as he would say.

Wallander left and managed to flag down a taxi right away. He sank into the back seat, and gave the name of his hotel.

When he got to his room, he reached for the phone to call Linda. Then he let it be. He would call her early tomorrow. He lay in bed for a long time, wide awake. Konovalenko. A name. Would it put him on the right track? He turned over in his mind everything that had happened since the morning Robert Åkerblom first came to his office. It was dawn before he fell asleep.

CHAPTER SIXTEEN

When Wallander arrived at the police station the next morning, he was told Lovén was already in a meeting with the team investigating Tengblad's killer. He got himself coffee, went to Lovén's office, and called Ystad.

After a brief pause Martinsson answered. "What's new?" he said.

"I'm focusing on a man who might be Russian and whose name could be Konovalenko," Wallander said.

"I hope you haven't found yourself another Balt," Martinsson said.

"We don't know if Konovalenko really is his name," Wallander said. "Or indeed if he is Russian. He may be Swedish."

"Alfred Olsson told us that the man who rented the house had a foreign accent," Martinsson said.

"Exactly what I was thinking," Wallander said. "But I doubt whether that was Konovalenko."

"Why so?"

"Just a hunch. The investigation is riddled with hunches. I don't like it at all. He also said that the man who rented the room was very fat. That doesn't fit with what we know of the man who shot Tengblad."

"Where does this African with the missing finger fit in?"

Wallander gave him a rapid rundown on his visit to the Aurora.

"You could be onto something," Martinsson said. "You'll be staying on in Stockholm?"

"I have to. One more day. All quiet in Ystad?"

"Åkerblom has asked through Pastor Tureson when he can bury his wife."

"There's nothing to stop him, is there?"

"Björk said I should talk to you."

"OK, now you have. What's the weather like?"

"As it should be."

"Meaning what?"

"It's April. It changes by the minute."

"Could you call my father again and tell him I'm still in Stockholm?"

"The last time he invited me to go and see him, but I just didn't have time."

"Can you do it?"

"Right away."

Wallander then dialled his daughter's number. He could tell that she was half asleep when she answered.

"You were supposed to call last night," she said.

"I had to work until very late," Wallander said.

"I can see you this morning."

"I'm afraid that's not possible. I'm going to be extremely busy for the next few hours."

"Maybe you'd rather not see me at all?"

"You know that's not true. I'll call you later."

Wallander hung up abruptly as Lovén stomped into the office. He knew he had offended his daughter. Why didn't he want Lovén to hear he was talking with Linda? He didn't know himself.

"You look like shit," Lovén said. "Did you get any sleep at all last night?"

"Maybe I slept too long," Wallander said evasively. "That does you in too. How's it going?"

"No breakthrough, but we're getting there."

"I have a question," Wallander said, deciding he would not yet disclose his visit to the Aurora. "They've had an anonymous call in Ystad to say that a Russian whose name could be Konovalenko might be mixed up in this police murder."

Lovén frowned. "Is that something we should take seriously?"

"The informant apparently sounded as though he knew what he was talking about."

Lovén thought for a while. "It's true that we have a lot of trouble with Russian criminal elements who are settling in Sweden. And it's likely to get worse over the next few years, and for that reason we have been doing some digging around the problem." He ferreted among some files in a bookcase before he found the one he was looking for. "We have a guy called Rykoff," he said. "Vladimir Rykoff. He lives out at Hallunda. If there's anybody by the name of Konovalenko in this town, he ought to know."

"Why?"

"He's said to be extremely well informed about what goes on in that particular circle of immigrants. We could drive out and say hello." Lovén handed Wallander the file. "Read through this," he said. "It'll tell you as much as we know."

"I can go and see him myself," Wallander said. "We don't both need to go."

Lovén shrugged. "I'd be glad not to go," he said. "Heaven knows, we have plenty more leads to follow up in the Tengblad case, even if there is no sign yet of a crucial lead. By the way, forensic thinks that your woman in Skåne was shot by the same weapon. They can't be 100% certain, of course, but more than likely it was the same weapon. Then again, we can't know if it was the same killer."

It was nearly 1 p.m. by the time Wallander had found his way to Hallunda. He stopped at a motel on the way and had lunch while reading through the material Lovén had given him about Vladimir Rykoff. When he located the apartment building, he paused for a while and studied the neighbourhood. It struck him that hardly any of the people in the streets were speaking Swedish.

This is where the future is, he thought. A kid growing up here, and maybe becoming a policeman, will have an experience of life very different from my own.

He found the name Rykoff in the entranceway and went up in the lift. A woman opened the door. Wallander could see at once that she was on her guard even before he had said who he was. He showed her his police ID.

"Rykoff," he said. "I have a few questions for him."

"What about?" She was foreign, probably from the Eastern bloc.

"That's a matter for me and him."

"He's my husband."

"Is he at home?"

"I'll get him for you."

As the woman disappeared through a door that he assumed led into the bedroom, he took a look around. The apartment was expensively furnished. Even so, he had the feeling everything was temporary. As if whoever lived there was ready to pack up at a moment's notice and move on.

The door opened and Vladimir Rykoff came into the living room. He was wearing a dressing gown that looked pretty expensive to Wallander. His hair was a mess. Wallander assumed he had been asleep.

Rykoff too was on his guard. Wallander realised that he was on the brink of a break in the investigation that had started almost two weeks ago when Robert Åkerblom came to his office and reported his wife missing. An investigation that had become bogged down in a maze of confusing tracks, criss-crossing without providing any shape he could come to grips with.

He'd had a similar feeling in previous investigations. The sense of being on the verge of a breakthrough, and often he had turned out to be right.

"I apologise for disturbing you," he said, "but I have some questions I'd like to ask you."

"What about?"

Rykoff had not invited him to sit down. His tone was brusque and dismissive. Wallander decided to take the bull by the horns. He settled in a chair and gestured to Rykoff and his wife to do the same.

"According to my information you came here as an Iranian refugee," Wallander said. "You were granted Swedish citizenship in the 1970s. The name Vladimir Rykoff doesn't sound especially Iranian."

"My name is my own business."

Wallander watched Rykoff's face intently. "Of course," he said. "But in certain circumstances the case for granting citizenship in this country can be re-examined. If, for example, it turns out that it was based on false information."

"Are you threatening me?"

"Not at all. What is your work?"

"I run a travel agency."

"Name?"

"Rykoff's Travel Service."

"Which countries do you organise trips to?"

"It varies."

"Give me some examples."

"Poland."

"And?"

"Czechoslovakia."

"Go on!"

"Shit! What is this all about?"

"Your agency is registered as an independent business with the local authority, but according to the tax office you have made no declarations for the last two years. As I naturally assume that you are not trying to evade taxes, I have to conclude that your business hasn't been operating these last years."

Rykoff stared at him, dumbstruck.

"We're living on the profits from the good years," said his wife all of a sudden. "There's no law that says you have to keep working every year."

"Of course there isn't," said Wallander. "Most people do, all the same, for whatever reason."

The woman lit a cigarette. She was nervous. Her husband stared at her in disapproval, at which very deliberately she got up to open a window. It was stuck, and Wallander was about to help her when she finally managed it.

"I have a lawyer who takes care of everything concerning the travel agency," Rykoff said. He was beginning to look agitated. Wallander wondered if that was due to anger or to anxiety.

"Let's be frank," Wallander said. "You have no more roots in Iran than I have. You come from Russia. Probably it would be impossible to strip you of Swedish citizenship, and in any case, that's not why I'm here. I am here because you are Russian, Rykoff, and you know what's going on in the Russian community here – not least among your fellow countrymen who are on the wrong side of the law. As you know, a policeman was shot here in Stockholm. That's the stupidest thing a man can do. We get angry in a very special way, if you know what I mean."

Rykoff seemed to have recovered his composure, but Wallander could see that the wife was still uneasy, although she was trying to hide it. She kept looking at the wall behind him.

He had seen a clock hanging there. Something's supposed to happen, he thought. And they don't want me here when it does.

"I'm looking for a man called Konovalenko," Wallander said calmly. "Do you know anyone of that name?"

"No," Rykoff said. "I know no-one of that name."

At that moment, three things became clear to Wallander. First, that Konovalenko existed. Second, that Rykoff knew exactly who he was. And third, that he was not at all happy that the police should be asking after him.

Wallander had glanced at Rykoff's wife as he put the question. The sudden twitch in her eye had given him the answer.

"Are you so sure? I thought Konovalenko was quite a common name."

"I don't know any Konovalenko." He turned to his wife. "We don't know anybody of that name, do we?"

She shook her head, saying nothing.

Oh yes, Wallander thought. You know Konovalenko all right, and we're going to get to him through you.

"That's a pity," Wallander said.

Rykoff stared at him in surprise. "Was that all you wanted to know?"

"For the time being, yes," Wallander said. "But I've no doubt you'll be hearing from us again. We won't give up until we've nailed whoever shot that policeman."

"I know nothing about that," Rykoff said. "I think like everybody else, of course, it's very sad when a young policeman gets killed."

"Indeed it is," Wallander said, getting to his feet. "There was just one other thing: you might have read in the newspapers about a woman who was murdered in the south of Sweden a couple of weeks ago? Maybe you saw something about it on TV. We believe that this Konovalenko was involved in that, too."

Wallander noticed something about Rykoff that did not register right away.

Then he got it: the man was totally expressionless. It was the question he had been expecting. Wallander started prowling around the room to conceal his reaction as his pulse quickened.

"Do you mind if I take a look around?" he said.

"As you wish," Rykoff said. "Tania, open all the doors for our visitor."

Wallander looked into every room. But his attention was focused on Rykoff. Lovén did not know how right he was. We have a lead in this apartment in Hallunda.

He was surprised at how calm he felt. He ought to have left the apartment right away, called Lovén, and suggested a full-scale search. The Rykoffs would have been subjected to interrogation, and the police would not have relaxed until they had admitted the existence of Konovalenko, and with luck also revealed where he could be found.

It was when he looked into the small room he assumed was for visitors that something seemed to catch his attention, although he could not say what it was. There was nothing striking about the room. A bed, a desk, a Windsor-style chair, and blue curtains. A few ornaments and books in a bookcase. Wallander did his best to identify what it was he had seen without having seen it. He memorised the details, then turned on his heel.

"Time to leave you in peace," he said.

"We have nothing to hide from the police," Rykoff said.

"Then you have nothing to worry about," Wallander said.

He drove back to the centre. Now we'll pounce, he thought. I'll tell Lovén and his boys this remarkable story, and we'll induce Rykoff or his wife to spill the beans.

But now we will get them, he was sure of it.

Konovalenko had very nearly missed Tania's signal. When he parked in front of the apartment block in Hallunda, he glanced up at the façade as usual. They had agreed that Tania would leave a window open if it was dangerous for any reason for him to come up. The window was shut. As he was on the way to the lift, he remembered the carrier bag with the two bottles of vodka in the car. He went back to fetch them, and from pure habit looked up again at the façade. The window was open. He got back into the car and waited.

When Wallander appeared at the entranceway, he knew immediately that this was the policeman Tania had warned him about. She confirmed his suspicions later on. He was called Wallander, and was a detective inspector. She had also noted from his ID that he came from Ystad.

"Why was he here?" Konovalenko said.

"He wanted to know if I knew anybody called Konovalenko," Rykoff said.

"Good," Konovalenko said.

Tania and Rykoff stared blankly at him.

"Of course it's good," Konovalenko said. "Who could possibly have told him about me? If you haven't? There's only one possibility: Mabasha. Through this policeman we can get to Mabasha."

Then he asked Tania for some glasses. They drank vodka.

Silently Konovalenko toasted the detective from Ystad. He was very pleased with himself.

Wallander went straight back to his hotel after the excursion to Hallunda. The first thing he did was to call his daughter.

"Are you free?" he said.

"Now? I thought you were working."

"I have an hour or two off. If you can make it."

"Where do you want us to meet? You don't know Stockholm at all."

"I know where the Central Station is."

"Why don't we meet there, then? In the middle of the big hall? In 45 minutes?"

"Sounds good."

Wallander went down to reception.

"I'm incommunicado for the rest of the afternoon," he said. "Whoever comes looking for me, whether in person or by telephone, gets the same message. I'm on important business and can't be contacted."

"Until when?" asked the receptionist.

"Until I tell you otherwise," Wallander said.

He crossed the road and walked to the Central Station. When Linda came into the big hall, he hardly recognised her. She had dyed her hair and cut it. She was also heavily made up. She was wearing black overalls and a bright red raincoat. Boots with high heels. Wallander saw how several men turned to look at her, and he felt angry and embarrassed. This was his daughter. But the lady who turned up was a self-assured young woman. No sign of the shyness so much a part of her in the old days. He gave her a hug, but felt there was something about it that wasn't quite right.

She said she was hungry. It had started raining, and they ran to a café on Vasagatan, across from the main post office. He watched her eat. He shook his head when she asked if he wanted anything.

"Mama was here last week," she announced in between chews. "She wanted to show off her new man. Have you met him?"

"We haven't spoken for more than six months," Wallander said.

"I don't think I like him," she said. "In fact, I felt that he was more interested in me than he was in Mama."

"Really?"

"He imports machine tools from France, but he went on and on about golf. Did you know Mama had taken up golf?"

"No," Wallander said, taken aback. "I didn't know that."

She stared at him for a moment. "It's not right that you don't know what she's up to," she said. "I mean, she is the most important woman in your life to date. She knows all about you. She knows about that woman in Latvia, for instance."

Wallander was surprised. He had never mentioned Baiba Liepa to his ex-wife.

"How does she know about her?"

"Somebody must have told her."

"Who?"

"Does it matter?"

"I just wondered."

She changed the subject. "What are you doing here in Stockholm?" she asked. "It isn't only to see me."

He recounted the case, from the day ten days ago when his father had announced he was going to get married, and Robert Åkerblom reported that his wife was missing. She listened attentively, and for the very first time he had the impression his daughter was a grown-up. A person who undoubtedly had much more experience in certain fields than he had himself.

"I've been missing somebody to talk to," he said when he'd finished. "If only Rydberg were still alive. Do you remember him?"

"Was he the one who always seemed so miserable?"

"That's the one. He could appear strict as well."

"I remember him. I hoped you'd never be like him."

Now it was his turn to change the subject. "What do you know about South Africa?"

"Not a lot. Just that the blacks are treated like slaves. And I'm against that, of course. We had a visit at school by a black woman from South Africa. You couldn't believe what she told us was true."

"You know more than I do in any case," he said. "When I was in Latvia last year, I often wondered how I could have reached 40 without having a clue about what was going on in the world."

"You just don't keep in touch," she said. "I remember when I was twelve, 13, and tried to ask you both things. Neither you nor Mama had the slightest idea about what was going on beyond your own back yard. All you wanted to know about was the house and the garden and your work. Nothing else. Is that why you divorced?"

"Is that what you think?"

"You had made your lives a matter of tulip bulbs and new taps in the bathroom. That's all you ever talked about, when you did talk to each other, that is."

"What's wrong with talking about flowers?"

"The flowers grew so high, you couldn't see anything that was happening beyond them."

He decided to put an end to that discussion. "How much time do you have?"

"An hour, at least."

"No time at all, really. How about meeting tonight, if you feel like it?"

They went out to the street when the rain had stopped.

"Don't you find those high heels difficult to walk in?" he said.

"Of course, but you get used to them. Do you want to try?"

Wallander was just happy that she existed. Something inside him eased up. He watched as she walked to the underpass, waving to him.

At that very moment it came to him what he had seen in the apartment in Hallunda, what had caught his attention, although he couldn't say why. Now he knew. On the bookshelf on the wall, there had been an ashtray. He'd seen one like it before. It might have been a coincidence, but he did not think so.

He remembered his meal at the Continental Hotel in Ystad. He'd started out in the bar. On the table in front of him was a glass ashtray. Exactly the same as the one in the Rykoffs' spare room. Konovalenko, he thought. At some time or other, he's been in the Continental Hotel. He might even have been sitting at the same table as me. He couldn't resist the temptation to take home one of their heavy glass ashtrays.

A human failing, one of the most common. He could never have imagined that a detective inspector from Ystad would take a look at the little room in Hallunda where he occasionally spends his nights.

Wallander went up to his hotel room, thinking that he might not be such an incompetent policeman after all. The times had not completely passed him by, not yet. Maybe he was still capable of solving the pointless and brutal murder of a woman who just happened to take a wrong turning not far from Krageholm.

He went over what he believed he had established so far. Louise Åkerblom and Klas Tengblad had been shot by the same weapon. Tengblad by a white man with a foreign accent. The black African who had been there when Louise Åkerblom was killed had been pursued by a man who also had a foreign accent, and was probably called Konovalenko. This Konovalenko was known to Rykoff, though he denied it. To judge by his build, Rykoff could well be the man who had rented the house from Alfred Olsson. And in Rykoff's apartment was an ashtray that suggested that somebody had been to Ystad. It was not a lot to go on, and but for the bullets, the link would have been tenuous. But he had his hunches, and he knew to pay attention to them. A search of the Rykoffs' apartment could provide the evidence they needed.

That evening he and Linda dined in a restaurant not far from the hotel. He felt more secure with her. When, shortly before 1 a.m., he got to bed, it occurred to him that it was the most pleasant evening he had spent for a long time.

Wallander arrived at the Kungsholmen police station before 8 a.m. the next morning. An audience of detectives there listened in astonishment to what he had discovered in Hallunda, and the conclusions he had drawn. He could feel their scepticism, but their desire to catch the man who had shot their colleague was overwhelming, and he felt the mood slowly change. In the end, nobody challenged his conclusions.

The morning saw continuous, rapid developments. The block in Hallunda was put under observation while preparations were made for a search. An energetic young prosecutor had no hesitation in approving the application for search and arrest warrants.

They were to go in at 2 p.m. Wallander kept himself in the background while Lovén and his colleagues went through what was going to happen. At about 10 p.m., in the middle of the most chaotic phase of the preparations, he made a call to Björk in Ystad from Lovén's office and told him of the action planned for that afternoon, and how the murder of Louise Åkerblom might soon be solved.

"I have to say it all sounds pretty improbable," Björk said.

"We live in an improbable world."

"Whatever happens, you've done a good job. I'll let everybody at this end know what's going on."

"No press conference, though," Wallander said. "And nobody is to discuss this with Åkerblom."

"Of course not," Björk said. "When do you expect to be back?"

"As soon as possible," Wallander said. "How's the weather?"

"Terrific," Björk said. "It feels like spring is on the way. Svedberg is sneezing like a man with hay fever. That's a sure sign of spring, as you well know."

As he put the phone down Wallander felt vaguely homesick, but his excitement at the imminent raid was stronger.

At 11 a.m. Lovén summoned everybody who would be involved. Reports from those watching the building suggested both Rykoff and his wife were in the apartment. It was not possible to establish whether anybody else was there.

Wallander listened closely to Lovén's summary. A raid in Stockholm was very different from anything he was used to. Operations of this size were virtually unknown in Ystad. He could only remember one such occasion, the previous year, when a man had barricaded himself into a summer cottage in Sandskogen, high on drugs.

Before the meeting Lovén had asked Wallander if he wanted to play an active role.

"Certainly," he said. "If Konovalenko is there, in a sense he's my baby. Half of him, anyway. Besides, I'm looking forward to seeing Rykoff's face."

Lovén brought the meeting to a close at 11.30 a.m.

"We don't know what we'll encounter," he said. "Probably just two people who'll go along with the inevitable. But it might turn out very different."

*

Wallander had lunch in the canteen with Lovén.

"Have you ever asked yourself what you've got involved in?" Lovén said, out of the blue.

"That's something I think about every day," Wallander said. "Don't most of us?"

"I don't know," Lovén said. "I only know what I think. And what I think depresses me. We're on the brink of losing control in Stockholm. I don't know how it is in a smaller district like Ystad, but being a criminal in this city must be a pretty carefree existence, at least as far as the chances of getting caught are concerned."

"We're still in control, I guess," Wallander said. "But the differences between districts are decreasing all the time. What's happening here is happening in Ystad too."

"A great many police officers in Stockholm can't wait to get posted to the provinces," Lovén said. "They think they'll have an easier time there."

"I reckon there are quite a few of ours who'd like to transfer here as well," Wallander said. "They think they lead too quiet a life out in the sticks, or in some small town."

"I doubt if I'd be able to change," Lovén said.

"Me neither," Wallander said. "Either I'm an Ystad policeman, or I'm not a policeman at all."

And then Lovén had things to do. Wallander found a sofa where he could stretch out. He thought he had not had a good night's sleep since the day that Robert Åkerblom had come into his office. He dozed off for a few minutes, and awoke with a start. Then he just lay there, thinking about Baiba Liepa.

The raid on the apartment in Hallunda began at exactly 2 p.m. precisely. Wallander, Lovén, and three other officers climbed the stairs. After ringing the bell twice without getting any reply, they broke down the door with a crowbar. Men with automatic weapons, from a special unit, were waiting in the background. All of the policemen on the stairs carried pistols, apart from Wallander. Lovén asked him if he wanted a gun, but he declined. On the other hand, he was glad to be wearing a bulletproof vest like the others.

They stormed into the apartment, spread out, and it was all over before it had begun. There was no-one there.

The officers looked at each other in bewilderment. Then Lovén took out his walkie-talkie and contacted the officer in charge down below.

"It's empty," he said. "There will be no arrests. You can call the special units off, but you can send in the forensic team."

"They must have left last night," Wallander said. "Or at the crack of dawn."

"We'll get them," Lovén said. "Within half an hour there'll be a country-wide APB."

He handed Wallander a pair of plastic gloves. "Maybe you'd like to do some dusting," he said.

While Lovén was talking to headquarters in Kungsholmen on his mobile, Wallander went into the little spare room. He put on the gloves and gently lifted the ashtray from the shelf. It was the model of the one he had been staring at a few nights ago, when he had had a skinful of whisky. He handed the ashtray to a forensic technician.

"There are bound to be fingerprints on this," he said. "Probably not in our files, but Interpol might have them." He watched the technician put the ashtray into a plastic bag. Then he went to the living room and absentmindedly contemplated the surrounding buildings and the grey sky. He remembered vaguely that this was the window that Rykoff's wife had opened to let the smoke out. Without really being able to decide whether he was depressed or annoyed at the failure of the raid, he went into the big bedroom. He examined the wardrobes. Many clothes were still there. On the other hand, there was no sign of a suitcase. He sat on one of the beds and opened a drawer in the bedside table. It contained only a cotton reel and a half-empty pack of cigarettes. He noted that Mrs Rykoff smoked Gitanes.

Then he bent down and looked under the bed. Only a pair of dusty slippers. He walked round the bed and opened the drawer in the other bedside table. Nothing in it. On the table were an ashtray and half a bar of chocolate. The cigarette butts had filters. He picked one of them up. A Camel.

He thought back to the previous day. The woman had lit a cigarette. Rykoff had immediately displayed his annoyance, and she had opened a window that was stuck. It was not usual for smokers to complain about others with the same habit. Especially when the room was not smoky. Did Tania smoke several different brands? That was hardly likely. So, Rykoff smoked too.

Thinking hard, he went back into the living room. He opened the same window the woman had opened. It was still sticking. He tried the other windows and the glazed door leading to the balcony. They all opened without difficulty.

He stood in the middle of the floor, frowning. Why had she chosen to open a window that stuck? And why was that window so difficult to open?

It suddenly dawned on him: there was only one possible answer. The woman had opened the window that stuck because there was some pressing reason for that of all the windows to be opened. And it was sticking because it was so seldom opened.

He went again to the window. If you were in a car in the car park, this was the window that could be seen most clearly. The other living room window was next to the projecting balcony. The balcony door itself was completely invisible from the car park.

He thought through the sequence one more time.

He'd cracked it. Tania seemed nervous. She had been looking at the clock on the wall behind his head. Then she opened a window – the signal to somebody in the car park that they should not come up to the apartment.

Konovalenko, it must have been. He had been that close.

When Lovén was done with his phone calls, Wallander took him to the window and passed on his conclusion.

"You may well be right," Lovén said. "Unless it was somebody else."

"Indeed," Wallander said. "Unless it was somebody else."

They drove back to Kungsholmen while the technicians continued their work. They were barely inside Lovén's office when the telephone rang. The technicians at Hallunda had found a tin containing the same kind of tear gas grenades that had been thrown into the disco.

"It's all falling into place," Lovén said. "Unless it's just getting more confusing. I don't understand what they had against that disco. In any case, the whole country is looking out for them. And we'll make sure there's wide coverage on the television and in the newspapers."

"Which means I can go back to Ystad tomorrow," Wallander said.

"When you pick up Konovalenko, maybe we can borrow him in Skåne for a while."

"It's always infuriating when a raid draws a blank," Lovén said. "I wonder where they have gone to earth."

The question remained unanswered. Wallander went back to his hotel and decided to pay a visit to the Aurora that evening. He had some more questions now for the bald man behind the bar.

The case was coming to a head.

CHAPTER SEVENTEEN

The man waiting outside the President's office was alone in the dimly lit antechamber. It was midnight, and he had been there since 8 p.m. A security guard occasionally looked in and sympathised at his being kept waiting. He was an old man in a dark suit. He had put all of the lights out just after 11 p.m., apart from the one lamp which was still burning.

Georg Scheepers had the feeling the man could easily have been employed at a funeral parlour. His discretion and unobtrusiveness, his humility bordering on servility, reminded him of the man who had taken care of his own mother's funeral. Perhaps President de Klerk is taking care of the last, dying remnants of the white South African empire? Maybe this is more of an outer office for a funeral parlour than the office of someone leading a great country into its future?

He had had plenty of opportunity to think during the hours he had been waiting. Now and then the security guard opened the door quietly and explained that the President was held up by some urgent business. At 10 p.m. he brought him a cup of lukewarm tea.

Scheepers did not know why he had been summoned to see the President that evening, Wednesday, May 6. The previous day, at lunchtime, he had been called by the secretary of his superior, Henrik Verwey. Scheepers was an assistant of the widely feared chief prosecutor in Johannesburg, whom he seldom saw him save in court or at their Friday meetings. Unlike this evening, he had been shown straight into the prosecutor's office. Verwey indicated a chair, and went on signing documents that a secretary was setting before him. Then they were left alone.

Verwey was a man feared not only by criminals. He was nearly 60, almost two metres tall, and sturdily built. Occasionally, performing various feats, he demonstrated his formidable strength. Some years ago, when his offices were being refurbished, he had alone carried out a cupboard that later took four men to lift on to a truck. But it was not his physical strength that made him so fearsome. During his many years as prosecutor he had always pressed for the death penalty whenever there was the slightest possibility of achieving it. When the court accepted his plea – and it was often – and sentenced a criminal to be hanged, Verwey was nearly always a witness to the sentence being carried out. That had given him the reputation of being a brutal man. Then again, no-one could accuse him of racial discrimination in applying his principles. A white criminal had as much to fear as a black one.

Scheepers sat there worrying whether he had done something to invoke censure. Verwey was known for his ruthless criticism of his assistants, if he considered it justified.

But the conversation turned out to be utterly unlike anything he had anticipated. Verwey had left his desk and sat in an easy chair beside him.

"Late last night a man was murdered in his hospital bed at a private clinic in Hillbrow," he began. "His name was Pieter van Heerden, and he worked for NIS. According to the CID, the evidence points to robbery with violence. His wallet is missing. Nobody saw anyone go into the room, nobody saw the murderer leave. It looks as if whoever did it acted alone, and there is some reason to think that he pretended to be a messenger from a laboratory used by the Brenthurst Clinic. As none of the nurses heard anything, the murderer must have used a gun with a silencer. It looks as though the police's theory is correct. On the other hand, we must also bear in mind that van Heerden worked for the intelligence service.

"There's another aspect which complicates matters," Verwey said. "What I'm about to say is confidential. You must be absolutely clear about that."

"I understand," Scheepers said.

"Van Heerden was responsible for keeping President de Klerk informed about secret intelligence activities outside the usual channels. In other words, his was an exceptionally sensitive post." Verwey fell silent. Scheepers waited tensely for him to continue.

"President de Klerk called me a few hours ago," he said. "He wanted me to select one of my prosecutors to keep him directly informed about the police investigation. He seems to be persuaded that the murder had to do with van Heerden's intelligence work. He has no proof, but he rejects outright the notion that this was a run-of-the-mill robbery."

Verwey looked at Scheepers. "We cannot know what van Heerden was keeping the President informed about," he said.

Scheepers nodded his understanding.

"I have picked you as the man to keep President de Klerk informed," he said. "You will drop all other matters and concentrate on the investigation into the circumstances surrounding van Heerden's death. Is that understood?"

Scheepers nodded. He was trying to absorb the implications of what Verwey had said.

"You will be summoned regularly by the President. You will keep no minutes of those meetings. You will report only to the President and speak only otherwise to me. If anybody in your section wonders what you're doing, the official explanation is that I've asked you to look into the recruitment policy for prosecutors over the next ten-year period. Is that clear?"

"It is," Scheepers said.

Verwey took a plastic folder from his desk, and handed it to Scheepers. "This is all the material the police have. Van Heerden has been dead for twelve hours. The investigation is being led by an Inspector Borstlap. I suggest you go to Brenthurst Clinic and speak with him."

That concluded the business.

"Do a good job," Verwey said. "I've chosen you because you have proved to be a good prosecutor. I don't like to be disappointed."

Scheepers went back to his office and tried to come to terms with what was being required of him. Then he thought he should buy himself a new suit. He had none that would be suitable for a meeting with the President.

Now he was in the antechamber, wearing a dark blue suit that had been very expensive. His wife wondered at the extravagance. He said he was to take part in an inquiry chaired by the Minister of Justice.

It was 12.40 p.m. before the security guard eventually came to tell him that the President was ready to receive him. Scheepers jumped up from his chair, acutely nervous. He followed the guard, who marched up to a high double door, knocked, and opened it for him.

Sitting behind a desk, illuminated by a single lamp, was the balding man he was destined to meet. Scheepers stood hesitating in the doorway until the man at the desk beckoned him to approach and gestured to a chair. Scheepers noticed that the President had large bags under his eyes. He came straight to the point. His voice had a sting of impatience about it, as if he was always having to deal with people who did not understand anything.

"The death of van Heerden had nothing to do with robbery, I am sure of that," said de Klerk. "It is your job to ensure the police investigators are properly aware of the fact that it's his intelligence work that lies behind the murder. I want all his computer files investigated, all his index files and documents, everything he's worked on over the last year. Is that understood?"

"Yes," Scheepers said.

De Klerk leaned forward so that the desk lamp lit up his face, giving it an almost ghost-like appearance.

"Van Heerden suspected there was a conspiracy in play that was a threat to South Africa as a whole," he said. "A plot that might lead to complete chaos. His death must be seen in this context. You don't need to know more than that. Chief Prosecutor Verwey selected you to keep me informed because he considers you to be completely reliable and loyal to the government authorities. But I want to stress the confidential nature of this assignment. Revealing what I have just told you would be high treason. You are a prosecutor, so I do not need to tell you what the punishment is for that crime."

"No, sir," Scheepers said, shifting uncomfortably on his chair.

"Talk to one of my secretaries whenever you have anything to report, and they will make an appointment. Thank you for coming." De Klerk turned back to his papers. Scheepers stood up, bowed, and walked across the thick carpet to the double doors.

The guard accompanied him down the stairs. Another armed guard escorted him to the car park. His hands were sweaty as he slid behind the wheel of his car.

A conspiracy, he thought. A plot that would lead the country into chaos? Aren't we there already?

He opened the glove compartment and took out his pistol. He checked the magazine, released the safety catch, and placed it on the seat beside him.

Scheepers did not enjoy driving at night. Armed robbery and assault were constant threats, and the scale of brutality was increasing. He drove home through sleeping Pretoria, through the South African night. He had much to think about.

CHAPTER EIGHTEEN

Days and nights had merged to form a vague whole from which he was no longer able to distinguish the parts. Mabasha did not know how long it was since he had left Konovalenko dead in the farmhouse in the south, yet the man had come back to life and shot at him when the disco filled with tear gas. He had killed Konovalenko with the bottle, he was sure of it. But despite the smarting in his eyes, he had recognised him through the clouds of smoke. Mabasha had made his escape from the premises by a back staircase full of people in a panic, kicking and screaming, desperate to flee the smoke. For a moment, he thought he was back in South Africa, where tear gas attacks on black townships were not uncommon, but he was in Stockholm and Konovalenko had risen from the dead and was now pursuing him to kill him.

He had reached town at dawn and spent hours driving around the streets, not knowing what to do. He was very tired, so weary he did not dare to trust his judgment. That scared him. He had always felt that his ability to think himself out of difficult situations with a clear head was his ultimate life insurance. He wondered whether to take a room in a hotel, but he had no passport, no documents at all to establish his identity. He was a nobody among all these people, an armed man without a name.

The pain in his hand kept coming back. Soon he would have to see a doctor. The black blood had seeped through the bandages. He could not afford to succumb to infections and fever. That would make him completely defenceless. But the bloody stump hardly affected him. His finger might never have existed. He had transformed it into a dream. He was born without an index finger on his left hand.

He slept in a cemetery. He was cold in spite of the sleeping bag he had bought. In his dreams he was pursued by the singing hounds. As he lay awake watching the stars, he thought of how he might never return to his homeland. The dry, red, swirling soil would never again be touched by the soles of his feet. He was stricken with a sorrow so intense that he could not remember feeling anything like it since the death of his father. It also occurred to him that in South Africa, a country founded upon an all-embracing lie, there was seldom room for simple untruths. He thought about the lie that formed the backbone of his own life.

The nights he spent in the cemetery were filled with the *sangoma's* words. It was there, surrounded only by the unknown dead – white people he had never met and would not meet until he entered the underworld, the world of spirits – that he thought of his childhood. He saw his father's face, his smile, and heard his voice. Perhaps the spirit world would be divided, just like South Africa. Perhaps even the underworld consisted of a black world and a white world? He was stricken with grief as he imagined the spirits of his forefathers forced to live in smoky, slummy townships. He tried to get his *sangoma* to tell him how it was, but all he could hear was the singing of the hounds, and their howls which he was unable to interpret.

On the second morning he left the cemetery at dawn, having hidden his sleeping bag in a tomb where he had managed to pry open an air vent. He stole another car. It all happened very quickly: an opportunity arose, and he grasped it without hesitation. His judgment was coming to his aid once more. He had come round a corner just as a man left his car with the engine running and disappeared into a doorway. There was nobody in sight. It was a Ford; he had driven lots of them. He got in, threw the man's briefcase onto the street, and drove off. Eventually he managed to find his way out of the city, looking for a lake where he could be alone with his thoughts.

He came upon the seashore. He supposed it had to be the seashore; he did not know which sea it was, but when he tasted the water it was salty. Not as salty as he was used to from the beaches at Durban and Port Elizabeth. But could there be salt lakes in this country? He clambered over some rocks and imagined he was gazing into infinity through a narrow gap between two islands in the archipelago. There was a chill in the air and he was cold. Even so, he remained standing on a rock as far out as he could get, thinking that this was where his life had taken him. A very long way. But what would the future hold?

Just as he used to do when he was young, he squatted down and made a spiral-shaped labyrinth from pebbles beneath the rock. At the same time he tried to reach so deep into himself that he would hear the voice of his *sangoma*. But the noise of the sea was too strong and his concentration too weak. The stones he had arranged to form a labyrinth were no help. He just felt scared. If he could not talk to the spirits, he would grow so weak he might even die. He would no longer have any resistance to sickness, he couldn't think straight, and his body would become a mere shell that cracked as soon as touched.

Feeling uneasy, he turned from the sea and went back to the car. He tried to focus on the important things. How could Konovalenko have traced him to the disco suggested by some Africans from Uganda he met in a burger bar? That was the first question. The second was: how could he leave this country and get back to South Africa?

He was going to have to do what he least wanted to do: find Konovalenko. He would be as hard to track down as a single springbok in the measureless African bush. Somehow he would have to entice Konovalenko. He had the passport. He hoped he would not need to kill anybody, apart from Konovalenko.

That evening Mabasha went back to the disco. There were not many people there, and he sat in a corner, drinking beer. When he went to the bar with his empty glass for another beer, the bald man spoke to him. Mabasha did not understand at first what he was saying. Then he understood that there had been two different people there the day before, looking for him. One of them was obviously Konovalenko. But the other one? The man behind the bar said he was a policeman, and that to judge by his accent he came from the southern part of the country.

The bald man nodded at Mabasha's filthy bandage. "He was looking for a black man missing a finger."

He left the disco without more ado. Konovalenko might come back again. He was not yet ready to confront him, even though his pistol was at the ready, tucked into his belt.

When he reached the street, he knew what he would do. The policeman was going to help him to find Konovalenko.

There was an investigation going on somewhere or other into the disappearance of a woman. Maybe they had found her body by now. But if they had managed to find out about him, they might also know about Konovalenko. I left a trace behind, he thought. A finger. Perhaps Konovalenko left something behind as well.

He spent the rest of the evening in the shadows watching the disco, but neither Konovalenko nor the policeman appeared. The bald man had given him a description of the policeman. It occurred to Mabasha that a white man in his forties was not going to be a regular customer at the disco.

Late that night he went back to the cemetery. The next day he stole another car, and that evening he parked in the shadows opposite the disco.

Just on 9 p.m., a taxi drew up at the entrance. Mabasha sank down so that his head was level with the steering wheel. As soon as the policeman had disappeared into the underworld, Mabasha drove across to the entrance and got out. He withdrew to the darkest shadows, and waited, his pistol now in his jacket pocket, within easy reach.

The man who emerged a quarter of an hour later and looked around vaguely or possibly lost in thought was not on his guard. He gave the impression of being completely harmless, a solitary, unprotected nocturnal prowler. Mabasha drew his pistol, took swift strides, and pressed the gun against the underside of the man's chin.

"Not a move," he said in English. "Not a single move."

The man gave a start, but he understood English. He did not move.

"Go to the car," Mabasha said. "Get into the passenger seat." The man did as he was told. He was obviously frightened.

Mabasha ducked into the car and punched the man on the chin. Hard enough to knock him out, but not hard enough to break his jaw. Mabasha could martial his strength when he was in control of the situation. Something that did not apply on that catastrophic last evening with the Russian.

He drove to an unlit street and went through the policeman's pockets. Strangely, no weapon. Mabasha was more than ever convinced he was in a very odd country, with policemen unarmed. He bound the man's arms to his chest and taped over his mouth. A thin trickle of blood was seeping from the side of his mouth. It was never possible altogether to avoid injuring someone. Presumably the man had bitten his own tongue.

During the hours available to Mabasha that afternoon, he had memorised the route. He knew where he was going and had no wish to risk a wrong turn. At the first red light, he took out the man's wallet and saw he was called Kurt Wallander, 44 years old.

The lights changed, and he moved on. He kept a close watch on the rear-view mirror.

The second time he had to stop at a red light he began to think he was being followed. Could there have been a backup? If so, there would soon be problems. When he came to a three-lane stretch of road, he accelerated. Perhaps he had been imagining things, they seemed to be on their own after all.

The man in the passenger seat started groaning and moving. Mabasha judged that he had hit him precisely as hard as he had intended.

He turned into the road leading to the cemetery and came to a halt in the shadow of a green building that housed a shop which sold flowers and wreaths during the day. Now it was in darkness. He turned off his lights and watched the cars taking the slip road. None of them seemed to be slowing down.

He waited another ten minutes. Nothing happened, apart from the policeman coming to.

"Not a sound," Mabasha said, ripping the tape from the man's mouth. A policeman understands, he thought. He knows when a man means what he says. He wondered if a man who abducted a policeman risked being hanged in Sweden.

He got out of the car, listened, and looked all around. Apart from the passing traffic there was no sound. He opened the passenger door and motioned to the man to get out. Then he led him to one of the iron gates and they soon disappeared in the darkness that swallowed up the gravel paths and gravestones.

Mabasha guided him to the vault where he had opened the iron door without difficulty. It smelled musty in the damp interior, but he was not scared by graveyards. He had often hidden among the dead in the past.

He had bought a hurricane lamp and an extra sleeping bag. At first the policeman refused to go with him into the vault, and put up a show of resistance.

"I'm not going to kill you," he said. "I'm not even going to hurt you. But you have to go in there."

He lit the lamp and, taking great care not to risk being kicked, put the policeman into one of the sleeping bags. He went outside to see if the light could be seen. But there was no sign of it.

Once again he stood and listened. The many years he had spent forever on the alert had developed his hearing. Something moved on a gravel path. The backup, he thought. Or some animal of the night.

In the end he decided it was not a threat. He went back into the vault and squatted opposite the man whose name was Kurt Wallander.

The fear Wallander had first felt had now become positive fright, even terror.

"If you do as I say no harm will come to you," Mabasha said. "But you must answer my questions. And you must tell the truth. I know you are a policeman. I can see you're all the time looking at my left hand and the bandage. That means you've found my finger. The one Konovalenko cut off. He was the one who killed the woman. It's up to you if you believe me or not. I only came to this country to stay for a short time, and I've decided to kill only one person. Konovalenko. But first you have to help me by telling me where he is. Once Konovalenko's dead, I'll let you go."

Mabasha waited for a reply. Then he remembered something he had forgotten.

"I don't suppose you have a shadow?" he said. "A car following you?" The man shook his head.

"You're alone?"

"Yes," the policeman said.

"I had to make sure you didn't struggle," Mabasha said. "But I don't think my punch did much damage."

"No," the man said, grimacing.

Mabasha sat there in silence. There was no rush for the moment. The man would feel calmer if everything was quiet. Mabasha did not blame him for being afraid. He knew how a man could feel when he was terrified and on his own.

"Konovalenko," he said quietly. "Where is he?"

"I don't know," Wallander said.

Mabasha eyed him up and down, and realised that the policeman knew who Konovalenko was, but not where he was. That was a pity. It would make everything more difficult, it would take more time, but it wouldn't really change anything. Together, they would be able to find him.

Taking his time, Mabasha recounted everything that had happened when the woman was killed. But he said nothing about why he was in Sweden.

"So he was the one who blew the house up?" Wallander said, when he had finished.

"You know what happened now," Mabasha said. "So it's your turn to put me in the picture."

The policeman had apparently calmed down, even if he did seem put out at being in a cold, damp burial vault. Behind their backs were caskets inside sarcophagi, stacked one on top of the other.

"Do you have a name?" he said.

"Just call me Goli," Mabasha said. "That'll do."

"And you come from South Africa?"

"That's not important."

"It's important for me."

"The only thing that's important for both of us is where is Konovalenko."

The last part of this declaration he spat out. The policeman understood. The fear returned to his eyes.

That very same moment Mabasha stiffened. He had not relaxed his guard while talking to the policeman. Now his sensitive ears had picked up a noise outside the vault. He gestured to the policeman to keep still. Then he took out his pistol and turned down the flame in the hurricane lamp.

There was somebody outside the vault. It was not an animal. The movements were too meticulously cautious.

He leaned rapidly over the policeman and grabbed him by the throat.

"For the last time," he hissed, "was there anybody tailing you?"

"No. Nobody. I swear."

Mabasha let go. Konovalenko, he thought in a fury. I don't know how you do it, but I do know now why Kleyn wants you working for him in South Africa.

They could not stay in the vault. He eyed the hurricane lamp. That was their chance.

"When I open the door, throw the lamp to the left," he said to the policeman, untying his hands at the same time. He turned up the flame as far as it would go, and handed it over.

"Jump to the right," he whispered. "Crouch down. Don't get in my line of fire." He could tell that the man wanted to protest, but he raised his hand and Wallander said nothing. Then he cocked the pistol and they got ready for action.

"I'll count to three," he said.

He kicked open the door and the policeman hurled the lamp to the left. Mabasha fired at the same moment. The policeman came stumbling behind him and he almost overbalanced. Just then he heard shots from at least two different weapons. He threw himself to the ground and crawled behind a gravestone. The policeman crawled off in some other direction. The hurricane lamp lit up the burial vault. Mabasha detected a movement in one corner and fired. The bullet struck the iron door and whined into the vault. Another shot shattered the hurricane lamp and everything went black. Somebody scampered away along one of the gravel paths. Then all was quiet.

Wallander could feel his heart pounding like a piston against his ribs. He seemed not to be able to breathe properly, and wondered if he'd been hit. But there was no blood, and he couldn't feel any pain apart from his tongue, which he had bitten some time ago. With great care he positioned himself behind a tall gravestone. He lay there motionless. His heart was still pounding. Mabasha was nowhere to be seen or heard. When he was sure he was alone, he started running. He ran along the gravel paths, towards the lights on the road and the noise of what traffic there still was. He kept running until he was outside the boundary fence of the cemetery. He stopped at a bus stop and waved down a taxi coming back into the city from Arlanda airport.

"Central Hotel," he gasped.

The driver eyed him up and down. "I don't know that I want you in my taxi," he said. "You'll make everything filthy."

"I'm a policeman, dammit," Wallander roared at him. "Just drive!"

When they got to the hotel Wallander paid without waiting either for a receipt or his change, and collected his key from the receptionist, who stared at his clothes in astonishment. It was midnight when he collapsed on to his bed. When he had calmed down, he called Linda.

"Why are you calling as late as this?" she said.

"I've been busy until now," he said. "I didn't have a chance to call earlier."

"Why do you sound so funny? Is something the matter?"

Wallander had a lump in his throat and was on the point of bursting into tears. But he managed to control himself. "It's nothing," he said.

"Are you sure everything's all right?"

"Everything's fine. Why shouldn't it be?"

"You know better than I do."

"Don't you remember from when you used to live at home that I was always out working at strange hours?"

"I suppose so," she said. "I'd forgotten."

He made up his mind on the spur of the moment.

"I'm coming over," he said. "Don't ask me why. I'll explain when I get there."

He took a taxi to where she lived in Bromma. They sat at the kitchen table, each with a beer, and he told her what had happened.

"They say it's good for the young to get some idea of what their parents get up to at work," she said, shaking her head. "Weren't you scared?"

"Of course I was. People like this have no respect for life."

"Why don't you send the police after them?"

"I'm the police myself. And I need to think."

"And meanwhile they can kill again."

"You're right," he said. "I'll go to the station at Kungsholmen. But I wanted to talk to you first."

"I'm glad you came."

She went out into the hall with him. "Why did you ask if I was at home?" she said. "Why didn't you say you stopped by yesterday?"

"What are you talking about?" he asked.

"I met Mrs Nilson from next door when I got home. She told me you'd been here asking if I was in. You have a key, don't you?"

"I haven't spoken to any Mrs Nilson," Wallander said.

"I must have got her wrong, then," Linda said.

A shiver suddenly ran down Wallander's spine. "One more time," he said. "You came home. You met Mrs Nilson. She said I'd been asking after you?"

"Right."

"Tell me again what she said, word for word."

"'Your Dad's been asking after you.' That's all."

Wallander was scared. "I've never met Mrs Nilson," he said. "How can she know what I look like?"

It was a while before she caught on. "You mean it could have been somebody else? But who? Why? Who would want to pretend they were you?"

Wallander switched off the light and went to one of the living room windows. The street below was deserted. He went back to the hall.

"I don't know who it was," he said. "But you're going back with me to Ystad tomorrow. I don't want you here on your own right now."

She could tell he was deadly serious.

"OK," she said simply. "Do I need to be frightened tonight?"

"You don't need to be frightened at all," he said. "It's just that you shouldn't be here on your own for the next few days."

"Don't say any more," she said. "Right now I want to know as little as possible."

She made up a bed for him on a mattress. He lay there in the dark, listening to her breathing. Konovalenko, he thought. When he was certain she was asleep, he got up and went over to the window.

The street was as empty as before.

Wallander found out that there was a train to Malmö at 7.03 a.m., and they left the apartment soon after 6 a.m.

He had slept restlessly, dozing off, then waking with a start. He needed to spend a few hours in a train. Flying would mean he got to Malmö too quickly. He needed rest, and he needed to think.

They came to a standstill just outside Mjölby with engine failure, and waited there nearly an hour. Wallander was grateful for the extra time. They occasionally exchanged a few words. But just as often Linda was buried in a book, and he was lost in thought. Fourteen days, he was thinking as he watched a lonely tractor ploughing what looked like a never-ending field. He tried counting the seagulls following the plough, but could not manage it. Fourteen days since Mrs Åkerblom had disappeared. The image of her must already be beginning to melt away from her two small children's consciousness. He wondered if Robert Åkerblom would be able to hold fast to his God. What sort of encouragement could Pastor Tureson give him?

He looked at his daughter, asleep with her cheek against the window. What did her mostly solitary anxieties look like? Was there a landscape where their abandoned thoughts could arrange to meet, without their knowing about it? We don't really know anybody, he thought. Least of all ourselves. Had Robert Åkerblom truly known his wife?

The tractor disappeared into a dip in the field. Wallander imagined it sinking into a bottomless sea of mud.

The train jerked into motion. Linda woke up and looked at him. "Are we there?" she said, drowsily. "How long have I been asleep?"

"A quarter of an hour, maybe," he said with a smile. "We haven't reached Nässjö yet."

"I could use a cup of coffee." She yawned. "How about you?"

They sat in the buffet car as far as Hässleholm. For the first time he told her the full story of his two journeys to Riga the previous year. She listened in fascination.

"It doesn't sound at all like you," she said when he had finished.

"That's how I feel too," he said.

"You could have died," she said. "Did you never think about me and Mama?"

"I thought about you," he said. "But I don't think I thought about your mother."

When they got to Malmö, they only had to wait half an hour for a train to Ystad. They were in his apartment shortly before 4 p.m. He made up her bed, and when he went to look for clean sheets it struck him that he had forgotten all about the time he had booked in the laundry room. At about 7 p.m. they went out to one of the pizzerias on Hamngatan and had dinner. They were both tired, and were back home again before 9 p.m.

She called her grandfather, and Wallander stood by her side, listening. She said she would go and see him the next day. He was surprised at how different his father could sound when he talked to her.

He thought he had better call Lovén. But he put it off, since he was not yet sure how he was going to explain why he did not contact the police immediately after he had got away from the cemetery. He could not understand it himself. It was a breach of duty, no doubt about it. Had he started to lose control over his own judgment? Or had he been so scared that he lost the ability to act?

Long after Linda had fallen asleep he stood in the window, looking down at the deserted street.

The images in his mind's eye were alternating between the African in the vault and the man known as Konovalenko.

While Wallander was standing at his window in Ystad, Rykoff was observing that the police were still taking an interest in his apartment. He was two floors up in the same building. It was Konovalenko who had once suggested they should have an escape route in case their own apartment ought not to be used. It was also Konovalenko who explained that the safest haven was not always the one furthest away. The best plan was the unexpected one. So Rykoff rented an identical apartment in Tania's name, two floors higher up. That made it easier to move the necessary clothes and other baggage.

Konovalenko had told them to leave the apartment. Having quizzed the couple, he concluded that the policeman was no fool. Nor could they exclude the possibility that the police would search the place. But above all, Konovalenko was afraid that Vladimir and Tania could be subjected to more serious interrogation.

Konovalenko had also wondered whether the best solution might not be to shoot them. But he still needed Rykoff's legwork. And the police would only get more excited than they already were.

They moved upstairs that same night. Konovalenko had given them strict instructions to stay at home for several days.

Among the first things Konovalenko had learned as a young KGB officer was that there were deadly sins in the intelligence service. Being a servant of secrecy meant joining a brotherhood in which the most important rules were written in invisible ink. The worst sin, of course, was being a double agent. Betraying one's own organisation, and in the service of an enemy.

There were other deadly sins. One was to arrive too late. Not just to a meeting, or clearing a secret letterbox, or a kidnapping, even for something as straightforward as a journey. Just as bad was being late with regard to oneself, one's own plans, one's own decisions.

And that is what happened to Konovalenko early in the morning of May 7. The mistake he made was to put too much faith in the BMW. His superiors had always taught him to plan a journey on the basis of two parallel possibilities. If one vehicle proved to be unserviceable, there should always be time to resort to a pre-arranged alternative. But that Friday morning, when his BMW stopped near St Erik's Bridge and refused to start again, he had no alternative plan. Of course, he could take a taxi or the underground. Besides, since he did not know if and when the policeman or his daughter would leave the apartment in Bromma, it was not even certain he would be too late, anyway. Nevertheless, it seemed to him that the mistake, the guilt, was his, not the car's. He spent nearly 20 minutes trying to restart it, but the engine was dead and he left the vehicle where it had died, by good fortune not in a conspicuous place. He gave up and hailed a taxi. He had planned to be outside the red-brick apartment by 7 a.m. at the latest. As it was, he did not get there until nearly 7.45 a.m.

It had been simple to find out that Wallander had a daughter and that she was the one living in Bromma. He called the police station in Ystad and was told that Wallander was staying at the Central Hotel in Stockholm. He claimed to be a policeman himself. Then he went to the hotel and discussed a block booking for a group of tourists later in the summer. When he was not being observed, he stole a look at a message left for Wallander and memorised a telephone number and the name Linda. He traced the number to an address in Bromma. He chatted to a woman on the stairs there, and swiftly discovered how things stood.

That morning he waited on the street outside the apartment until at 8.30 a.m. a woman came out. He wished her a good morning and she recognised him.

"They left early this morning," she said.

"Both of them?"

"Both of them."

"Are they going to be away long?"

223

"She promised to call."

"She told you where they were going, no doubt?"

"They were going abroad on holiday. I didn't quite catch where."

She was trying to remember. Konovalenko waited. "France, I think it was," she said eventually. "I'm not sure, mind you."

Konovalenko thanked her kindly and walked on. He would send Rykoff to go over the apartment in due course.

As he needed time to think and was in no special hurry, he walked to Brommaplan where he could no doubt find a taxi. He didn't believe that they had gone abroad. The policeman from Ystad was the cold, calculating type. He had found out that someone had been asking the old lady questions. Someone who would certainly come back and ask some more questions. So he left a false trail, pointing to a holiday overseas. Probably he had taken his daughter with him back to Ystad. On the other hand, he might have chosen some other haven that would be quite impossible to trace.

A temporary setback, thought Konovalenko. I'll give him a start, and I'll catch him up later.

Of this he could be sure: the policeman from Ystad was worried. Why else take his daughter with him? Konovalenko smiled at the idea that they were thinking along the same lines, he and the provincial policeman called Wallander. He recalled something a KGB colonel said to his new recruits: a superior education, a long line of ancestors, even a high level of intelligence is no guarantee to becoming an outstanding chess player.

The chief objective now was to find the African, he thought. Finish off what he had failed to do in the disco and the cemetery. Kill him.

With a feeling of unease, he recalled the previous night's conversation. He had called South Africa at midnight and spoken with Kleyn on his emergency number. He had rehearsed with some care what he would say. There were no excuses that would explain Mabasha's being still at large, so he had lied. He said Mabasha had been killed. A hand grenade next to his petrol tank. When the rubber band holding back the firing pin had been eaten away, the car exploded and Mabasha had perished.

In spite of this report, Konovalenko sensed a measure of dissatisfaction in his employer. A crisis of confidence between himself and the

South African intelligence service he could not afford. That could put his whole future at risk.

There was now no longer any time to spare. Mabasha had to be found and killed very soon.

The unfathomable dusk slowly set in, but Mabasha barely noticed it.

He was thinking about the man he was to kill. Kleyn would understand. He would allow him to retain his assignment. One of these days, he would have the South African President in his sights, and he would not hesitate.

He wondered if the President had any presentiment that his life was in the balance. Did white people have their own *sangomas* who came to them in their dreams? He concluded they must have. How otherwise could any man survive without being in contact with the spirit world that controlled our lives, that had power over life and death?

On this occasion the spirits had been kind to him. They had told him what it was he had to do.

Wallander woke soon after 6 a.m. For the first time since starting to track down Louise Åkerblom's killer, he felt rested. He could hear his daughter snoring through the half-open door. He stood in the doorway, watching her. He was overwhelmed by intense joy, and it occurred to him that the purpose of life was quite simply to take care of one's children. Nothing else. He went to the bathroom, took a long shower, and decided to make an appointment with the police doctor. It must be possible to get some kind of help to lose weight and be physically fitter.

Most mornings he thought of the night – a year ago – when he woke up in a cold sweat, and assumed he was having a heart attack. The doctor who examined him said it was a warning that there was something completely wrong in his life. Now, a year on, he had to admit he had done nothing at all to change the way he lived. And to make matters worse, he had put on at least three kilos.

He drank coffee at the kitchen table. There was a thick fog over Ystad, but soon spring would really have arrived. He made up his mind to talk with Björk this coming Monday about his holiday plans.

He left the apartment at a 7.15 a.m., after scribbling down his direct line number on a scrap of paper and leaving it on the kitchen table.

When he came out onto the street, the fog was so thick he could scarcely see his car only a short way down the street. Maybe he should leave it where it was, and walk to the station. Suddenly he thought he saw something move on the other side of the street. A lamppost seemed to sway. Then he saw there was a man standing there, enveloped by fog just like himself. It was Goli, returned to Skåne.

CHAPTER NINETEEN

Jan Kleyn did have one weakness, one pure secret. Her name was Miranda, and she was as black as a raven's shadow. She was his secret, the vital counterpoint in his life. Everyone who knew Kleyn would have thought it inconceivable. His colleagues in the intelligence service would have dismissed as preposterous fantasy the suggestion that they had anything at all in common.

They were the same age, and had been aware of each other since they were children. But they lived in two different worlds. Miranda's mother, Matilda, was a servant in Kleyn's parents' house on a hill outside Bloemfontein. She lived in one of a cluster of tin shacks where the Africans had their homes a few kilometres away. At first light, she would make her laborious way up the steep hill to the white house, where her first task of the day was to prepare and then serve the family breakfast. There were servants whose job was to take care of his brothers and sisters. Even so, he would often turn to Matilda. One day, when he was eleven, he began to wonder where she came from every morning, and where she went back to. He was not allowed to leave the walled-in garden on his own, but one day he followed her in secret when her day's work was done. It was the first time he had seen at close quarters the clutter of shacks where African families lived. He knew that the blacks lived in quite different conditions from his own. He was forever hearing from his parents how it was part of the natural order of things. Even so, he had never imagined their houses would be as awful as those he now saw.

But there was also something else that attracted his attention. Matilda was met by a girl of his own age, lanky and thin. Perhaps Matilda's daughter. He realised for the first time that Matilda had a family, a life apart from the work she did in his home. It was a discovery that affected him badly. He could feel himself getting angry. It was as if Matilda had deceived him.

Two years later she died. Miranda had never explained to him how it happened, just that something had eaten away her insides until all life left her. Her family had broken up. Miranda's father took two sons and a daughter with him to where he came from, the barren country far away on the Lesotho border. Miranda would grow up with one of Matilda's sisters. But Jan's mother, in a gesture of unexpected generosity, took Miranda under her wing. She was to live with the master gardener, who had a cottage in a remote corner of their grounds. Miranda would be trained to take on her mother's work. In that way, the spirit of Matilda would live on inside the white house. Jan's mother was a *Boer*. For her, keeping up traditions was a guarantee for the continuation of the family and Afrikaner society. Keeping the same family of domestic servants, generation after generation, helped to maintain a sense of permanence and stability.

Jan Kleyn and Miranda grew up near each other, but the distance between them was unchanged. Even though he could see she was very beautiful, there was in fact no such thing as black beauty. He heard young men his own age telling stories about Afrikaners travelling to neighbouring Mozambique in order to bed black women, but that just seemed to confirm the truth he had learned never to question. So he went on seeing Miranda without actually wanting to discover her. But she had started appearing in his dreams. The dreams sent his pulse racing when he recalled them the following day. Reality was transformed in his dreams. In them, not only did he recognise Miranda's beauty, he accepted it. In his dreams he was allowed to love her, and the girls of Afrikaner families he associated with normally faded in comparison with Matilda's daughter.

Their first real meeting took place when they were both 19. It was on a Sunday in January, when everyone else had gone to a family dinner in Kimberley. He stayed behind because he was still weak after a bout of malaria. He was sitting on the terrace, Miranda was the only servant in the house, and suddenly he stood up and went to her in the kitchen. He would often think he had never really left her after that. He had stayed in the kitchen. She had him in her power from that moment on. He would never be able to shake her off.

Two years later she got pregnant. He was studying at Rand University in Johannesburg. His love for Miranda was his passion and at the same time his horror. He was betraying his people and their traditions. He tried to break off contact with her many times, to escape from this forbidden relationship, but he could not. They would meet in secret, their moments together dominated by fear of being discovered. When she told him that she was pregnant, he beat her. The next moment it dawned on him that he would never be able to live without her, even if he could never live with her openly either. She gave up her position at the house. He arranged a job for her in Johannesburg. With the help of some English friends at the university, who had a different attitude towards affairs with black women, Kleyn bought a little house in eastern Johannesburg, in Bezuidenhout Park, and she lived there under the pretence of being a servant for an Englishman who spent most of his time on his farm in Southern Rhodesia. They could be together there, and there their daughter was born and, without any discussion being necessary, christened Matilda. They had no more children, and to the sorrow and sometimes even bitterness of his parents Kleyn never married. A *Boer* who did not form a family and have lots of children was a person who failed to live up to traditions. Kleyn became more and more of a mystery to his parents, and he would never be able to explain that he loved their servant Matilda's daughter, Miranda.

He lay in bed thinking about all this that Saturday morning of May 9. In the evening he would be visiting the house in Bezuidenhout Park. It was a routine he regarded as sacrosanct. Only something connected with his work for NIS could get in the way. That particular Saturday he knew his visit would be much delayed. He had an important meeting with Frans Malan which could not be postponed.

Kleyn had disciplined himself to get by on only a few hours of sleep, but that morning he allowed himself the luxury of sleeping late. He could hear faint noises from the kitchen where his servant, Moses, was making breakfast.

He thought about the telephone call he had received just after midnight. Konovalenko had given him the news he needed to hear. Victor Mabasha was dead. Not only did that mean a problem had been erased, it meant, that the doubts he had been entertaining over the last few days about Konovalenko's ability had been put to rest.

He was to meet Malan in Hammanskraal at 10 a.m. It was time to decide when and where the assassination would take place. Mabasha's successor had been chosen. Kleyn was certain that once again he had made the right choice. Sikosi Tsiki would do what was required of him. The selection of Mabasha had not been an error of judgment. Kleyn knew there were invisible depths in everybody, even the most uncompromising of people. That was why he had arranged for Konovalenko to test the man he had chosen. Mabasha had been weighed in Konovalenko's scales and found wanting. Tsiki would undergo the same test.

At 8.30 a.m. he left the house. Smoke was hanging low over the shanty town alongside the highway. He tried to imagine Miranda and Matilda being forced to live there, among the tin shacks, the charcoal fires constantly making their eyes water, homeless dogs all about. Miranda had been lucky and escaped from the inferno of the slums. Her daughter Matilda had inherited her good fortune. They had no need to share the hopeless lives of their African brothers and sisters.

It seemed to Kleyn that his daughter had inherited her mother's beauty, but there was a difference. Matilda's skin was lighter than her mother's. When eventually she had a child with a white man, the process would continue. Sometime in the future, long after he had gone, his descendants would have children whose appearance would hardly betray the black blood in their genes.

Jan Kleyn liked driving and thinking about the future. He had never been able to understand those who claimed it was impossible to predict what it would be like. As far as he was concerned, it was being shaped at that very minute.

Malan was waiting on the veranda at Hammanskraal. They shook hands and went straight in to where the table with the green baize cloth was waiting for them.

"Mabasha is dead," Kleyn said when they had sat down.

A broad smile lit up Malan's face. "I have been wondering," he said.

"Konovalenko killed him yesterday," Kleyn said. "The Swedes have always been very good at making hand grenades."

"We have some of them here," Malan said. "It's hard to get hold of them, but our agents can generally get around the problems."

"That's about the only thing we have to thank the Rhodesians for," Kleyn said.

In the course of his training for the intelligence service, he had learned from an old officer how almost 30 years ago the Southern Rhodesians had cracked the sanctions. It had taught him that all politicians have dirty hands. Those vying for power set up and break rules according to the state of the game. Despite the sanctions imposed by every country in the world apart from Portugal, Taiwan, Israel and South Africa, Southern Rhodesia had never run short of the goods they needed to import. Nor had their exports suffered any serious downturn. American and Soviet politicians offered their services. The Americans, mainly senators from the South, considered it important to support the white minority government. Through an ingenious network of intermediaries, they had taken it upon themselves to lift the sanctions by back-door methods. The Russians needed Rhodesian minerals for their industries. Soon there was nothing left but a mirage of isolation. Nevertheless, all over the world politicians continued to condemn the white racist regime and extol the success of the sanctions.

Kleyn realised later that white South Africa also had many friends throughout the world, although the support they received was less conspicuous than what the blacks were getting.

"Who'll replace him?" Malan said.

"Sikosi Tsiki. He was number two on the list I made earlier. He's 28, born near East London. He's managed to get himself banned by both the ANC and Inkatha. In each case for disloyalty and theft. He has such hatred for both organisations, I'd call it fanatical."

"There's generally something about fanatics that can't be completely controlled. They have absolutely no fear of death, but they don't always stick to the plans."

Kleyn was irritated by Malan's magisterial tone. "I'm the one calling him fanatical," he said calmly. "That doesn't necessarily mean he'll live up to the description in practice. His cold-bloodedness is scarcely less intense than yours or mine."

Malan had, as usual, no reason to doubt him.

"I've talked to our friends on the Committee," Kleyn said. "I asked for a vote, since we were talking about picking a replacement. Nobody disagreed."

Malan could picture the committee members round the oval-shaped walnut table slowly raising their hands one after another. There were never any secret votes. Decisions were always open, to make sure that members' loyalty never wavered. Apart from a shared determination to secure by any means the rights of Afrikaners and by extension those of all whites in South Africa, the members of the Committee had little or nothing to do with each other. The demagogue Terre Blanche was regarded with ill-concealed contempt by many of them, but his presence was a necessity. The chairman of the Two Oceans mining company, an elderly man whom no-one had ever seen laugh, was treated with the double-edged respect often inspired by extreme wealth. Judge Pelser, the Broederbond representative, was a man whose disdain for humankind was notorious, but he had great influence and was seldom contradicted. And finally there was General Stroesser, one of the air force high command, a man who was restless in the company of civil servants or mine owners.

They had voted to give Sikosi Tsiki the assignment. That meant he and Kleyn could proceed to implement their plans.

"Tsiki will leave here on the 12th," Kleyn said. "Konovalenko is ready to receive him. He'll fly to Copenhagen via Amsterdam on a Zambian passport, then go by ferry to Sweden."

Now it was Malan's turn. He took some black-and-white enlargements from his briefcase. He had taken the pictures himself and developed them in his darkroom at home. He had photographed the map at work.

"Friday, June 12," he began. "The local police think there'll be around 40,000 in the crowd. There are lots of reasons why this could be a suitable occasion for us to strike. To start with, there's a hill, Signal Hill, just south of the stadium. The distance from there to where the podium will be is about 700 metres. There are no buildings on the summit, but there is a serviceable access. Tsiki shouldn't have any problems getting there, or making his retreat. If necessary, he could lie low up there before making his way down later and mixing with the blacks who'll be milling around in the chaos that's bound to follow."

Kleyn studied the photographs, waiting for Malan to continue.

"My other argument," Malan said, "is that the assassination should take place in the heart of what we can call the English part of our country. Africans tend to react primitively. Their first reaction will be that somebody from Cape Town is responsible for the killing. Their rage will be directed at the locals. All those liberal-minded Englishmen who wish the blacks so well will be forced to face up to what is in store for them if ever the blacks come to power in our country. That will make it simpler to stir up a backlash."

Kleyn had been thinking along the same lines. He reflected briefly on what Malan had said. In his experience, every plan had some weakness.

"What is there against it?" he said.

"I cannot find anything at all," Malan said.

"There's always a weak point," Kleyn said. "We can't make a decision until we've identified it."

"I can only think of one thing that could go wrong," Malan said, after a few moments' silence. "Tsiki could miss."

Jan Kleyn looked surprised. "He won't miss," he said. "I only pick people who hit their targets."

"Seven hundred metres is a hell of a distance," Malan said. "A puff of wind. A flash of reflected sun. The bullet misses by a couple of centimetres. Hits somebody else."

"That won't happen," Kleyn said.

They might not be able to find the weak point in the plan they were developing, but Malan had found a weakness in Jan Kleyn. When rational arguments had run their course, he took refuge in fate. It could not happen.

But he said nothing, and after a servant had brought them tea they ran through the plan once more, spelled out details, listed questions that needed answering. Not until nearly 4 p.m. did they think they had gone as far as they could.

"We are now a month and three days to June 12," Kleyn said. "That means we don't have much time to make the plan final. We'll have to decide by next Friday if it's going to be Cape Town. By then we must have weighed everything, and answered all the outstanding questions. Let's meet here again on the 15th, in the morning. I'll get the whole Committee here at noon. Meanwhile we'll both go through the plans, independently, looking for cracks. We know the arguments in favour. We'll have to find the arguments against."

Malan had no objections. They shook hands and left the house at Hammanskraal ten minutes apart. Kleyn drove straight to the house in Bezuidenhout Park.

*

Miranda Nkoyi contemplated her daughter. She was sitting on the floor, staring into space. Miranda could see her eyes were not vacant, but alert. Sometimes when she looked at her daughter she felt, as if in a brief fit of giddiness, that she was seeing her mother. Her mother was as young as that, just 17, when she gave birth to Miranda. Now her own daughter was that very age.

What is she looking at? Miranda wondered. She sometimes felt a cold shudder run down her spine when she recognised those features characteristic of Matilda's father. Especially that look of intense concentration, even though she was staring into empty space. That inner vision that no-one else could understand.

"Matilda," she said tenderly, as if hoping to bring her back down to earth by treating her gently. The girl came out of her reverie with a start, and looked her straight in the eye.

"I know my father will soon be here," she said. "Since you won't let me hate him while he's here, I do it while I'm waiting. You can never take the hatred from me."

Miranda wanted to cry out that she understood her feelings, that she often thought that way herself. But she could not. She was like her mother, saddened by the endless humiliation of not being free to lead a satisfactory life in her own country. Miranda knew she had grown soft just like her mother, and remained in a state of impotence she could only make up for by constantly betraying the man who was the father of her daughter.

Soon, she thought. Soon I must tell my daughter that her mother has retained a little bit of her life force, despite everything. I shall have to tell her, in order to win her back, to show her that the gulf between us is not an abyss after all.

In secret, Matilda was a member of the ANC youth organisation. She was active, and had already undertaken several undercover assignments. She had been arrested by the police more than once. Miranda was terrified she would be injured or killed. Every time the coffins of dead blacks were being carried in swaying, chanting processions to their graves, she would pray to all the gods she believed in that her daughter might be spared. She turned to the Christian God, to the spirits of her ancestors, to her dead mother, to the *sangoma* her father used to speak about. But she never wholly believed that they had heard her.

Miranda could understand the confused feeling of impotence in her daughter, knowing that her father was a Boer, knowing herself to have been sired by the enemy. It was as if a mortal wound had been inflicted on her at the very moment of her birth.

Nevertheless, she knew a mother could never regret the existence of her daughter. Seventeen years ago she had loved Jan Kleyn as little as she loved him today. Matilda was conceived in fear and subservience. It was as though the bed they were lying in was floating in a remote, airless universe. Afterwards, she simply did not have the strength to throw off her subservience. The child would be born, it had a father, and he had organised a life for her, a house in Bezuidenhout, money to live on. She was resolved never to have another child by him. If Matilda would be her only offspring, so be it., Kleyn had never said that he wanted another child by her; his demands on her as far as love-making was concerned left her always feeling uninvolved. She let him spend nights with her, and could suffer it because she had learned how to take revenge by betraying him.

She observed her daughter, who had once again lost herself in a world to which her mother was denied access. Matilda had inherited her own beauty. The only difference was her lighter skin. She wondered sometimes what Kleyn would say if he knew that what his daughter most of all wanted was a darker skin.

My daughter betrays him as well, Miranda thought. But our betrayal is not malice. It's the lifeline we cling to, even as South Africa burns. Any malice is on his side. One of these days it will destroy him. The freedom we achieve will not primarily be the voting slips we find in our hands, but the release from those inner chains that have been holding us prisoner.

The car came to a stop by the security gate.

Matilda got up and looked at her mother.

"Why have you never killed him?" she said.

What Miranda heard was his voice in hers. But she had convinced herself that Matilda's heart was not an Afrikaner heart. Her appearance, her light skin, those were things she could do nothing about. But she had preserved her heart, hot and inexhaustible as it was. That was a line of defence, albeit the last one, which Kleyn could never overcome.

The shameful thing was that he never seemed to notice anything. Every time he came to Bezuidenhout his car was laden with food so that she could make him the meals, just as he remembered from his childhood. He never recognised that he was transforming Miranda into her own mother, the enslaved servant. He could never see that he was forcing her to play different roles: cook, lover, valet. He did not notice the resolute hatred in his daughter. He saw only a world that was unchanging, petrified, something he considered his main task in life to preserve. He did not see the dishonesty, the bottomless artificiality on which the country was built.

"Is everything OK?" he said as he laid the bags of food in the hall.

"Yes," Miranda said. "Everything's fine."

Then Miranda cooked while he tried to talk to his daughter, who was playing the shy and timid girl. He tried stroking her hair, and Miranda could see through the kitchen door how her daughter stiffened. They ate their meal of Afrikaner sausages, big chunks of meat and cabbage salad. Miranda knew that Matilda would go to the bathroom and force herself to throw up the whole meal when it was over. Then he wanted to talk about unimportant matters, the house, the wallpaper, the garden. Matilda withdrew to her room, leaving her mother alone with him, and she gave him the answers he was expecting. Then they went to bed. His body was as hot as only a freezing object can be. The next day would be Sunday. As they could not be seen together, they took their Sunday stroll inside the four walls of the house, walking around and around each other, eating, and sitting in silence. Matilda always went out as soon as she reasonably could and didn't come back until he had left. Only when Monday came would everything begin to return to normal.

When he had fallen asleep and his breathing was calm and steady, she got out of bed. She had learned how to move around the bedroom in perfect silence. She went to the kitchen, leaving the door open so she could the whole time check that he did not wake up. If he did, and wondered where she was, her excuse was a glass of water she had poured already.

As usual, she had hung his clothes over a chair in the kitchen, which he could not see from the bedroom. He did once ask why she always left his clothes in the kitchen rather than in the bed-room, and she explained she wanted to brush them for him in the morning.

She went through his pockets. She knew his wallet would be in the left inside pocket of his jacket, and his keys in the right-hand pocket of his trousers. The pistol he invariably carried was on the bedside table.

This was usually all she found in his pockets. That evening, however, there was a scrap of paper with something written on it in his hand-writing. With one eye on the bedroom, she swiftly memorised what was written.

Cape Town/12 June/Distance to location?/Wind direction?/Access road?

She put the paper back, folded exactly as it had been.

She could not understand what the words meant, but she would do what she was told to do whenever she found something in his pockets. She would tell the man she met every day after Kleyn had been to visit her. With their friends, they would try to work out what the words meant.

She drank the water and went back to bed.

He sometimes talked in his sleep. When that happened it was nearly always within an hour of his falling asleep. She would also memorise the words he mumbled, sometimes yelled out, and tell the man she met the following day. He would write down everything she could remember, just as he did with everything else that had happened during Kleyn's visit. Sometimes he would say where he had come from, and sometimes where he was going as well. But most often he said nothing at all.

A long time ago he had said he was working as a chief executive officer in the Ministry of Justice in Pretoria. Later, when she was contacted by the man who was looking for information and heard from him that Kleyn worked for NIS, she was told that she must never breathe a word to anyone about knowing where in fact he worked.

Kleyn left her house on the Sunday evening. Miranda waved goodbye as he drove away. He said that he would come back at the end of the following week.

As he drove, he decided he was looking forward to the week to come.

The plan had begun to take shape. He had everything that was going to happen under control.

What he did not know was that Mabasha was still alive.

On May 12, a month to the day before he was to carry out the assassination of Nelson Mandela, Sikosi Tsiki left Johannesburg on the KLM flight to Amsterdam. Tsiki had spent a long time wondering who his victim was to be. Unlike Mabasha, though, he had not concluded it must be President de Klerk. He left the question open. That it might involve Mandela had never crossed his mind.

On Wednesday, May 13, in the evening, a fishing boat pulled into the harbour at Limhamn. Tsiki jumped ashore and the fishing boat pulled out straightaway, headed back to Denmark. A strikingly fat man was waiting on the dock to welcome him.

On that afternoon there was a southwesterly gale blowing over Skåne. The wind did not die down until the evening. Then came the heat.

CHAPTER TWENTY

On Sunday afternoon, soon after 3 p.m., Peters and Norén were driving in central Ystad in their squad car, waiting for their shift to come to an end. It had been a quiet day with only one significant incident. They had been told by the emergency centre that a man had started demolishing a house in Sandskogen, and that he was stark naked. The wife had made the call. She explained that the man was in a rage because he had to spend all his free time repairing her parents' summer cottage. To ensure some peace and quiet in his life, he had decided to tear it down. He would prefer to sit by a lake, fishing, she had said, evidently terribly upset.

"You'd better go there and calm him down," the operator said.

"What's the charge?" Norén said, who was looking after the radio while Peters did the driving. "Disorderly conduct?"

"There's no such thing any more," the operator said. "But if the house belongs to his in-laws, you could say it's taking the law into his own hands. Who cares what the charge is? Just calm the man down."

They drove to Sandskogen without exceeding the limit.

"I understand the man," Peters said. "Having a house of your own is trouble enough. There's always something needing to be done. But you never have the time, or it costs too much. Having to take care of someone else's house makes it all the worse."

"Perhaps we should help him pull the house down," Norén said.

They found the address. A crowd had gathered on the road by the fence. Norén and Peters got out of the car and watched the naked man crawling over the roof, prying off tiles with a claw wrench. His wife came running up, still in tears. They listened to her incoherent account of what had happened.

They went over to the house and shouted up at the man, now sitting astride the roof ridge. He was so focused on dislodging tiles that he hadn't seen the police car. When he saw Norén and Peters he dropped the claw wrench. It came sliding down the roof, and Norén had to move smartly to avoid being hit.

"Careful!" Peters yelled. "You'd better come down. You have no right to be pulling down this house."

To their astonishment the man immediately obeyed them. He let down the ladder he had pulled up behind him, and climbed down. His wife met him with a dressing gown, which he put on.

"You going to arrest me?" the man said.

"No," Peters said. "But you'd better stop pulling the house down. After this, I can't see anyone asking you to do any more repairs."

"All I want to do is to go fishing," the man said.

As they drove back through Sandskogen, Norén telephoned his report to the station.

As they were about to turn into the Österlen highway, they saw him.

"Here comes Wallander," Peters said. Norén looked up from his notebook.

But apparently Wallander had not seen them. That would have been very strange if true, as they were in a marked patrol car painted blue and white. What attracted the attention of the two officers, however, was not Wallander's fixed stare. It was the man in the passenger seat. He was black. Peters and Norén looked at each other.

"Wasn't that an African in the car?" Norén said.

"Well," Peters said. "He was certainly black."

They were both thinking about the finger they had found a few weeks earlier, and the man they'd been searching for all over the country.

"Wallander must have caught him," Norén said hesitantly.

"Why is he going in that direction, then?" Peters said. "And why didn't he stop when he saw us?"

"It was as if he didn't want to see us," Norén said. "Like children do. If they close their eyes, they think nobody can see them."

Peters nodded. "Do you think he's in trouble?"

"No," Norén said. "But where did he manage to find the black man?"

Then they were interrupted by an emergency call about a motorcycle, suspected stolen, found abandoned in Bjäresjö. When they finished their shift, they asked about Wallander in the canteen, and discovered he had not appeared all day. Peters was about to tell everybody how they had seen him when he saw Norén put his finger to his lips.

"Why shouldn't I say anything?" he said, when they were in the locker room, getting ready to go home.

"If Wallander hasn't shown up, there must be some reason," Norén said. "Just what, is nothing to do with you or me. Besides, it could be some other African. Martinsson once said that Wallander's daughter had something going with a black man. It could have been him, for all we know."

"I still think it's weird," Peters said.

It was a feeling which stayed with him after he got back home to his terrace house on the Kristianstad road. When he had finished his dinner and played with his children for a while, he went out with the dog. Martinsson lived in the neighbourhood, so he decided to stop by and tell him what he and Norén had seen. The dog was a Labrador bitch and Martinsson had asked recently if he could join the waiting list for puppies.

Martinsson himself answered the door. He invited Peters in.

"I must get home pretty soon," Peters said. "But there is one thing I'd like to bounce off you. Do you have time?"

Martinsson had some position or other in the Liberal Party and was standing for a seat on the council; he had been reading some turgid political surveys the party had sent him. He lost no time collecting a jacket, and came out to join Peters.

"Are you positive?" Martinsson said.

"We can't both have been seeing things," Peters said.

"Most odd," Martinsson said thoughtfully. "I'd have heard right away if it was the African who's missing a finger."

"Maybe it was the daughter's boyfriend."

"Wallander said that was all over and done with."

They walked in silence for a while, watching the dog straining at its leash.

"It was as if he didn't want to see us," Peters said tentatively. "And that can only mean one thing. He didn't want us to know what he was up to."

"Or at least about the African with him," Martinsson said, lost in thought.

"There'll be some perfectly simple explanation," Peters said. "I mean, I don't want to suggest Wallander is up to something he shouldn't be."

"Of course not," Martinsson said. "But it was good you told me."

"I don't want to go spreading gossip," Peters said.

"This isn't gossip," Martinsson said.

"Norén will be mad," Peters said.

"He doesn't need to know," Martinsson said.

They parted company outside Martinsson's house. Peters assured him that he could buy a puppy when the time came.

Martinsson wondered if he ought to call Wallander. Then he decided to wait and talk to him the next day. With a sigh, he returned to his political documents.

When Wallander arrived at the police station the next morning, he had an answer ready for the question he knew would come. When, after much hesitation, he had decided to take Mabasha with him in the car, he thought the risk of bumping into a police colleague or anybody he knew was small. He had taken roads squad cars seldom used. But he ran into Peters and Norén. He saw them so late there was no time to tell Mabasha to crouch down and make himself invisible. Nor had he managed to turn off in some other direction. He could see in the corner of his eye that Peters and Norén had noticed the man in the seat beside him. They would want an explanation, no getting away from it. He cursed his luck, and wished he had never set out.

Then, when he had calmed down, he turned once more to his daughter for help.

"Herman Mboya will have to be resurrected as your boyfriend," he said. "If anybody should ask. Which is pretty unlikely."

She stared at him, then burst out laughing.

"Don't you remember what you told me when I was a kid?" she said. "That one lie leads to another? And eventually you get into such a mess, nobody knows what's true any more."

"I dislike this just as much as you do," Wallander said. "But it'll soon be over. He'll soon be out of the country. Then we can forget he was ever here."

"OK, I'll say Herman has come back," she said. "To tell you the truth, I sometimes wish he had."

So it was that when Wallander got to the station on Monday morning, he had an explanation ready for why there was an African in his car on Sunday. At a time when most things were threatening to slide out of control, that seemed the least of his problems. When he saw Mabasha on the street that morning in the fog, his first instinct was to run back to the apartment and summon his colleagues for assistance. But something held him back, something at odds with all his police logic. When they were in the cemetery that night in Stockholm, he had thought the black man was telling the truth. He might have been there, but he was not the killer of Mrs Åkerblom. It was the man called Konovalenko, who later tried to kill Mabasha as well. Very possibly Mabasha had tried to prevent what happened at the deserted house. Wallander had been turning over and over in his mind what could lie behind it all.

That was the spirit in which he took him back to the apartment, aware that he might be making a mistake. Wallander often used unconventional methods, to say the least, when dealing with suspects or convicted criminals. Björk had more than once felt obliged to remind Wallander of the correct police procedures. He had demanded of the black man that he surrender any weapon he was carrying. He accepted the pistol, and then frisked him. The man had seemed strangely unaffected, as if he expected nothing less of Wallander than an invitation to join him in his home. Wallander asked him how he had managed to track down his address.

"On the way to the cemetery," the man said, "I went through your wallet and memorised your address."

"You attacked me, Goddammit," he said. "And now you turn up at my home, many miles from Stockholm. You'd better have some damn good answers to the questions I'm going to ask you."

They sat in the kitchen, and Wallander closed the door so they wouldn't wake Linda. He would remember those hours as the most remarkable conversation he had ever had. It was not just that he received his first insight into the world from which Mabasha came and to which he would soon return. He also had to wonder how it was possible for a human being to be made up of so many incompatible parts: how a man could be a cold-blooded killer and at the same time be a rational, sensitive being with well-considered political views. He did not recognise that he was being taken in. Mabasha had seen how the wind was blowing. His seeming reliability could win him a passage home.

Wallander remembered most vividly what Mabasha said about a plant that grew only in the Namibian desert. It could live for two thousand years. It grew long leaves, like protective shades, to shield its flowers and its complicated root system. Mabasha took this plant as symbolic of the opposing forces in his homeland, and also of the struggle for supremacy in his own being.

"These privileges have become a habit with roots so deep," he said, "they've become a sort of extra limb. It's not all down to a racial defect. It's the whites who reap the benefits of this habit. If things had been different it could just as easily have been me and my brothers. But you cannot fight racism with racism. The habits of submission have to be broken and the whites must be made to understand that if they're to survive the immediate future, they have to hand back land to the deprived blacks. They have to give most of their riches to those who have nothing; they have to learn how to treat the blacks as human beings.

"Barbarism has always had a human face. That's what makes barbarism so inhuman. The blacks are so used to being submissive. It's so deeply ingrained. Progressing from being a nobody to being a somebody is the longest journey a human being can undertake.

"A peaceful solution is an illusion. The Apartheid system has gone so far, it's begun to flounder. A new generation of blacks has grown up who refuse to submit. They're impatient, they can see the imminent collapse. But progress is slow. Besides, there are many whites who think the same way, who refuse to go on accepting privileges requiring them to live as if all the blacks were invisible, as if they only existed to be servants or some strange sort of animals confined to remote shanty towns. In my country we have large nature reserves where wild animals can roam free, and we have large human reserves where the people are forever unfree."

Mabasha looked at Wallander as if expecting him to ask questions or make objections. It seemed to Wallander that all whites were the same to Mabasha, whether they lived in South Africa or anywhere else.

"A lot of my black brothers and sisters think this feeling of inferiority can be overcome by its opposite, a sense of superiority," Mabasha said. "That's wrong, of course. That leads to tensions between various groups where there should be co-operation. For instance, it can split a family in two. And where I come from if you don't have a family, you are nothing. For an African, the family is everything."

"I thought your spirits fulfilled that role," Wallander said.

"Spirits are part of our families," Mabasha said. "The spirits are our ancestors, keeping watch over us. They are invisible members of our family. We never forget them. That's why the whites have committed such a crime in driving us out of the land where we have lived for so many generations. Spirits don't like being forced to quit the land that once was theirs. The spirits hate even more than we do the shanty towns the whites have forced us to live in."

He stopped abruptly, as if the words he had just spoken had given him such terrible insight he had trouble absorbing it.

"I grew up in a family that was split from the start." After a long pause he said, "The whites knew they could break down resistance by splitting up our families. I watched my brothers and sisters behaving more and more like blind rabbits. They ran around in circles, no longer knowing where they came from or where they were going. I chose a different route. I learned to hate. I drank of the dark waters that arouse the desire for revenge. And I realised that despite their belief that their supremacy was God-given, the whites also had their weak points. They were frightened.

"They talked about making South Africa a perfect work of art, a white palace in Paradise. They could not see how impossible that dream was, and those who did refused to admit it. So the foundation on which everything was built became a lie; fear came to them in the night. They filled their houses with weapons. But fear found its way inside even so. Violence became a part of the everyday programme of fear. I could see all that, and I resolved to keep my friends close by me, but my enemies even closer. I would play the role of the black man who knew what white men wanted. I would feed my contempt by running errands for them. I would work in their kitchens, and spit in the soup before carrying it to their tables. I would go on being a nobody who in secret had become a somebody."

How much had Wallander really understood? How could it help him to understand what had brought Mabasha to Sweden?

"I have to know more," he said. "You haven't said who's behind all this, who sent you to Sweden?"

"Those ruthless people are mere shadows," Mabasha said. "Their ancestors abandoned them long ago. They meet in secret to plan the downfall of our country."

"And you run their errands?"

"Yes."

"Why?"

"Why not?"

"You kill people."

"Sooner or later others will kill me."

"What do you mean by that?"

"I know it will happen."

"But you didn't kill the woman at the farmhouse?"

"No."

"A man called Konovalenko did that?"

"Yes."

"Why?"

"Only he can tell you that."

"You come here from South Africa and another man comes from Russia. You meet at a farmhouse in Skåne. There is a radio transmitter there, and weapons. Why?"

"That's how it was arranged."

"By whom?"

"By the ones who asked us to make the journey."

We're going around in circles, Wallander thought. I'm not getting any answers.

But he forced himself to make one more effort.

"I've gathered this was some kind of preparation," he said, "for some crime or other that was going to take place back home where you come from. A crime you were to be responsible for. A murder? But who was going to be killed? Why?"

"I've tried to explain what my country's like."

"I'm asking you straight questions, and I want straight answers."

"Maybe the answers have to be what they are."

"I don't understand you," Wallander said. "You're a man who kills to order, if I understand you rightly. Yet you seem a sensitive person who's suffering as a result of circumstances in your country. I can't make it all add up."

"Nothing adds up for a black man living in South Africa."

Then Mabasha went on to explain how things were in his battered and bruised homeland. Wallander had difficulty believing his ears. When Mabasha was finished, it seemed to Wallander that he had been on a long journey. His guide had shown him places he never knew existed.

I live in a country where we've been taught to believe that all truths are simple, he thought. And also that the truth is clear and unassailable. Our legal system is based on that principle. Now I'm starting to realise that the truth is complicated, multi-faceted, contradictory. That lies are both black and white. If one's view of humans, of human life, is disrespectful and contemptuous, then truth takes on another aspect than if life is regarded as inviolable.

He contemplated Mabasha, who was looking him straight in the eye.

"Did you kill the woman at the farmhouse?" Wallander said, getting the impression that this was the last time he would ask. "Or the store-keeper."

"No," Mabasha said. "And I lost one of my fingers for the sake of the woman's soul. I didn't touch the man in the store."

"You still don't want to tell me what you're supposed to do when you get back?" Before Mabasha replied Wallander felt that something had changed. Something in the black man's face was different. Thinking about it later, he thought maybe it was that the expressionless mask suddenly started to melt away.

"I still can't say what," Mabasha said. "But it won't happen."

"I don't think I understand," Wallander said slowly.

"Death will not come from my hands," Mabasha said. "But I can't stop it coming from somebody else's."

"An assassination?"

"That was my job to carry out. But now I'm going to drop it and walk away."

"You're talking in riddles," Wallander said. "What are you going to drop? I want to know who was going to be assassinated."

But Mabasha did not answer. He shook his head, and Wallander accepted, reluctantly, that he would get no further. Afterwards he would also realise he still had a long way to go before he could recognise the truth in circumstances outside his normal range of experience. It was only later that it dawned on him that the last admission, when Mabasha allowed his mask to drop, was utterly false. He did not have the slightest intention of walking away from his assignment. But the lie was necessary if he were to receive the help he needed to get out of the country. To be believed, he had to lie – and to do so skilfully enough to deceive the Swedish policeman.

Wallander had no more questions then. He was tired, but he seemed to have achieved what he wanted to achieve. The assassination was foiled, at least Mabasha's involvement – if he was telling the truth. That would give his opposite numbers in South Africa more time to sort things out. I'll contact them via Interpol and tell them all I know. The only missing element is our friend Konovalenko. If I try to get Åkeson to have Mabasha arrested, there's a serious risk that everything could become even more confused. The chance of Konovalenko fleeing the country would only increase. I don't need to know any more. Now I can carry out my last illegal action as far as Mabasha is concerned.

Help him to get out of here.

His daughter had been present for the latter part of the conversation. She had woken up, and come into the kitchen. Wallander explained briefly who the man was.

"This is the man who hit you?"

"That's right. Goli, this is my daughter."

"And here he is drinking coffee with you?"

"Yes."

"Even you must think that's a little odd."

"A policeman's life *is* a little odd."

She asked no more questions. When she was dressed, she came back and sat quietly, listening. When they were finished, Wallander sent her to buy a bandage for the man's hand. He found penicillin in the bathroom and gave some to Mabasha, knowing that he ought to have called a doctor. Then, reluctantly, he cleaned up the wound and applied the clean bandage.

Next he called Lovén and got him almost right away. He asked for the latest news on Konovalenko and the others who had disappeared from the apartment block in Hallunda. He said nothing about the fact that Mabasha was there with him in his kitchen.

"We know where they went when we raided their apartment," Lovén said. "They moved two floors up in the same building. Cunning and convenient. They had an apartment there, in the wife's name. But they're gone from there too."

"Then we know something else as well," Wallander said. "They're still in this country. Presumably in Stockholm, where it's easiest to lose yourself."

"If need be I'll personally kick down the front door of every apartment in this town."

"Concentrate on Konovalenko. I think the African is less important."

"If only I could grasp the connection between them," Lovén said.

"They were in the same place when Louise Åkerblom was murdered," Wallander said. "Then Konovalenko did the bank job and killed an officer. The African wasn't with him then, and later Konovalenko tries to kill the African. One explanation is they started out friends but had a falling out."

"But where does your estate agent fit into this?"

"She isn't a part of it. I think she was there by sheer chance. Wrong place, wrong time. And Konovalenko is ruthless."

"All of which leaves us one single question," Lovén said. "Why?"

"The only person who can answer that is Konovalenko."

"Or the African," Lovén said. "You're forgetting him, Kurt."

After the call to Lovén, Wallander made up his mind to get Mabasha out of the country.

"The best thing you can do is to stay here in the apartment," he told Mabasha. "I still have a lot of questions I want answered. You might just as well get used to that."

Apart from the drive on Sunday afternoon, they spent the weekend in the apartment. Mabasha was exhausted, and slept most of the time. Wallander was worried that his hand would turn septic. At the same time he regretted ever having let him into his apartment. Like so often before, he had followed his intuition rather than his reason. Now he could see no obvious way out of his dilemma.

On Sunday evening he drove Linda to see his father. He dropped her on the main road so he would not have to deal with his father's complaints about his not even having time for a cup of coffee.

Monday finally came, and he returned to the police station. Björk welcomed him back. They got together with Martinsson and Svedberg in the conference room. Wallander reported selectively on what had happened in Stockholm. There were many questions, but nobody had much to say. The key to the whole business was finding Konovalenko.

"We just have to wait until he gets picked up," Björk said. "That'll give us time to sort out the stacks of other matters waiting for our attention."

They agreed the priorities. Wallander was assigned to find out what happened to three trotting horses that had been rustled from stables near Skårby. To the astonishment of his colleagues, he burst out laughing.

"It's a bit absurd," he said, apologetically. "A missing woman. And now missing horses."

He hardly got back to his office before he received the visit he was expecting. He was not sure which of them would actually turn up to ask the question. It could have been any one of his colleagues. But it was Martinsson who knocked and entered.

"Have you got a minute?" he said.

Wallander nodded.

"There's something I need to ask you."

Wallander could see he was embarrassed. "I'm listening," he said.

"You were seen with an African yesterday," Martinsson said. "In your car. I just thought . . ."

"What did you think?"

"I don't know really."

"Linda is back with her Kenyan again."

"I thought that would be it."

"A moment ago you said you didn't know what you thought."

Martinsson threw his arms wide and made a face. Then he retreated in a hurry.

Wallander ignored the case of the missing horses and sat down to think. What were the questions he still had to ask Mabasha? And how would he check his answers?

In recent years Wallander had dealt with people from abroad, both as victims and criminals, in connection with various investigations. It had occurred to him that what he used to regard as absolute truth when it came to right and wrong, guilt and innocence, might no longer apply. And what was held to be a crime might vary according to the culture one grew up in. He often felt helpless in such situations. In the course of the year before his mentor Rydberg had died, they had spent a lot of time discussing the enormous changes that were taking place in their country, and indeed in the world at large. The police would face quite different demands. Rydberg had sipped his whisky and prophesied that within ten years Swedish policemen would have to cope with more fundamental changes. This time, though, it would not just be organisational reforms, but it would affect police work on the ground.

"This is something I'm not going to have to face," Rydberg had said one evening as they sat on his cramped little balcony. "Sometimes I feel sad that I won't be around to see what comes next. It's bound to be difficult. But stimulating. You'll be there, though. And you'll have to start thinking along completely different lines."

"I wonder if I'll manage," Wallander said. "I ask myself more and more often whether there's life beyond the police station."

"If you're thinking of sailing to the West Indies, make sure that you never come back," Rydberg said. "People who go off somewhere and then do come back are seldom better off for their adventure. They haven't come to terms with the old truth: you can never run away from yourself."

"That's something I'll never do," Wallander said. "I don't have room in my psyche for such big plans. The most I can do is to wonder if there is some other job I'd rather have."

"You'll be a police officer as long as you live," Rydberg said. "You're like me. Face up to that."

Wallander banished thoughts of Rydberg, took out a note pad, and reached for a pen. Then he just sat there. Questions and answers, he thought. That's probably where I'm making the first mistake. Many people, not least those who come from continents a long way away, have to be allowed to tell the story their own way in order to be able to formulate an answer. That's something I ought to have learned by now, considering the number of Africans and Arabs and South Americans I've met. They are often put off by the hurry we're always in, and they think it's a sign of our contempt. Not having time for a person, not being able to sit in silence with somebody, that's the same as rejecting them, as being scornful of them.

Tell their own story, he wrote at the top of the page. That might put him on the right path. Tell their own story, that's all.

He pushed the pad to one side and put his feet on the desk. Then he called home and was told that everything was calm. He said he would be back in a couple of hours.

His mind elsewhere, he read the memo on the missing horses. It told him little more than that three valuable animals had disappeared on the night of May 5. They had been put into their stalls for the night. At about 5.30 a.m. the following morning, when one of the stable girls went in with their feed, the stalls were empty.

He glanced at his watch and decided to drive to the stables. He talked to three grooms and the owner's secretary. Wallander was inclined to think the whole thing was a sophisticated insurance fraud. He made a few notes and told them he would be coming back.

He stopped at a café for a cup of coffee on the way home to Ystad. He wondered if they had racehorses in South Africa.

CHAPTER TWENTY-ONE

Sikosi Tsiki landed in Sweden on Wednesday, May 13. That evening, Konovalenko told him, he would be staying in the southern part of the country. This was where his training would take place, and where he would leave from. He had considered setting up camp in the Stockholm area. There were possibilities, especially around Arlanda, where the noise of aeroplanes landing and taking off would drown out most other sounds. The shooting practice could take place there. Furthermore there was the problem of Mabasha, and the Swedish policeman. If they were still in Stockholm, he would have to be there until they had been disposed of. He had to take into account that the scale of police activity all over the country would be heightened as a result of the death of the officer. To be on the safe side, he advanced on two fronts. He kept Tania with him in Stockholm, but sent Rykoff to the country again to find a suitably isolated retreat. Rykoff had pointed out on a map an area to the north of Skåne called Småland, claiming it was much easier to find what they were looking for there, but Konovalenko wanted to be near Ystad. If they did not catch Mabasha and the policeman in Stockholm, they would turn up sooner or later in Wallander's home town. He was as sure of that as he was that some kind of unexpected relationship had formed between the African and Wallander. If he could find one of them, he was confident he would find the other.

Through a travel agency in Ystad, Rykoff rented a house northeast of Ystad, towards Tomelilla. The location could have been better, but next to the house was an abandoned quarry that could be used for target practice. As Konovalenko had decreed that Tania could go with them, Rykoff did not need to fill the freezer with food. Instead, at Konovalenko's instruction, he spent his time finding out where Wallander lived, and then keeping his apartment under observation. But Wallander did not appear. The day before Sikosi Tsiki was due to arrive, Tuesday, May 12, Konovalenko decided to stay in Stockholm.

None of the people he had sent out looking for Mabasha had seen him, but Konovalenko's instinct told him that he was lying low in the city. Also it was difficult to believe that a policeman as careful and well organised as Wallander would return directly to his home, which he would have to expect to be watched.

Nevertheless that is where Rykoff finally found him, late on Tuesday afternoon. The door opened and Wallander walked out. He was on his own, and Rykoff, who was sitting in his car, could see right away that he was on guard. Rykoff realised he would be spotted at once if he tried to follow him in his car. He was still there ten minutes later when the front door opened once again. Rykoff stiffened. This time two people. The girl had to be Wallander's daughter, whom he had never seen before. Behind her was Mabasha. They crossed the street, got into a car, and drove away. Rykoff did not follow them this time either. Instead he stayed where he was and dialled the number of the apartment in Järfälla. Tania answered. Rykoff greeted her briefly and asked to speak to Konovalenko. After hearing what Rykoff had to say, Konovalenko made up his mind right away. He and Tania would go to Skåne early the next day. They would stay there until they had collected Tsiki and killed Wallander and Victor Mabasha; the daughter as well, if necessary. Then they could make up their minds what to do next. But the apartment in Järfälla would be a possibility.

Konovalenko drove down to Skåne with Tania overnight. Rykoff met them at a car park on the western outskirts of Ystad. They went straight to the house he had rented. In the afternoon Konovalenko also paid a visit to Mariagatan. He spent some time observing the block where Wallander lived. On the way back, he stopped for a while on the hill where the police station was, observing it.

The situation seemed very simple to him. He could not afford to fail again. That would mean the end of his dreams about a future life in South Africa. He was already living dangerously. There was a risk, albeit a small one, that Kleyn had someone passing on information. Occasionally he had sent out scouts to see if they could identify anyone shadowing him. But nobody had come across any kind of surveillance.

Konovalenko and Rykoff spent the day deciding how to proceed. Konovalenko made up his mind from the very first to act resolutely and ruthlessly. It would be a brutal, direct attack.

"What kind of weapons do we have?"

"Practically anything you like short of a rocket launcher," Rykoff said. "We have various explosives, long-distance detonators, grenades, automatic rifles, shotguns, pistols, radio equipment."

Konovalenko drank a glass of vodka. What he most of all wanted was to take the policeman alive. There were questions he needed answering before he killed him. But he rejected the thought. He could afford no risks.

Then he made up his mind what to do. "Tomorrow morning when Wallander is out, Tania can go into the building and see what the staircase and apartment doors look like," he said. "You can be distributing leaflets. Pick up some from a supermarket. Then the building has to be kept under observation. If we know they're at home tomorrow evening, we'll make our move. We'll blow the door in, kill the pair of them and make our escape."

"There are three of them," Rykoff said.

"Two or three," Konovalenko said. "Nobody survives."

"The new man I'm picking up this evening, will he be in on it?" Rykoff said.

"No," Konovalenko said. "He waits here with Tania."

His expression was serious as he eyed Rykoff and Tania.

"The fact is, Mabasha has been dead for several days," he said. "That is what Tsiki has to believe. Is that clear?"

They both nodded.

Konovalenko poured another vodka for himself and Tania. Rykoff refused, since he was going to prepare the explosives. Besides, he was going to drive to Limhamn later to collect Tsiki.

"Let's put on a welcoming dinner for the man from South Africa," Konovalenko said. "None of us enjoys sitting at dinner with an African, but sometimes you have to do it for the sake of the job."

"Mabasha didn't like Russian food," Tania said.

"Chicken," Konovalenko said eventually. "All Africans like chicken."

At 6 p.m. Rykoff met Sikosi Tsiki off his boat at Limhamn. Now they were all sitting around the table. Konovalenko raised his glass. "You have a day off tomorrow," he said. "We get started on Friday."

Tsiki nodded. He was as laconic as his predecessor. Quiet people,

Konovalenko thought, but ruthless when necessary. As ruthless as I am.

Wallander devoted most of the first days after his return to Ystad to planning various forms of criminal activities. He arranged for Mabasha's escape from Sweden. He had decided after much soul-searching that it was the only way to get the situation under control. He had severe pangs of conscience: what he was doing was reprehensible. Even if Mabasha had not himself killed Louise Åkerblom, he was there when the killing took place. He had stolen cars and robbed a store at gunpoint and the storekeeper had died, though no shot was fired. Wallander convinced himself that this was a way of preventing the crime – whatever it was – that he had been preparing to commit in South Africa. This way Konovalenko could be stopped from murdering Mabasha. He would be charged with the murder of Mrs Åkerblom once he was caught. What he intended to do now was to send a message to his colleagues in South Africa via Interpol. But first he wanted Mabasha out of the country. He contacted a travel agency in Malmö. Mabasha had told him he could not get into South Africa without a visa. But with his fake Swedish passport, he did not need a visa for Zambia. He still had enough money for both an airline ticket and the journey home via Zimbabwe and Botswana. He would slip over the South African border at an unguarded point. The travel agent arranged a flight to London and thence a Zambia Airways flight to Lusaka. It meant Wallander would have to get him a false passport. That caused him the acutest problem, and also the worst worry. Arranging a forged passport in his own police station seemed to him a betrayal. It made things no better to have extracted from Mabasha a solemn promise to destroy the passport when he had passed the immigration desk in Zambia.

"The very same day," Wallander had insisted. "And it must be burned."

Linda took Mabasha to a booth for passport photographs in the port. The problem that could not be resolved until the last minute was how Mabasha would get through passport control. Even if he had a Swedish passport that was technically genuine and did not appear on the blacklist held by the border police, there was a risk that something would go wrong. Wallander decided to get Mabasha out through the hovercraft terminal in Malmö. He would buy him a first-class ticket. He assumed the embarkation card would help to ensure that passport officials were not especially interested in him. Linda would be his girl-friend. They would kiss goodbye right under the noses of the immi-gration officials, and Wallander would teach him a few phrases of Swedish.

The connections and the confirmed reservations were for the morning of May 15. Wallander would have to fix a passport for him by then.

On Tuesday afternoon he completed a passport application form for his father, and took with him two photographs. The procedures for issuing passports had lately been revised. The document was now produced while the applicant waited. Wallander hung around until the woman behind the counter had finished with the last of her customers and was about to close.

"Excuse me for being a little late," Wallander said. "But my father is going on a senior citizens' trip to France. He managed to throw away his old one when he was sorting some papers."

"These things happen," the woman said. "Does he have to have it today?"

"If possible," Wallander said. "I'm sorry I'm late."

"You can't solve the murder of that woman either," she said, taking the photos and the application form.

Wallander watched closely as she created the passport. Afterwards, when he had the document in his hand, he was confident he could do himself exactly what she had done.

"Impressively simple," he said.

"But boring," the woman said. "Why is it that all jobs get more boring when they're made easier?"

"Try being a policeman," Wallander said. "What we do is never boring."

"I am already a policewoman," she said. "Besides, I don't think I'd want to change places with you. It must be awful, pulling a body out of a well. What does it feel like, in fact?"

"I suppose it feels so awful," Wallander said, "that you get numb and you don't feel anything at all. But you can bet your boots there'll be a committee in the Ministry of Justice looking into what policemen feel when they pull dead women out of wells."

He stayed chatting while she locked up. All the bits and pieces you needed to make a passport were locked away in a cupboard. But he knew where the keys were kept.

Wallander had tried out many combinations of names to find out which ones Mabasha found easiest to pronounce. They settled on Jan Berg, Swedish citizen. Wallander knew from their conversations that the South African lived in close contact with a spirit world that was beyond his own comprehension. Nothing was coincidental, not even a change of name. Linda had been able to help him with some explanations of why Mabasha thought as he did. Mabasha spoke of his ancestors as if they were alive. Wallander was sometimes unsure whether what he described had taken place a hundred years ago or very recently. He could not help but be fascinated by the man. It became harder and harder to accept that this was a criminal preparing to commit a serious crime in his home country.

Wallander stayed in his office until late on Tuesday evening. To help the time pass he began a letter to Baiba Liepa in Riga. When he read through it, he tore the pages up. One of these days he would write her a letter and actually send it.

By about 10 p.m. only the night shift were still at the station. As he walked along the hall to the room where the passports were assembled, he thought of Mabasha's spirit world, and wondered if Swedish policemen had a special patron saint who would watch over them when they were about to do something illegal.

He had found a torch with a pale blue light since he could not risk turning on the light The key was in the filing cabinet. He paused, staring at the machine that converted the photographs and the completed application forms into a passport. Then he put on his rubber gloves and started work. At one point he thought he heard footsteps approaching. He turned the torch off and hid behind the machine. He could feel sweat streaming down under his shirt. In the end, though, he had a passport in his hand. He switched off the machine, locked the cupboard and put the key back in the cabinet. Sooner or later a routine check would show that a passport template was missing. Bearing the registration numbers in mind, it could happen the very next day, he thought. That would cause Björk a sleepless night or two, but nothing could be traced to Wallander.

Not until he was back in his office and sat at his desk did he realise that he had forgotten to stamp the passport. He cursed himself, and flung it onto the desk.

Just then the door opened and Martinsson marched in. He gave a start when he saw Wallander in his chair.

"Oh, excuse me," he said. "I didn't think you were here. I was just looking to see if I had left my cap."

"Cap?" Wallander said. "In the middle of May?"

"I have a cold coming on," Martinsson said. "I had it with me yesterday."

Wallander could not remember Martinsson having his cap when he and Svedberg had been in Wallander's office to go through the investigation.

"Look under the chair," Wallander said.

When Martinsson bent down, Wallander stuffed the passport into his pocket.

"Nothing there," Martinsson said. "I'm forever losing my caps."

"Ask the cleaner," Wallander said.

Martinsson was about to leave when something struck him. "Do you remember Peter Hanson?"

"How could I ever forget him?" Wallander said.

"Svedberg called him a few days ago and asked about a few details in the interrogation report. He told Peter Hanson about the break-in at your apartment. Thieves generally know what each other is up to. Svedberg thought it might be worth a try. Hanson called in today and said maybe he knew who did it."

"Well, I'll be damned!" Wallander said. "If he can get my records and tapes back, I'll forget about the stereo."

"Have a word with Svedberg tomorrow," Martinsson said. "And don't stay here all night."

"I was just about to leave," Wallander said, getting to his feet.

Martinsson paused in the doorway. "Do you think we'll get him?" he said.

"Of course we'll get him," Wallander said. "Konovalenko isn't going to get away."

"I do wonder if he's still in the country."

"We have to assume so."

"What about the African?"

"Konovalenko will point us in the right direction."

Martinsson nodded doubtfully. "One more thing," he said. "It's Mrs Åkerblom's funeral tomorrow."

Wallander looked at him, but he said nothing.

The funeral was to be at 2 p.m. Right up to the last minute Wallander was unsure whether or not he should go. He had no personal connection with the Åkerbloms. The woman they were burying had been dead before he first came into contact with the family. And maybe it would be misunderstood if someone from the police was there. Especially since the killer had not been found. For Wallander, was it curiosity? Or a guilty conscience? All the same, at 1 p.m. he had changed into a dark suit and spent some time looking for his white tie. Mabasha watched him tying the knot in front of the hall mirror.

"I'm going to a funeral," Wallander said. "The woman Konovalenko killed."

Mabasha stared at him in astonishment.

"Only now?" he said, surprised. "We bury our dead as soon as we can. That way they don't walk."

"We·don't believe in ghosts," Wallander said.

"Spirits aren't ghosts," Mabasha said. "I wonder sometimes how it is possible for white people to understand so little."

"Maybe you're right," Wallander said. "Or maybe you're wrong. It could be the other way around."

Then he went out. Mabasha's question had annoyed him. Does that black son of a bitch think he can come here and tell me what to think? he thought irreverently. Where does he think he would be without the help I've given him?

He parked his car some distance from the chapel at the crematorium and waited while the bells were ringing and the black-clad congregation entered. Only when a verger began to close the doors did he go in and sit in the back. A man two rows in front of him turned and greeted him. He was a journalist from the *Ystad Altehande*.

Then he listened to the organ music and felt a lump in his throat. Funerals were a great strain as far as he was concerned. He dreaded the prospect of his father's funeral. His mother's – eleven years ago – could still stir painful memories. He was to have made a short address, but he had broken down and rushed from the church.

He tried to master his feelings by observing the rest of the congregation. Åkerblom was in the front row with his daughters, both wearing white dresses. Pastor Tureson, who would take the service, was sitting with them.

Suddenly the handcuffs he found in a desk drawer at the Åkerbloms' house came into his mind. Policemen, he thought, have a sort of curiosity that goes beyond the immediate investigative work. Maybe it's an occupational hazard brought on by having to spend so many years delving into the most private parts of people's lives. I know that those handcuffs have nothing to do with the murder investigation. All the same I'm ready to spend time trying to find out what they meant to Louise Åkerblom, and maybe also her husband.

He shuddered at his train of thought, and concentrated on the service. At one point during Pastor Tureson's sermon he caught a glimpse of Robert Åkerblom. Even from a distance he could sense the depth of his sorrow and forlornness. The lump came back into his throat, and tears ran down his cheeks. To recover control of his emotions he started thinking about Konovalenko. Like most police officers in Sweden, no doubt, Wallander was secretly in favour of capital punishment. Apart from the scandal that it had been enforced against wartime traitors. Some killings, he felt, some assaults, certain drug offences were so appallingly immoral, so crass in their disregard of human dignity, that he could not escape the belief that those convicted of these crimes had forfeited all right to life themselves. Yes, his case was riddled with contradictions, and, yes, legislation to bring due punishment into effect would never be introduced. It was just his raw experience that shaped his thinking. What he was forced to deal with as a police officer.

After the burial, he shook hands solemnly with Robert Åkerblom and the other principal mourners. He avoided looking at the two daughters, afraid of bursting into tears.

Pastor Tureson took him to one side. "Your presence was very much appreciated," he said. "Nobody had expected the police to send a representative to the funeral."

"I'm only representing myself," Wallander said.

261

"So much the better that you came," Pastor Tureson said. "Are you still looking for the man behind the tragedy?"

Wallander nodded.

"But you will catch him?"

"Yes," Wallander said. "Sooner or later. How's Åkerblom taking it? And the daughters?"

"The support they're getting from the church is all-important to them just now," Pastor Tureson said. "And then, he has his God."

"You mean he still believes?" Wallander wondered aloud.

Pastor Tureson frowned. "Why should he abandon his God for something human beings have done to him and his family?"

"No indeed," Wallander said. "Why should he do that?"

"There'll be a meeting at the church in an hour," Pastor Tureson said. "You're welcome to come."

"Thanks," Wallander said. "But I've got to get back to work."

They shook hands and Wallander walked to his car. It dawned on him that spring really had arrived. Wait till Mabasha has left, he thought. Just wait until we've caught Konovalenko. Then I will devote myself to spring.

On Thursday morning Wallander drove his daughter to his father's house in Löderup. Once there, she decided out of the blue that she would stay there. She took one look at the overgrown courtyard and announced her intention to tidy it up before returning to Ystad. It would take her at least two days.

"If you change your mind, just give me a call," Wallander said.

"You should thank me for cleaning up your apartment," she said. "It looked awful."

"I know," he said. "And I am grateful."

"How much longer do I have to stay?" she asked. "I've got lots to do in Stockholm, you know."

"Not much longer," Wallander said, conscious of not sounding very convincing. Linda, to his surprise, did not argue.

When he got back, he had a long talk with Åkeson, the prosecutor, and then he gathered together all the investigation material with the help of Martinsson and Svedberg. He said goodbye to Ebba and left the station at about 4 p.m. He bought some food before driving home. Outside the apartment door was an unusually big heap of leaflets from some shop or other. He shoved them straight into the dustbin. Then he made dinner and went through all the details of the journey with Mabasha one more time. The lines he had memorised sounded better each time he spoke them. Mabasha would have an overcoat over his left arm to hide the bandage on his hand. He practised taking the passport from his inside pocket while keeping the coat over his left arm. Wallander was satisfied. Nobody would be able to see the injury.

"You'll fly to London with a British airline," he said. "SAS would be too risky. Swedish air hostesses probably read the newspapers and see the TV news. They'd notice your hand and raise the alarm."

Later in the evening, when there was nothing left to rehearse, silence fell and for a long time neither man seemed inclined to break it. In the end Mabasha got up and stood in front of Wallander.

"Why have you been helping me?" he said.

"I don't know," Wallander said. "I often think I ought to slip the handcuffs on you. I can see I'm taking a big risk in letting you go. Maybe it was you who killed Mrs Åkerblom after all. You say yourself how good a liar everybody becomes in your country. Maybe I'm letting a murderer go?"

"But you're doing it even so?"

"I'm doing it even so."

Mabasha took off his necklace and handed it to Wallander. The pendant was an animal's tooth.

"The leopard is the solitary hunter," Mabasha said. "Unlike the lion, the leopard goes its own way. During the day when the heat is at its height, it rests in the trees alongside the eagles. At night it hunts alone. The leopard is a skilful hunter. But the leopard is also the biggest challenge for other hunters. This is a tooth from a leopard. I want you to have it."

"I'm not sure I understood what you mean," Wallander said, "but I'll be glad to have the tooth."

"Not everything is understandable," Mabasha said. "A story is a journey without an end."

"That's probably the difference between you and me," Wallander said. "I'm used to stories having an end."

"That may be so, but it can be a good thing to know you'll never meet a certain person again. That means that something will live on."

"Perhaps, but I wonder if that's the way things really are."

An hour later Mabasha was asleep under a blanket on the sofa. Wallander sat gazing at the tooth he had been given. Suddenly he felt uneasy. He went out into the unlit kitchen and looked down at the street. No sign of life. Then he went into the hall and checked that the door was locked. He sat on a stool by the telephone, and thought that maybe he was just tired. Twelve more hours and Mabasha would be gone.

He examined the tooth once more. Nobody would believe me, he thought. If for no other reason, I'd better keep quiet about the days and nights I spent with a black man who had a finger cut off in a farmhouse in Skåne. That's a secret I'd better take to the grave.

When Jan Kleyn and Frans Malan met at Hammanskraal in the morning of Friday, May 15, they came swiftly to the conclusion there were no flaws in the plan. The assassination would now take place in Cape Town on June 12. Nelson Mandela would be addressing the crowded stadium. The summit of Signal Hill was the ideal position for a long-range shot. Then Sikosi Tsiki could make his escape unseen.

There were two things that Kleyn had not mentioned to Malan, nor to the other committee members. They were matters he had no intention of mentioning to anybody at all.

The first was that he was not prepared to take the risk of allowing Tsiki to live after he had carried out his assignment. That Tsiki could keep his mouth shut, he did not doubt, but just as the pharaohs killed those who had built the secret chambers in the pyramids, to ensure that any knowledge of their existence would be lost, he would sacrifice Tsiki. He would kill him himself, and make sure the body would never be found.

The second was that once Mandela's death was accomplished, he would decide whether or not he was ready to receive Konovalenko into South Africa. He trusted him to take care of the necessary training of Tsiki, but he did not exclude the possibility that even Konovalenko might have to go up in smoke, together with whoever his henchmen were. That whole unit needed a thorough spring cleaning. And he would not be delegating the job to anyone else.

In the week since they last met, Malan had been to Cape Town to study from all sides the stadium where Mandela would speak. He also spent a whole afternoon at the place on the hill from which Tsiki would fire his rifle. He made a videotape, which they watched three times on the television set in the room. The only thing still missing was a report on Cape Town's usual wind conditions. Claiming to be a visiting yachtsman, Malan had talked to the national weather centre, which was going to post him the information he had asked for. The name and address he gave would never be traced.

Kleyn had done no legwork. His contribution was a theoretical dissection of the plan, analysing unexpected developments. He kept at it until he was convinced that no unmanageable problem would crop up.

After two hours their work was done. "One last thing," Kleyn said. "We need to know well before June 12 how the Cape Town police will be deployed."

"I can take care of that," Malan said. "We can require all the police districts in the country to copy us their security plans – to give us time to consider the political measures that need to be taken given the scale of the anticipated crowds."

They waited on the veranda for the rest of the committee to arrive. They contemplated the view in silence. On the far horizon was a heavy blanket of smoke over a black shanty town.

"There'll be a bloodbath," Malan said.

"Think of it as a purification process," Kleyn said. "Besides, that's what we are hoping to achieve."

"Nevertheless," Malan said. "I can't help asking myself: will we be able to control what happens?"

"The answer to that is simple," Kleyn said. "We have to."

The familiar fatalism, Malan thought. Was Kleyn a psychopath hiding the violent truth about himself behind a mask that personified self-control? Malan did not like the thought, but all he could do was suppress it.

*

The formal meeting of the Committee lasted less than an hour. The decision was taken. In 28 days Nelson Mandela would die at the stadium near Cape Town.

The committee members left Hammanskraal at intervals of a few minutes. Kleyn was the last to leave.

CHAPTER TWENTY-TWO

The attack came just after midnight. Mabasha was asleep, wrapped in his blanket. Wallander was standing by the kitchen window, trying to decide whether he was hungry or whether all he wanted was a cup of tea. He was wondering whether his father and daughter were still up. He supposed they were. They always had a surprising number of things to talk about.

As he was waiting for the water to boil it came to him that it was 17 days since the hunt for Louise Åkerblom had begun. Now, they were pretty sure that she had been killed by a Russian called Konovalenko, who had in all likelihood shot the Stockholm policeman too.

Once Mabasha was out of the country – a few hours from now – he would be able to tell people what had happened. He would post an unsigned letter to the police. Not everyone would believe it. In the end everything depended on what they could make Konovalenko confess to. Not that everything he told them would be believed.

Wallander poured the boiling water into the teapot and left it to brew. Then he sat at the kitchen table. And at that moment the apartment door exploded. Wallander was thrown against the refrigerator by the blast. The kitchen rapidly filled up with smoke. He groped his way on all fours to the bedroom door. As he reached his bed and was fumbling for his pistol on the bedside table he heard four shots in close succession behind him. He flung himself to the floor. The shots had come from the living room.

Konovalenko, he thought frantically. He's coming for me. He wriggled as fast as he could under the bed. He was so shaken, he wasn't sure his heart could cope. Later on, he would recall thinking how degrading it would be, dying under one's own bed.

He heard some thuds and breathless groans from the living room. Somebody came into the bedroom, stood motionless for a moment, then went out again. Wallander heard Mabasha shouting something.

So he was still alive. Then came footsteps fading away into the stair-well. At the same time somebody started yelling, though he could not tell if it came from the street or from one of the neighbouring flats.

He eased himself from under the bed and carefully looked down into the street. The smoke was choking, and he had difficulty in making anything out. But then he saw two men dragging Mabasha between them. One of them was certainly Rykoff. Without thinking, Wallander flung open the bedroom window and fired straight up into the air. Rykoff let go of Mabasha and turned around. Wallander just managed to duck before a salvo from an automatic weapon demolished the window beside him. Glass showered down over his face. He heard shrieks and a car starting. He had time to see it was a black Audi before it disappeared. Wallander ran down the stairs and into the street, where half-dressed people were gathering. When they saw Wallander with a pistol in his hand, they jumped aside screaming. Wallander opened the door of his car with fumbling fingers, cursed as he stabbed at the igni-tion with his key before getting it in, then set off in the direction the Audi had taken. He could hear the distant wail of sirens. He decided to head for the Österlen highway and got lucky. The Audi came skid-ding around the corner from Regementsgatan and took off to the east. Wallander thought they might not realise it was him in the car. The only reason that the man who came into his bedroom had not looked under the bed must have been that it was still made, suggesting that Wallander was not at home. He did not normally make his bed in the morning, but that day his daughter, upset by all the mess, had cleaned the apartment and changed his bed linen.

They drove away from Ystad at high speed. Wallander kept his distance, and felt as if he was living a nightmare. Undoubtedly he was breaking all the rules on how to arrest dangerous criminals. He thought of turning back. Then he changed his mind and kept going. They had already passed Sandskogen, the golf course on the left, and Wallander began to wonder if the Audi would take a left to Sandhammaren or keep going straight on towards Simrishamn and Kristianstad.

Suddenly he saw the rear lights on the Audi shuddering, and getting closer. The car must have a puncture. He watched the car slide into the ditch and crash onto its side. Wallander stamped on his brakes outside the driveway to a house on the roadside, and turned in. When he got out of the car he saw a man standing in the doorway under a light.

Wallander had his pistol in his hand. When he started talking he made an effort to sound friendly and firm at the same time. "My name's Wallander and I'm a police officer," he said, noticing how breathless he was. "Call the police station in Ystad and tell them I'm chasing a Russian suspect, got that? Tell them where you live and tell them to prepare a search of the army training ground. Is that clear?"

The man nodded. He looked to be in his thirties. "I recognise you," he said. "I've seen you in the papers."

"Call at once," Wallander said. "You do have a telephone?"

"Of course I do," the man said. "Don't you need something more effective than that pistol?"

"I do," Wallander said. "But I don't have time to change right now."

Then he ran back to the road. The Audi was some way ahead. He tried to stick to the shadows as he approached it. He was still wondering how long his heart would hold out with the acute stress. He was glad, all the same, that he hadn't died under his bed. Now it seemed as if his fear was driving him on. He paused behind a road sign and listened. There was nobody in the car. Then he noticed that a section of the fence around the training ground had been cut open. Fog was drifting in from the sea and settling densely over the artillery range. He could see a group of sheep lying motionless on the ground, and he heard a bleat from a sheep he could not see through the fog, and another answering restlessly.

There, he thought. The sheep can guide me. He crouched and ran towards the hole in the fence, then lay on the ground, staring into the fog. He could neither see nor hear anything. A car approached from the direction of Ystad and slowed to a halt. A man got out. Wallander saw it was the man who had promised to call the police. He had a shotgun in his hand. Wallander crept back through the fence.

"Stay here," he said. "Back the car up about a hundred metres. Stay there and wait till the police arrive. Show them this hole in the fence. Say there are at least two armed men out there. One of them has some kind of automatic. Can you remember all that?"

The man nodded. "I brought this shotgun," he said.

Wallander hesitated a moment. "Show me how it works," he said. "I know next to nothing about shotguns."

The man looked at him in surprise. Then he showed him the safety catch and how to load. It was a pump-action model. Wallander took it and stuffed a handful of cartridges in his pocket.

The man went back to his car and Wallander crawled through the fence again. A sheep bleated once more. The sound came from the right, somewhere between a clump of trees and the slope down to the sea. Wallander tucked his pistol into his belt and started to edge his way towards where the sheep were bleating.

The fog was very thick by now.

Martinsson was woken by the call from headquarters. They told him about the shooting and the fire on Mariagatan, and also the message Wallander had sent from the outskirts of Ystad. He was immediately wide awake, and started getting dressed as he dialled Björk's number. It seemed to Martinsson it took forever for the message to penetrate Björk's sleepy brain, but half an hour later the largest squad the Ystad force could muster at such short notice was assembled outside the police station. Reinforcements were also on their way from surrounding districts. In addition, Björk had found time to wake up the police commissioner, who had asked to be informed as soon as the arrest of Konovalenko had been achieved.

Martinsson and Svedberg regarded the crowd of assembled officers with some irritation. A smaller squad would be as effective in a much shorter time. But Björk was going by the book, not risking criticism afterwards.

"This'll be a disaster," Svedberg said. "We should take care of this ourselves, you and me. Björk will just mess things up. If Wallander is out there on his own and Konovalenko is as dangerous as we think he is, he needs us right now."

Martinsson nodded and went over to Björk. "While you are organising the squad, Svedberg and I will go on ahead," he said.

"Out of the question," Björk said. "We have to follow the rules."

"You do that while Svedberg and I use our common sense," Martinsson said angrily, and walked away. Björk yelled after him, but Svedberg and Martinsson got into a squad car and drove off. They also signalled to Norén and Peters that they should follow. They allowed the patrol car to overtake them and lead the way with flashing blue lights and siren. Martinsson drove, with Svedberg at his side fumbling with his pistol.

"What have we got?" Martinsson said. "The training ground just before the turn-off to Kåseberga. Two armed men. One of them Konovalenko."

"We've got nothing," Svedberg said. "And I can't say I'm looking forward to this."

"Explosion and shooting on Mariagatan," Martinsson said. "How does it all hang together?"

"Let's hope Björk can work that one out with the help of his rule book," Svedberg said.

Outside the police station in Ystad things were deteriorating. Telephone calls were coming in from terrified people living on or near Mariagatan. The fire brigade was putting out the fire. Now it was up to the police to find out what was behind the shooting. The fire chief, Peter Edler, phoned in to say that the pavement in front of the house was covered with blood.

Björk was under pressure from all sides, but finally made up his mind to let Mariagatan take second place. The priority was to catch Konovalenko and the other man, and to give Wallander what assistance they could.

"Is there anybody here who knows how far the training ground extends?" Björk wanted to know. Nobody knew, but Björk was sure it stretched from the road right down to the beach. They had too little information to think of doing anything other than try to surround the whole area.

Cars kept arriving from nearby districts. Because they had the prospect of arresting someone who had killed a policeman, even off-duty officers were turning up.

Björk consulted a colleague from Malmö and decided they would make their plans for surrounding the place once they got there. A car had been sent to the army barracks to pick up some reliable maps.

The long caravan of police vehicles began leaving Ystad at 1 a.m. A few private cars that happened to be passing joined in out of curiosity. The fog was drifting down over central Ystad.

At the training ground they met the man who had spoken first with Wallander, and then with Martinsson and Svedberg.

"Any developments?" Björk said.

"None," the man said, just as a shot rang out somewhere in the middle of the training ground. It was followed shortly afterwards by a long burst of automatic fire. Then all was silent again.

"Where are Martinsson and Svedberg?" Björk said, in a voice that could not disguise his anxiety.

"They ran into the training ground," the man said.

"And Inspector Wallander?"

"I haven't seen him again since he went off into the fog."

The searchlights on the squad car roofs were lighting up a wall of fog and some sheep.

"We have to let them know we're here," Björk said. "We'll surround the place as best as we can."

A few minutes later his voice rang out over the training ground, the loudspeaker echoing spookily. Then the whole squad was divided into two and sent off in both directions around the fence in order to spread themselves around the perimeter. Then they settled down to wait.

Wallander had been completely swallowed up by the fog as soon as he had crawled into the training ground. Things happened very fast. He walked towards the bleating sheep. He was moving rapidly, as he had the strong sense that he was going to arrive too late. Several times he tripped over sheep on the ground, and they ran off bleating. He realised the sheep he was using to guide him were also betraying his whereabouts.

Then he came upon them. By now they were at the far side of the artillery range, where it started sloping down to the sea. It was like a still photograph from a film. Mabasha had been forced down on his knees. Konovalenko was standing in front of him, pistol in hand, and Rykoff a few paces to the side. Konovalenko repeated the same question over and over in English.

"Where's the policeman?"

"I don't know."

Mabasha's voice was defiant. That made Wallander see red. He hated the man who had killed Louise Åkerblom, and presumably the policeman Tengblad as well. At the same time his mind was racing as he tried to decide what he should do. If he crawled any closer, they would notice him. He doubted whether he could hit them with his pistol from where he was, and they were out of shotgun range. If he tried to run at them, he would simply be signing his own death warrant. The automatic pistol in Rykoff's hand would make short work of him.

The only thing he could do was wait and hope his colleagues would turn up soon. But he could hear Konovalenko getting more annoyed.

He had his pistol ready. He tried lying so that he could aim with steady hands. He was aiming straight at Konovalenko.

But the end came too soon. And it came so fast, Wallander had no time to react before it was too late. Looking back, he could see more clearly than ever in how short a time you can waste a life.

Konovalenko repeated his question. Mabasha gave his negative, defiant response. Then Konovalenko raised his pistol and shot Mabasha in the head.

Wallander yelled and fired. But it was too late. Mabasha had fallen backwards and was lying motionless. Wallander's shot had missed Konovalenko and now the real threat was Rykoff's automatic pistol. He aimed at the fat man and fired shot after shot. To his surprise, he saw Rykoff twitch, then fall in a heap. When Wallander turned his aim back to Konovalenko, he saw that the Russian had lifted Mabasha and was using him as a shield as he shuffled backwards to the beach. Mabasha was obviously dead, but Wallander could not bring himself to shoot. He stood up and yelled at Konovalenko to drop his gun and give himself up. His answer came in the form of a bullet. Wallander flung himself to one side. Mabasha's body had saved him. Not even Konovalenko could take a steady aim while holding a heavy corpse upright in front of him. In the distance he could hear a single siren approaching. The fog grew thicker as Konovalenko got closer to the sea. Wallander followed him, both of his weapons at the ready. Suddenly Konovalenko dropped the dead body and disappeared down the slope. Just then Wallander heard a sheep bleat behind him. He spun around and raised both the pistol and the shotgun.

Then he recognised Martinsson and Svedberg emerging from out of the fog. Their faces were pictures of astonished horror.

"Put your guns down!" Martinsson yelled. "It's us, can't you see!"

Wallander knew Konovalenko was about to escape yet again. There was no time for explanations.

"Stay where you are," he yelled. "Don't follow me!"

Then he started backing away, still pointing his guns. Martinsson and Svedberg did not move a muscle. Then he disappeared into the fog. Martinsson and Svedberg looked at each other in horror.

"Was that really Kurt?" Svedberg wondered.

"Yeah," Martinsson said. "But he seemed out of his mind."

"He's alive," Svedberg said. "He's still alive despite everything."

Cautiously they approached the slope down to the beach where Wallander had disappeared. They could detect no movement in the fog, but could hear the gentle lapping of the sea on the sand.

Martinsson contacted Björk, giving him precise directions, and called for ambulances.

"What about Wallander?" Björk said.

"He's still in one piece," Martinsson said. "But I can't tell you where he is just now." He switched off his walkie-talkie, before Björk could ask any more questions. He found Svedberg standing over the man Wallander had killed. Two entry marks just above the man's navel.

"We'll have to tell Björk," Martinsson said. "Wallander seemed completely out of his mind." Svedberg agreed. They had no choice. Then they made their way to where they had last seen Wallander and found the second body.

"The man without a finger," Martinsson said. "And now he's dead." He bent down and pointed to the bullet hole in his forehead. They were thinking the same thing. Louise Åkerblom.

Then the police cars arrived, followed by two ambulances. As the examination of the two bodies got under way, Svedberg and Martinsson took Björk aside. They told him what they had seen. Björk looked at them doubtfully.

"This all sounds very strange," he said. "Kurt can be pretty odd at times, but I can't imagine him going clean off his head."

"You should have seen what he looked like," Svedberg said. "He seemed to be on the verge of a breakdown. He pointed guns at us. He had one in each hand."

Björk shook his head. "And then he disappeared along the beach?"

"He was following Konovalenko," Martinsson said.

Björk said nothing, trying to let what he had heard sink in.

"We'd better send in dog patrols," he said after a few moments. "Set up roadblocks, and call in helicopters as soon as it gets light and the fog lifts."

A single shot rang out in the fog. It came from the beach, somewhere to the east of where they were standing. Everything went very quiet. Police, ambulance men and dogs all waited to see what would happen next. Finally a sheep bleated. The desolate sound made Martinsson shudder.

"We've got to help Kurt," he said eventually. "He's on his own out there in the fog. He's up against a man who won't hesitate to kill him. We've got to give him help. Now, Otto."

Svedberg had never heard Martinsson call Björk by his first name before. Even Björk was startled, as if he did not realise at first who Martinsson was talking to.

"Dog handlers with bulletproof vests," he said.

Within a short space of time the hunt was on. The dogs picked up the scent immediately, and started straining at their leashes. Martinsson and Svedberg followed close on the heels of the dog handlers.

About 200 metres from where the body of the black man was found the dogs discovered a patch of blood in the sand. They searched around in circles without finding anything else until one of the dogs set off in a northerly direction. They were on the perimeter of the training ground, following the fence. The trail the dogs found led over the road and then towards Sandhammaren.

After a couple of kilometres the trail fizzled out. The dogs whimpered and started backtracking the way they had come.

"What's going on?" Martinsson asked one of the handlers.

He shook his head. "The trail's gone cold," he said.

"Wallander can't have just gone up in smoke?"

"That's what it looks like," the handler said.

They kept on searching, and then dawn came. Roadblocks were erected. The whole southern Swedish police force was involved one way or another in the hunt for Konovalenko and Wallander. When the fog lifted, helicopters joined the search. But they found nothing. The two men had disappeared.

By 9 a.m. Svedberg and Martinsson were sitting with Björk in the conference room, all nursing cups of coffee. They were cold, very tired and soaked through from the fog. Martinsson had also the unmistakeable symptoms of a cold coming on.

"What do I tell the Commissioner?" Björk said.

"Sometimes it's best to give it to him straight," Martinsson said.

Björk shook his head. "Can't you just see the headlines? 'Crazed detective is Swedish police secret weapon in hunt for police killer.'"

"A headline has to be short," Svedberg said.

Björk stood up. "Go home and get something to eat," he said. "Get changed. Then we have to get going again."

Martinsson raised his hand, as if in a classroom. "I think I'll drive out to his father's place at Löderup. His daughter's there. She might be able to tell us something useful."

"You do that," Björk said. "But get moving." Then he went to his office and called the Commissioner.

When eventually he managed to bring the conversation to an end, he was seething with indignation, and he had been – just as he had anticipated – hauled over the coals. His face was red with anger.

He had received the negative criticism he was expecting.

Martinsson was sitting in the kitchen of the house in Österlen. Wallander's daughter was making coffee as they talked. When he arrived, he went straight out to the studio to say hello to Wallander's father. He said nothing to him about what had happened during the night, however. He wanted to talk to the daughter first.

He could see she was shocked. There were tears in her eyes.

"I should really have been sleeping at the apartment on Mariagatan last night, too," she said.

She served him coffee. He noticed her hands were shaking.

"I don't understand it all," she said. "That he's dead. Victor Mabasha. I just don't understand it."

Martinsson mumbled something vague in reply. He suspected she could tell him quite a lot about what had been going on between her father and the African. Obviously it had not been her Kenyan boyfriend in Wallander's car a few days earlier. But why had he lied?

"You've got to find Papa before anything worse happens," she said, interrupting his train of thought.

"We'll do what we can," Martinsson said.

"That's not good enough," she said. "You have to do much more."

Martinsson nodded. "Right," he said. "We'll do more than we can."

Martinsson left the house half an hour later. She had undertaken to tell her grandfather what had happened. He in turn had promised to keep her informed as things developed. Then he drove back to Ystad.

After lunch Björk sat down with Svedberg and Martinsson in the conference room. Björk did something most unusual. He locked the door.

"We need to be undisturbed," he said. "It's essential that we put a stop to this catastrophic mess before we lose control."

Martinsson and Svedberg stared down at the table. Neither of them knew what he was going to say next.

"Has either of you noticed any signs that Kurt was losing his mind?" Björk said. "You must have seen something. I've always thought he could be strange, but you're the ones who work with him on a daily basis."

"I don't think he's out of his mind," Martinsson said after a long pause. "Maybe he's overworked?"

"If that were anything to go by every police officer in the country would go off his rocker now and then," Björk said. "And they don't. Of course he's out of his mind. Or mentally unbalanced, if that sounds better. Does it run in the family? Didn't somebody find his father wandering around in a field a year or two back?"

"He was drunk," Martinsson said. "Or temporarily senile. Kurt isn't suffering from senility."

"Do you think he might have Alzheimer's?" Björk said.

"I don't know what you're talking about," Svedberg said suddenly. "For God's sake, let's stick to the facts. Whether or not Kurt has had some kind of breakdown is something only a doctor can decide. Our job is to find him. We know he was involved in a shoot-out in which two people died. We saw him out there in the training ground. He pointed his gun at us. But he wasn't dangerous. It was more like desperation. Or confusion. I'm not sure which. Then he disappeared."

Martinsson nodded slowly. "Kurt wasn't at the scene by chance," he said thoughtfully. "His apartment had been attacked. We must assume

277

the black man was there with him. What happened next we can only guess. But Kurt must be onto something, something he never had a chance to tell us about. Or maybe something he chose not to tell us about for the moment. We know he does that sometimes, and we get irritated. But right now only one thing matters, and that is finding him."

"I never thought I'd have to do anything like this," Björk said eventually. Martinsson and Svedberg at once understood what he meant.

"But you've got to do it," Svedberg said. "You have to get the whole force looking for him. Put out an APB."

"Awful," Björk muttered. "But I have no choice." There was nothing else to say. With a heavy heart, Björk went back to his office to put out an APB on his colleague and friend, Chief Inspector Kurt Wallander.

It was May 15, 1992. Spring had truly arrived in Skåne. It was a very hot day. In the late afternoon a thunderstorm moved in over Ystad.

The White Lioness

CHAPTER TWENTY-THREE

The lioness looked pure white in the light of the moon. Georg Scheepers held his breath as he stood in the back of the safari vehicle. She was lying by the river, not more than 30 paces away, motionless. He glanced at his wife Judith, standing beside him. He could tell she was scared. "It's not dangerous," he said. "She won't hurt us."

In the Kruger National Park, animals were used to people watching them from the back of open safari vehicles, even at midnight. But he could not forget that the lioness was unpredictable, governed by instinct and nothing else. She was young. Her strength and speed would never be greater than they were now. It would take her a very few seconds to shake herself out of her sprawling languor and bound to their car. The black driver did not seem to be alert. Neither of them carried a gun.

The lioness seemed to have read his thoughts. She lifted her head and stared at the car. Judith took hold of his arm. The lioness was looking straight at them. The moonlight was reflected in her eyes, making them luminous. Scheepers' heart beat faster. He wished the driver would start the engine, but perhaps – it occurred to Scheepers in horror – the man had fallen asleep.

At that moment the lioness got up from the sand. She never took her eyes off the people in the car for a second. Scheepers knew there was such a thing as freezing. You could think about being afraid and running away, but you had no strength to move.

She stood absolutely still, watching them. Her powerful shoulder muscles rippled under her skin. He thought how beautiful she was. He also thought that she was first and foremost a beast of prey. Being white was secondary. That thought stuck fast in his mind. It was a sort of reminder to himself of something he had forgotten about. He couldn't remember what.

"Why doesn't he drive away?" Judith whispered.

"It's not dangerous," he said. "She won't come over here."

The lioness stood still, watching the people in the car parked by the water's edge. The moonlight was very bright. The night was clear, and it was warm. Somewhere in the dark river they could hear the lazy sounds of hippos moving.

It seemed to Scheepers that the scene was a reminder. The feeling of imminent danger, which could at any moment become uncontrollable violence, was the everyday state of affairs in his country. Everybody waiting for something to happen, the creature watching them. It was like being there on the river bank, watched by a lion.

She was an albino. He thought of the myths attached to albino people and animals: that their strength was mighty, they could never die.

Suddenly the lioness moved, came straight towards them. Her concentration was unbroken, her movements stealthy. The driver hastily started the engine and switched on the headlights. The light blinded her. She stopped in mid-movement, one paw in the air. Scheepers felt his wife's fingernails piercing his khaki shirt. Drive, he thought. Go now, before she attacks. The driver engaged reverse. The engine coughed. Scheepers thought his heart would stop there and then when the engine almost died. But the driver revved the engine and the car started rolling backwards. The lioness turned her head to one side to avoid being blinded.

It was all over. Judith's fingernails were no longer digging into his arm. They clung to the rail as the safari vehicle bumped and jerked its way back to the bungalow where they were staying. The midnight adventure would soon be over, but the memory of the lioness, and the thoughts her lying there by the river aroused would stay with him.

Scheepers had suggested to his wife they should go up to the Kruger for a few days. He had spent a week or more trying to sort and make sense of the papers van Heerden left at his death. They would be away on Friday and Saturday, but on Sunday, May 17, he would try to master van Heerden's computer files. He wanted to do that when nobody was about. The police investigators had made sure all his material, all his disks, had been sent to the public prosecutor's office. His own chief, Verwey, had given the order for the intelligence service to hand over the material. Officially Verwey, in his capacity as chief public prosecutor of Johannesburg, should be going through the material himself. NIS had immediately classified it as top secret. When van Heerden's superiors refused to release the material until their own people had gone through it, Verwey threw a fit and at once got on to the Minister of Justice. A few hours later NIS relented. The material would be Verwey's responsibility, but it was Scheepers who would go through it.

They left Johannesburg early on the morning of Friday, May 15. They took the N4 and entered the Kruger National Park at the Nambi Gate. Judith had booked a bungalow in one of the remote camps, Nwanetsi, close to the Mozambique border. They had been there several times and liked going back. The camp appealed primarily to guests who went to bed early and got up at dawn to see the animals coming to the river to drink. During their two days there they were out on game drives all the time. They delighted in the animals and the scenery. After meals Judith would bury her head in one of the books she had brought, while Scheepers thought through what he now knew about van Heerden and his secret work.

He had started methodically, going through van Heerden's filing cabinet, and very soon realised he would have to step up his ability to read between the lines. In among formal memoranda and reports he found loose scraps of paper with scribbled notes. Making sense of them was slow work; the handwriting called to mind the work of a pedantic schoolteacher. They seemed to be sketches for poems, lyrical insights, sketches for metaphors and images. It was when he tried to penetrate this informal part of van Heerden's work that he had a premonition that something was going to happen. The reports, memos and loose notes – *divine poems*, as he began to regard them – went back a long way. At first they were often precise observations and reflections expressed in a cool, neutral style. But about six months before van Heerden died, a different, darker tone had crept into his thoughts. Something had changed dramatically either in his work or his private life. What had previously been certain became unsure, the clear voice became hesitant, tenuous. Scheepers thought he could see another change too. Before, the loose papers had been haphazard. From now on van Heerden noted down the date and sometimes even the time. Van Heerden had often worked late into the night. Many of the notes were timed after midnight. It all started to look like a poetically expressed diary. He tried to find a consistent theme as a starting point. Because van Heerden never referred to his private life, Scheepers assumed he was only writing about what happened at work. There was nothing concrete to guide him, only synonyms and parallels. Obviously, *Homeland* stood for South Africa. But who was *The Chameleon*? Who were *The Mother and Child*? Van Heerden had no wife or child, according to what Chief Inspector Borstlap of the Johannesburg police had written in a memo.

Van Heerden's language was evasive, as if he would prefer not to be associated with what he was writing. Scheepers often sensed a note of danger threatening. Sometimes a hint of confession. He wrote about a kingdom of death, seeming to imply that we all had it inside ourselves. In van Heerden there were feelings of guilt and sorrow, which grew dramatically during his last weeks.

He wrote all the time about the blacks, the whites, the *Boers*, God and forgiveness. But nowhere did he use the words conspiracy or plot. The thing I'm supposed to be looking for, the thing van Heerden warned President de Klerk about. *Why is there nothing about it?*

On the Thursday evening, the day before he and Judith left for Nwanetsi, he stayed in his office until very late. He had switched off all the lights apart from his desk lamp. Now and then he heard the guards talking outside his window, which he had left ajar.

Pieter van Heerden had been the ideal loyal servant, he thought. In the course of his work for the intelligence service that was growing more divided, acting more autonomously, he had come across something significant. A conspiracy against the state. A conspiracy whose aim was somehow or other to spark off a coup d'état. Van Heerden was attempting to track the core of the conspiracy. And yet he wrote poems about his anxieties and about the kingdom of death he had discovered inside himself.

Scheepers looked at his filing cabinet where he had locked the disks Verwey had demanded of van Heerden's superiors. That is where the solution must be, he thought. Van Heerden's increasingly introspective musings on loose scraps of paper could only be a part of the whole picture. The truth must be in his disks.

They left the Kruger Park early on Sunday, May 17. He took Judith home, and after breakfast he drove to the public prosecutors' office. The city centre was deserted, as if it had been evacuated and the people would never return. The armed guards let him in, and he walked along the echoing corridor.

The moment he walked through the door, he knew someone had been in his office. The smallest traces betrayed it. Presumably the cleaners, but he could not be sure of that. I'm letting my assignment get to me, he said to himself. Van Heerden's constant fear of being watched, threatened, is starting to affect me too.

He took off his jacket and opened his filing cabinet. Then he slid the first disk into his computer. After two hours' work he decided that the files revealed nothing significant, but he was struck by how immaculately everything was organised.

There was one disk left. Scheepers was sure that this was where van Heerden's secret testimony was to be found. The blinking message on his screen demanded a password before the disk could be opened. This is impossible, Scheepers thought. I could run the disk with a programme containing a whole dictionary. But is the password in English or Afrikaans? And surely, van Heerden would not lock his most vital diskette with a trivial password.

Scheepers rolled up his shirtsleeves, filled his coffee cup from the thermos he had brought with him, and started again looking through the loose papers. He was concerned that van Heerden might have programmed the disk so that it erased everything of its own accord after a certain number of wrong choices, but he had no option but to persevere.

By mid-afternoon, he was on the point of giving up. He had run out of ideas. He also felt that he was nowhere near finding the context even. Without expecting any particular help he turned to the memos and investigation documents he had received from Chief Inspector Borstlap. Maybe there would be something there which could help him. He read the autopsy report with distaste and looked at the photographs of the dead man. The long-winded police report gave him no clues nor could it convince him that van Heerden's death was simply a case of aggravated robbery after all.

The last item in Borstlap's file was an inventory of what the police had found in his office. Borstlap had made the comment that, of course, there was no way of knowing if van Heerden's superiors had removed any papers or objects they considered unsuitable for the police to get their hands on. He glanced casually down the list of ashtrays, framed photographs of his parents, some lithographs, a pen rack, diaries, blotting pad. He was just going to put it on one side when he noticed, among the items listed, a small ivory carving of an antelope. *Valuable, antique*, Borstlap had noted.

He typed *antelope* on the keyboard. The computer responded by asking for the correct password. Then he typed *kudu*. Same response. He picked up the telephone and called Judith.

"I need your help," he said. "Can you look up antelopes in our wildlife encyclopaedia?"

"What on earth are you doing?" she said.

"I am trying to write a paper on the development of our antelope species," he said. "I just want to be sure I don't forget any."

She read out the various species of antelope for him.

"When will you be home?" she asked, when she had finished.

"Either pretty soon, or very late," he said. "I'll let you know." As soon as he had rung off he knew which word it must be. *Springbok*, he thought to himself. National symbol. Precious carving on his desk. He keyed the word in slowly, pausing for a moment before the last letter. The computer responded at once. Negative.

One more possibility, he thought. Same word in Afrikaans. He keyed in *steenbok*. Immediately the screen flashed and a list of contents appeared. He had cracked it.

He noticed he was sweating. The elation of a criminal when he's just opened a bank vault, he thought. At almost 1 a.m., when he came to the end of the texts, he absolutely sure of two things. Van Heerden had been murdered because of the work he was doing. Second, his own premonition of imminent danger was justified.

He leaned back in his chair and stretched. Then he shuddered. Van Heerden had compiled his notes with precision. He was apparently a split personality. The further he penetrated into the conspiracy, the deeper he penetrated his own real life. The world depicted in the loose sheets of paper, and the surgical clarity of the records on the disk, were both aspects of the same person.

In a sense van Heerden had been close to his own destruction.

He stood up and walked to the window. He could hear police sirens in the distance.

Just what have we Afrikaners believed? he asked himself. Our dreams of an unchanging world? That the small concessions we made to the blacks would be sufficient? He was overcome by shame. For even if he was one of the new Afrikaners, one of those who did not regard de Klerk as a traitor, the years of passivity – on Judith's part and his own – had only contributed to the continuation of the Apartheid. He, too, had inside him the kingdom of death van Heerden had written of. The conspirators were counting on his passivity. His silent acceptance.

He sat down again in front of the screen. Van Heerden had done good work. The conclusions Scheepers was now able to draw, and which he would pass on to the President the very next day, were impossible to mistake.

Mandela was going to be murdered. During his last days van Heerden had worked frantically to find out where and when. He had not found the answer when he switched off his computer for the last time. But the indications were that it would be soon, during or on the occasion of a speech given by Mandela to a large gathering. Van Heerden had drawn up a list of locations and dates over the coming three months. Among them were Durban, Johannesburg, Soweto, Bloemfontein, Cape Town and East London, with dates attached. A professional killer was making preparations somewhere abroad. Van Heerden had managed to discover that a former KGB officer was hovering indistinctly in the assassin's background. There were many other things to be unravelled, including one crucial matter. Scheepers read again through the section where van Heerden analysed his way to the heart of the conspiracy. He spoke of a *Committee*, representatives of dominant groups among the Afrikaners. Van Heerden did not have all their names. The only ones he could identify for certain were Kleyn and Malan.

Scheepers was now convinced *The Chameleon* was Kleyn. He had not identified Malan's code name. Evidently, van Heerden judged this pair to be the main players. By concentrating on them, he hoped to be able to work out who the other members of the Committee were, and what they were plotting to achieve.

Coup d'état, van Heerden had written at the end of the last text, dated two days before he was killed. Followed by: *Civil war? Chaos?*

There was one more note, made the same day, the Sunday before he went into the clinic. *Next week*, van Heerden wrote, *Take it further. Bezuidenhout 559.*

His message to me from the grave, Scheepers thought. That's what he was going to do. Now I have to do it instead. But what is it? Bezuidenhout is a suburb of Johannesburg, and the number must surely be part of the address of a house.

He noticed he was suddenly very tired and very worried by the responsibility he had been given. He switched off the computer and locked the filing cabinet. It was 9 p.m. already, and dark outside. Police sirens were wailing non-stop, like hyenas, keeping watch in the night.

Without really having decided to do so, he drove to the eastern suburbs, to Bezuidenhout. It did not take him long to find what he was looking for. Number 559 was a house bordering the park that gave Bezuidenhout its name. He switched off the engine and put out his lights. The house was white, in glazed brick. A light was on behind drawn curtains. There was a car in the drive, inside the security fence.

He was too traumatised and exhausted by the discoveries of the day to be sure of how he should now proceed. He thought first of all of the white lioness by the riverbank. How she came towards them. The wild beast is almost upon us, he thought. Then it dawned on him what was the most important thing. If Mandela died the consequences would be horrific. Everything they were trying to achieve, this brittle attempt to reach a settlement between blacks and whites would be demolished. The dykes would be breached and the flood would rage over the whole country. And there were people who wanted this apocalyptic flood.

That was as far as his train of thought got. A man came out of the house and got into the car. At the same time one of the curtains was pulled back. A black woman, and behind her another one, younger. The older woman waved.

He could not see because it was dark. Even so, in the time it took for the security gates to swing open, in the floodlight over the gateway, he knew the man was Kleyn. He crouched down in his seat as the car passed. When he sat up again, the curtains were drawn tight.

He frowned. Two black women? Kleyn had come out of their house. *The Chameleon, Mother and Child?* He could not see the connection. But he had no reason to doubt van Heerden. If he had written that it was important, then it was so. Van Heerden had stumbled upon a secret, he thought. I must go down the same track.

The next day he called the President's office and asked for an appointment. The President could see him at 10 p.m. He spent the whole day writing his report. He was nervous as he sat waiting in the antechamber, having been welcomed by the same sombre security guard as before. This evening, however, he was not kept waiting. At exactly 10 p.m. the guard announced the President was ready to see him. Scheepers had the same impression as last time: President de Klerk was very tired. His eyes were dim and his face pale. The swollen bags under his eyes seemed to weigh him down.

As succinctly as possible he reported his findings. He said nothing, however, about the house in Bezuidenhout Park.

President de Klerk listened, his eyes half closed. For a moment, he thought the President had fallen asleep. Then de Klerk opened his eyes and looked straight at him.

"I often wonder how it is that I'm still alive," he said slowly. "Thousands of *Boere* regard me as a traitor. Even so, Mandela is this time the intended victim of an assassination attempt."

President de Klerk fell silent. Then he said, "There is something in your report that disturbs me. Let us assume that there are red herrings laid out in appropriate places. Let us imagine two parallel sets of circumstances. One is that it's me who is the intended victim. I'd like you to rethink your report with that in mind, Scheepers. I'd like you to consider also the possibility that these people intend to attack both my friend Mandela and myself. I'm not excluding the possibility that it really is Mandela these lunatics are after. I just want you to think critically about what you have uncovered. Van Heerden was murdered. That means there are eyes and ears everywhere. Experience has taught me that red herrings are an important part of intelligence work. Do you follow me?"

"Yes," Scheepers said.

"I'll be expecting your conclusions in the next two days. I can't give you any more time than that."

"I still believe van Heerden's notes strongly indicate that it's Mandela they intend to kill," Scheepers said.

"Believe?" de Klerk said. "I believe in God. But I don't *know* if he exists. Nor do I know if there is more than one."

Scheepers was dumbfounded by the response. But he understood what de Klerk meant. The President raised his hands, then let them drop on his desk. "A committee," he said, wearily, "of people and interests who mean to dismantle all we've achieved. Well, they will not be allowed to do that."

"Of course not," Scheepers said.

De Klerk was lost in thought once more. Scheepers waited. "Every day I expect some crazy fanatic to get to me," he said. "I think about what happened to my predecessor, President Verwoerd. Stabbed to death in Parliament. The same could happen to me. I am not frightened for myself. What does frighten me, though, is that there really isn't anybody who can take over after me." De Klerk looked at him, smiling slightly. "You are still young," he said. "But right now the future of this country is in the hands of two old men, Mandela and me. That's why it would be desirable for both of us to live a little bit longer."

"Shouldn't Mandela get an increased bodyguard?" Scheepers said.

"Mandela is a very special man," de Klerk said. "He's not fond of bodyguards. Outstanding men rarely are. Look at General de Gaulle. That's why everything will have to be handled with absolute discretion. I have of course arranged for his guard to be strengthened. He doesn't need to hear about it, though."

The audience was at an end.

"Two days," de Klerk said. "No more."

Scheepers got to his feet and bowed.

"One more thing: you must not for a minute forget what happened to van Heerden. Take good care."

It was not until he had left the government building that what the President said really sunk in. Unseen eyes were watching him as well. He broke into a cold sweat as he drove home, and his thoughts wandered once more to the lioness in the cold, clear moonlight.

CHAPTER TWENTY-FOUR

Kurt Wallander had always imagined death as black. Now, standing on the beach shrouded in fog, he realised that death was no respecter of colours. Here it was white. The fog enclosed him completely; he thought he could hear the lapping of waves, but it was the fog that dominated and strengthened his feeling of not knowing which way to turn.

When he had been higher up on the training ground, surrounded by invisible sheep, and it was all over, he did not have a single clear thought in his head. He knew Mabasha was dead, that he himself had killed a human being, and that Konovalenko had escaped again, swallowed up by the whiteness. Svedberg and Martinsson had emerged from the fog like two pale ghosts of themselves. He could see in their faces his own horror. He had felt simultaneously a desire to run away and never come back, but also to pursue the hunt for Konovalenko. Afterwards he recalled what happened in those few moments as something peripheral to him, something seen from a distance. It was a different Wallander standing there, waving his weapons, somebody who had temporarily possessed him. Only when he yelled at Martinsson and Svedberg to stay out of his way, then skidded and scrambled up the slope, finding himself alone in the fog, did it really begin to sink in. Mabasha was shot through the head, just like Louise Åkerblom. The fat man had started back and flung his hands in the air. He was dead, and Wallander had shot him.

He yelled out, like a solitary human foghorn. There's no turning back, he told himself desperately. I'll vanish into this fog. When it lifts, I won't exist any more.

He tried to gather the last vestiges of reason he might still have left. Go back, he told himself. Go back to the dead men. Your colleagues are there. You can search for Konovalenko together.

Then he walked away. He could not go back. If he had one duty left, it was to find Konovalenko, kill him if that could not be avoided, but preferably catch him and hand him over to Björk. Once that was done he could sleep. When he woke, the nightmare would be over. But that was not true. The nightmare would still be there. In shooting the fat man, he had done something he would never be able to shake off. So he might just as well go on hunting for Konovalenko. He had a vague feeling that he was already trying to find some way to atone for the killing of Rykoff.

Konovalenko was somewhere out there in the fog. Maybe close. Helplessly, Wallander fired a shot straight into the whiteness, as if trying to split the fog. He brushed aside the sweaty hair that was sticking to his forehead. Then he saw he was bleeding. He must have been cut when the window panes at Mariagatan were shattered. He saw too that his clothes were streaked with blood. It was dripping down onto the sand. He stood still, waiting for his breathing to calm. He could follow Konovalenko's tracks in the sand. He tucked the pistol into his belt. He held the shotgun cocked and ready, at hip level. It seemed to him from Konovalenko's footprints that he had been moving fast, probably running. He speeded up, following the traces like a dog. The thick fog gave him the impression he was standing still while the sand was moving. Just then, he noted that Konovalenko had stopped and turned around before going off in a different direction, back up to the cliff. Wallander realised that the tracks would disappear as they reached the grass. He scrambled up the slope and thought he must be at the eastern edge of the training ground. He stopped to listen. Far behind, he heard a siren fading into the distance. A sheep bleated, very close by. Silence. He followed the fence northwards. It was the only bearing he had. He half expected Konovalenko to loom out of the fog at any moment. Wallander tried to imagine being shot through the head. But he could not conjure up any feeling. The sole purpose of his life just now was to follow that fence along the perimeter of the training ground, nothing else. Konovalenko was there somewhere with his gun and Wallander was going to find him.

When Wallander reached the barbed wire fence that separated the training ground from the road to Sandhammaren, there was nothing to see but fog. He thought he could make out the dim shape of a horse on the other side, standing motionless, ears cocked. He wriggled under the bottom strand, got himself thoroughly wet in the dew in the grass, and then he stood in the middle of the road and urinated. In the distance he heard a car going by on the road to Kristianstad.

He started walking towards Kåseberga. Konovalenko had disappeared. He had got away again. Wallander was walking aimlessly, but walking was easier than standing still. He wished Baiba Liepa would walk out of the whiteness and embrace him. But there was nothing but him and the damp asphalt.

A bicycle leaned against an old milk pallet. It was unlocked, and it seemed to Wallander someone had left it there for him. He used the baggage rack for the shotgun and cycled off. As soon as possible he turned off the road onto the dirt roads criss-crossing the plain. Eventually he came to his father's house. There was only the single lamp outside the front door. He stood and listened. Then he hid the bicycle behind the shed. He tiptoed over the gravel. He found the spare keys hidden under a broken flowerpot on the outside stairs leading to the cellar. He unlocked the door to his father's studio. There was an inside room where he kept his paints and old canvases. He closed the door behind him and switched on the light. The brightness took him by surprise. It was as if he expected the fog to be here as well. He turned on the cold tap and tried to rinse the blood off his face. He did not recognise his reflection in the broken mirror. His eyes were staring, bloodshot, shifting. He heated water on the filthy electric hot plate and made some coffee. It was 4 a.m. His father generally got up at 5.30. He would have to be gone by then. What he needed right now was a hideaway. Various alternatives flashed through his mind, all of them impossible. In the end he drank his coffee, left the studio, crossed the courtyard, and carefully unlocked the door to the main house. He stood in the hall, and breathed in the acrid, old-mannish aroma. He listened. Not a sound. He went into the kitchen where the telephone was, closing the door behind him. To his surprise he remembered the number. With his hand on the receiver, he thought about what he was going to say.

Widén answered almost at once. Wallander could hear that he was already wide awake. Horsey people get up early, he thought.

"Sten? It's Kurt Wallander."

Once upon a time they had been very close friends. Wallander knew he hardly ever displayed a trace of surprise.

"I can hear that," he said. "Some things never change. And you're calling me at 4 a.m."

"I need your help."

Widén said nothing.

"On the road to Sandhammaren," Wallander said. "You'll have to come and get me. I need to hide in your house for a while. A few hours at least."

"Where are you?" Widén said. Then he started coughing. He's still smoking those cheroots, Wallander thought.

"I'll wait for you at the Kåseberga exit," he said. "What kind of car do you have?"

"An old Duett."

"How long will it take you?"

"If it's still thick fog, say 45 minutes. Possibly a little less."

"I'll be there. Thanks for your help."

He hung up and went back to the hall. Then he could not resist the temptation: he walked through the living room where the old television set was, and gently pulled aside the curtain to the spare bedroom. In the weak light from the lamp outside the front door, he could see Linda's hair and forehead, part of her nose. She was fast asleep.

Then he left the house and tidied up in the inside room of the studio, and put the keys back under the flowerpot. He cycled down to the main road and turned right. When he came to the Kåseberga exit he put the bicycle behind a telephone company hut and settled down to wait in the shadows. The fog was just as thick as before. A police car went by in the direction of Sandhammaren. Wallander thought he recognised Peters behind the wheel.

He had not seen Widén for more than a year. In the course of an investigation Wallander had called on him at his place near the ruined castle of Stjärnsund. He trained a number of trotting horses. He lived alone, probably drank too much, and had relationships with his stable girls. Once they had shared a common dream. Widén had a fine baritone voice and was going to become an opera singer, and Wallander was going to be his impresario. But the dream faded and their friendship dissolved.

Even so, he's perhaps the only real friend I've ever had, Wallander thought, as he waited in the fog. Not counting Rydberg. But that was something different. We would never have been as close if we hadn't both been policemen.

Forty minutes later the wine-red Duett came gliding through the fog. Wallander emerged from behind the hut and got into the car. Widén looked at his face, dirty, smeared with blood. But as usual he evidenced no surprise.

"I'll explain later," Wallander said.

"When it suits you," Widén said. He had an unlit cigarette in his mouth, and smelled of alcohol.

They passed the training ground. Wallander crouched down and made himself invisible. There were several police cars by the side of the road. Widén slowed down but did not stop. The road was clear, no roadblocks. He looked across at Wallander, who was still trying to hide, but he said nothing. They drove through Ystad, Skurup, then turned right to Stjärnsund. When they turned into the stable yard, a girl of about 17 stood yawning and smoking in front of the stalls.

"My face has been in the newspapers and on TV," Wallander said. "I'd rather be anonymous."

"Ulrika doesn't read papers," Widén said. "If she ever watches TV, it's just videos. I have another girl, Kristina. She won't say anything either."

They went into the untidy, chaotic house. It seemed to Wallander much as it had been the last time he was there. Widén asked him if he was hungry. Wallander nodded so he sat him down in the kitchen and made him some sandwiches and a cup of coffee. Widén occasionally went out into the next room. He came back each time with a fresh aroma of spirits.

"Thanks for coming for me," Wallander said.

Widén shrugged. "No problem," he said.

"I need a few hours' sleep. Then I'll tell you what's going on."

"The horses have to be looked after," Widén said. "I'll show you where you can sleep."

He got up and Wallander followed him. His exhaustion caught up with him. Widén showed him into a little room with a sofa.

"I doubt if I have any clean sheets. But you can have a pillow and a blanket."

"That's more than enough."

"You remember where the bathroom is?"

Wallander nodded. He took off his shoes. He could hear the sand crunching underfoot. He hung his jacket over a chair. Widén stood watching him in the doorway.

"How are things going?" Wallander said.

"I've started singing again," Widén said.

"You must tell me all about it."

Widén left the room, and Wallander heard a horse whinnying in the yard. The last thing he thought before falling asleep was that his friend was the same as ever. The same tousled hair, the same dry eczema on his neck. Nevertheless there was something different.

He was not sure where he was at first, when he woke up. He had a headache, and pain all over his body. He put his hand on his forehead and knew he had a temperature. He lay still under the blanket, which smelled of horse. When he went to check his watch, he discovered that he must have lost it during the night. The kitchen clock showed 11.30 a.m. He had slept for more than four hours. The fog was less dense but was still there. He poured himself a cup of coffee and opened various cabinets until he found some painkillers. The telephone rang. Wallander heard Widén come in and answer it. Something to do with hay. Then he came into the kitchen.

"Awake?" he said.

"I needed that sleep," Wallander said.

Then he told him what had happened. Widén listened in silence, expressionless. Wallander started with the disappearance of Louise Åkerblom. He talked about the man he had killed.

"I just had to get away," he concluded. "I know, of course, my colleagues will be looking for me now. But I'll have to tell them a white lie. Say I passed out and lay behind a bush. But I'd be grateful if you could do one thing for me. Call my daughter and tell her I'm OK. And tell her she should stay where she is."

"Should I tell her where you are?"

"No. Not yet. But you've got to convince her." He gave him the number. But there was no answer.

"You'll have to keep on trying until you reach her," Wallander said.

One of the stable girls came into the kitchen, and introduced herself as Kristina.

"You can go and get a pizza," Widén said. "Buy a few newspapers too. There isn't a bite to eat in the house." He gave the girl some money. She drove off in the Duett.

"You said you started singing again," Wallander said.

Widén smiled for the first time. Wallander remembered that smile, but it was many years since he had last seen it.

"I've joined the church choir at Svedala," he said. "I sometimes sing solos at funerals. I realised I was missing it. But the horses don't like it if I sing in the stables."

"Do you need an impresario?" Wallander wondered. "It's hard to see how I can keep going as a policeman after all this."

"You killed in self-defence," Widén said. "I'd have done the same thing. Just thank your lucky stars you had a gun."

"I don't think anybody can understand what it feels like."

"It'll pass."

"No, it won't. Not ever."

"Everything passes."

Widén tried calling Löderup again. Still no answer. Wallander went to the bathroom and took a shower. Widén lent him a shirt, which also smelled of horse.

"How's it going? The horse business," Wallander said.

"I've got one that's good. Three more that might become good. But Fog's got talent. She'll bring in the money. She might even be a possibility for the Derby this year."

"Is she really called Fog?"

"Yes. Why?"

"I was thinking about last night. If I'd had a horse I might have been able to catch up with Konovalenko."

"Not on Fog you wouldn't. She throws riders she doesn't know. Horses with real quality are often a handful. Like people. Full of themselves, and capricious. I sometimes wonder if she should have a mirror in her stall. But she runs fast."

The girl called Kristina came back with the pizza and some newspapers. Then she went out again.

"Isn't she going to eat?" Wallander said.

"They eat in the stables," Widén said. "We have a little kitchen there." He took the top newspaper and leafed through. One of the pages attracted his attention.

"It's about you," he said.

"I'd rather not know. Not yet."

"As you like."

The third time he called, Linda answered. Wallander could hear she was asking lots of questions, but Widén said only what he was supposed to.

"She was very relieved," he said when the call was over. "And she promised to stay put."

They ate their pizzas. A cat jumped up onto the table. Wallander gave it a piece. He noticed that even the cat smelled of horse.

"The fog is lifting," Widén said. "Did I ever tell you I'd been in South Africa? Apropos of what you were just saying."

"No," Wallander said, surprised. "I didn't know that."

"When nothing came of the opera singing business, I went away," he said. "I wanted to get away from everything, you'll remember that. I thought I might become a big game hunter. Or look for diamonds in Kimberley. Must have been something I'd read. And I actually went. Got as far as Cape Town. I stayed for three weeks, and by then I'd had enough. Ran away. Came back here. And so it was horses instead, when Dad died."

"Ran away?"

"The way those blacks were treated. I was ashamed. It was their country, but they were forced to go around cap in hand, apologising for their existence. I've never seen anything like it and I'll never forget it."

He wiped his mouth and went out. Wallander thought about what he had said. Then he realised that he could put it off no longer: he would have to go back to the police station in Ystad.

He went into the room where the telephone was, and found what he was looking for. A whisky bottle, half empty. He took a mouthful and then another. He watched Widén ride past the window on a brown horse.

First I get burgled. Then they blow up my flat. What next?

He lay down on the sofa again, and pulled the blanket up to his chin. His fever had been imagined, and his headache was gone. He would have to get up again soon. He did not wake up again for another four hours.

Widén was in the kitchen, reading an evening paper. "You're wanted," he said.

Wallander looked at him uncomprehendingly. "I'm what?"

"You're wanted. They've sent out an APB. You can also read between the lines that they think you've gone off your head."

Wallander grabbed the newspaper. There was a picture of him, and of Björk.

Widén wasn't exaggerating. He was a wanted man. He and Konovalenko. The reporter quoted a police source as saying that he might not be in full possession of his faculties.

Wallander stared in horror at the paper. "Call my daughter," he said.

"I already did," Widén said. "I told her you were *compos mentis*."

"Did she believe you?"

"Of course she did."

Wallander sat there for a while, then he made up his mind. He would play the role they had given him. A chief detective inspector, temporarily out of his mind, missing. That would give him the thing he needed above all else. Time.

When Konovalenko caught sight of Wallander in the fog, in the field with the sheep, he realised to his amazement that he was up against a worthy opponent. It was at the very instant that Mabasha was thrown backwards, dead before he hit the ground. Konovalenko heard a roar coming out of the fog, and turned around while crouching down. And there he was, the chubby provincial policeman who had defied him time and time again. He had underestimated him. Then Rykoff was hit by two bullets that ripped open his rib cage. Using Mabasha as a shield, Konovalenko withdrew to the beach, knowing that the policeman would come after him. He would not give up, and it was clear now that he was dangerous.

Konovalenko ran along the beach in the fog. At the same time, he called Tania on his mobile phone. She was waiting in Ystad with a car. He ran to the perimeter fence, scrambled onto the road, and found a sign pointing to Kåseberga. He directed her out of Ystad by telephone, talking to her all the time, urging her to drive carefully. He said nothing about Vladimir being dead. That would come later. All the time he kept an eye out behind him. Wallander was not far away and he was the first ruthless Swede he had come across. Yet he could not believe what had happened. The man was just a local police officer, after all. There was something about his behaviour that simply did not add up.

Tania arrived, Konovalenko took the wheel, and they drove to the house near Tomelilla.

"Where's Vladimir?" she said.

"We were forced to split up. I'll get him later."

"What about the African?"

"Dead."

"The policeman did that?"

Tania realised something had gone wrong when Konovalenko did not answer her question. He was driving too fast. Something had exasperated him. And Tania understood that Vladimir too was dead. She said nothing, and managed to keep up the façade until they got back to the house where Tsiki was sitting on a chair watching them, his face devoid of expression. Then she started screaming. Konovalenko slapped her, on the cheek with the flat of his hand at first, then harder and harder. But she kept on screaming until he managed to force some sedatives down her throat, so many they practically knocked her out. Tsiki watched them from the sofa, never moving. Konovalenko had the impression he was performing on a stage with Tsiki the only member of the audience. Once Tania had lapsed almost into unconsciousness, Konovalenko got changed and poured himself a glass of vodka. That Mabasha was at last dead did not give him the satisfaction he had anticipated. It solved certain immediate problems, not least the worry over his dealings with Kleyn. But the problem of the policeman was now exacerbated. He would come after him. He would pick up the trail once more.

Konovalenko poured another vodka. The African on the sofa is a dumb animal, he thought. He watches me all the time, not in a friendly way, not unfriendly, just watching. He says nothing, asks nothing. He could sit like that for days on end if anyone asked him to.

Konovalenko still had nothing to say to him. With every minute that passed, Wallander would be getting closer. What was needed now was an offensive on his part. Preparations for the assassination in South Africa would have to wait.

He knew what was the policeman's weak spot. That was what Konovalenko wanted to get at. But where was the daughter? Somewhere not far away, presumably in Ystad, but not in the flat.

It took him an hour to work out a solution. It was a plan fraught with risk. Since Tania was the key to his plan and she was going to be asleep for many hours, all he needed to do was to wait.

"I gather the big man won't be coming back," Tsiki said suddenly. His voice was very husky, his English singsong.

"He made a mistake," Konovalenko said. "He was too slow."

That was all Tsiki said that night. He got up from the sofa and went to his room. It occurred to Konovalenko that, despite everything, he preferred the replacement Kleyn had sent. He would mention this when he called South Africa the following night.

He was the only one awake. He went to bed shortly before 5 a.m.

Tania arrived at the police station in Ystad just before one in the afternoon on Saturday, May 16. She was still groggy, as a result of the sedatives Konovalenko had given her, and the shock of Vladimir's death. But she was also determined. The policeman who visited them in Hallunda had killed her husband. Konovalenko had described his death in a way that bore little resemblance to what had happened. As far as Tania was concerned, Wallander was a monster of uncontrolled, sadistic brutality. For Vladimir's sake she would play the part Konovalenko had given her. Eventually there would be an opportunity to kill him.

A woman in a glass cage in the reception area at the police station smiled at her. "How can I help you?" she said.

"My car has been broken into," Tania said.

"Oh dear," the receptionist said. "I'll see if there's anybody who can deal with you. The whole place is upside down today."

"I can imagine," Tania said. "Wasn't it awful, what happened?"

"I never thought we'd live to see anything like this happening in Ystad," the receptionist said.

She tried several extensions. Eventually someone answered.

"Is that Martinsson? Do you have time to deal with a car break-in?"

Tania could hear an excited voice at the other end of the line, harassed, negative. But the woman would not give up.

"We have to try and function normally, in spite of everything," she said. "I can't find anybody else. And it won't take long."

The man on the phone gave in.

"You can talk to Detective Inspector Martinsson," she said, pointing. "Third door on the left."

Tania knocked and walked into the office, which was extremely untidy. The man behind the desk looked worn out and harassed. His desk was stacked up with paper. He looked at her with ill-concealed irritation, but he invited her to sit down and started rummaging through a drawer for a form.

"Car break-in?" he said.

"Yes," Tania said. "The thief got away with my radio."

"They usually do," Martinsson said.

"Please excuse me," Tania said, "but could I have a glass of water? I have such a cough."

Martinsson looked at her in surprise. "Yes, of course," he said. "Of course you can have a glass of water." He got up and left the room.

Tania had already identified the address book in the mess on his desk. As soon as Martinsson went out, she picked it up and found the letter W. Wallander's home number at the Mariagatan apartment was listed, and his father's number as well. Tania wrote it quickly on a piece of paper in her bag. She replaced the address book and looked around the office.

Martinsson returned with a glass of water, and a cup of coffee for himself. The telephone started ringing, but he picked up the receiver and laid it on the desk. Then he asked his questions and she gave him details of the imaginary break-in. She gave the registration number of a car she had seen parked in the town. They had taken a radio, and a bag of several bottles of spirits. Martinsson wrote it all down, and when he had finished he asked her to read it through and sign it. She called herself Irma Alexanderson, and gave an address on the Malmö Road. She handed the form back to Martinsson.

"You must be very worried about your colleague," she said in a friendly tone. "What was his name? Wallander?"

"Yes," said Martinsson. "It's not easy."

"I'm sorry for his daughter," she said. "I used to be her music teacher once upon a time. But then she moved to Stockholm."

Martinsson looked up at her with somewhat renewed interest. "She's back here again now," he said.

"Really?" Tania said. "She must have been very lucky, then, when the apartment burned down."

"She's with her grandfather," Martinsson said, replacing the telephone receiver.

Tania got up. "I won't disturb you any longer," she said. "Thanks for your help."

"No problem," Martinsson said, shaking her by the hand.

Tania knew he would forget her the moment she left the room. The dark wig she was wearing over her own blonde hair meant he would never be able to recognise her.

She nodded to the woman in reception, passed a group of journalists waiting for a press conference due to begin any time now, and left the police station.

Konovalenko was waiting at the petrol station on the hill leading down to the town. She got into his car.

"Wallander's daughter is staying with his father," she said. "I've got his telephone number."

Konovalenko looked at her. Then he broke into a smile. "We've got her," he said quietly. "And when we've got her, we've got him as well."

CHAPTER TWENTY-FIVE

Wallander dreamed he was walking on water. The world he found himself in was a strange blue colour. The sky and its jagged clouds were blue, the edge of a forest in the far distance was blue, and the cliff face was cluttered with blue birds roosting. And the sea he was walking on too. Konovalenko was also somewhere in the dream. Wallander had been following his tracks in the sand. But then, instead of turning up towards the slope away from the beach, they went straight out to sea. In his dream it was obvious that he should follow them, so he walked on the water. It was like walking over a thin layer of fine glass splinters. The surface was uneven, but it bore his weight. Somewhere, beyond the last of those blue islets, close to the horizon, was Konovalenko.

He remembered the dream when he woke up early on Sunday morning, May 17. He was on the sofa in Widén's house. He went out into the kitchen and saw that it was 5.30 a.m. A quick look into Widén's bedroom revealed that he was already gone. Wallander poured himself a cup of coffee and sat at the kitchen table.

Last night he had tried to start thinking again. In one sense his situation was easy to assess. He was a wanted man, and they were looking for him. But he could be wounded, he could be dead. Moreover, he had threatened his colleagues with weapons and thereby demonstrated that he was out of his mind. To catch Konovalenko they would also have to track down Chief Inspector Wallander from Ystad. So far, so clear. Yesterday, when Widén told him what was in the papers, he had decided to play the part assigned to him. It would give him time to catch up with Konovalenko and, if necessary, to kill him.

He was taking the role of sacrificial lamb. He doubted whether Konovalenko could be arrested without officers being injured or killed. Therefore he would sacrifice himself. The thought terrified him, but he could not run away. He had to achieve what he had set out to do, regardless of the consequences.

Wallander tried to imagine what Konovalenko was thinking. He could not now ignore Wallander. He might not regard him as a worthy adversary, but he would have gathered that Wallander was a police officer who went his own way and did not hesitate to use a gun if necessary. That should have earned him a measure of respect. In reality Wallander was a policeman who never took unnecessary risks, was both cowardly and cautious. And if he acted in primitive fashion, it was because he was in desperate circumstances. But let Konovalenko go on thinking that he was the other Wallander.

He had tried to work out what Konovalenko was up to. He had come back to Skåne; he had found and now killed Mabasha. He couldn't be on his own. He had brought Rykoff with him, but how had he managed to get away without help? Rykoff's wife, Tania, must be around, and maybe other henchmen Wallander didn't know about. They had rented a house under a false name before.

Having got that far, Wallander realised there was another important question still waiting to be resolved. What happens after Mabasha? What about the assassination that was the mainspring of everything that's happened? What about the invisible organisation that's pulling all the strings, even Konovalenko's? Will the whole thing be called off? Or will these faceless men keep on?

He drank his coffee, and decided that there was only one course open to him. He had to make sure Konovalenko could find him. When they attacked the flat, they were looking for him as well. Mabasha's last words were that he didn't know where Wallander was. Konovalenko wanted to know.

He heard footsteps in the hall. Widén came in, dressed in dirty overalls and muddy boots.

"We're racing at Jägersro today," he said. "How about coming along?"

Wallander was tempted, just for a moment. He welcomed any diversion.

"Is Fog running?" he asked.

"She's running, and she's going to win," Widén said. "But I doubt whether the gamblers will have enough faith in her. That means you could earn a few kronor."

"How can you be so sure?"

"She's a temperamental beast," Widén said, "but today she's raring to go. She's restless in her box. She can sense the chips are down. And the opposition is not all that brilliant. There are a few horses from Norway I don't know much about. But I am confident she can beat them as well."

"Who's the owner of this horse?" Wallander said.

"A businessman by the name of Morell."

Wallander recognised the name. He had heard it not long ago, but could not remember the context. "Stockholmer?"

"No. From Skåne."

It came back to him. Peter Hanson and his pumps. A fence by the name of Morell.

"What line of business is this Morell in?"

"To tell you the truth, I think he's a little shady, or so rumour has it. But he pays his training bills on time. No business of mine where the money comes from."

"I don't think I'll come, thanks all the same," Wallander said.

"Ulrika brought in some food," Widén said. "We'll be taking the horses off in an hour or two. You'll have to look after yourself."

"What about the Duett? Will you leave it here?"

"Borrow it if you like," Widén said. "But remember to fill the tank. I keep forgetting."

Wallander watched the horses being led into the horsebox. Soon afterwards he too was on his way to Ystad. He took the risk of driving down Mariagatan. It looked pretty desolate. A yawning hole in the wall, ringed by scorched bricks where the window used to be. He stopped only briefly, before driving through town. As he passed the training ground he saw a squad car parked well back from the perimeter fence. Now the fog had lifted, the distance seemed shorter. He drove on and turned off to the harbour at Kåseberga. He knew he might be recognised, but the photograph of him in the newspapers was not a good likeness. The problem was that he might run into somebody he knew. He stopped by a phone booth and dialled his father's number. As he had hoped, his daughter answered.

"Where are you?" she said. "What are you up to?"

"Just listen," he said. "Can anybody overhear you?"

"How could anybody? Grandpa's painting."

"Nobody else?"

"There's nobody here, I told you!"

"Haven't the police put a guard there yet? Isn't there a car parked on the road?"

"Nilson's tractor is in one of the fields."

"What? Nothing else?"

"Papa, there's nobody here. Stop worrying."

"I'll be there in a few minutes," he said. "Don't say anything to your grandfather."

"Have you seen what they put in the papers?"

"We can talk about that later."

He replaced the receiver, thinking how pleased he was that it had not yet been confirmed that he killed Rykoff. Even if the police knew, they wouldn't release the information until Wallander was found. He was sure of that, after all his years in the force.

He drove straight to his father's house. He left the car on the main road and walked the last bit, taking a path on which he knew he could not be seen. She was standing at the door, waiting. When they got into the hallway, she hugged him. They stood in silence. He did not know what she was thinking. As far as he was concerned, though, it was proof that they were on the way to being so close that words were sometimes unnecessary.

They sat the kitchen table. "Grandpa won't show up for quite some time yet," she said. "I could learn a lot from his working discipline."

"Or stubbornness," he said. They both burst out laughing. Then he grew serious again. He told her slowly what had happened, and why he had decided to accept the role of a man on the run.

"What do you think you'll achieve? All by yourself?"

He could not make up his mind whether fear or scepticism lay behind her question. "I'll lure him out. I know I'm no-one-man army, but if this thing is going to be solved, I have to take the first step myself."

Quickly, as if in protest at what he had just said, she changed the subject. "Did he suffer a lot?" she asked. "Your African?"

"No," Wallander said. "I don't think he had any idea he was going to die."

"What'll happen to him now?"

"I've no idea," Wallander said. "There'll be an autopsy. Then it's a matter of whether his family want him buried here, or in South Africa. Assuming that is where he comes from."

"Who is he, in fact?"

"I don't know. I sometimes felt I'd made some kind of contact with him. But then he slipped away again. I don't know what he was thinking deep down. He was a remarkable man, very complicated. If that's how you get when you live in South Africa, it must be a country you wouldn't want to send your worst enemy to."

"I want to help you," she said.

"You can," Wallander said. "You can call the police station and ask to speak with Martinsson."

"That's not what I mean," she said. "I'd like to do something nobody else can do."

"That's not the kind of thing you plan in advance," Wallander said. "That just happens. When it happens."

She called the police station and asked to speak with Martinsson, but the switchboard could not track him down. She put her hand over the mouthpiece and asked what she should do. Wallander hesitated, but he realised he could not afford to wait, nor pick and choose. He asked her to get Svedberg instead.

"He's in a meeting," she said. "Not to be disturbed."

"Tell her who you are," Wallander said. "Say it's important."

It was a few minutes before Svedberg came to the phone. She handed the receiver to Wallander.

"It's me," he said. "Kurt. Don't say anything. Where are you?"

"In my office."

"Is the door closed?"

"Just a moment." Wallander could hear him slamming the door. "Kurt," he said. "Where are you?"

"I'm somewhere where you'll never be able to find me."

"Damn it, Kurt."

"Just listen. Don't interrupt. I need to see you, but only on condition that you don't say a word to anyone. To Björk, Martinsson, anybody. If you can't give me your word I'll hang up."

"We're in the conference room right now, discussing how to build

308

up the search for you and the Russian," Svedberg said. "It'll be ridiculous if I go back to that meeting and not say I've just been talking with you."

"That can't be helped," Wallander said. "I think I have good reason for doing what I'm doing. I'm intending to exploit the fact that I'm wanted."

"How so?"

"I'll tell you when we meet. Make up your mind, now!"

There was a long pause.

"I'll come," Svedberg said, eventually.

"Are you sure?"

"Yes."

Wallander told him the way to Stjärnsund. "Two hours from now. Can you manage that?"

"I'll have to make sure I can," Svedberg said.

Wallander hung up.

"Somebody has to know what I'm doing," he said.

"In case something happens?"

Her question came so suddenly Wallander had no time to think of an evasive answer. "Yes," he said. "In case something happens."

He stayed for another cup of coffee. As he was getting ready to leave, he hesitated. "I don't want to make you any more worried than you already are," he said, "but I don't want you to leave these four walls for the next few days. Nothing's going to happen to you. It's to make me sleep easier at night, that's all."

She patted his cheek. "I'll stay here," she said. "Don't you worry."

"Just a few more days," he said. "It can hardly be more than that. This nightmare will be over in that time. Then I'll have to get used to the fact that I killed a man."

He left before she had a chance to say anything more. He could see in the rear-view mirror that she had followed him to the road and was watching him drive away.

Svedberg was there on time. It was 2.50 p.m. when he turned into the courtyard. Wallander put on his jacket and went out to meet him. Svedberg looked at him and shook his head.

"What are you up to?" he said.

"I think I can handle it," Wallander said. "And thanks for coming."

They walked to the bridge over the old moat around the ruined castle. Svedberg leaned over the rail and contemplated the green sludge below, and Wallander told him what Mabasha had revealed to him, and what Konovalenko's part in the plot had been.

"It's hard to grasp that this sort of thing can happen," Svedberg said, horrified.

"We think we can stop something happening just by refusing to acknowledge it," Wallander said.

"But why Sweden? Why choose Sweden as their starting point?"

"The African had a possible explanation," Wallander said. "He claimed that it was partly because this is where Konovalenko was established, of course, but the crucial thing for the people behind this business is that nothing can be tracked down. Sweden is a country where it's easy to get lost; it's simple to cross the border, and it's easy to disappear. He had a simile for it. Mabasha said South Africa is a cuckoo, she often lays her eggs in other people's nests."

"I've never been here before," Svedberg said. "I wonder what it was like, being a policeman, as it were, when the castle was in its prime."

They wandered around the crumbled ruins of what had once been high walls.

"You have to understand: Martinsson and I were really shaken. You were covered in blood, your hair was standing on end, and you were waving guns at us in both hands."

"Yes, I realise that," Wallander said.

"All the same, it was wrong of us to tell Björk that you appeared to be out of your mind."

"I wonder sometimes if I am, in fact."

"What are you going to do?" Svedberg said.

"I'm thinking of ways of enticing Konovalenko to come after me. That's the only way I can think of to get him to come out of wherever he's hiding."

Svedberg stared at him, grimly. "That's dangerous," he said.

"It's less risky when you can anticipate the danger," Wallander said, wondering as he did so if that really meant anything at all.

"You've got to have backup," Svedberg said.

"He wouldn't come out in that case," Wallander said. "It's not enough for him to think I'm on my own. He won't pounce until he's absolutely certain."

"What do you mean, pounce?"

Wallander shrugged. "He'll try to kill me, but he won't succeed."

"How so?"

"I don't know yet."

Svedberg stared at him in amazement, but he said nothing.

They started back, and stopped again on the bridge.

"There's something else," Wallander said. "I'm worried about Linda. Konovalenko's unpredictable. I want her to have a bodyguard."

"Björk will want an explanation."

"That's why I'm asking you. You can talk with Martinsson. Björk doesn't need to know."

"I'll try," Svedberg said. "I can understand your being worried."

They left the bridge and puffed their way up the hill.

"By the way, somebody who knows your daughter came to see Martinsson," Svedberg said, trying to change the subject to something less solemn.

Wallander stared at him in alarm. "At home?"

"In his office. She was reporting a theft from her car. She'd been your daughter's teacher or something. I don't remember exactly."

Wallander stopped dead. "One more time," he said. "Repeat that."

Svedberg told him again.

"What was her name?"

"I've no idea."

"What did she look like?"

"You'll have ask Martinsson that."

"Try and remember precisely what he said."

"We were having coffee," Svedberg said. "Martinsson was complaining about being interrupted the whole time. He says he'll get an ulcer from all the work piling up. 'At least they could stop breaking into cars at a time like this. A woman came in, someone had broken into her car. She asked about Wallander's daughter. If she was still living in Stockholm.' Something along those lines."

"What did he tell her? That Linda is here?"

"I can't tell you what he told her."

"We have to call Martinsson," Wallander said. He started running towards the house, with Svedberg after him.

"Get him on the phone," Wallander said, when they were inside. "Ask him if he told the woman where Linda is right now. Find out who she is. If he asks why, just tell him that you'll explain later."

Svedberg nodded. "You don't believe there was a car theft?"

"I have no way of knowing, but I can't take any risks."

Svedberg was put through to Martinsson almost right away. He wrote a few notes in the margins of yesterday's paper. Wallander could hear that Martinsson was perplexed by Svedberg's questions. By the time their conversation was over, Svedberg had started to share Wallander's worry.

"He says he told her."

"Told her what?"

"That she was staying with your father at Österlen."

"Why did he do that?"

"She asked him."

Wallander looked at the kitchen clock. "You'd better make the call," he said. "My father may answer. He's probably eating now. Ask to talk to Linda. Then I'll take over."

Wallander gave him the number. It rang for a long time before anybody answered. It was Wallander's father. Svedberg asked to speak to his granddaughter. When he heard the reply, he cut the conversation short.

"She went down to the beach on her bike," he said.

Wallander felt a stabbing pain in his stomach. "I told her to stay indoors."

"She left half an hour ago," Svedberg said.

They took Svedberg's car and drove fast. Svedberg glanced at him occasionally, but Wallander did not say a word.

They came to the Kåseberga exit.

"Keep going," Wallander said. "Next turning."

They parked as near to the beach as they could safely get. There were no other cars. Wallander raced onto the sands with Svedberg alongside him. The beach was deserted. Wallander could feel panic rising. Once again the invisible Konovalenko was breathing down his neck.

"She could be behind one of the sand dunes," he said.

"Are you sure this is where she'll be?" Svedberg said.

"This is her beach," Wallander said. "If she goes to the beach, this is where she comes. You go that way, I'll go this way."

Svedberg walked back towards Kåseberga while Wallander continued to the east. He tried to convince himself nothing had happened to her. But why hadn't she stayed inside the house as she had promised? Was it possible that she had not understood how serious it was? In spite of everything that had happened?

Every minute he turned and looked back at Svedberg.

Wallander found himself thinking of Åkerblom. He would have said a prayer in this situation. I have no god to pray to. I don't even have any spirits, like Mabasha. I have my own joy and my own sorrow, that's all.

There was a man with a dog on top of the slope, gazing out to sea. Wallander asked him if he had seen a girl walking by herself, or with a bicycle along the beach. He had been on the beach with his dog for 20 minutes, but he had seen no-one in all that time.

"Not even a man by himself?" The man shook his head.

Wallander walked on. He felt cold though there was a trace of spring warmth in the wind. He started walking faster. The beach seemed endless. Then he looked around again. Svedberg was a long way away now, but Wallander could see somebody standing next to him. Svedberg started waving.

Wallander ran the whole way. When he got to Svedberg and his daughter he was exhausted. He looked at her without saying anything while he waited to get his breath back.

"You were supposed not to leave the house," he said. "Why did you?"

"I didn't think a walk along the beach would do any harm," she said. "Not when it's light. It's night-time when things happen, isn't it?"

Svedberg drove and they put the bicycle in the boot.

"What shall I tell Grandpa?" Linda said.

"Nothing," Wallander said. "I'll talk to him tonight. I'll play cards with him tomorrow. That will cheer him up."

They separated on the road not far from the house. Svedberg drove Wallander back to Stjärnsund.

"I want that guard starting tonight," Wallander said.

"I'll go and tell Martinsson right away," Svedberg said. "We'll arrange it somehow."

"A police car parked on the road," Wallander said. "I want it to be obvious that the house is being watched."

Svedberg got ready to leave.

"I need a few days," Wallander said. "Until then, keep on looking for me. But I'd like you to call me here from time to time."

"What shall I tell Martinsson?"

"Tell him it was your idea, guarding my father's house," Wallander said. "Find whatever way you think best to convince him."

"You really don't want me to tell Martinsson the truth?"

"It's enough that you know where I am."

After Svedberg left, Wallander fried a couple of eggs. Two hours later the horsebox returned.

"Did she win?" Wallander said, as Widén came into the kitchen.

"She won," he said. "But only just."

Peters and Norén were in their patrol car, drinking coffee.

They were both in a bad mood. They had been ordered by Svedberg to guard the house where Wallander's father lived. The longest shifts were always when your car was standing still. They would be here until someone came to relieve them, many hours away yet. It was 11.15 p.m. and pitch dark.

"What do you think's happened to Wallander?"

"No idea," Norén said. "How many times do I have to say it? I don't know."

"It's hard not to think about it," Peters said. "I'm sitting here wondering whether he might be an alcoholic."

"Why should he be?"

"Do you remember that time we caught him drunk?"

"That's not the same as being alcoholic."

"No. But still."

The conversation petered out. Norén got out of the car and stood legs apart to urinate. That was when he saw the fire. At first he thought it was the reflection from a car's headlights. Then he noticed smoke barrelling up from where the fire was burning.

"Fire!" he shouted to Peters.

Peters got out.

"Can it be a forest fire?" Norén said. The blaze was in a clump of trees on the far side of the nearest group of fields. It was hard to see where the heart of it was because of the slope in front of the trees.

"We'd better drive over and take a look," said Peters.

"Svedberg said we weren't to leave our posts, no matter what."

"It'll only take a few minutes," Peters said. "We have no choice but to act if we find a fire."

"Call Svedberg first and get permission."

"It'll take maximum ten minutes," Peters said. "What are you scared of?"

"I'm not scared," Norén said. "But orders are orders."

Nevertheless, they did as Peters wanted. They reached the fire by way of a muddy tractor track. When they got there, they found only an oil drum that had been filled with paper and plastic to make a good blaze. The fire was almost out.

"Funny time to burn garbage," Peters said, looking round. The place was deserted.

"Let's get back," Norén said.

Twenty minutes had passed they were at the house again. All was quiet. The lights were out. Wallander's father and daughter were asleep. Many hours later they were relieved by Svedberg himself.

"All quiet," Peters said. He did not mention the excursion to the burning oil drum.

Svedberg sat dozing in his car. Dawn broke, and developed into morning.

By 8 a.m. he was wondering why there was no sign of anybody being up. He knew that Wallander's father was an early riser. By 8.30 a.m., he had the distinct impression something was wrong. He got out of his car, crossed the courtyard to the front door and tried the handle. The door was not locked. He rang the bell and waited. Nobody opened. He entered the dark hall and listened. Not a sound. Then he thought he could hear a scratching sound somewhere. It sounded like a mouse trying to get through a wall. He followed the noise until he found himself in front of a closed door. He knocked. By way of answer he could hear a muffled bellowing. He flung open the door. Wallander's father was lying in bed. He was tied up, with a length of black tape over his mouth.

Svedberg stood stock still. Then he very gently removed the tape and untied the ropes. Then he searched the whole house. The room in which he assumed Wallander's daughter slept was empty. There was nobody else in the house.

"When did it happen?" he asked.

"Last night, just after 11 p.m."

"How many of them were there?"

"One."

"One?"

"That's right. But he had a gun."

Svedberg's mind was a complete blank. He went to the telephone to call Wallander.

CHAPTER TWENTY-SIX

The acrid smell of winter apples. That was the first thing she noticed. But after that, when she opened her eyes in the darkness, there was nothing but being alone and terrified. She was lying on a stone floor, but it smelled of damp earth. There was not a sound, even though fear sharpened all her senses. She felt the rough surface of the floor with one hand. It was made of individual slabs fitted together. She was in a cellar. In Österlen, where her grandfather lived and where she had been brutally woken and abducted by an unknown man, there was a similar floor in the potato cellar.

When there was nothing more for her senses to register, she felt dizzy and her headache got steadily worse. She could not say how long she had been there in darkness and silence; her watch was still on her bedside table. Nevertheless she guessed that it was many hours since she had been woken up and dragged away.

Her arms were free, but she had a chain around her ankles. When she felt it with her fingers she discovered there was a padlock. The feeling of being confined by an iron lock turned her cold. People were usually tied up with ropes. They were softer, more flexible. Chains belonged to the past, to slavery and medieval witch trials.

But worst of all during this waking up period were the clothes she had on. She could feel at once that they were not hers. They were unfamiliar – their shape, the colours she could not see but seemed to think she could feel with her fingertips, and the smell of a strong washing powder. Somebody must have dressed her in them. Somebody had taken off her nightie and dressed her in everything from underclothes to tights and shoes, an outrage that made her feel sick. The dizziness immediately grew stronger. She put her head in her hands and rocked backwards and forwards. It's not true, she thought in desperation. But it was true, and she could even remember what had happened.

She had been dreaming something but could no longer think of the context. She was woken by a man pressing a handkerchief over her nose and mouth. A pungent smell, then she was overcome by a feeling of numbness and fading senses. The light from the lamp outside the kitchen door produced a faint glow in her room. She could see a man in front of her. His face was very close when he bent over her. Now when she thought about him she recalled a strong smell of shaving lotion even though he was unshaven. He said nothing, but although it was almost dark in the room she could see his eyes and had time to think she would never forget them. Then she remembered nothing else until she woke up on the damp stone floor.

It did not take her long to understand why it had happened. The man who bent over her and drugged her must be the one who was hunting, and being hunted by, her father. His eyes were Konovalenko's eyes, just as she had imagined them. The man who killed Victor Mabasha, who had already killed a policeman and wanted to kill her father. He was the one who had crept into her room, dressed her and put chains around her ankles.

When the hatch in the cellar ceiling opened, she was utterly unprepared. It occurred to her afterwards that the man had probably been standing up there, listening. The light shining through the hole was very strong, perhaps deliberately to dazzle her. She caught a glimpse of a ladder being dropped down and a pair of brown shoes, a pair of trouser legs approaching her. Then, last of all, the face, the same face and the same eyes that had stared at her as she was being knocked out. She looked away so as to avoid the brilliant light, and because her fear had returned and was paralysing her. She saw that the cellar was larger than she had supposed. In the darkness the walls and ceiling seemed close to her. Maybe she was in a cellar the length of the whole ground floor of a house.

The man stood in such a way that he shielded her from the light streaming down. He had a torch in one hand. In the other he had a metal object she could not at first make out.

Then she realised it was a pair of scissors.

She screamed. Shrill, long. She thought he had climbed down the ladder in order to kill her, and that he would do it with the scissors. She grabbed the chains around her legs and started pulling at them,

318

as if she could break free despite everything. All the time he was staring at her, and his head was no more than a silhouette against the strong background light.

Then he turned the torchlight onto his own face. He held it under his chin so that his face looked like a lifeless skull. She fell silent. Her screaming had only increased her fear. And yet she felt strangely exhausted. It was already too late. There was no point in offering resistance.

The skull suddenly started talking. "You're wasting your time screaming," Konovalenko said. "Nobody will hear you. Besides, there's the risk I'll get annoyed, and might hurt you. Better to keep quiet."

His last words were like a whisper.

Papa, she thought. You've got to help me.

Then everything happened very quickly. With the same hand in which he held the torch, he grabbed her hair, pulled it and started cutting it off. She started back, in pain and surprise. But he was holding her so tightly, she could not move. She could hear the dry sound of the sharp scissors snipping away around the back of her neck, just under her earlobes. It was over in no time, and he let her go. The feeling of wanting to vomit came back. Cropping hair was another outrage, like him dressing her without her being aware of it.

He rolled the hair into a ball and put it into his pocket. He's sick, she thought. He's crazy, a sadist, a madman who kills and feels nothing. Her thoughts were interrupted by him talking again. The torch was shining on her neck, on her necklace. It was in the form of a lyre. Her parents had given it to her for her 15th birthday.

"The necklace. Take it off."

She did as she was told and was careful to avoid touching his hands when she held it out. Without a word he left her, climbed up the ladder, and returned her to the darkness. She crawled away until she came to the wall, and groped her way along it until she came to a corner, still within the radius of the chain. And there she tried to hide.

After having carried off his plan to kidnap Wallander's daughter, Konovalenko had ordered Tania and Tsiki out of the kitchen. He had a great need to be alone, and the kitchen suited him best. The house, the one Rykoff had rented, was arranged so that the kitchen was the biggest room. It was in old-fashioned style, with exposed beams, a deep baking oven, and open china dressers. Copper pans were hanging along one wall. Konovalenko was reminded of his childhood in Kiev, the big kitchen in the *kolkhoz* where his father had been a political superintendent.

He was discovering that he missed Rykoff. It was not just a feeling of having now to shoulder a greater part of the work. There was also a feeling that could hardly be called melancholy or sorrow, but which nevertheless made him feel depressed. During his many years as a KGB officer, the value of life, for everybody but himself and his two children, had gradually been reduced to calculable resources or, at the opposite pole, to expendable persons. He was forever surrounded by sudden death, and emotional reactions gradually vanished. But Rykoff's death had affected him, and it made him hate even more this provincial Swedish police officer, who was always getting in his way. He was going to get his come-uppance. But he had the daughter in his hands, and she would be the bait that would lure him into the open. Yet the prospect of revenge could not liberate him entirely from his depression. He sat in the kitchen drinking vodka, careful not to get too drunk, and occasionally seeing himself in a mirror on the wall. It occurred to him that his face was ugly. He must be starting to get old. Had the collapse of the Soviet empire brought on the softening of his ruthless and implacable nature?

At 2 a.m., when Tania was asleep or at least pretending to be asleep, and Tsiki had shut himself away in his room, he telephoned Kleyn. He decided there was no reason to conceal the fact that one of his assistants was dead. It would do no harm for Kleyn to be aware that Konovalenko's work was not without its risks. Then he resolved to lie to him one more time. He would say that the damned nuisance of a policeman had been liquidated. He was so sure he would get him, now that he had his daughter locked in the cellar, that he dared to declare Wallander dead.

Kleyn made no special comment. Konovalenko knew Kleyn's silence was the most approval he would get for his efforts. Then Kleyn said that Tsiki should return to South Africa soon. He asked if there was the least doubt about his suitability, if he had displayed any sign of weakness, as Mabasha had done. Konovalenko said no, but in fact he had been able to devote very little time to Tsiki so far. The impression he had was chiefly of a man devoid of emotion. He hardly ever laughed, and was as controlled as he was impeccably dressed. Konovalenko reckoned that once Wallander and his daughter were out of the way he would spend a few intensive days teaching the African all he needed to know. But he said Tsiki would not let them down and Kleyn seemed satisfied. He told Konovalenko to call again in three days to receive instructions for Tsiki's return journey.

The conversation with Kleyn restored some of the energy he thought he had lost in the wake of Rykoff's death. He sat at the kitchen table and reflected that the abduction of Wallander's daughter had been almost embarrassingly easy. It had taken him only a few hours to find her grandfather's house, once Tania had been to the Ystad police station. He made the call himself and a housekeeper answered the phone. He said he was from the telephone company and was calling to know if there was likely to be a change of address before the next edition of the telephone directory went to press. Tania bought a large-scale map of Skåne from the bookshop, and then they drove to the house and kept it under observation from a distance. The housekeeper went home late in the afternoon, and a few hours later a police car parked on the road. When he was satisfied that there were no other guards posted, he rapidly devised a diversion. He drove back to the house in Tomelilla, prepared an oil drum he found in a shed, and told Tania what she had to do. They rented a car from a nearby petrol station, then drove back to the house in two cars, saw the police car, decided on a time and set to work. Tania made the fire blaze up as intended and then left the scene before the police arrived to investigate. Konovalenko knew that he did not have much time, but that was just an extra challenge for him. He forced open the outside door, silenced the old man in his bed and tied him up, then chloroformed the daughter and carried her to the waiting car. The whole operation took less than ten minutes, and he had made his escape before the police car got back. Tania had bought some clothes for the girl during the day, and dressed her while she was still unconscious. Then he carried her down into the cellar and secured her legs with a padlock and chain. It was all so easy, and he wondered whether things would continue so straightforwardly. He had noticed her necklace and thought her father would be able to identify her by it. But he also wanted to give Wallander a different picture of the circumstances, something threatening that would leave no doubt as to what he was prepared to do. Cropped female hair smells of death and ruin, he thought. He's a policeman, he'll get the picture.

Konovalenko poured himself another glass of vodka and gazed out of the window. Dawn was in the sky, and there was warmth in the air. He thought about how he would soon be living in constant sunshine, far from this climate in which you never knew from one hour to the next what the weather would be like.

The hatch leading down to the cellar where Wallander's daughter was imprisoned was just behind his chair. He listened for any noises, but everything was silent. Then he got up, found an envelope and put the cropped hair and the necklace into it.

He went to bed for a few hours. When he woke up he looked at his wristwatch. It was 9.15 a.m., Monday, May 18. Wallander must know by now that his daughter has been abducted. He would be waiting for Konovalenko to contact him.

Well, he can wait a bit longer, Konovalenko thought. The silence will grow increasingly unbearable with every hour that passes, and his worry greater than his ability to control it.

The news hit Wallander like an attack of vertigo. It made him desperate and furious. Widén happened to be in the kitchen when the telephone rang, answered it, and looked on in astonishment as Wallander tore the instrument from the wall and hurled it through the open door into the office. But he saw at once how frightened Wallander was. His fear was raw, naked. Sympathy often aroused ambivalent reactions in him, but not this time. The man's agony over what had happened to his daughter and the fact that nothing could be done about it had hurt him terribly. He squatted down beside his friend and patted him on the shoulder.

Meanwhile Svedberg had worked up a frenzy of energy. Once he had made sure that Wallander's father was uninjured and did not seem to be especially shocked, he called Peters at home. His wife answered, and said her husband was still asleep after his night shift. Svedberg's bellowing left no doubt in her mind that he should be woken immediately. When Peters came to the phone, Svedberg gave him half an hour to get hold of Norén and be at the house they were supposed to have been guarding. Peters asked no questions and promised to hurry. He called Norén, and when they arrived at Wallander's father's house, Svedberg wasted no time before confronting them with what had happened.

"All we can do is tell you the truth," Norén said, who had been uneasy the previous evening that there was something odd about the burning oil drum.

Svedberg listened to what he had to say. It was Peters who insisted that they should investigate the fire, but of that he said nothing. In his report he said that the decision was a joint one.

"I hope nothing happens to Wallander's daughter, for your sakes," Svedberg said.

"But abducted, and by whom? And why?" Norén said.

Svedberg gave them a long, serious look before answering. "I'm going to make you promise me something," he said. "If you keep that promise, I'll try and overlook that you acted in complete disregard of clearly expressed orders last night. If the girl comes out of this unharmed, nobody will get to know a thing. Is that clear?"

They both nodded.

"You heard nothing, and you saw nothing last night," he said. "And most important of all, Wallander's daughter has not been abducted. In other words, nothing has happened."

Peters and Norén stared at him, nonplussed.

"I mean what I say," Svedberg said again. "Nothing has happened. That's what you have to remember. You'll just have to believe me when I say it's important."

"Is there anything we can do?" Peters said.

"Yes," Svedberg said. "Go home and get some sleep."

Then Svedberg searched in vain for clues in the courtyard and inside the house. He searched the clearing where the oil drum had been. There were tyre tracks into the area, but no other clue. He went back to the house and spoke again with Wallander's father. He was in the kitchen drinking coffee, and was scared stiff.

"What's happened?" he asked, worried. "There's no sign of Linda."

"I honestly don't know," Svedberg said. "But it'll all work itself out, that's for sure."

"You think?" Wallander's father said. His voice was full of doubt. "I could hear how upset Kurt was on the telephone. Where is he, come to that? What's going on?"

"I think it'll be best if he explains that himself," Svedberg said, getting to his feet. "I'm going to see him now."

"Say hello from me," the old man said. "Tell him I'm doing just fine."

"Thanks. I'll do that," Svedberg said.

Wallander was barefoot in a patch of sun on the gravel outside Widén's house when Svedberg drove up. It was nearly 11 a.m. Still in the courtyard, Svedberg set out in every detail he knew what must have happened. He did not leave out how easily Peters and Norén had been fooled into leaving for the short time it took for his daughter to be taken. Finally, he passed on the message from his father.

Wallander listened attentively all the time. Even so, Svedberg saw that there was something distant about him. Normally he could look Wallander in the eye when he spoke to him, but now his eyes were wandering aimlessly about. Svedberg could see that, mentally, he was with his daughter, wherever she might be.

They went into the house.

"I've been trying to think," Wallander said, when they were sitting in the kitchen. Svedberg could see his hands were shaking. "This is Konovalenko's work, of course. Just as I'd feared. It's all my fault. I ought to have been there. Now he's using Linda to get hold of me. He's apparently working on his own."

"He must have at least one assistant," Svedberg said, cautiously. "If I understood Peters and Norén right, he couldn't possibly have had time to light the fire himself, get back to the house, break in, tie up your dad and get away from the house with your daughter."

Wallander thought for a moment. "OK. The oil drum was lit by Tania," he said. "Rykoff's wife. So there are two of them. We don't know where they are. Presumably in a house somewhere not far from Ystad. A remote place. A house we could have found if circumstances were different. We can't now."

Widén came discreetly to the table with coffee. Wallander looked at him. "I need something stronger," he said.

Widén came back with a half-empty bottle of whisky. Wallander took a gulp straight from the bottle.

"I've been trying to work out what'll happen next," he said. "He'll get in touch with me. And he'll use my father's house. That's where I'll wait until I hear from him. I don't know what he'll propose. At best my life for hers. At worst, God only knows what."

He turned to Svedberg. "That's how I see it," he said. "Do you think I'm wrong?"

"It sounds right," Svedberg said. "The question is just what are we going to do about it."

"Nobody should do anything," Wallander said. "No police near the house, nothing. Konovalenko will smell the slightest hint of danger. I'll have to be alone in the house with my father. Your job will be to make sure nobody goes there."

"You can't handle this on your own," Svedberg said. "You've got to let us help you."

"I don't want my daughter to die," Wallander said quite simply. "I have to sort this out myself."

Svedberg realised the conversation was over. Wallander had made up his mind.

"I'll take you to Löderup," Svedberg said.

"That won't be necessary. You can take the Duett," Widén said.

Wallander nodded. He almost fell as he stood up. He grabbed the edge of the table. "No problem," he said.

Svedberg and Widén stood in the courtyard, watching him drive off.

When Wallander reached Löderup his father was painting in his studio. He had abandoned for the first time ever his unvarying theme, a landscape in the evening sun, either with or without a wood grouse in the foreground. This time he was painting a different landscape, darker, more chaotic. The picture did not hang together. Woods were growing directly out of a lake, and the mountains in the background overwhelmed the scene.

He put down his brushes after Wallander had been standing behind him for a while. When he turned around, Wallander could see he was scared.

"Let's go in," his father said. "I sent the housekeeper home." His father placed his hand on Wallander's shoulder. He could not remember the last time the old man had made a gesture like that.

When they were inside Wallander told him everything that had happened. He could see his father was incapable of making sense of the various incidents as they crisscrossed one another. Even so, he wanted to give him an idea of what had been going on these last three weeks. He did not want to hide the fact that he had killed another human being, or that his daughter was in great danger. The man holding her prisoner, who had tied him up in his own bed, was absolutely ruthless.

When he was finished, his father sat looking down at his hands.

"I can deal with it," Wallander said. "I'm a good policeman. I'll stay here until this man contacts me. It could be any time now. Or he may wait until tomorrow."

The afternoon was close to being evening, and still no word from Konovalenko. Svedberg called twice, but Wallander had nothing new to tell him. He sent his father out to the studio to go on painting. He couldn't stand having him sitting in the kitchen, staring at his hands. His father would normally have been furious at having to do what his son told him, but now he stood up and went.

Wallander paced up and down, sat down on a chair for a moment, then got up again straightaway. Sometimes he would go into the court-yard and gaze over the fields. Then he would come back in and start pacing again. He tried eating twice, but he had no appetite. His anguish, his worry and his helplessness made it impossible for him to think straight. On several occasions Åkerblom came into his mind. But he sent him packing, scared that the very thought could be a bad omen for what might happen to his daughter.

Evening came and still no contact. Svedberg called to say he could be reached at home from now on. Wallander called Widén, but did not really have anything to say. At 10 p.m. he sent his father to bed. It was still warm and light outside. He sat on the steps outside the kitchen door for a while. When he was sure his father was asleep, he called Baiba Liepa in Riga. No reply the first time. But she was home when he tried again half an hour later. He was icily calm as he told her his daughter had been taken hostage by a very dangerous man. He said he had no-one to talk to, and just then he felt he was telling the absolute truth. He apologised for the night when he had been drunk and woken her with his call. He tried to articulate his feelings for her, but the words he needed were beyond his grasp of English. Before hanging up he promised to keep in touch. She listened to what he had to say, but hardly said anything herself from start to finish. Afterwards he wondered whether he really had been talking to her, or whether it had all been in his imagination.

He spent a sleepless night. Occasionally he slumped down into one of his father's worn old armchairs and closed his eyes. But just as he was about to doze off, he would wake again with a start. He started pacing up and down once more, and it was like reliving the whole of his life. Towards dawn he stood staring at a solitary hare sitting motionless in the courtyard.

It was now Tuesday, May 19. Shortly after 5 a.m. The wind got up and it started raining.

The message came just before 8 a.m.

A taxi from Simrishamn turned into the courtyard. Wallander heard the car approaching from some way off, and went out onto the steps when it came to a halt. The driver got out and handed him a fat envelope.

The letter was addressed to his father.

"It's for my father. I'll take it," he said. "Where is it from?"

"A lady handed it in at the office in Simrishamn," the driver said, who was in a hurry and did not want to get wet. "She paid for it to be delivered. I don't need a receipt."

Wallander nodded. Tania, he thought. She has taken over her husband's role as errand boy.

The taxi disappeared. Wallander was alone in the house. His father was already in his studio.

It was a padded envelope. He examined it carefully before starting to open it along one of the short sides. At first he could not see what was inside. Then he saw Linda's hair, and the necklace he had once given her.

He sat still as a statue, staring at the cropped hair lying on the table in front of him. Then he started crying. His pain had passed another limit, and he could not fight it anymore. What had Konovalenko done to her? It was all his fault, getting her involved in this.

Then he forced himself to read the letter. Konovalenko would be in touch again in twelve hours' time. They needed to meet in order to sort out their problems, he wrote. Wallander would just have to wait until then. Any contact with the police would put his daughter's life in grave danger. The letter was unsigned.

He looked again at his daughter's hair. The world was helpless in the face of such evil. How could he stop Konovalenko?

He supposed that these were exactly the reflections Konovalenko wanted him to be having. He had also given him twelve hours with no hope of doing anything other than what Konovalenko had dictated.

Wallander sat frozen like a statue on his chair. He had no idea what to do.

CHAPTER TWENTY-SEVEN

A long time ago, Karl Evert Svedberg had decided to become a police-man for a very particular reason, and for that only – a reason he tried to keep secret. He was terrified of the dark. Ever since he was a child he had slept with the bedside lamp on. Unlike most people's, his fear of the dark did not recede as he grew older. On the contrary, it became worse when he was a teenager. And so had his feeling of shame at suffering from a defect that could hardly be classified as other than cowardice.

His father had been a baker who got up at 2.30 a.m. every morning; he suggested to his son that he should follow him into the business. He would sleep in the afternoons, so the problem would solve itself. His mother was a milliner, considered by her dwindling clientele very skilful at creating individual and expressive ladies' hats. She took her son to a child psychologist, who was convinced that the problem would disappear in time. But he became even more scared. He could never resolve what was the cause of it. In the end he decided to become a policeman. He thought his fear of the dark might be driven out if he developed his physical courage. But now, this spring day, Tuesday, May 19, he woke up with his bedside lamp on. Moreover, his habit was always to lock the bedroom door. He lived alone in an apartment in central Ystad. He was born in the town, and disliked leaving it – even for short periods.

He put the light out, stretched, and got up. He had slept badly. What was happening to Kurt Wallander had made him upset and alarmed. He could see that he had somehow to help him. During the night he had worried about what he could do without breaking his promise of silence to Wallander. In the end, shortly before dawn, he made up his mind. He would try to find the house where Konovalenko was hiding. He thought it highly likely that Wallander's daughter was being held prisoner there.

329

He got to the police station just before 8 a.m. His only starting point was what had happened at the military training ground at Fskjutfalt. It was Martinsson who had gone through the belongings he found in the dead men's clothes. There was nothing exceptional. Nevertheless, Svedberg decided to go through the material one more time. He went to the room where the various pieces of evidence and other finds from several crime scenes were kept, and identified the relevant plastic bags. Martinsson had found nothing at all in the African's pockets, which seemed significant in itself. Svedberg replaced the bag containing nothing more than a few grains of dust. Then he carefully tipped out onto the table the contents of the other bag. Martinsson's list had cigarettes, a lighter, grains of tobacco, unclassifiable bits of dust, and odds and ends. Svedberg contemplated the objects in front of him. His interest was immediately focused on the lighter. It had an advertising slogan that was almost worn away. Svedberg held it up to the light and tried to read what it said. He replaced the bag, and took the lighter to his office. At 10.30 a.m. they were due at a meeting to establish how things were going in the attempt to track down Konovalenko and Wallander. He wanted the time before that meeting to himself. He took a magnifying glass from a drawer, adjusted the desk lamp, and started to study the lighter. After a minute or so, his heart started beating faster. He had managed to decipher the text. If the clue would lead anywhere was too early to say, of course, but the lighter's slogan was for the ICA in Tomelilla. Not conclusive in itself; could have been picked it up more or less anywhere. But if the man had been at the ICA shop in Tomelilla, it was not impossible that a checkout assistant might be able to remember a man who spoke broken Swedish, and most obviously of all, was hugely fat. He put the lighter in his pocket and left the station without saying where he was going.

He drove to Tomelilla, went into the ICA, showed his ID, and asked to see the manager. This turned out to be a young man by the name of Sven Persson. Svedberg showed him the lighter and explained what he wanted to know. The manager thought for a while, then shook his head. He could not recall a strikingly fat man having been in the shop recently.

"Talk to Britta," he said. "The girl at the check out. But I'm afraid she has a pretty poor memory. Well, she's scatterbrained, put it that way."

"Is she the only person on the till?" Svedberg said.

"We have an extra one on Saturdays, but she's not in today."

"Call her," Svedberg said. "Ask her to come here at once."

"Is it that important?"

"Yes, it is. Call her now please."

"Yes. Immediately." The manager disappeared to make the call. Svedberg waited until Britta, a woman in her fifties, was through with the customer she was dealing with and who had produced a wad of coupons for discounts and special offers. Svedberg identified himself.

"I want to know if you've had a big and very fat man shopping here recently," he said.

"We get lots of fat people shopping here," the woman said.

Svedberg rephrased the question. "Not just fat, positively obese. In fact, absolutely enormous. And who speaks bad Swedish as well. Has anyone of that description been here?"

She tried to remember, but Svedberg could tell that her growing curiosity was affecting her concentration.

"He hasn't done anything in the least bit exciting," Svedberg said. "I just want to know if he's been in here."

"No," she said. "If he was that fat, I'd have remembered. I'm dieting myself, you see. So I do look at people."

"Have you been away at all lately?"

"No."

"Not even for an hour?"

"Well, I sometimes have to go on an errand."

"Who does the till then?"

"Sven."

Svedberg could feel any hope he had ebbing away. He thanked her for her assistance and wandered around the shop while waiting for the part-timer. As he did so, his mind was working overtime, trying to work out what to do if this lead went nowhere. Where to find another starting point?

The girl who worked Saturdays was, he thought, no more than 17. She was quite fat herself, and Svedberg dreaded having to ask her about other fat people. The manager introduced her as Annika Hagström and withdrew discreetly. They were standing by some shelves stacked with dog and cat foods.

"You work here on Saturdays," Svedberg said.

"I'm out of work," she said. "There aren't any jobs. Sitting here on Saturdays is all I do."

"It can be pretty tough just now," Svedberg said, trying to sound understanding.

"Actually, I've wondered about joining the police," the girl said.

Svedberg stared at her in surprise.

"But I'm not sure I'm the type to wear a uniform," she said. "Why aren't you wearing a uniform?"

"We don't always have to," Svedberg said.

"Maybe I'll think again, then. Anyway, what have I done?"

"Nothing at all," Svedberg said. "I only wanted to ask if you'd seen a male person in this shop who looked a little unusual."

He groaned inwardly at his clumsy way of putting it.

"What do you mean, unusual?"

"A man who is very fat, and speaks bad Swedish."

"Oh, him," she said immediately. "He was here last Saturday."

Svedberg took a notebook out of his pocket. "What time," he said.

"A little after 9 a.m."

"Was he alone?"

"Yes."

"Do you remember what he bought?"

"Quite a lot. Several packets of tea, among other things. He filled four bags."

That's him, thought Svedberg. Russians drink tea like we drink coffee.

"How did he pay?"

"He was carrying money loose in his pocket."

"How did he seem? Was he nervous? Or what?"

Her answers were all immediate and specific.

"He was in a hurry. He practically stuffed the food into the bags."

"Did he talk to you?"

"No."

"How do you know he had a foreign accent?"

"He said hello and thank you. You could tell right away."

"Just one more question. You don't happen to know where he lives, I suppose?" he wondered.

Her brow furrowed and she thought hard. Surely she can't have an answer for that one as well, Svedberg thought quickly.

"He lives somewhere in the direction of the quarry," she said.

"The quarry?"

"Do you know where the college is?"

Svedberg nodded. He knew.

"Drive past there, then take a left," she said. "Then left again."

"How do you know he lives there?"

"The next person in line was an old man called Holgerson," she said. "He always gossips when he pays. He said he'd never seen anyone as fat as that before. Then he said he'd seen him outside a house down by the quarry. There are quite a few empty houses there. Holgerson knows about everything that happens in Tomelilla."

Svedberg put his notebook away. "I'll tell you something." he said. "You really should join the police force."

"What did he do?" she said.

"Nothing," Svedberg said. "If he comes back it's very important you don't say somebody's been asking about him. Least of all a policeman."

"I won't say a word," she said. "Would it be possible to come and see you at the police station some time?"

"Just call and ask for Svedberg. That's me. I'll show you around."

Her face lit up. "I'll do that," she said.

"Wait a few weeks though. We're pretty busy right now."

He left and followed her directions. When he came to the road leading to the quarry, he took the pair of binoculars he kept in the glove compartment and walked to the quarry and climbed up to the cabin of an abandoned stone crusher.

There were two houses on the other side of the quarry, several hundred metres apart. One of them was rather decrepit, the other seemed to be in better condition. He could see no cars in the yard, and the house looked deserted. Even so, he had the feeling that this was the place. It was remote. There was no road nearby. Nobody would take that track unless they had business at the house. He waited, binoculars ready. It started drizzling.

After almost half an hour, the door opened and a woman stepped out. Tania, he thought. She stood quite still, smoking. Svedberg could not see her face because she was half hidden by a shrub.

333

He put down his binoculars. That's the place. The girl in the shop had her wits about her, and a good memory too. He waited until Tania had gone back inside, then climbed down from the stone crusher and went back to his car. It was after 10 a.m. He decided to call in and report sick. He had no time to sit around in meetings. And he must now talk to Wallander.

Tania threw down her cigarette and stubbed it out with her heel. She was in the yard, in the drizzle. The weather was in tune with her mood. Konovalenko was closeted with the new African. She had no interest in whatever they were talking about. Vladimir used to tell her what was going on. Some politician in South Africa was to be killed, but she had no idea who or why. Probably Vladimir had told her, but she had forgotten.

She went out to the yard to have a few minutes to herself. She still had barely had time to come to terms with the consequences of Vladimir's death. Their marriage had never been more than a practical arrangement that suited them both, but she was stricken by the sorrow and pain she was feeling. When they fled the collapsing Soviet Union, they were able to give each other some support. When they came to Sweden, she gave her life some purpose by helping Vladimir with his various undertakings. All that changed when Konovalenko turned up. At first Tania was quite attracted to him. His decisive manner, his self-confidence, stood in sharp contrast to Vladimir's personality, and she did not hesitate when Konovalenko had started to take a serious interest in her. It did not take her long to see that he was just using her, however. His lack of emotion and his fierce contempt for other people horrified her. He began totally to dominate their lives. Occasionally, late at night, she and Vladimir had talked about getting out, starting all over again, far from Konovalenko's influence. But nothing had come of it, and now Vladimir was dead. She was standing in the yard, thinking about how much she missed him.

She had no idea what would happen next. Konovalenko was obsessed with killing this policeman who had killed Vladimir and had caused him so much trouble. Thoughts about the future would have to wait until it was all over, the policeman dead and the African back in South

Africa to carry out his assignment. She was dependent on Konovalenko, whether she liked it or not. She was in exile, and there was no going back. She had occasional but increasingly vague thoughts about Kiev, the city both she and Vladimir grew up in. What hurt was not all the memories, but her conviction that she would never again see the place and the people who used to be the foundation of her life. The door had slammed inexorably behind her. The last hopes had vanished with Vladimir.

She thought about the girl in the cellar. That was the only thing she had asked Konovalenko about these last days. What would happen to her? He said they would let her go once he had captured the father. But she wondered from the first if he meant that. She shuddered at the thought of him killing her as well.

Tania had trouble sorting out her feelings on this matter. She could feel unmixed hatred for the girl's father, for having killed her husband, and barbarically too, although Konovalenko had not told her what he meant by that. But sacrificing the daughter as well was going too far. At the same time, she knew she could do nothing to prevent it. The slightest sign of resistance on her part would only result in Konovalenko turning his deadly attention on her as well.

She was shivering in the rain, no longer a drizzle, and went back into the house. The mumbling sound of Konovalenko's voice could be heard from behind the closed door. She went into the kitchen and looked at the hatch in the floor. The clock on the wall indicated it was time to give the girl in the cellar something to eat and drink. She had already prepared a plastic carrier bag with a flask and some sandwiches. The girl had not once touched the food. Each time Tania came back up with what she had taken down last time. She switched on the light Konovalenko had rigged up. She carried a torch in one hand.

Linda had crept into a corner. She lay rolled up, as if suffering severe stomach cramps. Tania shone the torch on the chamber pot they had left on the stone floor. It was unused. She was full of pity for the girl. At first she had been so preoccupied with the pain she felt after Vladimir's death, there had been no room for anything else. But now, when she saw the girl rolled up, paralysed with fear, she had the feeling there was no limit to Konovalenko's cruelty. There was absolutely no reason why the girl should be in a dark cellar, with chains on her legs.

She could have been locked in one of the rooms upstairs, tied so she could not leave the house.

The girl did not move, but she followed Tania's movements with her eyes. Her cropped hair made Tania feel sick. She crouched down beside her. "It'll be over soon," she said.

The girl did not answer. Her eyes stared straight into Tania's.

"You must try and eat something," she said. "It'll be over soon."

Her fear has already started to consume her, Tania thought. It's gnawing away at her from the inside. She knew now that she would have to help the girl. It could cost her her life, but she had no choice. Konovalenko's evil was too great to bear, even for her.

"It'll be over soon," she whispered, placing the bag by the girl's head and going back up the stairs. She closed the hatch and turned around.

Konovalenko was standing there. She gave a start and squealed softly. He had a way of creeping up on people without a sound. She sometimes had the feeling his hearing was unnaturally well developed. Like a nocturnal animal, she thought. He hears what others can't.

"She's asleep," Tania said.

Konovalenko looked at her sternly. Then he smiled and left the kitchen without saying a word. Tania flopped into a chair and lit a cigarette. Her hands were shaking. But the resolve that had formed within her was irreversible.

Svedberg called Wallander shortly after 1 p.m. Wallander picked up the receiver after the first ring. Svedberg had been sitting at home for some time, trying to work out how to convince Wallander not to challenge Konovalenko on his own again. He recognised Wallander had reached a point where emotional impulses were as strong as reason in guiding his actions. In a way he is not responsible for his actions, Svedberg thought. He is being driven by the fear of what might happen to his daughter. There's no telling what he might do.

"I've found Konovalenko's house," Svedberg said. He had the feeling that Wallander winced. "I found a clue in the stuff Rykoff had in his pockets," he said. It led me to an ICA store in Tomelilla. A check-out girl with a phenomenal memory pointed me in the right direction. The house, which used to be a farmhouse, is just to the east of Tomelilla, not far beyond a quarry that doesn't seem to be in commission any more. It's got a yard and out buildings and there's no house close to it. I saw the woman too."

"I hope nobody saw you," Wallander said.

Svedberg could hear how tense and tired he was. "Not a soul," he said. "Don't worry."

"How could I not worry?" Wallander said.

Svedberg did not answer.

"I think I know where that quarry is," Wallander said. "If you are right, that gives me an advantage over Konovalenko."

"Have you heard from him again?"

"Twelve hours means 8 p.m. tonight. He'll be on time. I'm not going to do anything until he contacts me."

"It'll be disastrous if you try to take him on your own," Svedberg said. "I can't bear to think what would happen."

"You know there's no other way," Wallander said. "I'm not going to tell you where I am going to meet him. I know you mean well, but I can't take the risk. Thank you for finding the house for me. I won't forget that." And he hung up.

Svedberg was left sitting there with the receiver in his hand. What should he do now? It had not occurred to him that Wallander might simply not pass on the vital information. He replaced the receiver, convinced that, whatever Wallander might think, he needed help. The only question was who he could get to go with him.

He went over to a window and looked out at the church tower half hidden by the rooftops. When Wallander was on the run after that night at the training ground, he had chosen to contact Widén. Svedberg had never met the man before. He had never even heard Wallander mention him. Nevertheless, they were obviously friends who had known each other for a long time. He was the one Wallander had turned to for help. Svedberg decided to do the same thing. He left the flat and drove out of town. The rain was heavier, and a wind was getting up. He followed the coast road, thinking how all the things that had happened lately must soon come to an end. It was all too much for a little police district like Ystad.

He found Widén in the stables. He was standing in front of a stall fitted with bars in which a horse was pacing restlessly up and down and occasionally delivering a vicious kick at the woodwork. Svedberg said hello and stood beside him. The restless horse was very tall and thin. Svedberg had never sat on a horse's back in his life. He had a great fear of the creatures and could not understand how anyone would voluntarily spend his life training them and looking after them.

"She's sick," Widén said. "But I don't know what's the matter with her."

"She seems a bit restless," Svedberg said, cautiously.

"That's the pain," Widén said.

Then he drew the bolt and entered the stall. He took hold of the halter and the horse calmed down almost immediately. Then he bent down and examined her left foreleg. Svedberg leaned tentatively over the edge of the stall to look.

"It's swollen," Widén said. "Can you see?"

Svedberg could not see anything of the sort, but he muttered something non-committal. Widén stroked the horse's neck for a while, then emerged from the stall.

"I need to talk to you," Svedberg said.

"Let's go inside."

Svedberg saw an elderly lady sitting on a sofa in the untidy living room. She did not seem to fit in with Widén's surroundings. She was strikingly elegant, heavily made up, and wearing expensive jewellery.

"She's waiting for her chauffeur to fetch her," Widén said, as they sat in the kitchen. "She owns two horses I have in training."

"So that's it," Svedberg said.

"A master builder's widow from Trelleborg. She'll be on her way home soon. She comes over from time to time and just sits there. I think she's very lonely." Widén's understanding surprised Svedberg.

"I don't really know why I'm here," he said. "Or rather, I do know, of course. But what exactly is involved, if I ask you to help, I have no idea." He explained about the house near the quarry outside Tomelilla. Widén got up and ferreted about in a drawer crammed full of papers and racing programmes. At last he produced an old, torn map. He unfolded it on the table and Svedberg used a blunt pencil to show where the house was.

"I've no idea what Wallander intends to do," Svedberg said. "All I know is that he intends to confront Konovalenko on his own. He can't risk involving his colleagues because that would compromise the safety

338

of his daughter. Which I understand. The problem is simply that Wallander hasn't a remote chance in hell of getting Konovalenko into custody on his own."

"So you're intending to help him?" said Widén.

Svedberg nodded. "But I can't do that on my own either," he said. "I couldn't think of anybody to talk to apart from you. Besides, I gave him my word that I wouldn't. That's why I came here. You know him, you're his friend."

"Maybe," Widén said.

"Maybe?" Svedberg said, puzzled.

"It's true we've known each other for a long time, but we haven't been in close touch for over ten years or more."

"I didn't know that," Svedberg said. "I obviously got it wrong."

A car turned into the yard. Widén got up and went out with the builder's widow.

"What exactly do you have in mind?" Widén said, when he returned to the kitchen. Svedberg told him. Some time after 8 p.m. he would telephone Wallander. He would not be able to find out exactly what Konovalenko had said. Nevertheless, Svedberg hoped to persuade Wallander to tell him when the meeting was to take place, if nothing else. Once he knew the time of the meeting, he and preferably someone else as well, would go to the house so they would be there on hand, out of sight, in case Wallander needed help.

Widén listened, expressionless. When Svedberg had finished, he got up and left the room. Svedberg wondered if he had gone to the bathroom, perhaps. But when he reappeared, he had a rifle in his hand.

"We'd better see what we can do to help him," he said abruptly. He sat down to examine the rifle. Svedberg put his pistol on the table to show that he was armed as well. Widén made a face.

"Not much to go hunting a desperate madman with," he said.

"Can you leave the horses?"

"Ulrika sleeps here," Widén said. "One of the girls who works here."

Svedberg felt hesitant in Widén's presence. His taciturnity and odd personality made it hard for Svedberg to relax. But he was glad he would not be on his own.

He left for home at 3 p.m. They agreed that they would be in touch as soon as he had spoken to Wallander. On the way to Ystad he bought the evening papers that had just arrived. He sat in the car leafing through them. Konovalenko and Wallander were still big news, but they had already been relegated to the inside pages.

Svedberg's attention was suddenly caught by a headline. The headline he had been dreading more than anything else. And a photograph of Wallander's daughter.

He called Wallander at 8.20 p.m. Konovalenko had made contact.

"I know you won't want to tell me what's going to happen," Svedberg said. "But at least tell me when."

Wallander hesitated before replying. "At 7 a.m. tomorrow."

"Not at the house, though," Svedberg said.

"No, somewhere else. But no more questions now."

"What's going to happen?"

"He's promised to let Linda go. That's all I can tell you."

But you know more, Svedberg thought. You know he'll try to kill you.

"Be careful, Kurt," he said.

"Sure," Wallander said, and hung up.

Svedberg was certain that the meeting would be at the house by the quarry. Wallander's reply had come a little bit too readily.

Then he called Widén. They would meet at Svedberg's place at midnight, then drive to Tomelilla.

They drank a cup of coffee in Svedberg's kitchen.

It was still raining when they set out at 1.45 a.m.

340

CHAPTER TWENTY-EIGHT

The man outside her house in Bezuidenhout Park was there again. It was the third morning in succession Miranda had seen him standing on the other side of the street, waiting. She could see him through the thin curtains in the living-room window. He was white, dressed in a suit and tie, and looked like a lost soul in this world of hers. She had noticed him first not long after Matilda left for school. She reacted immediately, for people very rarely loitered in her street. Every morning the men living in the detached houses drove off to the centre of Johannesburg. Later on the women would set out in their own cars to do the shopping, go to the beauty parlour, or simply to get away. Bezuidenhout was the haunt of frustrated and restless members of the white middle class. The ones who could not quite make it into the very top white echelons. Miranda knew that many of these people were thinking about emigrating. Another fundamental truth was about to be revealed. For these people South Africa was not the natural father-land where soil and blood had run in the same veins and furrows. Even if they had been born here, they did not hesitate to start thinking about running away from the moment that de Klerk made his speech to the nation in February. Mandela had been released from prison, and a new age was dawning. A new age that would surely see other blacks besides Miranda living in Bezuidenhout.

The man in the street was a stranger. He did not belong there, and Miranda wondered what he wanted. Anyone standing about on a street in the early morning must be looking for something, something lost or dreamed about. She had stood at the window for a long time, watching him; in the end she decided that it must be her house he was keeping under observation. At first that scared her. Was he from one of those incomprehensible surveillance organisations that were still governing the lives of blacks in South Africa? She had expected him to announce his presence, to ring the bell. But the longer he stood there, hardly moving, the more she began to doubt that. Besides, he was not carrying a briefcase and he had nothing in his hands.

That first morning, Miranda kept returning to the window to check if he was still there. She thought of him as a sort of statue no-one was sure where to put. By shortly before 9 a.m., the street was empty. But the next day he was back again, in the same place, staring straight at her windows. She had a nasty suspicion he might be there because of Matilda. He could be from the secret police; in the background, invisible to her, there could be cars waiting, full of uniformed men. But something about his behaviour made her hesitate. That was when she first had the idea that he might be standing there precisely for her to see him, and realise he was not dangerous. He was not a threat, but was giving her time to get used to him.

Now it was the third morning, Wednesday, May 20, and he was there again. Suddenly he looked around, then crossed the street and rang the bell at her gate. That morning Matilda had a headache and a temperature when she woke, possibly malaria, and she was asleep in her room. Miranda carefully closed her bedroom door before going to answer the bell. He had rung only once. He knew somebody was at home, and it seemed he was also sure somebody would answer. She released the gate.

He's young, Miranda thought, when she confronted him at the front door.

"Miranda Nkoyi? I wonder if I might come in for a moment? I promise not to disturb you for long." Alarm bells were ringing somewhere inside her. But she let him in even so, showed him into the living room and invited him to take a seat.

As usual, Georg Scheepers felt insecure when he was alone with a black woman. It did not happen often in his life. Mostly it would be one of the black secretaries that had begun to appear in the prosecutor's office when the race laws were relaxed. This was in fact the first time he had ever sat with a black woman in her own home.

He had spent the last days delving as far as possible into Jan Kleyn's secret. He knew now that Kleyn regularly visited this house in Bezuidenhout. For many years in fact, since Kleyn moved to Johannesburg after graduating from the university. With Verwey's help and through some of his own contacts, he had also managed to get around the bank confidentiality regulations, and discovered that Kleyn transferred money to Miranda Nkoyi every month.

One of the most respected members of NIS, an Afrikaner who carried this high esteem with pride, secretly lived with a black woman. For her sake he was prepared to take the greatest of risks.

But Scheepers had the impression that he was only scraping the surface of the secret, and decided to visit the woman. He would not explain who he was, and it was possible she might tell Kleyn that he had been there. If she did, he would very soon work out who the visitor was, but he would not be sure why; he would be afraid that his secret had been exposed and that Scheepers would have a hold over him in the future. There was a risk that Kleyn would decide to kill him. But Scheepers believed that he had insured himself against that possibility as well. He would make sure that Miranda understood that other people, too, were aware of Kleyn's secret life outside the closed world of the intelligence service.

She looked at him, looked through him. She was very beautiful. Her beauty had survived; it survived everything, subjugation, compulsion, pain, as long as the spirit of resistance was there. Ugliness, stunted growth, degeneration, all those things followed in the wake of resignation.

He forced himself to tell her how things stood. That the man who paid her visits, paid for her house, and was presumably her lover, was a man under grave suspicion of conspiracy against the state and the lives of certain individuals. He sensed that she knew some of what he was telling her, but that some parts were new to her. At the same time he had a strange feeling that she was relieved, that she had been expecting, even fearing, something different. What, he asked himself, could that be? It had something to do with this hidden life of hers, he thought. There was another secret door, he thought, waiting to be opened.

"You shouldn't think," he said, "that I'm asking you to testify against your husband. But what is as stake is a threat to the whole country. So grave that I cannot even tell you who I am."

"But you are his enemy," she said. "When the herd senses danger, some animals run off on their own. And they are doomed. Is that how it is?"

"Maybe," Scheepers said. "Perhaps it is."

He was sitting with his back to the window. When Miranda was talking about the animals and the herd, he detected the slightest of movements at the door directly behind her. It was as if someone had started to turn the handle but then thought better of it. It dawned on him he had not seen the young woman leave the house that morning. The young woman who must be Miranda's daughter.

It was one of the strange circumstances he had discovered while doing his research these last few days. Miranda Nkoyi was registered as the single housekeeper for a man named Sidney Houston, who spent most of his time on his cattle ranch miles away in the plains east of Harare. Scheepers had no difficulty in seeing through this business of the absentee rancher, especially when he found out that Kleyn and Houston had been together at university. But the other woman, Miranda's daughter? She did not exist. And now here she was, standing behind a door, listening to their conversation.

He was overwhelmed by the thought. Afterwards, he would see his prejudices had misled him, the invisible racial barriers that ruled his life. He understood who the listening girl was. Kleyn's secret had been exposed. It was like a fortress finally giving way under siege. It had been possible to conceal the truth for so long because it was quite simply unthinkable. Kleyn, the star of the intelligence services, the ruthless Afrikaner, had a daughter with a black woman, a daughter he presumably loved above all else. Perhaps he thought that Mandela would have to die so that his daughter could continue to live alongside, and be refined by her proximity to, the whites of this country. As far as Scheepers was concerned, this hypocrisy deserved nothing more than scorn. He felt that all his own resistance had now been broken down. At the same time he thought he could understand the enormity of the task President de Klerk and Mandela had taken upon themselves. How could they possibly create a feeling of kinship among peoples if everybody regarded everybody else as traitors?

Miranda did not take her eyes off him. He could not imagine what she was thinking, but he could see she was upset.

He let his gaze wander, first to her face and then to a photograph of the girl on the mantelpiece.

"Your daughter," he said. "Jan's daughter."

"Matilda."

Scheepers recalled what he had read about Miranda's past.

"Like your mother."

"Like my mother."

"Do you love your husband?"

"He's not my husband. He's her father."

"What about her?"

"She hates him."

"She's behind her door now, listening to our conversation."

"She's sick. She has a fever."

"Even so, she's listening."

"Why shouldn't she listen?"

Scheepers nodded. He understood. "I need your help," he said. "Please, think carefully. The slightest thing might help us to find the men who are plotting to throw our country into chaos. Before it's too late."

It seemed to Miranda the moment she had been awaiting for so long had arrived. She had always imagined nobody else would be there when she confessed to how she went through Kleyn's pockets at night, and wrote down the words he uttered in his sleep. There would only be the two of them, herself and her daughter. But now things would be different. She wondered why, without knowing even his name, she trusted him so implicitly. Was it his own vulnerability? His lack of confidence in her presence? Was weakness the only thing she dared to trust?

The joy of liberation, she thought. That's what I feel. Like emerging from the sea and knowing I'm clean.

"I thought for ages he was just an ordinary civil servant," she said. "I knew nothing about his crimes. But then I heard."

"Who from?"

"I might tell you. But not yet. You should only say things when the time is ripe."

He regretted having interrupted her.

"He doesn't know that I know," she said. "That has been the advantage I had. Maybe it was my salvation, maybe it'll be my death. But every time he came to visit us, I got up during the night and emptied his pockets. I copied even the smallest scrap of paper. I listened to the words he muttered in his sleep. And I passed them on."

"Who to?"

"To the people who look after us."

"I look after you."

"I don't even know your name."

"My name doesn't matter."

"I spoke with black men who lead lives just as secret as Jan's."

He had heard rumours. But nothing had ever been proved. He knew the intelligence service, both the civilian and military branches, were always running after their own shadows. There was a persistent rumour that the blacks had their own intelligence service. Maybe linked to the ANC, maybe an independent organisation. They investigated what the investigators were doing. Their strategies and their identities. This woman, Miranda, was confirming the existence of these people. And Kleyn is a dead man, he thought. Without his knowing it, his pockets have been picked by the people he regards as the enemy.

"Only the last few months," he said. "But what have you found recently?"

"I've already passed it on, and forgotten," she said. "Why should I bother myself to remember?"

He could see she was telling the truth. He tried appealing to her one more time. He had to talk with one of the men whose job it was to interpret whatever she found in Kleyn's pockets or heard him saying aloud in his sleep.

"Why should I trust you?" she asked.

"You don't have to," he said. "There are no guarantees in this life. There are only risks."

She sat in silence, and seemed to be thinking. "Has he killed a lot of people?" she asked. She was speaking very loudly, and he gathered this was so that her daughter could hear.

"Yes," he said. "He's killed a lot of people."

"Blacks?"

"Blacks."

"Who were criminals?"

"Some were. Some weren't."

"Why did he kill them?"

"They were people who preferred not to talk. People who had rebelled. Causers of instability."

346

"Like my daughter."

"I don't know your daughter."

"But I do."

She stood up suddenly. "Come back tomorrow," she said. "There might be somebody here who wants to meet you. Go now."

He left the house. When he got to his car parked on a side street, he was sweating. He drove off, thinking about his own weakness. And her strength. Was there a future in which they could be reconciled?

Matilda did not leave her room when he left. Her mother left her in peace. But that evening she sat on her bed for a long time. The fever came and went in waves.

"Are you upset?" Miranda said.

"No," Matilda said. "I hate him even more now."

Scheepers would remember his visit to Kliptown as a descent into a hell he had thus far in his life managed to avoid. By sticking to the white path mapped out for Afrikaners from the cradle to the grave, he had trodden the path of the one-eyed man. Now he was forced to take the other path, the black path, and what he saw he thought he would never forget. It moved him, it had to move him, because the lives of 20 million people were affected. People who were not allowed to live normal lives and never given the opportunity to develop, who died early, after lives that were artificially restricted.

When he went back to the house in Bezuidenhout at 10 a.m. the next day, Miranda answered the bell, but it was Matilda who would take him to the man who had said he would talk to him. He felt he had been granted a great privilege. Matilda was as beautiful as her mother. Her skin was lighter, but her eyes were the same. He had difficulty making out any features of her father in her face. Perhaps she kept him at such a distance, she simply prevented herself from growing to look like him. She greeted him very shyly, merely nodding when he offered his hand. Again he felt insecure, in the presence of the daughter as well, though she was only a teenager. He felt uneasy too about what he had let himself in for. Perhaps Kleyn's influence over this house was altogether different from what he had been led to believe? But it was too late to back out now. An old rusty car, its exhaust pipe trailing almost to the ground and the fenders missing, was parked in front of the house. Without a word, Matilda opened the door, and turned to him.

"I thought he'd be coming here," Scheepers said, doubtfully.

"We're going to visit another world," Matilda said.

He got into the back seat and was hit by a smell he only later recognised as reminiscent of his childhood's henhouse. The man behind the wheel had a baseball cap pulled down over his eyes. He turned and looked at him, but said nothing. Then they drove away, and the driver and Matilda started a conversation in Xhosa, which Scheepers recognised but did not understand. Scheepers thought the man was driving much too fast. Soweto, Scheepers thought. Is that where they're taking me?

But they were not headed for Soweto. They passed Meadowland, where the choking smoke lay thick over the dusty countryside. Not far beyond the sea of crumbling houses, dogs, children, hens, wrecked and burned-out cars, the driver slowed down and came to a halt. Matilda came to sit beside him in the back seat. She had a black hood in her hand.

"You're not allowed to see from now on," she said. He protested and pushed her hand away.

"What is there to be afraid of?" she asked. "Make up your mind."

He took hold of the hood. "Why?" he asked.

"There are a thousand eyes," she said. "You are not to see anything. And nobody's going to see you, either."

"That's not an answer," he said. "It's a riddle."

"Not for me it isn't," she replied. "Make up your mind now!"

He pulled the hood over his head. They set off again. The road was getting worse all the time, but the driver did not slow down. Scheepers rode with the bumps as best he could. Even so he banged his head on the car roof several times. He lost all track of time. The hood was irritating his face, and his skin started to itch.

The car slowed down and came to a halt. Somewhere a dog was barking furiously. Music from a radio was coming and going in waves. Through the hood he could smell smoke from wood fires. Matilda helped him out of the car. Then she removed the hood. The sun shone straight into his unprotected eyes, blinding him. When his eyes grew accustomed to the light, he could see that they were in a mass of shacks cobbled together from corrugated iron, cardboard boxes, sacks, sheets of plastic, venetian blinds. There were huts where a car wreck formed one of the rooms. There was a stink of garbage, and a skinny, mangy dog was sniffing at one of his legs. He observed the people who lived out their lives in this destitution. None of them seemed to notice he was there. There was no threat, no curiosity, merely indifference. As far as they were concerned he did not exist.

"Welcome to Kliptown." Matilda said. "Maybe it's Kliptown, maybe it's some other shantytown. You'd never find your way here anyway. They all look the same. The destitution is just as bad in all of them, the smells are the same, the people who live here are the same."

She led him into the cluster of shacks. It was like a labyrinth that soon swallowed him up, robbed him of his past. After a few paces he had lost all sense of direction. He thought how absurd it was that he was here with Kleyn's daughter. But absurdity was their inheritance, something that was about to be disturbed for the first time, and then destroyed.

"What can you see?" she said.

"The same as you," he said.

"No!" she said sternly. "Are you shocked?"

"Of course."

"I'm not. Shock is a staircase. There are many steps. We are not standing on the same one."

"Maybe you're at the very top?"

"Nearly."

"Is the view different?"

"You can see further. Zebra grazing in herds, on alert. Antelopes leaping and leaving gravity behind. A cobra that has hidden itself away in an empty termite mound. Women carrying water."

She stopped and turned to face him. "I see my own hatred in their eyes, but your eyes can't see that."

"What do you want me to say?" he said. "It's obviously sheer hell, living like this. The question is, is it my fault?"

"It might be," she said. "That depends."

They continued deeper into the labyrinth. He would never find his way out alone. I need her, he thought. As we have always needed the blacks. And she knows it.

Matilda halted outside a shack that was slightly bigger than the others, even if it was made from the same materials. She squatted by the door, which was roughly made from a sheet of hardboard.

"Go on in," she said. "I'll wait here."

Scheepers went in. He had difficulty distinguishing anything at all in the darkness. Then he made out a simple wooden table, wooden chairs, and a smoking kerosene lamp. A man detached himself from the shadows. He gazed at him with a hint of a smile. Scheepers thought he must be about the same age as himself, but the man facing him was more powerfully built, had a beard, and radiated the same kind of dignity he had found in both Miranda and Matilda.

"Georg Scheepers," said the man, bursting into laughter. Then he pointed to one of the chairs.

"What's so funny?" Scheepers said. He had trouble concealing his growing unease.

"Nothing," the man said. "You can call me Steve."

"You know why I want to meet you," Scheepers said.

"You don't want to meet me. You want to meet somebody who can tell you things about Kleyn you don't know already. That person happens to be me. But it could as easily have been somebody else."

"Can we get to the point?"

"White men are always short of time," Steve said. "I've never been able to understand why."

"Kleyn," Scheepers said.

"A dangerous man," Steve said. "Everybody's enemy, not just ours. The ravens cry in the night. And we analyse and interpret and think we know something is going to happen, something that could turn the country upside down. And we wouldn't want that. Neither the ANC nor de Klerk. That's why you must first tell me what you know. Then perhaps we can combine to illuminate some of the darkest corners."

Scheepers did not tell him everything. But he did divulge the most important points. Even that was a risk. He did not know who he was talking to. But he had no choice. Steve listened, stroking his chin slowly the while.

"So it's gone that far," he said when Scheepers had finished. "We've been expecting this. But we really thought some crazy *Boer* would first try to slit the throat of the traitor de Klerk."

"A professional killer," Scheepers said. "No face, no name. But he might have cropped up before. Perhaps working for Kleyn. Those ravens you were talking about could perhaps do some listening. The man could be white, he could be black. I've found an indication that he could be due for a lot of money. A million rand, possibly more."

"It ought to be possible to identify him," Steve said. "Kleyn only picks the best. If he's a South African, black or white, we'll find him."

"Find him and stop him," Scheepers said. "Kill him. We have to work together."

"No," Steve said. "We're meeting now. But this is the only time. We're going from two different directions, on this occasion and in the future. Nothing else is possible."

"Why not?"

"We don't share each other's secrets. Everything is still too unsure, too uncertain. We avoid all pacts and agreements unless absolutely essential. Don't forget we're enemies. And the war in our country has been going on for a very long time. Although you don't want to recognise that fact."

"We see things differently," Scheepers said.

"Yes," Steve said. "We do." He got to his feet. The conversation had lasted only a few minutes.

"Miranda exists," Steve said. "You can contact my world through her."

"Yes," Scheepers said. "She exists. And we both have to stop this assassination."

"Right," Steve said. "But I guess you are the ones who are going to have to do it. You are still the ones with the resources. I have nothing. Apart from my tin hut. And Miranda. And Matilda. Just imagine what would happen if the assassination came off."

"I'd rather not think about it."

Steve stared at him for a moment in silence. Then he disappeared through the door without saying goodbye. Scheepers followed him into the bright sunlight. Matilda led him back to the car. Once again he sat in the back seat with a hood over his head. In his darkness he was already preparing what to say to President de Klerk.

De Klerk had a recurring dream about termites. He was in a house where every floor, every wall, every piece of furniture had been attacked

351

by the hungry insects. What he was doing in the house, he had no idea. Grass was growing between the floorboards, the windowpanes were smashed, and the furious chewing of the termites was like an itch in his own body. In his dream he had a very short time in which to write an important speech. His usual secretary had disappeared, and he had to do the work himself. But when he started typing, termites came pouring out from under the keys.

At that point he usually woke up. He would lie in the dark, thinking how the dream might anticipate coming reality. Maybe everything was too late already? What he wanted to achieve – to rescue South Africa from disintegration while preserving the influence and status of the whites as far as possible – could well be already beyond black impatience. Only Mandela could convince him there was no other course to take. De Klerk knew they shared the same fear. Uncontrolled violence, a chaotic collapse that no-one could manage, a familiar precondition for a military coup intent on revenge, or various ethnic groupings that would fight each other until nothing was left.

It was 10 p.m. on Thursday, May 21. De Klerk knew that the young lawyer Scheepers was in his anteroom. But de Klerk did not feel ready to receive him just yet. He was tired, his head bursting with the problems he had to solve. He got up from his desk and went to one of the high windows. He was sometimes petrified by the responsibility resting on his shoulders. Too much for one man to bear. He sometimes felt an urge to run away, to make himself invisible, to go straight out into the bush and simply disappear. But he knew he would not do that. The God he found increasingly difficult to talk to and believe in was maybe still shielding him after all. He wondered how much time he still had. His mood was constantly changing. From being convinced he was already living on borrowed time, he could start believing he had another five years after all. And time was what he needed. His grand design – to delay the transition to a new kind of society, and meanwhile to encourage more black voters into his own party – needed time. But he could also see that Mandela would refuse to allow him time that was used other than to pave the way for the transition.

It seemed to him there was an element of artificiality in everything he did. I too am really an upholder of the impossible dream, that my country will never change. The difference between me and a fanatic madman who wants to defend the impossible dream with open violence is very small.

Time was running out for South Africa, it seemed to him. What was happening now ought to have happened many years ago. But history does not follow invisible guidelines.

He returned to his desk and rang the bell. Scheepers came in. De Klerk had come to appreciate his energy and thoroughness. He overlooked the streak of naïve innocence he also detected in the lawyer. Even this young Afrikaner had to learn that there were sharp rocks under the soft sand.

He listened to Scheepers's report with half-closed eyes. The words that got through to him piled up in his consciousness. When Scheepers had finished, de Klerk looked searchingly at him.

"I take it for granted everything I've just heard is true," de Klerk said.

"Every word of it, sir."

De Klerk thought for a moment before proceeding. "So they kill Mandela," he said. "Some miserable contract killer selected and paid by this secret committee. The murder to take place in the near future when Mandela is making one of his public appearances. The consequence will be chaos, a bloodbath. A group of influential *Boere* waiting in the wings to take over the government. The constitution will be overturned, a regime imposed, equal parts from the military, the police and civilian interests. The future will be one long-drawn-out state of emergency. Is that right?"

"Yes," Scheepers said. "If I may venture a guess, I would say the assassination attempt will be on June 12."

"Why then?"

"Mandela is to speak in Cape Town. I have learned that the army information office has been displaying an exceptional interest in the plans for dealing with the occasion by the local police. There are other indications. It is a guess, but it's an informed guess."

"Three weeks," de Klerk said. "Three weeks in which to stop these lunatics."

"We must work, too, on the assumption that June 12 and Cape Town are a red herring. The people involved in this are very cunning. The assassination attempt could as easily take place tomorrow."

"In other words, any place, at any time," de Klerk said.

Scheepers waited.

"I must speak with Mandela," de Klerk said. "He has to know what's afoot."

Then he turned to Scheepers.

"These people must be stopped without delay," he said.

"We don't know who they are," Scheepers pointed out. "How can we stop something we don't know about?"

"What about the gunman they've hired?"

"We don't know who he is either."

De Klerk looked thoughtfully at him. "You have a plan," he said. "I can see it in your face."

Scheepers felt himself blushing. "Mr President," he said. "I think the key to all this is Jan Kleyn. He has to be arrested immediately. There is a risk he won't talk. Or he might prefer to commit suicide. But I can see no alternative to interrogating him."

"Let's do that," de Klerk said. "In fact we have quite a few skilful interrogators. They can usually get to the truth."

From blacks, Scheepers thought. Who then die in mysterious circumstances. "I think it would be best if I could conduct the interrogation," he said. "I know most about it."

"Do you think you can handle him?"

"Yes, sir."

The President rose. The audience was over.

"Kleyn will be arrested tomorrow," de Klerk said. "I want reports from now on every day." He shook Scheepers warmly by the hand.

Scheepers nodded to the old guard in the antechamber. Then he drove home through the night, with his pistol on the seat beside him.

De Klerk stood at his window for a long time, deep in thought. Then he worked at his desk for three long hours.

In the antechamber, the guard ambled round straightening out ridges in the carpets and smoothing cushions on chairs. All the time he was thinking over what he had overheard with his ear to the door of the President's private office. The situation was extremely serious. He went into the modest room that served as his own office. He removed the telephone from the plug routed through the switchboard. Behind a loose wooden panel was another socket only he knew about. He lifted the receiver and got a direct line out. Then he dialled a number.

The answer came almost at once. Kleyn was not yet asleep.

Countdown to a Void

CHAPTER TWENTY-NINE

Tsiki skewered a mouse with a well-aimed throw of a knife. Tania had already gone to bed. Konovalenko was waiting until it was late enough to call Kleyn. He was going to raise the question of his own future as an immigrant to South Africa.

There was not a sound from the cellar. Tania had been down to look at the girl and said she was asleep. For the first time in a long time, Konovalenko felt content. He had made contact with Wallander; he had demanded an unsigned letter of safe conduct from him, in return for getting his daughter back unharmed. Wallander would give him a week's start, and personally ensure that the police search was wrongly directed. Konovalenko was going to make his way back to Stockholm immediately; Wallander would make sure the search for him was concentrated in Skåne.

None of this was true, of course. Konovalenko would shoot him and the girl. He wondered whether Wallander really believed what he had said. If so he would go back to being the kind of policeman Konovalenko had begun by assuming he was, the naïve provincial drudge. But he would not underestimate the man again.

During the day he had devoted many hours to Tsiki. Just as in preparing Mabasha, he had run through various possible turns of events in connection with the assassination. Tsiki was more quick witted than Mabasha. Moreover, he seemed unruffled by the passing but unambiguous racist remarks Konovalenko could not resist making. He intended to provoke him even more over the next few days, to see if he could press him to the limit of his self-control. There was one characteristic Tsiki shared with Mabasha; Konovalenko wondered if it was a typical African trait, this introversion – the impossibility of reading their thoughts. It irritated him. He was used to being able to see straight through people, and hence give himself an opportunity to anticipate their reactions.

He gazed at the man who had just dispatched a mouse with his strangely curved knife. He'll do a good job, Konovalenko thought. A few more days of planning and weapons training, and he'll be ready to go home. He'll be my entrance visa to South Africa.

Tsiki retrieved his knife with the mouse speared on the end of it. Then he went into the kitchen and dropped it into a rubbish bin and rinsed the blade. Konovalenko observed him, occasionally taking a sip of vodka from his glass.

"A knife with a curved blade," he said. "I've never seen one like that before."

"My ancestors used to make them over a thousand years ago," Tsiki said.

"But why the curved blade?"

"Nobody knows. It's still a secret. The day the secret is revealed, the knife will lose its power."

Konovalenko was annoyed by the mysterious reply, but Tsiki disappeared into his room. He heard the key turned in Tsiki's bedroom door.

He went round the room turning off the lights, apart from the lamp next to the table where the telephone was. He checked the time. Half past midnight. He listened at the cellar hatch. Not a sound. He poured himself another glass of vodka. He would save it until after he had finished speaking with Kleyn.

The call to South Africa was brief.

Kleyn listened without comment to Konovalenko's reassurance that Tsiki would cause no problems. There was no doubt about his mental stability. Then Kleyn announced his verdict. He wanted Tsiki to return to South Africa within a week at the most. It was now Konovalenko's job to make the arrangements, immediately, to get him out of Sweden, and make sure the return journey to Johannesburg was booked and confirmed. Konovalenko had the impression Kleyn was in a hurry, that he was under pressure. He had no way of confirming his hunch. But it was enough to put him off his stride when it came to discussing his own journey to South Africa. The call ended without his having been able to raise the subject. He felt annoyed with himself afterwards. He drained his glass and considered whether Kleyn was going to double-cross him. But he dismissed the thought. They needed his talents and experience in South Africa. He drank another glass of vodka, then went out onto the porch to urinate. It was raining. He gazed into the mist. He should be pleased with himself. A few more hours and his problems would be over, for this particular job. The assignment was almost at an end. Then he would have time to devote to his future. Not the least of the decisions he would have to make was whether to take Tania with him, or if he should do what he had done with his wife and leave her behind.

He locked the door, retired to his own room and lay down. He did not get undressed, but just pulled a blanket over him. Tania could sleep alone tonight. He needed rest.

She was lying awake in her room, and heard Konovalenko shut the door and lie down on the bed. She lay still, listening. She was scared. Deep down, she judged it would be impossible to get the girl out of the cellar and leave the house without Konovalenko hearing. Nor would it be possible to lock the door to his room without the noise waking him. She had tried it earlier in the day, when Konovalenko and the African were shooting rifles in the quarry. Besides, he could jump out of the window even if the door had been locked. She wished she had some sleeping pills. She could have dissolved them in one of his vodka bottles. But she had only herself, and she had to try. She had prepared a small case with some money and clothes. She hid it in the barn. She also left her rain clothes there, and a pair of boots.

She checked the time once more: 1.15 a.m. She knew the meeting with the policeman was to be in the early morning. She and the daughter would have to be well away by then. As soon as she heard Konovalenko start to snore, she would get up. He was a very light sleeper, she knew, and woke often, but rarely during the first half-hour after falling asleep.

She still was not sure why she was doing this. She knew she was risking her own life. But she did not feel the need to justify her actions to herself. Some things were just dictated by life itself.

Konovalenko turned over and coughed. 1.25. Some nights he chose not to sleep, just lay on his bed resting. If this was one of those nights, there was nothing she could do to help the girl. That made her feel even more frightened. It was a threat that seemed to her greater than any danger she might herself run.

At 1.40 a.m. she finally heard that Konovalenko was snoring. She listened for a minute. Then she carefully got out of bed. She was dressed. All the time she had been clutching the key to the padlock on the chains round the girl's ankles. She slowly opened the door of her room and avoided the floorboards she knew would creak. She closed the door behind her and crept into the kitchen, switched on her torch and started very carefully easing up the hatch. It was a critical moment: the girl might scream. That had not happened so far. But it could. Konovalenko was snoring. She listened. Then she climbed cautiously down the ladder. The girl was curled into a ball. Her eyes were open. Tania squatted beside her and whispered while stroking her cropped hair. She said they were going to run away, but she would have to be very, very quiet. The girl did not react. Her eyes were expressionless. Tania was suddenly afraid she would not be able to move. Perhaps she was immobilised by fear? She had to turn her over on her side to get to the padlock, and at once the girl suddenly kicking and punching. Tania just managed to clamp her hand over the girl's mouth before she started screaming. Tania was strong, and pressed as hard as she could. One half-stifled yell would be enough to wake Konovalenko. She gasped at the thought. Konovalenko was quite capable of nailing down the hatch and leaving them both there in the darkness. Tania tried to whisper to her at the same time as she pressed. The girl's eyes had come alive, and Tania hoped she would understand now. She slowly took away her hand, unlocked the padlock, and gently removed the chains.

At the same moment she noticed Konovalenko had stopped snoring. She held her breath. Then it started again. She hurriedly got to her feet, reached for the hatch, and closed it. The girl had understood. She sat up, and was quiet.

Tania suddenly thought her heart would stand still. She heard footsteps in the kitchen. Someone was walking around above them. The footsteps stopped. Now he'll open the hatch, she thought, shutting her eyes. He's heard me.

Then came relief in the form of the clinking of a bottle. Konovalenko had got up for another glass of vodka. The footsteps padded away. Tania shone the torch on her own face and tried to smile. Then she took the girl's hand and held it while they waited. After ten minutes she opened the hatch cautiously. Konovalenko was snoring again. She told the girl what was going to happen. They would approach the front door as quietly as they could. Tania had oiled the lock. She thought it would be possible to open it without a click. If all went well they would then hurry from the house together, collect Tania's case and boots. But if something did happen, if Konovalenko did wake up, Tania would simply fling the door open and they would race off in different directions. Was that clear? Run, run for their lives. There was a fine drizzle and a mist that should make it harder for them to be seen. But she should just keep on running, without looking back. When she came to a house or saw a car on the road, she should give herself up. But the main thing was to run for her life.

Did she understand? Tania thought so. The girl's eyes were animated, she could move her legs, even if she was weak and unsteady. Tania listened again. Then she nodded to the girl. It was time to move. Tania climbed up first, listened one more time, then reached down to help the girl. Now speed was of the essence. Tania made herself hold back so as to avoid the stairs creaking. The girl emerged into the kitchen. She screwed up her eyes, even though the light was very weak. She's practically blind, thought Tania. She held her firmly by the arm. Konovalenko was snoring. Then they started walking towards the hall and the front door, one step at a time, painfully slow. There was a heavy curtain in the hall doorway. Tania took great care in pulling it to one side, with the girl hanging onto her arm. Then they were at the door. Tania was drenched in sweat. Her hands were trembling as she took hold of the key. At this point she almost dared to believe it would be OK. She turned the key. There was a point, a certain resistance, where it would click if she turned it too quickly. She could feel the resistance and kept on turning as steadily as she could. She was past the critical point. There had not been a single sound. She nodded to the girl. Then she opened the door.

As she did so, something crashed behind her. She gave a start and turned around. The girl had bumped into a stand for coats and umbrellas. It had fallen. Tania had no need to listen in order to know what was already happening. She flung the door open, shoved the girl out into the rain and mist, and yelled at her to run. At first the girl seemed petrified. But Tania pushed her, and she started running.

Within a couple of seconds she had disappeared into the greyness.

Tania knew it was already too late as far as she was concerned. But she would try even so. Most of all she did not want to turn around. She ran in the opposite direction to divert Konovalenko, make him unsure about where the girl was for a few more precious seconds.

Tania got to the middle of the yard before Konovalenko caught up with her. "What are you doing?" he yelled. "Are you sick?"

Then she realised Konovalenko did not know the hatch was open. He would not understand what had happened until they were back inside the house. The girl's head start would be sufficient. Konovalenko would never find her again.

Tania suddenly felt very tired, but what she had done was right.

"I don't feel well," she said, pretending to be dizzy.

"Let's go inside," Konovalenko said.

"Just a minute," she said. "I need some air." I'll do the best I can for her. Every breath gives her a better chance. The game is up for me.

She ran at the night. At the rain. She had no idea where she was, she just ran. She kept falling, but simply scrambled back onto her feet and kept running. She came to a fence and over it into a field. All around her frightened hares were bounding off in different directions. She felt like one of them, a hunted animal. The mud was clinging to her shoes. In the end she took them off and kept on running in her stockinged feet. The field seemed to go on forever. Everything was engulfed by the mist. Only she and the hares existed. Eventually she came to another fence and a road, and had no strength left to run any further. She walked along the gravel road. The sharp edges of the stones hurt her feet. Then the gravel came to an end and she found herself on an asphalt road. She could see the white line down the middle. She had no idea which direction to take. But she kept on walking. She did not dare to think about what had happened. She could still feel a vague sense of evil somewhere behind her. It was neither human nor animal, rather a sort of cold breeze; but it was there all the time, forcing her to keep going.

Then she saw a pair of headlights approaching. It was a man who had been visiting his girlfriend. During the night they had started quarrelling. He had decided to go home. Now he was thinking that if only he had the money, he would go away. Anywhere would do, anywhere far away. The windscreen wipers were squeaking, and visibility was poor. He suddenly saw something in front of the car. At first he thought it was an animal, and slammed on the brakes. Then he stopped altogether. It was a human being, he could see that. He could hardly believe his eyes. A young girl, with no shoes, covered in mud, her hair a short-cropped mess. Maybe there had been a car crash. He saw her sit down in the middle of the road. He got slowly out of the car, and went up to her.

"What happened?" he said.

She did not answer. He could not see any blood, nor was there any sign of a car in the ditch. He lifted her up and led her to his car. She could barely stand.

"What happened?" he said again.

Widén and Svedberg left the flat in Ystad at 1.45 a.m. It was raining hard as they got into Svedberg's car. Three kilometres out of town Svedberg knew that he had a puncture in one of the back tyres. He pulled into the side, worrying that the spare might be no good. It was OK when they fitted it, but the lost minutes had thrown out their schedule. Svedberg had assumed Wallander would approach the house before it got light. That meant they would have to set off earlier to avoid bumping into him. It was nearly 3 a.m. by the time they parked the car on a track into a wood a mile from the quarry and the house. They needed to catch up their schedule and moved quickly through the mist. They crossed a field on the north side of the quarry. Svedberg had suggested a position as near the house as they dared. They did not know which direction Wallander would come from, and they would have to have a view on all sides if they were to avoid being seen. They agreed that Wallander would probably take the western approach. It was slightly hilly on that side. There were high, dense clumps of bushes growing right up to the edge of the property. On that basis they decided to approach from the east. Svedberg had noticed a haystack on a narrow strip of ground between two fields. If necessary they could burrow into the stack itself. They were in position by 3.30 a.m. Both of them had their guns ready and loaded.

The house shimmered before them in the mist. Everything was still. Without knowing why, Svedberg had the feeling that something was not quite right. He took out his binoculars, wiped the lenses, and then examined the house wall bit by bit. There was a light in one window, probably the kitchen. He could see nothing unusual. He thought it unlikely Konovalenko was asleep. He would be there, waiting. He might even be outside the house. Each of them waited on tenterhooks, lost in a world of his own.

It was Widén who spotted Wallander. It was 5 a.m. As they had anticipated, he appeared on the western side of the house. Widén had good eyesight, and thought at first it was a hare or a deer moving among the bushes. But then he began to wonder, nudged Svedberg's arm gently, and pointed. Svedberg took out his binoculars. He could just make out Wallander's face among the bushes.

Was Wallander acting according to the instructions he had received from Konovalenko? Or had he decided to try and take him by surprise? And where was Konovalenko? And Wallander's daughter?

They could only wait. There was no movement around the house. Widén and Svedberg took turns observing Wallander's expressionless face. Again Svedberg was moved by a sense that something wasn't right. He looked at his watch. Wallander would soon have been lying in the bushes for an hour. There was still no sign of life in the house.

Suddenly Widén passed the binoculars to Svedberg. Wallander was on the move. He was wriggling his way towards the house, then stood there pressed against the wall. He had his pistol in one hand. So, he's decided to take Konovalenko on, Svedberg thought, and he could feel a lump in his stomach. There was nothing they could do but keep watching. Widén had taken aim with his rifle, pointing it at the front door. Wallander ducked under the windows as he ran to the front door. Svedberg could see that he was listening. He tried the handle. The door was unlocked. Without hesitation he flung it open and rushed in. Widén and Svedberg scrambled out of the haystack.

They had not agreed what their next move would be; they just knew that they had to follow Wallander. They ran to the corner of the house and took cover. It was still deathly quiet inside.

Svedberg realised why he had been uneasy. "They've moved out," he said. "There's nobody there."

Widén stared at him in disbelief. "How do you know?"

"I just know," Svedberg said, stepping out of the shadow of the wall.

He shouted Wallander's name. Wallander came out onto the steps. He did not seem surprised to see them.

"She's gone," he said. He looked deadbeat. It was possible that he had already passed the limit of being so exhausted he might collapse at any moment.

They went into the house together and tried to interpret the clues. Widén stayed in the background and kept watch, while Wallander and Svedberg searched the house. Wallander did not refer to their having followed him to the house. Svedberg suspected that deep down he knew they would not abandon him. Perhaps he was even grateful.

It was Svedberg who found her. He opened the door to one of the rooms, and looked at the unmade bed. Without knowing why, he bent down and peered under it. There she was. For one horrible moment he thought it was Wallander's daughter, but it was the older woman, in the clothes he had seen her in earlier. Before telling the others what he had found, he swiftly checked under the other beds. He looked in the refrigerator and all the cupboards. Only when he was certain that Linda was not lying hidden somewhere did he attract their attention. They moved the bed to one side. When Wallander saw her head he turned on his heel, rushed out of the house and threw up.

She had no features left. Just a bloody mass in which it was impossible to pick out any features. Svedberg took a towel and laid it over her head. Then he examined the body. There were five bullet wounds. They formed a pattern, and that made him feel even worse than he did already. She had been shot in both feet, then in her hands, and finally through the heart.

They left her, and continued going through the house in silence. Neither of them said a word. They lifted the hatch to the cellar, and went down. Svedberg managed to hide the chain which he assumed had been used to tie up Wallander's daughter, but Wallander knew she had been kept down there in the darkness. Svedberg could see him biting his lips. He wondered how much longer Wallander could keep going. They went back to the kitchen. Svedberg discovered a cauldron full of blood-coloured water. When he stuck his finger in, he could feel traces of lingering heat. It slowly dawned on him what had happened. He went through the house one more time, painstakingly trying to follow up the various clues, make them reveal what had happened.

In the end, he proposed they should all sit down. Wallander was almost apathetic by this stage. Svedberg thought long and hard. Did he dare? The responsibility was enormous. But in the end he resolved to go ahead.

"I don't know where your daughter is," he said. "But she's still alive. I'm sure of that."

Wallander looked at him without saying anything.

"I think this is what happened," Svedberg said. "I can't be sure, but I'm trying to interpret the clues, piece them together, and see what kind of a story they tell. I think the dead woman tried to help your daughter to escape. I can't know whether or not she managed it. Maybe she got away, maybe Konovalenko stopped her? There are signs to suggest both possibilities. He killed Tania in such a sadistic fury, we have to believe that Linda has escaped. It could also have been a reaction to the fact that she even tried to help Linda. Tania let him down, and that was enough to trigger his brutality, which seems to be limitless. He scalded her face with boiling water. Then he shot her in the feet, that was for the escape, and then in the hands and finally through the heart. I would prefer not to try and imagine what her last hour in this life was like. Then he left. That is another indication that Linda escaped. If she managed to get away, Konovalenko could no longer regard the house as safe. But it could also be that Konovalenko was afraid somebody might have heard the shooting. That's what I think happened. But, of course, it could all have been quite different."

It was 7 a.m. now. Nobody said a word.

Svedberg went to the telephone. He called Martinsson, and had to wait as he was in the bathroom.

"Do me a favour," he said. "Drive to the railway station in Tomelilla. I'll be there in an hour. And don't tell anybody where you're going."

"Are you going off your rocker as well?" Martinsson said.

"No," Svedberg said. "I am in dead earnest."

He hung up and looked at Wallander. "Right now there's nothing you can do apart from get some sleep. Go home with Sten. Or we'll take you to your father's."

"How could I sleep?" Wallander said, as if in a dream.

"By lying down, for a start," Svedberg said. "You'd better do as I tell you. If you're going to be in any condition to help your daughter, you have to get some sleep. The state you're in, you'd only be a nuisance."

"I think I should go to my father's place," Wallander said.

"Where did you leave the car?" Widén said.

"Let me go and get it," Wallander said. "I need the air."

He went out. Svedberg and Widén stared at each other, too weary and upset to talk.

"By God, I'm glad I'm not a policeman," Widén said, gesturing towards the room where Tania was, as the Duett trundled into the yard.

"Thanks for your help," Svedberg said. He watched them drive away, wondering when the nightmare would end.

Widén stopped to drop Wallander at his father's house. They had not exchanged a single word during the journey.

"I'll be in touch before the day's over," Widén said.

He watched Wallander making his way slowly to the house. Poor devil, he thought. How much longer can he keep going?

His father was at the kitchen table. He was unshaven, and Wallander could smell that he needed a bath. He sat opposite him. Neither of them spoke for a long time.

"She's asleep," his father said eventually.

Wallander hardly heard what he said.

"She's sleeping calmly," repeated his father.

The words slowly penetrated Wallander's befuddled head.

"Who is?" he said, wearily.

"I'm talking about my granddaughter," his father said.

Wallander stared at him. For ages. Then he slowly got to his feet and went to the bedroom. Slowly, he opened the door. Linda was in bed, asleep. Her hair was cropped on one side of her head. But it was her all right. Wallander stood in the doorway. Then he walked to the bed and knelt down. He just looked. He did not want to know what had happened, he could not know what had taken place or how she had got home. He just wanted to look at her. Somewhere in the back of his mind, he knew that Konovalenko was still out there. But just for the moment, he didn't care about Konovalenko. Right now she was the only person who existed.

He lay on the floor beside the bed. He curled up and went to sleep. His father put a cushion under his head and a blanket over him and closed the door. Then he went to his studio and carried on painting. He had reverted to his usual motif. He was putting the finishing touches to a grouse.

Martinsson arrived at the railway station in Tomelilla a little after 8 a.m. He got out of his car and greeted Svedberg.

"What's so important, then?" he said, not bothering to disguise his annoyance.

"You'll see," Svedberg said. "But I must warn you it's not a pretty sight."

Martinsson frowned. "What's happened?"

"Konovalenko," Svedberg said. "He's struck again. We have another body to deal with. A woman."

"Good God!"

"Follow me," Svedberg said. "We have a lot to talk about."

"Is Wallander mixed up in all this?"

Svedberg did not hear. He was on the way to his car.

CHAPTER THIRTY

She cut her own hair in the late afternoon. That was how she hoped to erase the ugly memories. Then she started describing what had happened. Wallander had tried in vain to persuade her to let him call a doctor, but she refused.

"My hair will grow again in its own good time," she said. "No doctor can make it grow any faster than it wants to."

Wallander was afraid of what was coming next. What scared him was that his daughter might blame him for what had happened to her. It would be hard to defend himself. It was his fault, dragging her into all this.

She had made up her mind not to see a doctor for the moment. Only once during the day did she start crying. Out of the blue, just as they were going to sit down for lunch. She looked at him and asked what had happened to Tania. He told her the truth, that she was dead. But he did not say that she had been tortured by Konovalenko. Wallander hoped the newspapers would leave out the details. He also told her that Konovalenko was apparently still at large.

"He's on the run," he said. "He's a hunted man; he can't attack whenever he likes any more."

Wallander suspected that this was not necessarily true. Konovalenko was probably just as dangerous now as before. He also knew that he himself, once again, would be setting out to find him. But not yet, not this Wednesday, when his daughter had come back to him from the darkness, silence and terror.

At one point in the evening he spoke with Svedberg on the telephone. Wallander asked for one more night to catch up on sleep and do some thinking. He would come out into the open on Thursday. Svedberg told him about the search going on at full scale. There was no trace of Konovalenko.

"He's not alone," Svedberg said. "There was somebody else in that house. Rykoff is dead. Tania too. The man called Victor Mabasha died some days ago. Konovalenko ought to be on his own, but he isn't. There was somebody else in that house. The question is: who?"

"I don't know," Wallander said. "A new, unknown henchman?"

Shortly after Svedberg had hung up, there was a call from Widén. Wallander assumed that he and Svedberg were in touch with each other. Widén asked about Wallander's daughter, and Wallander replied that she would no doubt be OK.

"I'm thinking about that woman," Widén said. "I'm trying to understand how anybody could possibly do something like that to another human being."

"There are such people," Wallander said. "Unfortunately there are more of them than we care to imagine."

When Linda had fallen asleep, Wallander went to the studio where his father was painting. Although he suspected it was just a temporary state of affairs, he felt they had both found it easier to talk with each other during the terrors of the last days. He also wondered just how much of what had happened his father had understood.

"Are you still determined to get married?" Wallander said, sitting on a stool out in the studio.

"You shouldn't joke about serious matters," his father said. "We're getting married in June."

"My daughter has been invited," Wallander said. "But I haven't."

"You will be."

"Where are you going to get married?"

"Here."

"Here? In the studio?"

"Why not? I'm going to paint a big backdrop."

"What do you think Gertrud will have to say about that?"

"It's her idea."

His father turned around and smiled at him. Wallander burst out laughing. He couldn't remember the last time he had a good laugh.

"Gertrud is an unusual woman."

"She must be," Wallander said.

On Thursday morning Wallander woke up refreshed. His joy at the fact his daughter had emerged unscathed filled him with renewed energy. Konovalenko was a constant presence at the back of his mind. He began to feel again that he was ready to go after him.

Wallander called Björk just before 8 a.m. He had prepared his excuses meticulously.

"Kurt," Björk said. "For God's sake! Where are you? What's happened?"

"I guess I had a bit of a breakdown," Wallander said, trying to sound convincing by speaking softly and slowly. "But I'm better now. I just need a few more days of peace and quiet."

"You must take sick leave, of course," Björk said, firmly. "I don't know if you realise we've had a search on for you, and for Linda, of course. All very unpleasant. I'll call off the search right away, and I'll issue a press statement. The missing chief inspector has returned after a short illness. Where are you, by the way?"

"In Copenhagen," Wallander said.

"What the hell are you doing there?"

"I'm staying at a little hotel and getting some rest."

"And no doubt you're not going to tell me what that hotel is called? Or where it is?"

"I'd rather not."

"We need you as rapidly as possible. But in good health. Some horrible things are happening here. Martinsson and Svedberg and the rest of us feel helpless without you. We'll be asking for assistance from Stockholm."

"I'll be there on Friday. And sick leave won't be necessary."

"You'll never know how relieved I am. We've been extremely worried. What actually happened out there in the fog?"

"I'll write a full report, and I'll be with you on Friday."

He put the telephone down and started thinking about what Svedberg had said. Who was this other person? Who was hanging on Konovalenko's coat-tails now? He lay in bed, staring up at the ceiling. He went over all that had happened since the day poor Åkerblom had come into his office. He thought of the many summaries he had tried to write, attempting to find some kind of path through all the confusing tracks. The sense of being caught up in an investigation that could never quite be pinned down came to him once more, and he still did not know the real cause of it all.

He called Svedberg late in the afternoon.

"We haven't been able to find any clue as to where they've gone," he said. "On the other hand, I think my theory about what happened during the night is correct. There's no other plausible explanation."

"I need your help," Wallander said. "I have to drive out to that house again tonight."

"You don't mean you're thinking of going after Konovalenko on your own again?" Svedberg said, horrified.

"Not at all," Wallander said. "My daughter dropped a piece of jewellery while she was being held there. I don't suppose you found it?"

"Not as far as I know."

"Who's on guard there tonight?"

"I expect there'll just be a patrol car checking up now and then."

"Can you keep that patrol car out of the way between 9 p.m. and 11 p.m.? I'm in Copenhagen, as you might have heard from Björk, and everybody has to know that."

"Yes," Svedberg said.

"How can I get into the house?"

"We found a key in the gutter on the right-hand corner of the house, seen from the front, that is. It's still there."

Wallander wondered whether Svedberg had really believed him. Searching for a piece of jewellery was a pretty feeble excuse. If it was there, then of course the police would have found it. Then again, he had no idea what he thought he might find. During the last year Svedberg had developed into a skilful crime scene investigator. Wallander thought he might one day get up to Rydberg's level. If there had been anything significant there, Svedberg would have found it. All Wallander might be able to do was to see new connections.

In any case, that was where he had to start. It was most likely, to his way of thinking, that Konovalenko and his companion had returned to Stockholm.

He left for Tomelilla at 8.30 p.m. It was a warm evening, and he drove with the window open. It crossed his mind that he had never discussed his holiday entitlement with Björk.

He parked in the yard and retrieved the key. When he got into the house he started by switching on all the lights. He looked around, but he felt unsure where he should start. He wandered around the house, trying to isolate what it was he was looking for. A track leading to Konovalenko. A destination. An indication of who the unknown companion might be. Something that would reveal what was behind it all. He sat down in one of the chairs and thought back to when he checked the rooms first time around. At the same time he let his gaze wander. He saw nothing that seemed to him odd, or in any way remarkable. There's nothing here, he thought. Even if Konovalenko left in a hurry, he'll have covered his tracks. The ashtray in Stockholm was a fluke. Besides, Nyberg must have picked the house clean.

He got up from the chair and went around the house again, more slowly this time, and more carefully. He paused occasionally, lifted up a tablecloth, leafed through magazines, felt underneath the seats of chairs. Nothing. He went through the various bedrooms, leaving until last the room where they had found Tania. Nothing. In the rubbish bin, which Svedberg would have been through already, he found a dead mouse. Wallander poked at it with a fork and saw it had not been killed by a mousetrap. Somebody had stabbed it to death. A knife, he thought. He remembered that Mabasha had had a knife. But he was in the morgue. Wallander left the kitchen and went into the bathroom. Konovalenko had left nothing behind. He returned to the living room and sat down again. He picked a different chair this time, so he could see the room from another angle. There's always something, he thought. It's just a case of finding it. He set off to search through the house once more. Nothing. By the time he sat down again, it was already 10.15 p.m. He would have to leave soon. Time was running out.

Whoever used to live in this house had been very well organised. There was a place for every object, every piece of furniture, every light fixture. He looked to see if he could find anything out of place. After a while his eye settled on a bookcase against one of the walls. All the books were standing in straight lines. Except on the bottom shelf, where the back of one book was sticking out. He got up and picked out the book. It was a road atlas. He noticed a piece of the cover had been torn off and was inserted between the pages. He opened the atlas and found himself looking at a map of eastern Sweden, including sections of Småland, Kalmar County, and the island of Öland. He studied the map. Then he sat down at a table and adjusted the lamp. He could see some traces of pencil marks here and there. As if somebody had been following a route with a pencil, occasionally letting it touch the paper. One of the faint pencil marks was at the point where the Öland bridge starts out from Kalmar. Right down at the bottom of the page, more or less level with Blekinge, he found another mark. He thought for a while. Then he turned to the map of Skåne. There were no pencil marks there. He went back to the previous page. The faint marks followed the coastal road to Kalmar. He put the atlas down, went to the kitchen and called Svedberg at home.

"I'm still here," he said. "If I say Öland, what does that mean to you?"

Svedberg pondered. "Nothing," he said.

"You didn't find a notebook when you searched the house? No telephone book?"

"Tania had a little pocket diary in her purse," Svedberg said. "But there was nothing in it."

"No loose scraps of paper?"

"If you look in the woodstove, you'll see somebody has been burning paper," Svedberg said. "We went through the ashes. There was nothing there. Why do you mention Öland?"

"I found an atlas," Wallander said. "But I don't suppose it means anything."

"Konovalenko has probably gone back to Stockholm," Svedberg said. "I think he's had enough of Skåne."

"You're probably right," Wallander said. "Sorry to disturb you. I'll be leaving soon."

"Just one thing," Svedberg said. "Linda's mother keeps calling."

"Keep her away from Linda until the weekend," Wallander said and hung up.

He returned the atlas to the bookcase.

He went to the kitchen and poured himself a glass of water. He noticed that the telephone was nesting on a directory. He picked it up and opened it. Somebody had written an address on the inside cover: 14 Hemmansvägen. It was written in pencil. He thought for a moment. Then he called directory enquiries. When they answered he asked for the number of a subscriber by the name of Wallander who lived at 14 Hemmansvägen in Kalmar.

"There is nobody called Wallander at the address you gave," the operator said.

"It could be that the phone is in his boss' name, but I can't remember what he's called."

"Could it be Edelman?"

"That's it," Wallander said.

He was given the number, thanked the girl and hung up. Was it possible? Did Konovalenko have another safe house, this time on Öland?

He put the lights out behind him, locked up and replaced the key in the gutter. There was a breeze blowing. The warmth of the evening suggested early summer. His mind had been made up for him. He drove away from the house and headed for Öland.

He stopped in Brösarp and called home. His father answered.

"She's asleep," he said. "We've been playing cards."

"I won't be home tonight," Wallander said. "But don't worry. I just have to catch up with a stack of routine stuff. I'll be in touch tomorrow morning. And don't tell *anyone* she's there."

"I've already sent two reporters packing, and your man Björk. You come when you're ready," his father said.

Wallander replaced the receiver. Their relationship might indeed be improving after all. Let's hope it lasts, he thought. Maybe something good will come of this nightmare after all.

He reached the bridge across to Öland at 4 a.m. He had stopped twice on the way, once to fill up with petrol, and once to take a nap. Now that he had arrived, he no longer felt tired. He contemplated the mighty bridge looming up before him, and the water glittering in the early morning light. In the car park where he stopped there was a telephone box with a tattered directory. Hemmansvägen was evidently on the other side of the bridge. He took his pistol out of the glove compartment and checked to make sure it was loaded. There came to him the time, many years ago, when he had visited Öland with his sister Kristina and their parents. There was no bridge then. He had a faint memory of the little ferry that took them over the sound. They spent a week camping that summer. He remembered that week as a happy experience rather than a series of separate incidents. A vague feeling of something lost forever possessed him for a moment. Then he redirected his thoughts to Konovalenko. He tried to convince himself that he was probably wrong. The pencil marks in the atlas and the address in the directory need not have been made by Konovalenko. He would soon be on his way back to Skåne.

He stopped when he came to the Öland side of the bridge. There was a large road map of the island there, and he got out to study it. Hemmansvägen was a turning just before the zoo entrance. There was still not much traffic. After a few minutes he found the right road. He left the car in a car park. Hemmansvägen was a mixture of old and new houses, all of them with large gardens. He started walking. The first house had a number three on the fence. A dog eyed him suspiciously. He kept going, and calculated which one must be number 14. He noted that it was one of the older houses, with bay windows and elaborate ornamentation. He walked back the same way as he had come. He wanted to try approaching the house from the rear. He could not afford to take any risks. Konovalenko and his unknown companion might be there after all.

There was a sports field at the back of the houses. He clambered over the fence, ripping his trousers high up on one leg. He reoriented himself and approached number 14 from behind a wooden pavilion, That was painted yellow, with two storeys and a tower in one corner. There was a boarded-up hot-dog stand next to the fence. Crouching down, he left the shelter of the pavilion and ran over to the hut. Once there, he took his pistol out of his pocket. He stood there for five minutes, watching the house. Everything was quiet. There was a tool-shed in one corner of the garden. That was where he would hide. He looked again at the house. Then he got down onto his knees and crawled to the fence behind where the shed was. It was broken-down and diffi-cult to climb. He almost fell backwards, but regained his balance and jumped down into the narrow space behind the shed. He was breathing heavily. That's due to all the evil, he thought. Carefully he stuck his head out and contemplated the house from his new position. All was still quiet. The garden was overgrown. Next to him was a wheelbarrow full of last year's leaves. Perhaps the house was deserted. After a while he was more or less convinced it was. He left the protection of the shed and ran to the back wall of the house. Then he followed it to the right to get round to the front. He gave a start when he stepped on a hedgehog. It hissed and raised its spikes. Wallander had put his pistol back in his pocket. Now, without being quite sure why, he took it out again. The sound of a foghorn drifted in from the sound. He crept around the corner of the house and found himself at the far gable end. What am I doing here? If there is anybody in the house, it's bound to be some old couple waking up after a good night's sleep. What on earth will they say if they find a runaway detective inspector sneaking around in their garden? He kept going to the next corner. Then he peered around it.

Konovalenko was standing barefoot on the gravel path by a flag-pole, urinating. He was dressed in trousers and an open shirt. Wallander did not move. Even so, something alarmed Konovalenko, possibly an instinct for danger that never waned. He turned around. Wallander had his pistol drawn. For a split second they both assessed the situation. Wallander realised Konovalenko had made the mistake of leaving the house without his gun. Konovalenko could see Wallander would either kill him or intercept him before he could reach the front door. Konovalenko found himself in a situation that gave him no choice. He flung himself to one side with such force that just for a moment, Wallander lost sight of him. Then he ran as fast as he could, dodging from side to side, and jumped over the low front wall. He was in the road before Wallander began chasing him. It had all happened in a flash, and Wallander did not see the African standing in a window, watching what was going on.

Tsiki knew something alarming had happened. He did not know what, but he realised the instructions Konovalenko had given him the day before must now be followed. "If anything happens," Konovalenko told him, handing over an envelope, "follow the instructions inside here. That way you'll make it back home. Get in touch with the man you already met, the one who gave you your money and your last set of instructions."

He waited by the window only for a short while. Then he sat at a table and opened the envelope. An hour later he was on his way.

Konovalenko had about a 50-metre head start. Wallander wondered how he could run so incredibly fast. They were going in the direction of where Wallander had parked his car. Was Konovalenko's car in the same car park? Wallander cursed and ran faster, but the distance between them got no shorter. He was right. Konovalenko headed for a Mercedes, ripped open the door, which was unlocked, and started the engine. It all happened so fast Wallander realised the key must have been in the ignition. Konovalenko was prepared, even if he had made the mistake of leaving the house without a gun. Just then Wallander saw a flash. He threw himself to one side. The bullet whined past and struck the asphalt. Wallander huddled behind a bicycle stand and hoped he was invisible. Then he heard the car make a racing start.

He rushed towards his own car, fumbling with the keys and thinking he had surely lost Konovalenko already. He was sure he would want to get off Öland as quickly as possible. If he stayed on the island he would be cornered sooner than later. Wallander slammed down the accelerator. He caught sight of the Mercedes at the roundabout just before the bridge. Wallander overtook a slow-moving truck at high speed and nearly lost control of the car as he clipped the flower bed in the centre of the roundabout. Then he raced onto the bridge. The Mercedes was in front of him. He must think of something. If it came to a car chase, he wouldn't stand a chance.

It all came to a head at the highest part of the bridge.

Konovalenko was going at very high speed, but Wallander had managed to keep on his tail. When he was sure of not hitting a car coming in the opposite direction, he stuck his pistol out of the window and fired. His aim was just to hit the car. The first shot missed. But the second was on target, and by an incredible stroke of luck he managed to burst one of the rear tyres. The Mercedes flew into a skid. Wallander slammed on his brakes and watched as Konovalenko careered into the concrete barrier on the outside edge of the bridge. There was a violent crash. Wallander could not see what had happened to Konovalenko behind the wheel. But without a second thought he shifted into first gear and drove straight into the back of the wrecked car. He felt a searing pain as the seat belt bit into his chest. Wallander wrestled with the gears to find reverse. With tyres screeching, he backed off and prepared for another ram. Then he repeated the manoeuvre one more time. The Mercedes was slammed a few more metres forward. Wallander backed off again, flung open the door, and took cover. Cars were already lining up behind him. When Wallander waved his pistol and yelled at the drivers to keep out of the way, several tumbled out of their cars and ran for it. Wallander could see a similar line of cars on the other side of the bridge. Still no sign of Konovalenko. Even so, he fired a shot at the crumpled car.

After the second bullet, the petrol tank exploded. Wallander never knew for sure afterwards if it was his bullet that caused the fire, or whether the leaking petrol had ignited for some other reason. The car was engulfed by roaring flames and thick smoke. Wallander approached the car.

Konovalenko was on fire. He was trapped on his back with half his upper body sticking out through the windscreen. Afterwards, Wallander would remember his staring eyes, indicating he could not believe what was happening to him. Then his hair started burning, and a few seconds later it was obvious to Wallander he was dead. Sirens were approaching in the distance. He walked slowly back to his own car and leaned against the door.

He gazed out over Kalmar Sound. The water glistened. There was a smell of the sea. His mind was a blank; he could not think at all. Something had come to an end, and he felt stupefied. Then he heard a voice from a megaphone ordering someone to lay down their arms. It was a while before he realised the voice was talking to him. He turned round and saw fire engines and patrol cars on the Kalmar side. Konavalenko's car was still ablaze. Wallander looked at his pistol. Then he threw it over the side of the bridge. Armed police were walking towards him.

Wallander waved his ID. "Chief Inspector Wallander," he yelled.

He was soon surrounded by suspicious local officers.

"I'm a policeman and my name's Wallander," he said. "You might have read about me in the papers. There's been an APB on me since last week."

"I recognise you," said one of the officers in a broad local accent.

"The man on fire in the car is Konovalenko," Wallander said. "He's the one who murdered our colleague in Stockholm. And a few others besides."

Wallander looked around. Something that might have been joy, or maybe relief, was beginning to well up inside him. "Shall we go?" he said. "I could do with a cup of coffee. It's all over here."

CHAPTER THIRTY-ONE

Kleyn was arrested in his office at NIS headquarters at about midday, Friday, May 22. Soon after 8 a.m. Chief Prosecutor Verwey had listened to Scheepers's account of the circumstances and President de Klerk's decision late the previous night. Then, without comment, he signed a warrant for Kleyn's arrest and another to search his house. Scheepers requested that Inspector Borstlap, who had made a good impression in connection with the murder of van Heerden, should handle the arrest. When Borstlap had deposited Kleyn in an interrogation room, he went to a nearby room where Scheepers was waiting. He was able to report that the arrest had taken place without any problems, but he had observed something that seemed to him important, and possibly worrisome. His information about why somebody in the intelligence service should be brought in for interrogation was scanty. Scheepers had stressed the secrecy surrounding everything to do with state security. Nevertheless, Borstlap had been told in confidence that President de Klerk was aware of what was happening. Borstlap had therefore felt instinctively that he ought to report what he had seen.

Kleyn had not been surprised by his arrest. Borstlap had seen through his indignation as a poorly performed charade. Somebody must have warned Kleyn what was going to happen. Since it was clear to Borstlap that the decision to arrest Kleyn had been made a very short time before, he realised that Kleyn either had friends in circles close to the President or there must be a mole operating in the public prosecutor's office. Scheepers listened to what Borstlap had to say. It was less than twelve hours since de Klerk had made his decision. Apart from the President only Verwey and Borstlap knew what was going to happen. Scheepers knew that he must at once warn de Klerk that his office was bugged. He asked Borstlap to wait outside while he made the call. The President's secretary said he was in a meeting and could not be disturbed until later in the afternoon.

Scheepers decided to keep Kleyn waiting. He had no illusions about his being worried that he was not told why he had been arrested. But it was more that Scheepers felt a degree of uncertainty about the imminent confrontation.

Borstlap drove them to Kleyn's house outside Pretoria. Scheepers was slumped in the back seat. He was thinking about the white lioness. A symbol of Africa, he thought. The animal at rest, the calm before it gets to its feet and musters all its strength. The beast of prey one cannot afford to wound, but which has to be killed if it starts to attack.

Scheepers wondered whether the grand design worked out by de Klerk and Mandela, involving the ultimate retreat of the whites, would succeed. Or would it lead to the doomsday they had tried to contain like an evil genie in a bottle?

They stopped outside the gates of Kleyn's house. Borstlap had told him on his arrest that the house would be searched, and requested the keys. Kleyn played up his outraged dignity and refused. Borstlap said he would break down the front door. In the end he got the keys. There was a guard outside the house, and a gardener. Scheepers introduced himself. He looked around the walled garden. Straight lines. And it was so well tended that it had lost all signs of life. That's what Kleyn must be like himself, he thought. His life is an extension of straight ideological lines. There is no room for divergence, not in his thoughts, his emotions, or his garden. The exception is his secret: Miranda and Matilda.

They went into the house. A black servant stared at them in astonishment. Scheepers asked him to wait outside while they searched the building. They asked him to tell the gardener and the guard not to go away until they had received his permission to do so.

The house was sparsely but expensively furnished. Kleyn favoured marble, steel, and substantial wood in his furniture. Lithographs hung on the walls. The motifs were taken from South African history. There were also fencing swords, old pistols and game bags. A stuffed kudu head with powerful, curved horns was mounted over the mantelpiece. While Borstlap went through the house, Scheepers shut himself into Kleyn's study. The desk was empty. There was one filing cabinet. Scheepers looked for a safe but found nothing. He went downstairs to the living room where Borstlap was searching through a bookcase.

"There must be a safe," Scheepers said.

Borstlap picked up Kleyn's keys and showed them to him. "No key, though," he said.

"You can be sure he's chosen a place for the safe he thinks is the last place we'd think of looking," Scheepers said. "So that's where we'll start. Where's the last place we'd think of looking?"

"Right in front of our very eyes," Borstlap said. "The best hiding place is often the most obvious one."

"Concentrate on finding the safe," Scheepers said. "There's nothing on the bookshelves." He went back to the study. He sat at the desk and opened the drawers in turn. Two hours later he had found nothing at all relevant to the investigation. Kleyn's papers mostly concerned his private life and contained nothing remarkable, or they were to do with his coin collection. To his surprise Scheepers learned that Kleyn was chairman of the South African Numismatic Society, and did noble work on behalf of the country's coin collectors. Another peculiarity, he thought. But hardly significant.

Borstlap had made two thorough searches, top to bottom, and found no safe.

"There is one, nevertheless," Scheepers said.

Borstlap called in the servant and asked him where the safe was. The man stared at him uncomprehendingly.

"A secret cupboard," Borstlap said. "Hidden, always locked?"

"There isn't one," the man said.

Borstlap sent him out again in annoyance. Then they started again. Scheepers tried to see if there were any irregularities in the house's architecture. It was not unusual for South Africans to have secret chambers built into their houses. He found nothing. While Borstlap was up in the cramped loft searching around with a flashlight, Scheepers went into the garden. He observed the house from the back. The solution struck him more or less immediately. The house had no chimney. He went back inside and squatted in front of the open hearth. He shone his torch up into the chimney. The safe was cut into the wall. When he tried the handle he discovered to his astonishment that it was unlocked. Just then Borstlap came downstairs.

"A well chosen hiding place," Scheepers said. Borstlap was annoyed that he had failed to find it himself.

Scheepers sat at the marble table sorting through the papers. Borstlap had gone outside for a cigarette. There were insurance policies, envelopes containing old coins, the house deeds, about 20 stock certificates, and some government bonds. He pushed them all to one side and concentrated on a small black notebook. He leafed through the pages. They were full of cryptic notes, a mixture of names, places and combinations of numbers. He decided to take the book with him.

He replaced the papers in the safe and went out to Borstlap. A thought struck him. He beckoned to the three men who squatted watching them.

"Were there any visitors late last night?" he said.

"Only Mofolo, the night watchman, can tell you that," the gardener said.

"And he's not here, of course."

"He comes in the evenings." Scheepers nodded. He would come back.

They drove back to Johannesburg. On the way they stopped for a late lunch. They parted at 4.15 p.m. outside the police station. Scheepers could put it off no longer. He would have to start the interrogation now. But first he would try again to reach the President.

When the security guard called close to midnight, Kleyn had been surprised. He knew, of course, that a young prosecutor by the name of Scheepers had been given the assignment of trying to unravel the suspicions of a conspiracy. But he was confident all the time of being a sufficient number of steps ahead of the man trying to track him. Now he realised Scheepers was closer to him than he had imagined. He got up, dressed, and prepared to be up all night. He guessed he had until at least 10 the following morning. Scheepers would need an hour or two the next day to arrange all the papers needed for his arrest. By then he would have to have made sure that he had issued all the necessary instructions to ensure the operation would not run into trouble. He went down to the kitchen and made tea. Then he sat down to write a summary. There was a lot to keep in mind, but he would manage.

Getting arrested was an unexpected complication, but he had considered the possibility. The situation was annoying, but not impossible to resolve. As he could not be sure how long Scheepers was thinking of holding him, he must plan on the basis that he would be detained until the assassination of Mandela had been carried out.

That was his first task. To turn what would happen the following day to his own advantage. As long as he was detained, they would not be able to accuse him of being involved in the various activities. He thought through what was going to happen. It was 1 a.m. before he decided to call Malan.

"Get dressed and come over," he said.

Malan was only half-awake and confused. No name, nothing more. "Get dressed and come over."

Malan asked no questions. An hour later, at exactly 2 a.m., he was in Kleyn's living room. The curtains were closed. The night watchman who opened the gate for him was threatened with instant dismissal if he ever revealed the visitors who came to the house late in the evening or during the night. Kleyn paid him a high wage in order to guarantee his silence.

Malan was nervous. Kleyn hardly let him sit down before explaining what had happened, what would happen the next morning, and what must be fixed that night. What Malan heard increased his alarm. His own responsibility would grow beyond where he was really happy with it.

"We don't know how much Scheepers has managed to figure out," Kleyn said. "But we must take certain precautions. The most important one is to dissolve the Committee, and divert attention from Cape Town and June 12."

Malan stared at him in astonishment. Could he be serious? Would all the executive responsibility fall on his shoulders?

"I'll be out very soon," he said. "Don't worry. Then I'll take back the responsibility."

"I hope so," Malan said. "But dissolving the Committee . . ."

"We have no choice. Scheepers might have penetrated deeper and further than we can know."

"But how has he done that?"

Kleyn shrugged in annoyance. "What do we always do?" he asked. "We use all our skills, all our contacts. We bribe, threaten, and lie our way to the information we need. There are no limits to what we can do. And so there are no limits for those who keep watch over our activities.

The Committee must not meet again. It will cease to exist. That means it has never existed. We will contact all the members tonight. But before that there are other things we have to do."

"If Scheepers knows we're planning something for June 12, we'll have to postpone it," Malan said. "The risk is too great."

"It's too late," Kleyn said. "Besides, Scheepers can't be certain. A well-laid trail in another direction will convince him that Cape Town and June 12 are an attempt to mislead him. We turn the tables on him."

"How?"

"During the interrogation I'll be subjected to tomorrow, I'll have the chance to trick him into starting to believe something else."

"But that's hardly enough."

"Of course not."

Kleyn took out a little black notebook. When he opened it, Malan could see all the pages were blank.

"I'll fill this with nonsense," Kleyn went on. "But here and there I'll note down a place and a date. All except one will be crossed out. The one that is left will not be Cape Town, June 12. I'll leave the book in my safe. I'll leave it unlocked, as if I'd been in a great hurry and tried to dispose of incriminating papers."

Malan nodded. He was beginning to think Kleyn was right. It would be possible to set false trails.

"Tsiki is on his way home," Kleyn said, handing over an envelope to Malan. "It will be your job to receive him, take him to Hammanskraal, and give him his final instructions the day before June 12. Everything is written down inside this envelope. Read through it now and see if anything is unclear. Then we'll start making our calls."

While Malan was reading the instructions, Kleyn started filling the notebook with meaningless combinations of words and numbers. He used several different pens to give the impression the notes had been made over a long period. He thought for a while before deciding on Durban, July 3. The ANC were holding an important meeting there on that day. That would be his red herring.

Malan put down the papers. "It doesn't say anything about what gun he should use," he said.

"Konovalenko has been training him to use a particularly long-range rifle," Kleyn said. "There is an exact copy in the underground store at Hammanskraal."

Malan nodded.

"No more questions?"

"No," Malan said.

Kleyn had three separate lines. They made calls all over the country. Men fumbled for receivers, only to become instantly wide awake when they recognised the callers.

The Committee was dissolved. It had never existed because it had disappeared without trace. All that remained was a rumour of its existence. It could be re-created at short notice. For the time being it was no longer needed, and could be a danger. But the state of readiness to bring about their solution for the future of South Africa was as high as ever. They were all ruthless men who never rested. Their ruthlessness was real, but their ideas were based on a mixture of illusions, lies and fanatical despair. For some of the members it was a matter of pure hatred.

Malan drove home through the night.

Kleyn tidied up his house and left the safe door unlocked. At 4.30 a.m. he went to bed and prepared to get a few hours' sleep. He wondered who had provided Scheepers with all the information. He could not dislodge the feeling that there was something he did not understand. Somebody had betrayed him, but he could not figure out who it was.

Scheepers opened the door of the interview room.

Kleyn was sitting on a chair against one of the walls, smiling at him. Scheepers had decided to treat him in a friendly and correct manner. He had spent an hour going through the notebook. He was still doubtful whether the assassination attempt had been switched to Durban. He had weighed the reasons for and against without reaching any conclusion. He saw no prospect of Kleyn actually telling him the truth. He might just be able to lure him into providing snippets of information which could indicate indirectly how things stood.

Scheepers sat facing Kleyn. This was Matilda's father he was looking at. He knew the secret, but he knew he would not be able to make use of it. It could only compromise the two women. Kleyn could not be detained indefinitely. He already looked like a man who was ready to leave the interview room at any moment.

A clerk came in and sat down at a table to one side.

"Jan Kleyn," he said. "You have been arrested because there are strong grounds for believing you are involved in and possibly even responsible for subversive activities, and plotting to commit murder. What do you have to say?"

Kleyn continued smiling as he replied. "My response is that I will not say anything until I have a lawyer present."

Scheepers was momentarily put off his stride. The normal procedure was that when a person is arrested, the first step is to give him the opportunity of contacting a lawyer.

"Everything has been conducted by the book," Kleyn said, as if he could see right through Scheepers' hesitation. "But my lawyer, who was available this morning, as you apparently were not, hasn't arrived back yet this afternoon."

"We can start with personal details, then," Scheepers said. "You don't need a lawyer present for that."

"Of course not."

Scheepers left the room as soon as he had recorded all the details. He left instructions to send for him the moment the lawyer appeared. When he got to the prosecutor's waiting room, he was drenched in sweat. Kleyn's nonchalant superiority unnerved him. How could he be so indifferent when faced with charges which, if proven, could result in his being sentenced to death?

Scheepers wondered if he would be able to handle him as required. Should he contact Verwey and suggest that a more experienced interrogator be called in? On the other hand, he knew Verwey was expecting him to carry off the assignment. Verwey never gave anyone the same challenge twice. His career would be under threat if he failed. He took off his jacket and rinsed his face with cold water. Then he ran one more time through the questions he planned to put to Kleyn.

He also managed to reach the President, and passed on his suspicion that the President's office was bugged. De Klerk heard him through without interrupting.

"I'll have that looked into," he said. That was the end of the conversation.

It was 6 p.m. before at last Kleyn's lawyer arrived. He returned to the interview room immediately. The lawyer at Kleyn's side was about 40 and called Kritzinger. They shook hands, greeting each other coolly. Clearly Kritzinger and Kleyn were old acquaintances. It was possible that Kritzinger had deliberately delayed his reappearance in order to give Kleyn breathing space and at the same time unnerve his chief interrogator. The effect on Scheepers was quite the opposite. He was now perfectly calm. All the doubts he had experienced over the last few hours had disappeared.

"I have examined the detention order," Kritzinger said. "These are serious charges."

"Undermining national security is a serious crime," Scheepers said.

"My client rejects all the charges," Kritzinger said. "I demand that he be released immediately. Is it sensible to detain people whose daily task it is to uphold precisely that national security you refer to?"

"For the moment I am the one asking the questions," Scheepers said. "Your client is the one required to supply the answers."

Scheepers glanced at his papers. "Do you know Frans Malan?" he said.

"Yes," Kleyn said, without hesitation. "He works in the military sector which deals with the most sensitive security measures."

"When did you last see him?"

"In connection with the terrorist attack on the restaurant outside Durban. We were both called in to assist with the investigation."

"Are you aware of a secret group of *Boers* who call themselves simply 'the Committee'?"

"No."

"Are you sure?"

"My client has already answered once," Kritzinger said.

"Nothing will prevent my asking the same question twice," Scheepers said, sharply.

"I am not aware of any such committee," Kleyn said.

"We have reason to believe that the assassination of one of the black nationalist leaders is being plotted by that committee," Scheepers said. "Various places and dates have been mentioned. Do you know anything about that?"

"No."

Scheepers produced the notebook. "When your house was searched, the police found this book. Do you recognise it?"

"Of course I recognise it. It's mine."

"There are various notes in it about dates and places. Can you tell me what they mean?"

"What is all this?" Kleyn said, turning to his lawyer. "These are private notes about birthdays and meetings with friends."

"What do you have planned for Cape Town on June 12?"

Kleyn's expression did not waver as he replied. "I have nothing planned at all," he said. "I had thought of going there for a meeting with some of my fellow numismatists. But it was cancelled."

Kleyn seemed totally unconcerned.

"What do you have to say about Durban on July 3?"

"Nothing."

"You have nothing to say?"

Kleyn turned to his lawyer and whispered something.

"My client declines to answer that question for personal reasons," Kritzinger said.

"Personal reasons or not, I want an answer," Scheepers said.

"This is lunacy," Kleyn said, with a gesture of resignation.

Scheepers noticed Kleyn was sweating. Moreover one of his hands, resting on the table, had started trembling.

"Your questions so far have been lacking in substance," Kritzinger said. "I shall very soon demand an end to all this and insist on the immediate release of my client."

"When it comes to investigations concerning threats to national security, the police and prosecutors have wide powers," Scheepers said. "Now, will you please answer my question."

"I have a friendship with a woman in Durban," Kleyn said. "As she is married, I have to meet her in discreet circumstances."

"Do you meet her regularly?"

"Yes."

"What's her name?"

Kleyn and Kritzinger protested with one voice.

"We'll leave the name out of it for the time being," Scheepers said. "I'll come back to that. But if it's true you meet her regularly and, moreover, note down various meetings in this book, is it not a little odd that there's only one reference to Durban?"

"I get through at least ten notebooks a year," Kleyn said. "I throw full ones away all the time. Or burn them."

"Where do you burn them?"

Kleyn seemed to have recovered his composure.

"In the garden," Kleyn said. "As you obviously know, my fireplace has no chimney."

The interrogation continued. Scheepers reverted to questions about the Committee, but the answers were always the same. Kritzinger protested at regular intervals. After three hours of questioning, Scheepers rose to his feet and said curtly that Kleyn would remain in custody. Kritzinger was furious, but Scheepers reminded him that the law allowed him to detain Kleyn for at least another 24 hours.

It was already evening by the time he went to report to Verwey, who had promised to remain in his office until he arrived. The corridors were deserted as he hurried to the chief prosecutor's office. The door was ajar. Verwey was asleep in his chair. Scheepers knocked and went in. Verwey opened his eyes and looked at him.

"Kleyn has not admitted to any knowledge whatsoever of a conspiracy or an assassination," he said. "Nor do I think he will. Moreover, we have no evidence to connect him with either offence. When we searched his house, we found only one item of interest. There was a notebook in his safe, with various dates and locations. All of them were crossed out except one. Durban, July 3. We know that Mandela will be giving a public address on that day. The date we first suspected, Cape Town June 12, is crossed out in the book."

Verwey quickly adjusted his chair to the upright position and asked to see the notebook. Scheepers had it in his case. Verwey leafed through it slowly under the light of his desk lamp.

"What explanation did he give?" Verwey said, when he got to the end.

"Various meetings. As far as Durban is concerned, he claims he is having an affair there with a married woman."

"Start with that tomorrow," Verwey said.

"He refuses to say who she is."

"Tell him he won't be released unless he tells us."

Scheepers looked at Verwey in surprise. "Can we do that?"

"Young man," Verwey said. "You can do anything when you are chief prosecutor and as old as I am. Don't forget that a man like Kleyn knows how to eradicate every trace of where he's been. He must be beaten in battle. Even if one has to resort to dubious methods."

"I sometimes got the feeling he was insecure," Scheepers said, hesitantly.

"He knows we're snapping at his heels in any case," Verwey said. "Put him under real pressure tomorrow. The same questions, over and over again. From different angles. But the same thrust, the same thrust every time."

Scheepers nodded. "There was one more thing," he said. "Inspector Borstlap who made the arrest had the strong impression Kleyn had been warned. Only a very few people knew only a short time in advance that it was to happen."

Verwey looked at him for a long time before responding. "This country of ours is at war," he said. "There are ears everywhere, human and electronic. Penetrating and stealing secrets is often the best weapon. Don't forget that."

Scheepers left the building and paused on the steps, enjoying the fresh air. He felt very tired. As he went to his car, one of the parking attendants emerged from the shadows.

"A man left this for you," he said, handing him an envelope.

"Who?"

"A black man," the attendant said. "Didn't say his name. Just that it was important."

Scheepers handled the letter carefully. It was thin, and could not contain a bomb. He nodded to the attendant, unlocked the car and got in. Then he opened the envelope and read by the light of the dashboard what the note said.

Assassin probably a black man by the name of Victor Mabasha. Steve.

Scheepers felt his heart beating faster. At last, he thought. Then he drove straight home. Judith was waiting for him with a meal. But before sitting down, he called Borstlap at home.

"Victor Mabasha," he said. "Does the name mean anything to you?"

There was a pause before Borstlap replied. "No," he said.

"Tomorrow morning, go through all the files and everything you have in the computer. Victor Mabasha is a black, and probably the assassin we are looking for."

"Have you managed to break Kleyn?" Borstlap said.

"No," Scheepers said. "I got that information elsewhere."

Victor Mabasha, he thought as he sat down to dinner, if you're the one, we'll put a stop to you before it's too late.

CHAPTER THIRTY-TWO

That day in Kalmar, Kurt Wallander began to realise how bad he actually felt. Later, when the murder of Louise Åkerblom and the sheer nightmare that followed in its wake had become a series of unreal events, a desolate charade in a distant landscape, he would insist stubbornly that it was not until Konovalenko was sticking out of his windscreen on the Öland bridge with staring eyes and his hair on fire that it really struck him how profoundly unwell he was. That was the moment of insight, and he would not budge from that view, even though the memories and all the painful experiences came and went like shifting patterns in a kaleidoscope. It was in Kalmar that he lost his grip on himself. He told his daughter that it was as if a countdown had started, a countdown to nothing but a void. The doctor in Ystad, who began treating him in mid-June and tried to sort out his increasing gloom, wrote in his journal: *According to the patient, the depression started over a cup of coffee at the police station in Kalmar while a man was being burned alive in a car on a bridge.*

There he sat in the police station in Kalmar, drinking coffee, feeling exhausted and drained. Everybody who saw him hunched over his cup that half-hour thought he was preoccupied or aloof. Or was he just thoughtful? In any case, nobody went to keep him company or to ask him how he was doing. The strange officer from Ystad was treated with a mixture of respect and hesitation. He was simply left in peace while they dealt with the chaos on the bridge and the flow of telephone calls from newspapers, radio and television.

After half an hour he jumped to his feet and demanded to be taken to the yellow house on Hemmansvägen. When they passed the place on the bridge where Konovalenko's car had become a smoking shell, he stared straight ahead of him. When he got to the house he immediately took command, forgetting that the investigation was being led by a Kalmar detective called Blomstrand. But they deferred to him, and he worked up an enormous level of energy over the next few hours. He seemed to have put Konovalenko right out of his mind already. There were two things that especially interested him. He wanted to know who owned the house. He also kept going on about Konovalenko not being alone. He ordered a house-to-house search of the street, and he wanted taxi drivers and bus conductors contacted. Konovalenko was not alone, he kept repeating. Who was the man or woman he had with him, who had now obviously disappeared? None of his questions could be answered straightaway. The property register and the neighbours who were questioned gave conflicting answers as to who owned the yellow house. The owner, a widower called Hjalmarson who worked at the provincial records office, had died about ten years earlier. His son lived in Brazil. According to one of the neighbours he was a representative for a Swedish firm, and an arms dealer according to others. He had come home for the funeral. It had been a worrying time for Hemmansvägen, according to a retired department head at the council offices in Kronoberg, who emerged as a spokesman for the neighbours. So there was considerable relief when the "For Sale" sign was taken down and a removal van drove up with all the belongings of a retired reserve officer. He used to be something as antiquated as a major in the Scanian hussars, a bizarre relic from a former age. He was called Gustav Jernberg, and he announced his presence to the world at large by friendly bellowing. The worries returned, however, when it became apparent that Jernberg would spend most of his time in Spain, on account of his rheumatism. When he was away, the house was occupied by a grandson in his mid-thirties, who was arrogant and rude. He was Hans Jernberg, and all anyone knew was that he was some kind of businessman who paid fleeting visits, sometimes with strange companions.

The police immediately started looking for the young Jernberg. They tracked him down in the early afternoon to an office in Göteborg. Wallander spoke with him on the telephone. At first he claimed to have no idea what they were talking about, but Wallander was in no mood to wheedle and coax people into telling the truth that day. He threatened to hand him over without delay to the Göteborg police, hinting also that it would be impossible to keep the press out of it. Halfway through the call one of the Kalmar officers stuck a note on the table next to Wallander. They had run a search through various files: Jernberg had links with neo-Nazi movements in Sweden. Wallander stared at the note before the obvious question to ask the man at the other end of the line struck him.

"Can you tell me your views on South Africa?" he asked.

"I can't see what that has to do with it," Jernberg said.

"Answer the question," Wallander said, brusquely.

The reply came after a short silence. "I consider South Africa to be one of the best organised countries in the world," Jernberg said. "I regard it as my duty to do all I can to support the whites living there."

"And you do that by renting out your house in Kalmar to the Russian Mafia who run errands for the South Africans? Is that it?"

This time Jernberg was genuinely surprised. "I don't know what you're talking about."

"Oh yes you do," Wallander said. "But you can answer another question instead. Which of your friends has had access to the house during the past week? Think carefully before you answer. The slightest evasion and I'll ask the Göteborg prosecutors to issue a warrant for your arrest. And that's what will happen, believe you me."

"Ove Westerberg," Jernberg said. "He's an old friend of mine who runs a construction firm here in town."

"Address?"

It was all very confusing, but effective work on the part of the police in Göteborg threw light on what had happened at the yellow house over the last few days. Westerberg was also a friend of South Africa. He had had a query some weeks ago as to whether the house could be rented to some South African guests, who would pay good money. As Jernberg was abroad at the time, Westerberg had not told him about it. Wallander also suspected that the money had gone no further than Westerberg's pocket. But Westerberg had no idea who these guests from South Africa were. He did not even know whether they had been there.

That was as far as Wallander got that day. The Kalmar police would have to delve further into contacts between Swedish neo-Nazis and the upholders of Apartheid in South Africa. There was still no indication who had been in the yellow house with Konovalenko. While neighbours, taxi drivers and bus conductors were being questioned, Wallander made a thorough search of the house. Two of the bedrooms had been used, and the house had been abandoned in a hurry. Konovalenko must have left something behind this time. Presumably the other visitor had taken Konovalenko's belongings with him. Maybe there was no limit to Konovalenko's caution. Maybe he anticipated the possibility of a burglary every night and hid his belongings before going to bed? Wallander summoned Blomstrand, who was scouring the toolshed. Wallander wanted the house searched for a bag. He couldn't say what it looked like or how big it might be.

"A bag with some things in it," he said. "There must be one somewhere."

"What kind of things in it?" Blomstrand said.

"Papers, money, clothes," Wallander said. "Maybe a weapon. I don't know."

Various bags and cases were carried down to where Wallander was waiting on the ground floor. He blew the dust off a leather briefcase containing old photographs and letters, most of them starting with *Dearest Gunvor* or *My dear Herbert*. Another one, as dusty, unearthed in the attic, was crammed with exotic starfish and seashells. But Wallander waited patiently. There had to be traces of Konovalenko somewhere, and also of his companion. While he was waiting, he spoke with his daughter and with Björk. News of what had happened that morning had spread all over the country. Wallander told Linda that he felt OK, and that it really was all over now. He would be home that night, and they could take the car and spend a few days in Copenhagen. He could tell she was not convinced he was well, or that it was all over. He reflected afterwards that he had a daughter who could read him like a book. The conversation with Björk came to an abrupt end when Wallander lost his temper and slammed down the receiver. That had never happened in all the years he had worked with Björk. But Björk had begun to question Wallander's judgment because, without telling anybody, he had set out after Konovalenko on his own. Wallander could see there was a lot to be said for Björk's point of view, of course, but what upset him was the fact that Björk started going on about that now, when he was at a critical stage of the investigation. Björk regarded Wallander's outburst as an unfortunate sign that he was still mentally disturbed. "We'll have to keep an eye on Kurt," Björk told Martinsson and Svedberg.

It was Blomstrand who uncovered the right bag, hidden behind a neat row of boots in a cupboard in the corridor between the kitchen and the dining room. It was a leather suitcase with a combination lock. Wallander wondered whether the lock might be booby-trapped. What would happen if they forced open the case? Blomstrand drove to Kalmar airport, and had it put through the X-ray machine. Nothing to suggest it might blow up. Wallander took a screwdriver and forced the lock. There were a number of papers in the case, tickets, several passports, and a large sum of money. There was also a small pistol, a Beretta. The passports all belonged to Konovalenko, and were issued in Sweden, Finland, and Poland. He had a different name in each passport. As a Finn he was called Konovalenko Mäkelä, and as a Pole he had the German-sounding name of Hausmann. There were 47,000 Swedish kronor and $11,000 in the case. But what interested Wallander most was whether the other documents would indicate who the companion might be. To his disappointment and annoyance, most of the notes were written in what he assumed was Russian. They seemed to be some sort of journal since there were dates in the margin.

Wallander turned to Blomstrand. "We need someone with Russian," he said, "who can translate this on the spot."

"We could try my wife. She's very interested in Russian culture. Especially 19th-century writers," Blomstrand said.

Wallander closed the suitcase and tucked it under his arm. "Let's go and see her," he said. "She'd only get distracted if we brought her to this circus."

Blomstrand lived in a terrace house north of Kalmar. His wife was an intelligent, straightforward woman, and Wallander took an immediate liking to her. While they were drinking coffee and eating sandwiches in the kitchen, she took the papers into her study and looked up a few words in the dictionary. It took her nearly an hour to translate the text and write it down. But then it was ready, and for Wallander, it was like reading about his own experiences from a different point of view. Many details of what had happened now became clear. The main thing, the answer to the question of who had been Konovalenko's final companion, who had managed to leave the yellow house without being seen, was quite different from what he had expected. South Africa had sent a substitute for Mabasha. Another African called Sikosi Tsiki.

He had entered the country from Denmark. "His training is not perfect," Konovalenko wrote, "but sufficient. And his ruthlessness and mental resilience are greater than those of V.M." Konovalenko also referred to a man in South Africa by the name of Kleyn. Wallander assumed he was an important go-between. There was no clue about the organisation Wallander was now certain must be behind it all. He explained to Blomstrand what the notebook had revealed.

"There's an African who even now is in the process of leaving the country," Wallander said. "He was in the yellow house this morning. Somebody must have seen him, somebody must have driven him somewhere. He can't have walked over the bridge. We can rule out the possibility he's still on Öland. There is a chance that he had his own car or has stolen one. More important is the fact that he's trying to leave Sweden. Where, we don't know, but we have to pull out all the stops to prevent him leaving."

"That won't be easy," Blomstrand said.

"But not impossible," Wallander said. "There can only be a limited number of black men going through Swedish border controls each day."

Wallander thanked Blomstrand's wife. They returned to the police station. An APB went out on the unknown African. At about the same time the police found a taxi driver who had picked up an African that morning from a car park at the end of Hemmansvägen, after the car burned and the bridge was closed. Wallander assumed the African had first hidden somewhere outside the house for an hour or two. The taxi driver took him to the centre of Kalmar. Then he paid, got out, and disappeared. The driver could not give much of a description. The man was tall, well built, and wore light-coloured trousers, white shirt, dark jacket. That was about all he could say. They had spoken English.

It was almost evening and there was nothing more Wallander could do in Kalmar. Once they picked up the fugitive, the last piece of the puzzle could be fitted into all the others.

They offered to drive him to Ystad, but he wanted to be on his own. He said goodbye to Blomstrand, apologised for shamelessly taking over command for a few hours in the middle of the day, and left Kalmar.

*

He had studied a map and come to the conclusion that the shortest way home was via Växjö. The forest seemed to go on forever. Everywhere was the same mood of silent detachment he had experienced inside himself. He stopped in Nybro for a meal. Although he would have preferred to forget all that had happened to him, he forced himself to call Kalmar and find out if the African had been traced yet. There was still no sign of him. He got back in the car and kept on driving through the endless forest. He got as far as Växjö and hesitated whether to take the Älmhult route or to go via Tingsryd. In the end he chose Tingsryd so that he could at least start heading southwards.

He had passed through Tingsryd and turned off towards Ronneby when a moose loomed up on the road in the gathering dusk. For one desperate moment, with the brakes screeching in his ears, he was convinced he had reacted too late. He would run smack into the enormous bull moose, and his safety belt was not even fastened. But all of a sudden the moose shied away, and without knowing how, Wallander shot past and did not even touch it.

He stopped at the side of the road and sat there, his heart beating madly, his breath coming in gasps, feeling ill. When he had calmed down he got out of the car and stood motionless in the silent forest. A hair's breadth from death yet again, he thought. I can't have any get-out-of-jail-free cards left. He wondered why he did not feel jubilant at having been miraculously saved from being crushed by the bull moose. What he did feel was more like a vague guilty conscience. The bottomless depression that had taken possession of him that morning returned. What he most wanted was to leave the car where it was, walk into the forest and disappear without trace. Not to disappear for ever, but for long enough to recover his equilibrium, to fight off the dizziness that had taken hold of him as a result of all he had been through these last weeks. But he got back into the car and kept on driving, now with his safety belt fastened. He came to the main road to Kristianstad, and turned off to the west. He stopped at an all-night café and ordered a cup of coffee. Some long-distance lorry drivers were sitting in silence at a table and a group of youths were whooping it up around a games machine. Wallander did not touch his coffee until it was cold, but he did drink it in the end, and went back to his car.

Shortly before midnight he turned into the yard outside his father's house. Linda came out onto the steps to greet him. He smiled wearily and said everything was fine. Then he asked if there had been a telephone call from Kalmar. She shook her head. The only calls had been from journalists who had found out her grandfather's telephone number.

"Your flat has been repaired already," she said. "You can move back in."

"That's great," he said.

He wondered if he ought to call Kalmar, but he was too tired. Tomorrow would do.

They sat up late, talking. But Wallander said nothing about the feeling of melancholy weighing down on him. For the moment, that was something he wanted to keep to himself.

Tsiki took the express bus from Kalmar to Stockholm. He got to Stockholm just after 4 p.m. His flight to London would leave at 7 p.m. He looked everywhere but could not find the airport bus, so he took a taxi to Arlanda. The driver was suspicious of foreigners and demanded the fare in advance. He had handed over a 1,000 kronor note and settled down in the corner behind the driver. Tsiki had no idea that every emigration officer in Sweden was on the lookout for him. All he knew was that he should leave the country as a Swedish citizen, Leif Larson, a name he had very quickly learned to pronounce. He was completely calm, as he trusted Konovalenko. His taxi had taken him over the bridge, and he could see something had happened, but he did not doubt that Konovalenko had disposed of the man who had turned up in the garden that morning.

Tsiki took his change when they got to Arlanda, shaking his head when asked if he wanted a receipt. He went into the departure hall, checked in, and stopped to buy some English newspapers on the way to passport control.

If he had not stopped at the newspaper stand, he would have been arrested at passport control. But during those very minutes he took choosing and paying for his newspapers, the passport officers changed shifts. One of the new ones went to the toilet. The other, Kerstin Anderson, had arrived for work at Arlanda very late. Her car wouldn't start and she turned up at the last moment. She was conscientious and ambitious and would normally have been early enough to read through all the notices that had arrived that day, lists of people to look out for, as well as the lists still current from previous days. As it was, she had no time to do so, and Tsiki went through passport control with his Swedish passport and smiling face, no problem. The door closed behind him just as Kerstin Anderson's colleague came back from the toilet.

"Is there anything special to look out for this evening?" Kerstin Anderson said.

"A black South African," her colleague said.

Kerstin remembered the African who had just gone through. But he was Swedish. It was 10 p.m. before the supervising officer checked with the officers to make sure that all was in order.

"Don't forget the African," he said. "We have no idea what he's called, or what passport he'll be travelling on."

Kerstin Anderson could feel a sudden tightening of her stomach. "He was a South African, surely?" she said.

"Presumably," the supervisor said. "But that won't tell us what nationality he'll claim when he leaves Sweden." She told him immediately what had happened a few hours earlier. After some hectic activity, they established that the man with the Swedish passport had taken the British Airways flight to London at 7 p.m.

The aeroplane had taken off on time. It had already landed in London, and the passengers had been through customs. Tsiki had used his time in London to tear his Swedish passport into small pieces and flush it down a lavatory. Now he was a Zambian citizen, Richard Motombwane. Since he was in transit, he had not been through passport control with either his Swedish or his Zambian passport. Moreover, he had two separate tickets. He had no check-in baggage, so the girl in Sweden had only seen his ticket to London. At the transit desk in Heathrow he showed his ticket to Lusaka. He had left the first ticket and the boarding card on the plane from Stockholm.

At 11.30 p.m. the Zambia Airways DC-10 Nkowazi took off for Lusaka. Tsiki arrived there at 6.30 on Saturday morning. He took a taxi into town and paid for a South African Airways ticket for the afternoon flight to Johannesburg. It had been booked some days earlier. This time he used his own name. He returned to the airport, checked in, and had lunch in the departure hall restaurant. He boarded at 3 p.m., and shortly before 5 p.m. his plane landed at Jan Smuts Airport outside Johannesburg. He was met by Malan, who drove him straight to Hammanskraal. He showed Tsiki the deposit receipt for the half-million rand which constituted the second to last part of the payment. Then he left him on his own, saying he would be back the next day. Meanwhile, Tsiki was not to leave the house and compound. When Tsiki was alone, he took a bath. He was tired, but contented. The journey had passed without problems. The only thing that concerned him was what had happened to Konovalenko. He was, strangely, less curious about the identity of the person he was being paid so much to shoot. Could any individual be worth so much money, he asked himself. But before midnight he had settled down between cool sheets and fallen asleep.

On the morning of Saturday, May 23, two things happened more or less simultaneously. Kleyn was set free in Johannesburg. Scheepers told him that he could expect to be called in for further questioning.

He stood by a window, watching Kleyn and the lawyer Kritzinger making their way to a car. Scheepers had asked for him to be watched around the clock. He took it for granted Kleyn was expecting that, but thought it would at least force him to be passive.

He had managed to extract no information from Kleyn that gave concrete weight to the suspicions surrounding the Committee, but Scheepers now felt certain that the real scene of the assassination was to be Durban on July 3, and not Cape Town on June 12. Every time he had come back to the notebook Kleyn displayed signs of nervousness, and Scheepers did not believe it was possible for anybody to fake reactions such as sweating and shaking hands.

At about the same time as Kleyn was getting into his lawyer's car, Kurt Wallander arrived at the Ystad police station. He received the congratulations and good wishes of those colleagues who were at work that Saturday morning. He smiled his lopsided smile and mumbled something inaudible in response. When he got to his office he closed the door. His whole body felt like he had been raving drunk the night before. He had feelings of remorse. His hands were shaking. He was sweating. It took him nearly ten minutes to summon the strength to call the Kalmar police. Blomstrand passed on the disappointing news that the African they were looking for had almost certainly left the country the night before, from Arlanda.

"How is that possible?" Wallander said, indignantly.

"Carelessness and bad luck," Blomstrand said, explaining what had happened.

"Why the hell do we bother?" Wallander said.

When their conversation was over, he left the receiver off the hook. He opened the window and stood listening to a bird singing in a tree outside. It was going to be a hot day. It would soon be June. The whole month of May had passed without him really noticing that the trees were in leaf and flowers were starting to grow. The scents of early summer were in the air.

He went back to his desk. There was something he could not postpone until the following week. He fed a sheet of paper into his typewriter, took down his English dictionary, and started slowly to write a report for his unknown colleagues in South Africa. He set out what he knew about the planned assassination and described in detail what had happened to Victor Mabasha. When he got to the end of Mabasha's life, he inserted another sheet of paper into the typewriter. He continued typing for an hour, and finished with the most important information: that a man by the name of Sikosi Tsiki was Mabasha's replacement. Most regrettably he had managed to slip out of Sweden. It could be assumed that he was on his way back to South Africa. He gave his name, found the telex number to the Swedish section of Interpol, and invited them to get in touch with him if they needed any more information. He gave the secretary instructions to send it urgently to South Africa.

Then he went home. He crossed the threshold again for the first time since the explosion. He felt like a stranger in his own flat. The furniture that had been damaged by the smoke was covered by plastic sheeting. He pulled a chair out, and sat down. The atmosphere was stifling.

He wondered how he was going to come to terms with everything that had happened.

*

At about this time his telex arrived in Stockholm. A temp., not fully familiar with procedures, was instructed to send the message to South Africa. Because of technical problems and careless checking, the second page of Wallander's report was never sent. And so the South African police were informed that night, May 23, that a hitman by the name of Victor Mabasha was on his way to South Africa. The police in the Johannesburg section of Interpol were puzzled by this message. It was unsigned, and was obviously written by someone for whom English was not their first language, and perhaps that explained why the message ended as it did. Nevertheless, they had been requested by Inspector Borstlap to send all telex messages from Sweden to his office. As the telex arrived late on Saturday, Borstlap did not receive it until Monday morning. He called Scheepers immediately.

They now had confirmation of what was in the letter signed by the secretive Steve. The man they were looking for was called Victor Mabasha. Scheepers, too, thought that the telex was oddly abrupt and was concerned that it was unsigned. But since it was merely a confirmation of something he already knew about, he let the matter rest.

From now on all resources were concentrated on the hunt for Victor Mabasha. Every border post was put on standby. They were ready.

CHAPTER THIRTY-THREE

The day he was released, Kleyn called Malan from his house in Pretoria. He had to assume his telephones were tapped, but he had another line nobody knew about, apart from the NIS special intelligence officers in charge of security-sensitive communications centres throughout South Africa. There were several telephone lines that did not exist officially.

Malan was surprised. He did not know Kleyn had been released. As there was every reason to suspect Malan's telephone also was tapped, Kleyn used an agreed code word to prevent Malan from saying anything that should not be mentioned on the telephone. The call was camouflaged as a wrong number. Kleyn asked for Horst, then apologised and rang off. Malan looked up his special code list to check the meaning. Two hours after the call, he was to make contact from a specified public phone box to another one.

Kleyn was eager to find out what had been happening while he was under arrest. Malan must also be clear that he would continue to take main responsibility. Kleyn did not doubt his ability to shake off shadows. Even so it was too risky for him to make personal contact with Malan or to visit Hammanskraal, where Tsiki presumably already was or shortly would be.

It took Kleyn very few minutes to locate the car tailing him. He knew there would also be another car in front, but he did not worry about that for the moment. They would be curious when he stopped to make a call from a phone box. It would be reported, but they would never find out what was said.

Kleyn was surprised that Tsiki had arrived already. He was also wondering why there was no word from Konovalenko. In their plan was an agreement to inform Konovalenko that Tsiki had indeed arrived. That check should be no later than three hours after the assumed arrival time. Kleyn gave Malan some brief instructions. They also agreed to call from two other phone boxes the next day. Kleyn tried to detect whether Malan seemed especially anxious. But he could hear nothing beyond Malan's usual slightly nervous way of expressing himself.

He went to have lunch at one of the most expensive restaurants in Pretoria. He was pleased at the thought of the reaction when his shadow handed his expenses to Scheepers. He could see the man at a table at the far end of the dining room. Kleyn had already decided that Scheepers was unworthy of continuing to live in a South Africa which, within a year or so, would be well organised and faithful to its old ideals, created and then defended forever by a close community of Boers.

There were moments when Kleyn was assailed by the awful thought that the whole plan was doomed, yet that there was, after all, no turning back. But he soon recovered his self-control. It was just a moment of weakness, he told himself. I've allowed myself to be influenced by the negative approach South Africans of British origin have towards us *boere*. They know the real soul of the country is to be found in us, not in them, so they cherish this unholy envy.

He paid for his meal, smiled as he passed the table where his shadow was sitting, a small, overweight man sweating profusely. As he drove home he could see that he had a new shadow. When he had put his car away in the garage, he continued his methodical analysis of who could possibly have betrayed him and provided Scheepers with information.

He poured himself a little glass of port and sat down in the living room. He drew the curtains and switched off all the lights apart from a discreet lamp illuminating a painting. He always thought best in a dimly lit room.

The hours he had spent with Scheepers had made him hate the current regime more than ever. It was an intolerable humiliation for him, a superior, trusted, and loyal civil servant in the intelligence service, to be arrested under suspicion of subversive activities. What he was doing was the exact opposite of that. If it were not for what he and the Committee were doing in secret, the risk of national collapse would be real rather than imaginary. As he sipped his port, he no longer regarded the death of Mandela as an assassination, but as an execution in accordance with the unwritten constitution he represented.

There was another element that added to his irritation. It was clear to him from the moment that his trusted security guard on the President's personal staff called him, that somebody must have supplied Scheepers with information it should have been impossible for him to obtain. Someone close to Kleyn had betrayed him. He had to find out who it was, and quickly. What worried him was that Malan could not be excluded. Not he, nor any member of the Committee. Apart from these men there could possibly be two, or at most three, colleagues in NIS who could have decided, for whatever reason, to sell him down the river.

He sat in the darkness thinking about each of these men in turn, dredging his memory for clues. But he found none.

He worked from a process of intuition, facts and elimination. He asked himself who had anything to gain by exposing him, who disliked him so much that revenge could be worth the risk of being found out. He reduced the group of possibilities from 16 to eight, then started all over again, and each time there were fewer possible solutions. In the end, there was nobody. His question remained unanswered.

It was then he thought for the first time that perhaps it was Miranda. Only when there was no other possible culprit was he forced to accept that she too was a possibility. The very idea appalled him. It was impossible. Nevertheless, the suspicion was there, and he had no choice but to confront her with it. As he was certain she could not lie to him without his noticing, it would be resolved the moment he spoke to her. He must shake off his shadows within the next few days and visit her and Matilda in Bezuidenhout.

He put both his thoughts and his papers on one side, and devoted himself instead to his coins. Studying the beauty of the various coins and imagining their value always gave him a feeling of calm. He picked up an old, shiny, gold coin. It was an early Kruger rand, and had the same kind of timeless durability as the Afrikaner traditions. He held it up to the desk lamp and saw that it had acquired a small, almost invisible stain. He took out his neatly folded polishing cloth and rubbed the golden surface until the coin shone again.

He visited Miranda and Matilda in Bezuidenhout on Wednesday afternoon. As he did not want his shadows to follow him even as far as

Johannesburg, he had decided to lose them while he was still in central Pretoria. A few simple manoeuvres were sufficient to shake off Scheepers's men. All the same, he kept a close eye on the rear-view mirror on the highway to Johannesburg. He also did a few circuits of the business centre, just to be sure he was not mistaken, before he turned into the streets that would take him to Bezuidenhout.

It was very unusual for him to visit them in the middle of the week, nor had he given them advance notice. It would be a surprise. Just before he got there, he stopped at a grocer's and bought food for dinner. It was about 5.30 p.m. by the time he turned into the street.

At first he thought his eyes were deceiving him. But it was so. He saw that the man on the pavement had come out of Miranda and Matilda's security gate. A black man.

He drew up at the curb and watched the man walking towards him on the other side of the road. He lowered the sun visor on each side of the windscreen so that he would not be recognised.

He knew who he was. It was a man he had been keeping under observation a long time. Although they had never managed to prove it, NIS were certain he belonged to a group in the most radical faction of the ANC, thought to be behind a number of bomb attacks on shops and restaurants. He used the aliases of Martin, Steve and Richard.

Kleyn watched the man walk past. His mind was in turmoil, and it took some time to recover. But there was no getting away from it: the suspicions he had refused to take seriously were now real. When he eliminated one after the other of his suspects and ended up with none at all, he had been on the right track. The only other possibility was Miranda. It was both true and inconceivable at the same time. For a moment he was overwhelmed by sorrow. Then he turned ice-cold. The temperature inside him fell as his fury grew, or so it seemed. In the twinkling of an eye, love turned to hate. It was aimed at Miranda, not Matilda: he regarded her as innocent, a second victim of her mother's treachery. He gripped the wheel tightly. He controlled his urge to drive up to the house, beat down the door, and look Miranda in the eye for the last time. He would not approach the house until he was utterly calm. Uncontrolled anger was a sign of weakness. That was something he had no desire to display in front of Miranda or her daughter.

Kleyn could not understand. What he did not understand angered him. He had dedicated his life to the fight against disorder. For him disorder included everything that was unclear. What he did not understand must be fought against, just as all other causes of society's increasing confusion and decay must be defeated.

He remained in his car for a long time. Darkness had fallen before he drove up to the security gates. He noticed a movement behind the curtains in the big living room window and then the gates swung open. He drove in and picked up the bags of supplies.

He smiled at her when she opened the door. There were moments, so short that he barely managed to notice them, when he wished it were all in the imagination. But now he knew what was true, and he needed to know what lay behind it.

The darkness inside made it difficult to read her expression.

"I thought I'd surprise you," he said.

"You've never done this before," she said.

It seemed to him her voice was rough and strange. He wished he could see her more clearly. Did she guess that he had seen the man leaving the house?

At that moment Matilda came out of her room. She looked at him without saying a word. She knows, he thought. She knows her mother has betrayed me. How will she be able to protect her except by staying silent?

He put down the bags of food and took off his jacket.

"I want you to leave," Miranda said.

He must have misheard her. He turned, his jacket still in his hand. "Are you asking me to go?"

"Yes."

He contemplated his jacket for a moment before letting it drop to the floor. Then he hit her, as hard as he could, right in the face. She lost her balance but not her consciousness. Before she could manage to scramble up off the floor, he took hold of her blouse and dragged her to her feet.

"You are asking me to leave," he said, breathing heavily. "If anybody is going to leave, it's you. But you aren't going anywhere."

He dragged her into the living room and flung her onto the sofa. Matilda moved to help her mother, but he shouted at her to stay back.

411

He sat down on a chair right in front of her. The darkness in the room suddenly made him furious. He leapt to his feet and switched on every light he could find. Then he saw she was bleeding from both her nose and her mouth. He sat down again and stared at her.

"A man came out of your house," he said. "A black man. What was he doing here?"

She did not answer. She was not even looking at him. Nor did she pay any attention to the blood dripping from her face.

It was a waste of time. Whatever she said or did, she had betrayed him. There was no going on. He did not know what he would do with her. He could not imagine a form of revenge that was harsh enough. He looked at Matilda. She still had not moved. Her face bore an expression he had never seen before. He could not say what it was. That made him insecure as well. Then he saw Miranda was looking at him.

"I want you to go now," she said. "And I don't want you ever to come and visit me again. This is your house. You can stay, and we'll move out."

She's challenging me, he thought. How dare she? He felt his rage rising again. He forced himself not to beat her again.

"No-one's leaving," he said. "But you will tell me what's going on."

"What do you want to know?"

"Who you've talked to. About me. What you've said. And why."

She looked him straight in the eye. The blood under her nose and on her chin had already congealed. "I've told them what I found in your pockets whenever you were sleeping here. I listened to what you said in your sleep, and I wrote it down. Maybe it was insignificant, but I hope it ruins you."

She spoke in that strange, rough voice. He realised that was her normal voice, and that the one she had used all those years had been a sham. Everything had been a sham.

"Where would you have been without me?" he said.

"Maybe dead," she said. "But maybe I'd have been happy."

"You'd have been living in the slums."

"Maybe we'd have helped to pull them down."

"You leave my daughter out of this."

"You are the father of my daughter, Jan Kleyn, but you do not have a child. You have nothing but your own ruin."

There was an ashtray on the table between them. Now that words were beyond him he grabbed it and flung it with all his might at her head. She managed to duck. The ashtray bounced onto the sofa beside her. He leapt up from his chair, shoved the table aside, took hold of the ashtray and held it over her head. At the same moment he heard a hissing noise, as if from an animal. He looked at Matilda, who had moved towards him. She was hissing through clenched teeth. He could not make out what she was saying, but he could see she had a gun in her hand.

Then she fired. He was hit in the chest and lived only for a minute after collapsing to the ground. They stood above him looking down, and he could see them although his vision was fading. He tried to say something, tried to hold on to his life as it ebbed away. But there was nothing to hold. There was nothing.

Miranda felt no relief, but neither did she feel fear. She looked at her daughter, who had turned her back on the corpse. Miranda took the pistol from her hand. Then she went to call the man who had been to see them, the one called Scheepers. She had looked for his number earlier, and written it down beside the telephone. Now she realised why she had done that.

A woman answered, giving her name as Judith. She called out to her husband, who came straightaway to the telephone. He said he would come at once to Bezuidenhout and asked her to do nothing until he got there.

He told Judith that dinner would have to be late, but he did not say why, and she suppressed her wish to ask. His special assignment would soon be over, he had explained. Then everything would return to normal, and they could go back to the Kruger and see if the white lioness was still there, and if they were still scared of her. He called Borstlap, trying various numbers before tracking him down. He gave him the address, but asked him not to go in before he got there himself.

When he arrived in Bezuidenhout, Borstlap was standing waiting by his car. Miranda opened the door to them and he saw with shock the bruises on her face. Before they went into the living room, Scheepers put his hand on Borstlap's shoulder. "The man lying dead in there is Kleyn," he said. Borstlap turned and stared at him in frank astonishment.

It was striking how pale he looked, and how thin his face seemed to be. It was almost skeletal. Scheepers tried to make up his mind whether what he was witnessing was the end of an evil story or of a tragic one.

"He hit me," Miranda said. "I shot him."

As she said that, Scheepers happened to be looking at the daughter. He could tell she was shaken to hear what her mother had said. She was the one who had killed him, had shot her father. He could see from her bloodstained face that Miranda had been beaten. Did Kleyn have time to realise what was happening? That he was going to die, and it was his daughter who was holding the gun.

He said nothing, but indicated to Borstlap that he should accompany him to the kitchen. He shut the door behind them.

"I don't care how you do it," he said, "but I want you to get that body out of here and make it look like a suicide. Kleyn has been arrested and interrogated. That hurt his pride. He salvaged his honour by committing suicide. That will do for a motive. Covering up incidents involving the intelligence service doesn't seem to be all that difficult. I'd like you to take care of this right now."

"I'll be putting my job on the line," Borstlap said.

"I give you my word that you're not risking anything at all."

Borstlap stared at him for what seemed like an eternity.

"Who are these women?" he said.

"People you've never met," Scheepers said.

"Of course, it's all about the security of South Africa," Borstlap said, and Scheepers appreciated his weary irony.

"Yes," he said. "Exactly so."

"That's another lie. Our country is a production line for lies, 24 hours a day. What'll happen when the whole thing collapses?"

"Why are we trying to prevent an assassination?" Scheepers said.

Borstlap nodded slowly. "OK, I'll do it," he said.

"On your own."

"Nobody will see me. I'll leave the body somewhere in the countryside. And I'll make sure I'm in charge of the investigation."

"I'll tell them," Scheepers said. "They'll open the gates for you when you come back."

Borstlap left the house.

Miranda had put a blanket over Kleyn's body. Scheepers suddenly felt tired of all the lies, lies that were partly in him too.

"I know it was your daughter who shot him," he said. "But that doesn't matter. Not as far as I'm concerned, at least. If it matters to you, I'm afraid that's something you'll have to deal with yourselves. But the body will disappear later tonight. The officer who came here with me will come back and take it away. He's going to arrange it as suicide. Nobody will find out what really happened."

Scheepers thought he saw a gleam of surprised gratitude in Miranda's eyes.

"In a sense, maybe it was suicide," he said. "A man who lives like him maybe shouldn't expect anything else."

"I can't even cry over him," Miranda said. "There's nothing there."

"I hated him," Matilda said. Scheepers could see she was crying.

Killing a human being, he thought. However much you hate somebody, no matter how desperate you were, there will be a wound in your soul that will never heal. He was her father, the father she didn't choose and couldn't escape.

He did not stay. He could see that they needed each other more than anything else. But when Miranda asked him to return, he promised to do so.

"We will move out," she said.

"Where to?"

She threw her arms wide. "That's something I can't decide alone. Maybe it's best if Matilda decides?"

Scheepers drove home for dinner. He was thoughtful and distant.

"It'll be over soon," he said.

Borstlap called just before midnight.

"I thought I'd better tell you Kleyn has committed suicide," he said. "They'll find him – probably not before tomorrow morning – in a car park between here and Pretoria."

Who is the strong man now? Scheepers wondered. Who will direct the Committee now?

Inspector Borstlap lived in the suburb of Kensington, one of the oldest in Johannesburg. His wife was a nurse on permanent night duty at the big army camp in town. As their three children had left the nest,

Borstlap spent most weekday evenings alone in the house. He was generally so tired when he came home from work, he did not have the strength to do anything but watch television. He sometimes went down to a little hobby room he had made for himself in the basement. He cut out silhouettes. It was an art he had learned from his father, although he had never managed to be as skilful as he was. But it was a restful occupation, carefully but boldly cutting out faces in black paper. That particular evening, when he had driven Kleyn in his own car to the car park he knew about because there had been a murder there not long ago, he found it impossible to relax when he got home. He was going to cut out silhouettes of his children, but he was also thinking about the work he had been doing these last few days with Scheepers. He had enjoyed working with the young lawyer. He was intelligent and energetic, and he had imagination to boot. He listened to what others had to say, and he did not hesitate to admit it when he was wrong. But Borstlap wondered what his assignment really was. It was something serious, a conspiracy, a threatened assassination of Mandela that had to be prevented. But apart from that, his knowledge was pretty scanty. He suspected there was a gigantic conspiracy, but the only one he knew was involved was Kleyn. He thought he was taking part in an investigation with a blindfold on. He said as much to Scheepers, who told him he understood, but that there was nothing he could do to help. His hands were tied by the need for secrecy his work demanded.

When the telex message from Sweden had landed on his desk that Monday morning, Scheepers had gone into high gear. After a couple of hours they tracked down Mabasha in the register and he felt the tension increase when it was established that he had been suspected of being a contract killer. He had never been convicted. Reading between the lines of the case histories, it was plain that he was highly intelligent and always went about his business with skilful camouflage and security arrangements. His most recent known address was the township of Ntibane just outside Umtata. Borstlap had contacted his colleagues in Umtata without delay, and they confirmed that they kept an eye on Mabasha all the time. The same afternoon Scheepers and Borstlap drove there. With local detectives they raided Mabasha's shack at dawn. It was empty. Scheepers had trouble concealing his disappointment. They agreed that the official reason for the manhunt, should be that Mabasha was wanted for violent attacks on white women in the province of Transkei. Strong warnings were issued that no word of this was to reach any of the media. There were teams working around the clock now, but still they failed to find any trace of the man. And now Kleyn was dead.

Borstlap yawned, put down his scissors and stretched. They would have to start all over again, he thought. But there was still time, whether the crucial date was June 12 or July 3. Borstlap was not as convinced as Scheepers that the evidence pointing to Cape Town was a red herring. It seemed to him he ought to act as devil's advocate with regard to Scheepers's conclusions, and keep a close eye himself on the trail leading to Cape Town.

On Thursday, May 28, Borstlap met Scheepers at 8 a.m.

"Kleyn's body was found at 6 this morning," Borstlap said. "A motorist stopped to take a leak. He informed the police right away. I spoke to a patrol car that was first on the scene. They said it was obviously a suicide."

Scheepers could see that he had made a good choice when he had asked for Inspector Borstlap as his assistant.

"There are two weeks to go before June 12," he said. "Just over a month to July 3. In other words, we still have time to track down Victor Mabasha. I'm not a policeman, but I would think that gives us long enough."

"It depends," Borstlap said. "Mabasha is an experienced criminal. He can remain hidden for long periods. He could disappear into some township or other, and we might never find him."

"We have no choice," Scheepers said. "Don't forget that the authority I've been given means that I can call up almost unlimited resources."

"That's not the way to find him," Borstlap said. "You could get the army to besiege Soweto and then send in paratroops, but you'd still never find him. On the other hand, you'd have a revolt to deal with."

"What would you do?"

"Me? I would put it about that there was a reward of 50,000 rand. A similarly discreet message to the underworld that we'd be prepared to pay for information enabling us to nail Mabasha. That'll give us a sporting chance of tracking him down."

Scheepers eyed him doubtfully. "Is that how the police go about their business?"

"Not often. But it happens, sometimes."

"Well, you're the one who knows about these things," Scheepers said. "I'll take care of the money."

"The word will be out tonight."

Scheepers turned his attention to Durban. They should take a look at the stadium where Mandela would address a large crowd. They must find out what security measures the police were taking. They needed a strategy for how to proceed if they did not manage to find Mabasha.

Borstlap was worried that Scheepers was not taking the other alternative as seriously as Durban. He said nothing, but made up his mind to get in touch with a colleague in Cape Town and ask him to do some legwork. That same day Borstlap contacted some of the informers he regularly received more or less useful rumours from. Fifty thousand rand was a lot of cash. The hunt for Mabasha had now begun in earnest.

CHAPTER THIRTY-FOUR

Chief Inspector Wallander was sent on sick leave with immediate effect on Wednesday, June 10. According to the doctor, who regarded Wallander as taciturn and very uptight, he was vague, and not sure exactly what was pestering him. He talked about nightmares, insomnia, stomach pains, nocturnal panic attacks when he thought his heart was about to stop beating – in other words, all the symptoms of stress that could easily lead to a breakdown. At this point, Wallander was seeing the doctor every other day. His symptoms varied, and on each visit he had a different opinion as to which ones were worst. He had also had bouts of violent sobbing. The doctor, who finally ordered him to take sick leave on the grounds of acute depression, and prescribed anti-depressants for him, did not doubt the seriousness of the situation. Within a short space of time he had killed one human being and actively contributed to another being burned alive. Nor could he wash his hands of responsibility for the woman who died while helping his daughter to escape. But most of all he felt guilty about the death of Victor Mabasha. It was natural that the reaction should set in with the death of Konovalenko. There was no longer anyone to chase, and no-one hunting him. Paradoxically, the onset of depression indicated that the pressure on Wallander had eased. Now that he would have the time to set his own house in order, his melancholy broke through all the barriers he had so far managed to erect. After a few months, some of his colleagues began to doubt whether he would ever return. Occasionally, when news reached the police station of his peculiar journeys to places near and far, to Denmark, to the Caribbean islands, there were those who thought he ought to be granted early retirement. The very thought caused much gloom. But, in fact, it did not happen. He did come back, even though it took a long time.

The day after he had been ordered to take sick leave was a hot, windless day in southern Skåne, and Wallander was sitting in his office. He still had some paperwork to attend to before he could clear his desk and go in search of a cure for his depression. He felt a nagging sense of uncertainty, and wondered when he would be fit to return to work.

He had arrived at the police station at 6 a.m., after a sleepless night at home. Through the silent hours of the morning he had at last completed his detailed report on the murder of Louise Åkerblom and everything that followed in its wake. He read through what he had written, and it was like descending into an underworld again, repeating a journey he wished he had never made. Moreover, he was about to submit a report that was in some respects untruthful. It was a mystery to him why some parts of his strange disappearance and his secret collaboration with Mabasha had not been exposed. His extremely feeble, and in some particulars contradictory, explanations of some of his remarkable behaviour had not, as he had expected, aroused widespread scepticism. He could only think it was because he was surrounded by sympathy mixed with a rather vague *esprit de corps*, because he had killed a man in the line of duty.

He put the fat report on his desk and opened the window wide. Somewhere he could hear a child laughing.

What about my own report? he thought. I found myself in a situation where I had no control over what happened. I made every mistake a police officer can make, and the worst of all was that I put my own daughter's life at risk. She has assured me she doesn't blame me for those horrific days when she was chained up in a cellar, but do I really have any right to believe her? Have I not caused her suffering which might come to the surface at some time in the future, in the form of angst, nightmares, a ruined life? That's where my report has to begin, the one I'll never write. The one which ends today with my being so shattered that a doctor has put me on indefinite sick leave.

He went back to his desk and flopped down onto his chair. He had not slept a wink all night, it was true, but his weariness came from somewhere else, from the depths of his depression. Could it be that his fatigue was in fact clinical depression? He thought about what would happen to him now. The doctor had suggested he should immediately start confronting his experiences through counselling. Wallander had taken that as an order that had to be obeyed. But what would he actually be able to say?

In front of him was an invitation to his father's wedding. He did not know how many times he had studied it since it arrived in the post a few days ago. His father was going to marry his home help the day before Midsummer Eve. In ten days' time. He had talked several times to his sister, Kristina, who had come on a short visit and thought she had managed to put an end to the whole idea. Now Wallander had no more doubts about whether or not it would happen. Nor could he deny that his father was in a much better mood than he could ever remember. He had painted the gigantic backdrop in the studio, where the ceremony was to take place. It was exactly the same scene that he had been painting all his life: the static, romantic woodland landscape. The only difference was that he had now reproduced it giant-sized. Wallander, too, had talked with Gertrud, the woman he was going to marry. Actually it was she who had wanted to talk to him, and he recognised that she had a genuine affection for his father. He had felt quite touched, and said he was happy about what was going to happen.

Linda had gone back to Stockholm a week earlier. She would return for the wedding, and then go straight to Italy. That had brought home to Wallander the frightening realisation of his own solitude. Wherever he turned, things seemed to be just as bleak. After Konovalenko's death he had taken the car back to Widén and drank nearly all his whisky. He got very drunk, and started talking about the feeling of hopelessness that was dragging him down. He thought it was something he shared with Widén, even if his old friend had his stable girls to go to bed with occasionally, thereby creating a superficial glimmer of what might be called companionship. Wallander hoped the renewed contact with Widén would turn out to be lasting. He had no illusions about their being able to revive the friendship they had shared in their youth. That was gone forever.

His train of thought was interrupted by a knock at the door. He jumped. He had noticed last week at the police station that he was scared of being with people. The door opened and Svedberg looked in, hoping he wasn't disturbing him.

"I hear you're going away for a while," he said.

Wallander immediately felt a lump in his throat.

"It seems to be necessary," he said, blowing his nose.

Svedberg, seeing he was emotional, changed the subject.

"Do you remember those handcuffs you found in a drawer at Åkerblom's house?" he said. "You mentioned them once in passing. Do you remember?"

Wallander nodded. To him, the handcuffs had come to represent the mysterious side of everybody's character. Only the day before, he had been wondering what his own hidden handcuffs were.

"I was clearing out a cupboard at home yesterday," Svedberg said. "There were lots of old magazines I'd decided to get rid of. But you know how it is. I ended up sitting down and reading them. I happened to come across an article about variety performers over the last 30 years. There was a picture of an escape artist, and he'd used the fanciful professional name of Houdini's Son. His real name was Davidsson, and he eventually gave up wriggling out of chains and metal boxes and the like. Do you know why he stopped?"

Wallander shook his head.

"He saw the light. He became a born-again Christian. Guess which denomination he joined."

"The Methodists."

"Exactly. I read the whole article. At the end it said he was happily married and had several children. Among them a daughter called Louise. Née Davidsson, later married to a man called Åkerblom."

"The handcuffs," Wallander said. "Good grief!"

"A souvenir of her father," Svedberg said. "As simple as that. I don't know what you thought. I have to admit a few thoughts I wouldn't repeat in front of children entered my head."

"Mine, too," Wallander said.

Svedberg got up. He paused in the doorway and turned round.

"There was one other thing," he said. "Do you remember Peter Hanson?"

"The thief?"

"Yes. You may remember that I asked him to keep his eyes open in case the things stolen from your flat turned up on the market. He called me yesterday. Most of your stuff has been disposed of, I guess. You'll never see it again. But oddly enough he managed to get hold of a CD he claims is yours."

"Did he say which one it was?"

"I wrote it down."

Svedberg searched through his pockets and eventually came across a crumpled scrap of paper.

"*Rigoletto*," he read. "Verdi."

Wallander smiled. "I've missed that," he said. "Send my regards to Peter Hanson, and thank him."

"He's a thief," Svedberg said. "You don't thank creeps like that." He left the room with a laugh. Wallander started going through the remaining stacks of paper. It was nearly 11 a.m. by now, and he wanted to be finished by noon.

The telephone rang. At first he thought he would ignore it. Then he picked it up.

"There's a gentleman here who wants to talk with Chief Inspector Wallander," said a voice he did not recognise. He assumed it was the temp for Ebba, who was on leave.

"Put him through to somebody else," Wallander said. "I'm not receiving visitors."

"He's adamant he wants to talk with Chief Inspector Wallander," the receptionist said. "He says he has important information for you. He's Danish."

"Danish?" Wallander said in surprise. "What's it about?"

"He says it has to do with an African."

Wallander thought for a moment. "Send him along," he said.

The man who came into Wallander's office introduced himself as Paul Jørgensen, a fisherman, from Dragør. He was tall and big. When Wallander shook hands with him, it was like being gripped by an iron claw. He pointed to a chair. Jørgensen sat down and lit a cigar. Wallander was glad the window was open. He hunted in his drawers before finding an ashtray.

"I have something to tell you," Jørgensen said. "But I haven't yet made up my mind whether I'm going to or not."

Wallander raised his eyebrows. "You should have made your mind up before coming here," he said. In normal circumstances he would probably have been annoyed. Now he could hear that his voice was far from convincing.

"It depends whether you can overlook a minor breach of the law," Jørgensen said.

Wallander began to wonder whether the man was making a fool of him. If so, he had chosen a most unfortunate moment. He could see he had better get a grip on the conversation, which looked like it was going off course almost before it had begun.

"I was told you had something important to tell me about an African," he said. "If it really is important, I might be able to overlook any minor breach of the law. But I can't promise anything. You must make up your own mind. I have to ask you to do so right now, though."

Jørgensen screwed up his eyes and gazed at him from behind a cloud of smoke.

"I'll risk it," he said.

"I'm listening."

"I'm a fisherman on Dragør," Jørgensen said. "I make just about enough to pay for the boat, the house, and a beer in the evenings. But nobody turns down the chance for some extra income, if the opportunity arises. I take tourists out for little sea trips now and then, and that produces some pocket money. Sometimes I'm asked to take somebody over to Sweden. That doesn't happen often, maybe once or twice a year. It could be passengers who have missed a ferry, for instance. A few weeks ago I did a trip over to Limhamn one afternoon. One passenger on board."

He stopped, as if expecting a reaction. But Wallander had nothing to say. He nodded to Jørgensen, telling him to go on.

"It was a black man," Jørgensen said. "He only spoke English. Very polite. He stood in the wheelhouse with me all the way. Maybe I should mention there was something special about this trip. It had been booked in advance. There was this Englishman who spoke Danish, and he came down to the harbour one morning and asked if I could do a trip over the sound, with a passenger. I thought it sounded a bit suspicious, so I asked a pretty high fee in order to get rid of him. I asked for 5,000 kronor. The funny thing was, he took out the money right away and paid in advance."

Wallander was extremely interested by this. Just for a moment he forgot all about himself and concentrated on what Jørgensen had to say.

"I went to sea as a young man," Jørgensen said. "I learned quite a bit of English. I asked the guy what he was going to do in Sweden. He said he was going to visit some friends. I asked how long he'd be staying, and he said he'd probably be going back to Africa in a month, at the latest. I suspected there was something fishy going on. He was probably trying to get into Sweden illegally. Since it's not possible to prove anything now that happened so long ago, I'm taking the risk of telling you."

Wallander raised his hand. "Let's dig a little deeper," he said. "What day was this?"

Jørgensen leaned forward and studied Wallander's desk diary.

"Wednesday, May 13," he said. "About 6 p.m."

That could fit, Wallander thought. It could have been Mabasha's replacement.

"He said he would stay for about a month?"

"I guess."

"Guess?"

"I'm sure."

"Go on," Wallander said. "Don't leave out any detail."

"We chatted about this and that," Jørgensen said. "He was open and friendly. But all the time I somehow felt he was on his guard. I can't really put it any more exactly than that. We got to Limhamn. I docked, and he jumped ashore.

"Since I'd already been paid, I backed out again right away and I wouldn't have given it another thought if I hadn't happened across a Swedish evening paper the other day. There was a photograph on the front page of a man I thought I recognised. A man who got killed in a gun battle with the police."

He paused briefly.

"With you," he said. "There was a picture of you as well."

"When was the paper from?" Wallander said, although he already knew the answer.

"It was a Thursday paper, possibly," Jørgensen said, hesitantly. "It could have been the next day. May 14."

"Go on," Wallander said. "We can check up on that if it's important."

"I recognised that photo," Jørgensen said. "But I couldn't place it. I didn't catch on to who it was until the day before yesterday. When I dropped that African off in Limhamn, there was a giant of a man waiting for him on the quay. He stayed in the background, as if he didn't want to be seen, but I have pretty good eyes. It was him all right.

Then I started thinking about it all. I thought it might be important. So I took a day off and came here."

"You did the right thing," Wallander said. "I'm not going to pursue the fact that you were involved in illegal immigration into Sweden. But that assumes, of course, that you have nothing more to do with it."

"I've already packed it in," Jørgensen said.

"That African," Wallander said. "Describe him to me."

"About 30. Powerfully built, strong and supple."

"Nothing else?"

"Not that I can remember. Maybe it's not important."

Wallander put down his pen. "It's extremely important," Wallander said. He stood up. "Thanks for coming to tell me, and please leave a note of your address with the receptionist. I'll see that you are refunded your travel expenses."

"That's OK," Jørgensen said, leaving.

Wallander looked for the copy he had kept of the telex he had sent to Interpol in South Africa. He pondered for a moment. Then he called Swedish Interpol in Stockholm.

"Chief Inspector Wallander, Ystad," he said when they answered. "I sent a telex to Interpol in South Africa on Saturday, May 23. I wonder if there's been any response."

"If there had been, you'd have heard right away."

"Look into it, would you, just to be on the safe side."

He got an answer a few minutes later. "A telex of one page went to Interpol in Johannesburg in the evening of May 23. There has been no response beyond confirmation of receipt."

Wallander frowned. "*One* page?" he said. "I sent two pages."

"I have a copy of it in front of me right now. The thing does seem to stop in mid-air."

Wallander looked at his own copy on the desk in front of him.

If only the first page had been transmitted, the South African police would not know that Mabasha was dead, and that a replacement had probably been sent. Furthermore, it could be assumed that the assassination attempt would be made on June 12, as Tsiki had told Jørgensen the latest date he would be going home. Wallander could see the implications right away. The police in South Africa had spent two weeks searching for a man who was dead. Today was Thursday,

June 11. The assassination attempt would probably be made on June 12. Tomorrow.

"How the hell is this possible?" he shouted. "How come you only sent half my telex?"

"I have no idea," the voice said. "You'll have to talk to whoever was in charge."

"Some other time," Wallander said. "I'll be sending another telex shortly. And this one must go to Johannesburg without delay."

"We send everything without delay."

Wallander slammed down the receiver. He could not understand how the hell such incompetence was possible.

He put a sheet of paper into his typewriter and composed a brief message. *Victor Mabasha is no longer relevant. Look instead for a man named Sikosi Tsiki, 30 years of age, well-proportioned* (he looked the phrase up in the dictionary, and rejected "powerfully built"), *no obvious peculiarities. This message replaces all previous ones. I repeat that Victor Mabasha is no longer relevant. Tsiki is presumably his replacement. We have no photograph. Fingerprints will be investigated.*

He signed the message and took it to reception.

"This must go to Interpol in Stockholm immediately," he said. He had never seen the receptionist before.

He stood over her and watched her send the message. Then he returned to his office. He thought it might be too late.

If he were not on sick leave, he would have demanded an immediate investigation into who was responsible for sending only half of his telex. But as things stood, he couldn't be bothered.

He continued to attack the stacks of paper on his desk. It was nearly 1 p.m. by the time he was finished. He had cleared his desk. Without a backward glance, he left his office and closed the door behind him. He saw nobody in the corridor, and managed to get away from the station without being seen by anybody apart from the receptionist.

There was just one more thing he had to do. Once that was done, he was finished.

He walked down the hill, passed the hospital, and turned left. All the time he thought everybody he met was staring at him. He tried to make himself as invisible as possible. When he got as far as the square, he stopped at the optician's and bought a pair of sunglasses. Then he

427

continued down Hamngatan, crossed over the Österlen highway, and found himself in the docks. There was a café that opened for the summer. About a year ago he had sat there and written a letter to Baiba Liepa in Riga, but he had never posted it. He had walked onto the pier, ripped it to pieces, and watched as the scraps floated away over the harbour. Now he intended to make another attempt to write to her, and this time he would send it. He had paper and a stamped envelope in his inside pocket. He sat down at a table in a sheltered corner, ordered coffee, and thought back to that occasion a year ago. He had felt pretty gloomy then, too. But that was nothing compared to the situation he found himself in now. He started writing whatever came into his head. He described the café he was sitting in, the weather, the white fishing boat with the light-green nets moored not far from where he sat. He tried to describe the sea air. Then he started writing about how he felt. He had trouble finding the right words in English, but he persevered. He told her that he was on sick leave for an indefinite period, and that he was not sure whether he would ever return to his post. *I may well have concluded my last case,* he wrote. *And I solved it badly, or rather, not at all. I'm beginning to think I am unsuitable for the profession I have chosen. For a long time I thought the opposite was true. Now I'm not sure any more.*

He read through what he had written, and decided he was not up to rewriting it, even if he was dissatisfied with how he had expressed himself. It seemed wooden and unclear. He folded up the sheet of paper, sealed the envelope, and asked for his bill. There was a postbox in the marina. He walked over and posted his letter. Then he continued walking out onto the pier, and sat down on one of the stone piles. The ferry from Poland was on its way into the harbour. The sea was steel grey, blue and green in turn. He suddenly remembered the bicycle he had found there that foggy night. It was still behind the shed at his father's place. He decided to return it that same evening.

After half an hour he got to his feet and walked through the town to Mariagatan. He opened the door, then stood staring.

In the middle of the floor was a brand-new stereo system. There was a card on top of the CD player.

Get well soon and hurry back. Your colleagues.

He remembered that Svedberg still had a spare key so he could let the workmen in to do the repairs after the attack. He sat on the floor and gazed at the equipment. He was touched, and only with difficulty held back tears of emotion. But he didn't think he deserved it.

On Thursday, June 11, there was a fault in the telex lines between Sweden and South Africa between noon and 10 p.m. Wallander's message was therefore delayed. It was 10.30 p.m. before the night operator eventually transmitted it to South Africa. It was received, registered, and placed in a basket of messages to be distributed the next day. But somebody remembered a memo from some prosecutor by the name of Scheepers about sending all copies of telexes from Sweden to his office immediately. The officer in the telex room could not remember what they should do if messages arrived late in the evening or in the middle of the night. Nor could they find Scheepers' memo, although it ought to have been in the special file for running instructions. One of the men on duty thought it could wait until the next day, but the other was annoyed because the memo was missing. If only to keep himself awake, he started looking for it. Half an hour later, he found it – filed in the wrong place. Scheepers' memo stated categorically that late messages should be conveyed to him immediately by telephone, regardless of the time. The sum total of all these mishaps and delays, most of which were due to human error and sheer incompetence, was that Scheepers was not telephoned until three minutes past midnight on Thursday, June 11. Even though he was sure in his own mind that the assassination attempt would be in Durban, he had difficulty in getting to sleep. Judith was asleep, but he was still tossing and turning in bed. He thought it was a pity he hadn't taken Borstlap with him to Cape Town after all. If nothing else it would have been an edifying experience. He also worried that Borstlap thought it so odd they had received not a single tip about where Mabasha was hiding, despite the reward. Several times Borstlap had said he thought there was something fishy about the apparent disappearance of Mabasha. When Scheepers tried to pin him down, he said it was just a hunch, nothing he could put his finger on. His wife groaned when the bedside telephone rang. Scheepers reached for the receiver as if he had been waiting for a call all the time. He listened to what the Interpol duty officer read out for him. He picked up a pen from the bedside table, asked to hear it one more time, then wrote two words on the palm of his left hand.

Sikosi Tsiki.

He hung up and sat there motionless. Judith was awake now and asked him what had happened.

"Nothing of danger to us," he said. "But it could be dangerous for somebody else."

He dialled Borstlap's number. "A new telex from Sweden," he said. "They say it's not Victor Mabasha. It's a man called Sikosi Tsiki. The attempt will probably take place tomorrow. Well, today."

"Goddammit!" Borstlap said. They agreed to meet at Scheepers' office.

Judith could see her husband was extremely shocked. "What's happened?" she asked again.

"The worst that possibly could happen," he said.

Then he went out into the darkness. It was 12.19 a.m.

CHAPTER THIRTY-FIVE

Friday, June 12, dawned a clear but somewhat cool day in Cape Town. In the morning a bank of fog drifted into Three Anchor Bay from the sea, but it would blow off later. The cold season was approaching in the Southern Hemisphere. You could already see lots of Africans on their way to work in woollen hats and thick jackets.

Mandela had arrived in Cape Town the previous evening. When he woke at dawn, he thought about the coming day. It was a custom he had grown used to during the many years he spent as a prisoner. So many memories, so many bitter moments, but such a great triumph in the end.

He was an old man now, more than 70 years old. His time was limited, but he ought to live a few more years at least. Together with President de Klerk, he had to steer his country along the difficult, painful, but also wonderful path that would lead to the end of the Apartheid system forever. The last fortress of colonialism on the black continent would fall. Once they had achieved that goal, they could withdraw, even die if need be. But he still had a great lust for life. He wanted to see it all through, and enjoy the sight of the black people liberating themselves from hundreds of years of subjugation and humiliation.

Mandela knew he would be elected the first black President of South Africa. That was not something he was striving to achieve, but he would have no grounds for declining.

It is a long way, he thought to himself. A long way to go for a man who has spent almost half his adult life in captivity.

He smiled at the thought. But then he grew serious again. He thought about what de Klerk told him when they last met, a week ago. A group of *boere* had formed a conspiracy to kill him in order to create chaos and drive the country to the brink of civil war.

Could that really be possible? He knew there were fanatical *boere*, people who hated all blacks. But did they really think they could prevent what was happening in the country by means of such a desperate conspiracy? Could they be so blinded by hatred – or was it fear? – that they thought it possible to return to the old South Africa? Could they not see they were a dwindling minority? Admittedly with widespread influence, but even so. Were they really prepared to sacrifice the future on a bloodstained altar?

Mandela shook his head. He had difficulty believing that was true. De Klerk must have been exaggerating or misreading the information he had received. He was not afraid of anything happening to him.

Tsiki had also arrived in Cape Town on Thursday evening, but unlike Mandela, he arrived unnoticed. He came by bus from Johannesburg, and when he had recovered his bag, he allowed himself to be swallowed up by the darkness.

He had spent the night in the open, sleeping in a hidden corner of Trafalgar Park. At daybreak, roughly same time as Mandela had woken and stood at his window, he climbed up the hill as far as he needed to, and installed himself there. Everything was in accordance with the map and the instructions he had received from Malan at Hammanskraal. He was pleased to be supported by such good organisers. There was nobody in sight; the barren slope was not suitable for picnics. The path to the summit, 350 metres high, meandered up on the other side of the hill. He had never used an escape car. He always felt freer on foot. When it was all over he would walk quickly down the hill and blend in with the furious crowds demanding revenge for the death of Mandela. Then he would leave Cape Town.

Now he knew it was Mandela he was going to kill. He realised it the day Malan told him when and where the shooting was to take place. He had read in the papers that Mandela was to speak at the Green Point Stadium on the afternoon of June 12. He contemplated the oval-shaped arena stretched out in front of him, some 700 metres away. The distance did not worry him. His telescopic sights and the long-range rifle satisfied his requirements of precision and power.

He had not reacted to the news that it was Mandela who was to be his target. His first thought was that he ought to have been able to work it out for himself. If these crazy *boere* were to have the slightest chance of creating chaos in the country, they would have to get rid of Mandela first. As long as he continued to stand up and speak, the black masses would keep their self-control. Without him everything was more uncertain. Mandela had no obvious successor.

As far as Tsiki personally was concerned, it would be an opportunity to right a personal wrong. It was not actually Mandela who had kicked him out of the ANC, but as he was the overall leader, he could nevertheless be regarded as responsible.

Tsiki looked at his watch. All he had to do now was wait.

Scheepers and Inspector Borstlap landed at Malan Airport on the outskirts of Cape Town just after 10 a.m. They were tired and looked washed out after being on the go all night, trying to find out about Sikosi Tsiki. Detectives had been hauled from their beds, computer operators with access to various police registers had turned up in overcoats over pyjamas, collected by patrol cars. But when it was time to go to the airport, the result was depressing. Tsiki was not in any of the registers. Nor had anyone ever heard of him. He was totally unknown. By 7.30 p.m. they were on their way to Jan Smuts Airport. During the flight they tried with increasing desperation to formulate a strategy. They could see that their chances of stopping this Sikosi Tsiki were limited, perhaps non-existent. They had no idea what he looked like, they knew nothing about him. As soon as they landed in Cape Town, Scheepers went to call President de Klerk to ask him, if possible, to persuade Mandela to cancel his appearance that afternoon. Only when he threatened to have every police officer at the airport arrested did he manage to convince them who he was, and they left him alone in a room. It took almost ten minutes to reach the President. Scheepers told him as succinctly as possible what had happened during the night. But de Klerk had responded in ice-cold fashion to his suggestion, saying it would be pointless. Mandela would never agree. Besides, they had got the time and place wrong before. It could happen again. Mandela had agreed to an increase in his bodyguard. There was nothing more the President could do now. When the conversation was over, Scheepers had the uncomfortable feeling again that de Klerk was not prepared to go to all possible lengths to protect Mandela from assassination. Was that really possible, he wondered indignantly. Have I misunderstood his position? But he had no time to go on thinking about President de Klerk. He found Borstlap, who had meanwhile picked up the car the police had ordered from Johannesburg. They drove straight to Green Point Stadium, where Mandela was due to speak in three hours' time.

"Three hours is not long enough," Borstlap said. "What do you think we'll have time to do?"

"We have to stop the man," Scheepers said. "It's as simple as that."

"Or stop Mandela," Borstlap said.

"That's just not possible," Scheepers said. "He'll be on the platform at 2 p.m. De Klerk refused to plead with him."

They showed their Ids and were allowed into the stadium. The podium was already in place. ANC flags and colourful streamers were everywhere. Musicians and dancers were getting ready. Soon the audience would start arriving from the townships of Langa, Guguletu and Nyanga. They would be greeted by music. For them, the political meeting was also a festival.

Scheepers and Borstlap stood on the podium and looked around.

"There's a crucial question we must face up to," Borstlap said. "Are we dealing with a suicide killer, or somebody who will try to get away afterwards?"

"The latter," Scheepers said. "We can be sure of that. An assassin prepared to sacrifice his own life is dangerous because he's unpredictable. But there's also a big risk that he would miss the target. We are dealing with a man who is expecting to get away."

"How do we know he'll be using a gun?" Borstlap said.

Scheepers stared at him with a mixture of surprise and irritation. "What else could he do?" he said. "A knife at close range would mean he'd be caught and lynched."

Borstlap nodded gloomily. "Then he has lots of possibilities," he said. "Just look around. He could use the roof, or a deserted radio cabin. He could choose a spot outside the stadium."

Borstlap pointed to Signal Hill, which loomed up half a kilometre from the stadium.

"He has, from our viewpoint," he said, "only too many choices."

They could both see what this implied. They would be forced to choose, to take a chance. Impossible to investigate everything. Scheepers thought that they might have time to check maybe one in four.

"We have two hours and 35 minutes," Scheepers said. "If Mandela is on time, that's when he'll start speaking. I assume an assassin won't hang about."

Scheepers had requested ten experienced police officers to assist him. They were under the command of a young sergeant.

"Our assignment is very simple," Scheepers said. "We have a couple of hours in which to turn this stadium inside out. We're searching for an armed man. He's black, he's dangerous, and he must be put out of action. If possible we should take him alive. If there's no other choice, he has to be killed."

"Is that all?" the sergeant said, when Scheepers had finished. "Don't we have a description?"

"We don't have time to argue," Borstlap said. "Arrest anybody who seems to be acting at all strangely. Or is somewhere he shouldn't be. We can find out if we have the right person or not later."

"There has to be some kind of description," the sergeant said, and was supported by murmurs from his officers.

"There has to be nothing of the kind," Scheepers said. "We'll divide the stadium into sections and get started right away."

They searched cleaners' cupboards and abandoned storerooms, crept around on the roof and out onto girders. Scheepers left the stadium, crossed over Western Boulevard, the broad High Level, and then started climbing up the hill. He stopped after about 200 metres. It seemed to him the distance was too great. A potential assassin couldn't possibly pick a spot outside the stadium itself. He returned to Green Point soaked in sweat and short of breath.

Tsiki had seen him from where he was hidden behind some bushes, and thought it was a security officer checking the area around the stadium. He was not surprised; he had expected something like this. What worried him was that they might use dogs to comb the area. But the man scrambling up the slope was on his own. Tsiki crouched low, a pistol with a silencer ready. When the man turned back without even going as far as the top, he knew nothing could go wrong. Mandela had only a couple of hours to live.

Crowds were already flocking into the stadium. Scheepers and Borstlap fought their way through the teeming mass. All around drums were beating, people were singing and dancing.

An hour later, 30 minutes before the meeting was due to commence with Mandela's arrival at the stadium, Scheepers was in a panic. Borstlap tried to calm him.

"We haven't found him," Borstlap said. "We have very little time left to continue the search now. We have to ask ourselves what we might have missed."

He looked round. His eyes focused on the hill beyond the stadium.

"I was there already," Scheepers said.

"What did you see?"

"Nothing," Scheepers said.

Borstlap nodded, lost in thought. He was beginning to think they would not find the assassin before it was too late.

They were pushed backwards and forwards by the massive crowds.

"I just don't get it," Borstlap said.

"It was too far away," Scheepers said.

Borstlap looked at him questioningly. "What do you mean?" he asked. "Too far away?"

"Nobody could hit a target from there," Scheepers said angrily.

It was a while before Borstlap realised that Scheepers was still talking about the hill outside the stadium. Suddenly he was deadly serious.

"Tell me exactly what you did," he said, pointing to the hilltop.

"I climbed up part way. Then I turned back."

"You didn't actually go to the top of Signal Hill?"

"It's too far away, I told you!"

"It's not too far away at all," Borstlap said. "There are rifles that can kill at more than a kilometre. That's 800 metres at most."

Just then an enormous cheer went up from the dancing crowd, followed by intense drumming. Mandela had arrived in the stadium. Scheepers caught a glimpse of his greyish-white hair, his smiling face, and his waving arms.

"Come on!" yelled Borstlap. "If he's here at all, he has to be somewhere on that hillside."

Through his powerful telescopic sights Tsiki could see Mandela in close-up. He had removed the sights from the rifle and followed him from the moment he stepped out of his car at the stadium entrance. Tsiki could see he had only a few bodyguards. There did not seem to be any conspicuous alert or unrest around the white-haired man.

He remounted the sights on the rifle, checked the loading mechanism, and sat down in the position he had selected. He had rigged up a stand made of light metal. It was his own invention, and would give his arms the support they needed.

He glanced up at the sky. The sun was not going to cause him any unexpected problems. No shadows, no reflections, no glare. The hilltop was deserted. He was alone with his gun and a few birds hopping around on the ground.

Five minutes to go. The cheering in the stadium hit him at full volume, in spite of the distance.

Nobody would hear the shot, he thought.

He had two spare shells. They were lying on a handkerchief in front of him, but he did not expect to have to use them. He would save them as a souvenir. Maybe one day he would turn them into an amulet. That would bring him good luck for the rest of his life.

He avoided thinking about the money. He had to carry out his mission first.

He raised his rifle, put his eye to the telescopic sight and watched Mandela coming to the podium. He would shoot at the first opportunity. No reason to delay. He put down the gun and tried to relax his shoulders, taking deep breaths. He felt his pulse. It was normal. Everything was normal. Then he raised the rifle again, placed the butt against his right cheek and closed his left eye. Mandela was just below the podium, partly shielded by other people. Then he broke away from the group and strode towards the microphone. He raised his arms over his head like a victor. His smile was very wide.

Tsiki pulled the trigger.

But a fraction of a second before the bullet flew out of the barrel of the rifle at tremendous speed, he felt a thump on his shoulder. He couldn't stop his finger on the trigger. The shot rang out. But the thump had nudged him nearly five centimetres. That meant the bullet did not even hit the stadium, but smacked into a car parked on a street a long way away.

Tsiki turned around. There were two men, breathing heavily and staring at him. Both had pistols in their hands.

"Put down the gun," Borstlap said. "Slowly."

Tsiki did as he was told. He had no choice. The two white men would not hesitate to shoot, he could see that. What had gone wrong? Who were they?

"Place your hands on your head," Borstlap said, handing Scheepers a pair of handcuffs. He stepped forward and locked them on Tsiki's wrists.

"Get up," Scheepers said.

Tsiki stood up.

"Take him down to the car," Scheepers said. "I'll be there in a moment."

Borstlap led Tsiki away.

Scheepers listened to the cheering from the stadium. He could hear Mandela's unmistakable voice over the loudspeakers. The sound seemed to come from very far away.

He was soaked in sweat. He could still feel traces of the horror he had felt when it seemed they wouldn't find the man they were looking for. The sense of relief had still not caught up with him.

What had just happened, he knew, was a historic moment, but it was a historic moment that nobody would ever know about. If they had not managed to get up the hill in time, if the stone he had thrown in desperation at the man had missed, a different kind of historic moment would have taken place. And that one would have been more than just a footnote in the pages of history.

I am an Afrikaner myself, he thought. I ought to be able to understand these lunatic people. Even if I don't want it that way, they are my enemies today. Maybe they haven't understood deep down that the future of South Africa will force them to reassess everything they've been used to. Many of them will never manage that. They would rather see the country destroyed in an cataclysm of blood and fire. But they will not succeed.

He gazed over the sea. As he did so, he wondered what he was going to say to President de Klerk. Verwey was also expecting a report. And he had a visit to make to a house in Bezuidenhout Park. He was looking forward to meeting the two women again.

What would happen to Tsiki, he had no idea. That was Inspector Borstlap's problem. He put the rifle and the cartridges back into their case. He folded the metal frame.

*

438

Suddenly he thought of the white lioness on the river bank in the moonlight. He would take Judith back to the safari park. Maybe the lioness would again be there.

He was deep in thought as he descended the hillside. He had realised something that had not been clear to him before, what it was that the white lioness in the moonlight had meant to him. That first and foremost he was not an Afrikaner, a white man. He was an African.

EPILOGUE

This novel was written almost a year before the first free elections in South Africa: April 27, 1994. It is sobering to recall what Nelson Mandela had already said: "A watershed has finally been reached. In the long term, the outcome can already be predicted, albeit with the natural reservations that apply to all political prophesies: the establishment of a democratic society based on the rule of law."

The medium or long-term outcome, in terms of civil peace, was far from certain then. Not all commentators were willing to predict that civil war could be avoided.

Many individuals have contributed – sometimes without realising it – to the South African sections of the novel. Had it not been for Iwor Wilkins's and Hans Strydom's essential work in exposing the realities behind the Afrikaner secret society, the Broederbond, its secrets would have been concealed from me as well. Reading Graham Leach's writings on Boer culture was also a veritable adventure. And to round things off, Thomas Mofololo's stories cast light on African customs, not least with regard to the spirit world.

There are many others whose personal testimony and experiences have been significant. I thank them all, without naming individuals.

Because this is a novel, the names of characters and places, and also the timing, are not always authentic. Since the first publication, in Swedish, in 1993 some towns and districts in South Africa have been renamed. The names then in use are retained here.

The conclusions, and indeed the story as a whole, are my own responsibility. No-one else can be blamed for any shortcomings.

H. M.
Maputo, Mozambique